COLD ENERGY
Part 1
The Alex Cave Series Book 2

Written by James M. Corkill.

Copyright 2014, James M. Corkill. All rights reserved.

No part of this publication may be reproduced, stored in a retrieval system, or transmitted by any form or by any means, electronic, mechanical, recording, or otherwise, without the written permission of the author.

The characters and events in this book are fictitious. Any similarity to real persons, living or dead is coincidental and not intended by the author.

Chapter 1

ALASKA. A TINY ISLAND IN THE ALEUTIAN CHAIN:

Geophysics instructor Alex Cave entered the opening in the rock face of the volcano and saw the light from his flashlight reflecting off a mirror surface. He followed the mirror deeper into the volcano until he reached the airlock doors of the alien spacecraft and stepped into a large, circular room. His light reflected off a six-foot diameter sphere with a mirror surface before he aimed the flashlight at the floor, exposing the powdered remains of a human-shaped body in a one-piece silver suit. As he picked up the shiny fabric, the powder flowed through the material onto the floor. "Tough luck for the first time traveler."

He set it aside while removing all his clothes and stepped into the suit. "I hope this works." He cautiously placed his palms against the mirror surface of the sphere, felt an electrical shock, and vanished.

***

SEVEN DAYS EARLIER.

PACIFIC OCEAN SIXTY MILES WEST OF VANCOUVER, BRITISH COLUMBIA.

On board the sophisticated research ship *Mystic*, billionaire Mike Tanner was ready to try his new high-powered ultrasound unit, hoping to find methane hydride in extremely deep water. He pressed the button, and the unit activated.

***

SEATTLE FEDERAL BUILDING. FEMA REGIONAL OFFICE:

"Listen up everybody," Director Charles Simson hollered across the control room. "We've just received a report there has been a major seismic event on Vancouver Island. It hit Victoria the hardest, but the United States' San Juan Islands also felt some seismic activity. Call your contacts and find out the extent of the damage so we can get the emergency response teams moving. Make it happen, people."

The USGS, (United States Geological Survey), supervisor from the sixth floor, Sharon Aniston, stepped out of the elevator and hurried across the room into Simon's office. "Charlie, it didn't register as a major earthquake."

Simson stared up at her. "What do you mean?"

"We don't know what it was. All we know is the ground suddenly rose beneath Victoria and only affected that specific area."

"Is that even possible?"

"Logically? Not a chance. We don't have a clue how to explain what happened."

"Do you think it's a prelude to a major earthquake in the Pacific Northwest?"

"I don't want to speculate because we just don't have enough information. I'll tell you one thing, Charlie. If whatever caused the destruction in Victoria happens here, in Seattle, there won't be anything left standing. There's a helicopter on its way to pick me up on the roof. I'll look at the damage and try to figure out where it started, and I'll call you when I have more information."

Simson stood from behind his desk. "I need to see the San Juan Islands to get a better idea of what I'm dealing with, so I'm going with you."

"It's only a two-person helicopter, but I'll let you know what I find out."

Simson sat back down. "Okay. Thanks, Sharon."

***

Sharon left the elevator and climbed the stairs to the roof access door, then stopped to look at the digital thermostat mounted on the wall. The outside ambient temperature was close to eighty-nine degrees Fahrenheit, when it should be in the upper seventies, but global warming was changing the weather patterns across the planet, and no one country had enough influence to stop the major contributors to the problem.

She stepped out onto the roof, hurried across to the two-person Bell helicopter, and climbed in next to the pilot, Steve Bolton. A few moments later, they were flying north over the Puget Sound. The damage to the San Juan Islands appeared to be minimal, so she asked Steve to drop lower for a closer view of the damage to Victoria.

She stared down through the smoke and saw the devastation was far worse than she had imagined. The beautiful castle was now a pile of shattered marble, and large sections of the majestic hotels had collapsed into mounds of concrete and shattered glass. The mooring docks had been tossed around the harbor like rubber bands, and beautiful yachts lay smashed into tangled heaps of sunken wood, fiberglass, and sail masts. Dozens of emergency workers and dogs were searching through the rubble for survivors, and bodies were stacked in long rows on what remained of the streets. For registering as a minor tremor, the damage was horrific.

"I've seen enough, Steve. Take me back to the Federal Building."

She leaned back in her seat and stared out the front window as the helicopter turned south, back to Seattle. She only knew of one who might have a theory about how this could happen. An old hermit volcanologist named Wesley Patterson, but since the Mount Saint Helens eruption, he was no longer consulting with the USGS.

***

Steve set the helicopter down on the roof of the Federal Building, and Sharon climbed out and hurried across to the door to get out of the heat. She entered the building and went down the stairs to wait for the elevator, and when the doors opened, her own geophysics expert, Patrick Chandler, was waiting inside.

She entered and looked at the thin stack of papers in his hand. "I hope you've figured out where this started, Patrick."

Patrick shook his head no. "This was unlike any seismic disturbance we've dealt with before, and we have no idea where the epicenter was. What did it look like from the air?"

"The damage in Victoria is extensive and very precise, as if planned to hit only that specific city. I need to find out if the CIA knows of any terrorist activity in the area."

"You can't be serious, Sharon. It was a seismic disturbance, not a bomb."

Sharon sighed in exasperation and leaned back against the wall. "You're probably right. I'm just frustrated and searching for answers."

The doors opened, and they stepped into the hallway of the USGS Command Center, where they collected and analyzed all the seismic data for the western region of North America. Using sophisticated software, her team was trying to pinpoint the origin of the event.

A young woman ran up and handed Sharon a sheet of paper, so they stopped walking while she read the information. She finished and gave it to Patrick. "This day just keeps getting worse by the hour. The tsunami warning detectors in the northern Bering Sea activated at the same time as the seismic event in Victoria." She looked at the young woman. "We need to find out if there was any seismic activity in that area. Put it up on screen number three, please."

Sharon turned and moved across the room to study the information displayed on one of the large video screens. The image changed, showing no seismic activity in the Bering Sea.

Patrick had stopped while he read the report, and then caught up to her. "This is very bad, Sharon. If this is happening along the entire northwest coast, it means there is some major tectonic activity along the Pacific Rim. I'm just surprised we haven't noticed an increase in volcanic activity."

"Did you try calling Wesley Patterson about this? He must be monitoring the activity here in the Pacific Northwest."

"Three times, but he didn't answer."

"After the Mount Saint Helens incident, can you blame him?"

Patrick looked down at the floor for a moment as he remembered what had happened. He had ignored Patterson's warning about an imminent eruption, and many lives were lost. He stared up at the monitor. "I guess not. Even so, he must have noticed what happened."

They stopped in front of a large display showing all the seismic detectors in Western North America, and the only flashing red dot was in Victoria. The tsunami sensors in the Bering Sea showed a ten-foot surge radiating south toward the Pacific Ocean, with nearly no surge past the Aleutian Islands.

"That's a bit of luck," stated Patrick. "It seems the islands broke up the surge before it reached the Pacific."

Sharon folded her arms across her chest and continued to stare at the screen. "I don't think luck plays any part in all this. If it wasn't an earthquake that created the surge, what did?"

"I know. None of this makes any sense."

***

MONTANA STATE COLLAGE, BOZMAN:
Alex Cave sat on the edge of his old wooden desk, looking at his

second year geology students while they headed toward the door. He heaved a deep sigh at the thought of having to teach the same old material to his *first*-year students. The subject was becoming so routine he could do it in his sleep. Ever since the Dead Energy operation, he yearned for the adrenalin rush of being on the hunt again.

David Conway waited until the last student walked out of the room before strolling over to Alex. He noticed the nearly healed scar just above his left eyebrow. "What did you do last weekend to get so banged up?"

Alex grinned. The physics student was like the little brother he never had. "Just a field trip, David. You never can tell when a few rocks might fall when you go underground."

"Speaking of a fall, Greta Bernstein, the English Literature teacher, seems to be really interested in you. She keeps asking me if you're gay, since you never accept her offer to go out on a date." He noticed the look in Alex's eyes change to one of deep sorrow, and realized Alex was still mourning the death of his wife in Holland not too long ago.

"I'm sorry, Alex. Hey, listen. I thought you might find this interesting. I logged into one of NASA's northern imaging satellites and it was taking pictures over the Arctic Ocean when a small section of ice suddenly changed color from white to clear."

"That's interesting. Could it just be a refraction of the light through the ice?"

"It's possible, but that's not what it looked like to me. It took several seconds before the satellite moved out of range, but even when the angle changed, the ice was still transparent."

"Have you contacted facilities who were watching at the same time?"

"I've been trying, but so far, no one has responded to my request."

"Let me know what you find out."

"I will."

Chapter 2

C.H.A.R.S., (CANADIAN HIGH ARCTIC RESEARCH STATION), CAMBRIDGE BAY, NUNAVUT:

Sonja Hanspevin studied the computer map of the Polar Ice Sheet north of Canada. One of the GPS units on was flashing a warning the elevation had just increased by two hundred meters in only three minutes. "This cannot be right," she whispered.

She grabbed her phone and entered the number for her District Manager, Peter Hendrix. "Hallo, Peter. We are getting a warning from GPS unit 635. I want to fly out to look for myself, but I need your approval for the helicopter."

"Tom is scheduled to pick up the Regional Director at the airport in three hours. Can it wait until he returns?"

"I would rather not. We could have a serious problem."

"What kind of problem?"

"The elevation of the ice sheet has gained two hundred meters in only a few minutes. Peter?"

"I'm still here. That's impossible. It has to be a malfunction."

"There is only one way to find out. If it *is* a malfunction, I will exchange the unit and be back in time for Tom to pick up the Director, but we need to be sure."

"Okay. I'll call Tom and tell him you're coming."

"Thank you, Peter."

***

Thirty minutes later, Sonja and the helicopter pilot, an American named Tom Hatfield, thought they were seeing an illusion. Directly ahead, a vertical wall of transparent ice had risen two hundred feet out of the Arctic Ocean.

Tom whistled softly. "Now that's different."

Sonja was speechless as they closed the distance to the ice wall. "Take us higher, Tom."

When Tom increased their altitude, she saw the transparent block of ice was ten miles wide, and extended three hundred miles south into the

Beaufort and East Siberian seas. "This is not logically possible, Tom. We should find the GPS unit and retrieve the data. That will help us determine how this could happen."

Tom gave her a nod and entered the new coordinates into the navigation system. "If all this happened as quickly as you say, I would imagine it made a powerful wave."

The surface of the newly formed ice block was as transparent as the sides, and Sonja's heart broke at the sight of dozens of white pilot whales frozen in the surface. "I do not understand what could have caused the water to freeze that quickly."

Tom set the helicopter down fifty feet from the GPS receiver and brought the engine's speed down to idle. Sonja opened the side door and noticed the air felt extremely cold. When she stepped out, the rubber sole of her shoe touched the ice and immediately stuck to the surface. She struggled to pull it free, and when it tore loose, chunks of the gray rubber sole remained stuck to the ice, so she slid back inside onto the seat.

"The ice is extremely cold, and I do not think we should stay here. We will have to come back with different equipment."

"That works for me."

Tom shoved the throttle forward and pulled up on the collective, but the helicopter runners were frozen to the ice in a vice-like grip. He shoved the throttle to full power, but when he pulled up on the collective, the runners remained frozen to the ice and vibration threatened to tear the helicopter apart.

He let go of the collective and pulled back on the throttle until the engine was idling. "We're stuck here until the ice melts."

"Can I do something to help?"

"If we can't break free with the rotors, there's nothing we can do."

"Call for another helicopter to pick us up."

"Are you kidding? No one else can land to get us, because they would get stuck, too. Until something changes radically, we're trapped out here."

Sonja wrung her hands together on her lap while she tried to think of a way out of their situation. "Call the research station and tell them what happened. We have many intelligent people working at the facility, and perhaps someone will think of a way to help us."

Tom entered the research facility's frequency into the radio. "Chars research station, this is chars helicopter one. Come in, please?"

No one responded, so he tried again, but after several minutes without a response, he changed frequencies. "This is the Chars research helicopter calling anyone on the emergency radio frequency. Please, respond." When no one answered, he looked over at Sonja. "Something must be interfering with the radio signal."

"Do you have any survival equipment?"

"Not much. Spare water, a small supply of power bars, first aid equipment, and signal flares."

"If we do not return to the station, they will send a search and rescue unit to find us."

"Even if they do, they still can't land to pick us up, and without radio communication, we don't have any way to warn them about the ice, and they'll be stranded out here with us. When our fuel runs out, it's going to get freezing cold in here."

"How long do we have before that will happen?"

Tom looked at the digital readout. "Even leaving the engines at idle, we'll run out of fuel in less than four hours, and without heat, we'll be dead thirty minutes later. I'm sorry, Sonja."

Chapter 3

MOUNT BAKER, WASHINGTON STATE:
Wesley Patterson ignored the messages from the USGS, but his seismic detector on Mount Baker had registered a significant disturbance deep beneath his sleeping volcano. His personal seismic activity center was his workshop, near the Mount Baker National Forest and State Park, where he had studied the volcano for ten years. The problem was the activity was coming from several thousand feet beneath the surface, and that could only occur if the sleeping giant was awakening because of new tectonic activity.

He studied the picture on a thirty-two inch flat screen television sitting on a beat up wooden desk, and it displayed the seismometer reading recorded during the event. What puzzled him was the absence of seismic activity deep below the surface, so why was it affecting his mountain?

He rewound the recording back to the time of the event in Victoria and moved the cursor to an area just past the end of the sensor needle. He clicked the mouse to zoom in on the black line, and when he saw the magnified view, he leaned back in his chair and released a slow sigh of astonishment. "What is going on?"

***

BOZEMAN MONTANA:
Alex Cave threw a yellow tennis ball for his dog to chase and then grabbed the ringing phone from his front pants pocket. As he walked up onto the back porch and sat in one of the green plastic chairs, he recognized the caller ID from the USGS headquarters in Washington and answered. "This is Alex Cave."

"Hello, Mister Cave. I'm Sharon Aniston, from the USGS in Seattle. Sorry to bother you, but we've had a major seismic event in this area. It did significant damage to Victoria earlier today and we've just had another event in the San Juan Islands. This may sound impossible, but they did not register as major earthquakes. None of our people know what caused them, and we're worried it could be a prelude to a major event in the Pacific Northwest."

"I live in Montana, so I'm not sure what I can do to help."

"We have a mutual friend in Yellowstone National Park. Jerry Mercer spoke highly of you and said you were the one person he could count on when all other ideas fail. I was hoping you could help me with this problem."

"Jerry is exaggerating, but I'll make some calls and try to figure out what happened."

"Thanks, Mister Cave."

When Alex turned off his phone, his dark brows bunched together in thought. He grew up in the Pacific Northwest and there was very little seismic activity. Still, the amount of energy required to destroy an entire city could only be on a tectonic level. So, why didn't it register as an earthquake?

He tried to remember the name of a man he had met at a conference in Iceland three months ago. He lived in Washington, and his particular field is volcanism, the study of volcanoes, and was currently studying the activity in the Pacific Northwest.

His dog, Barney, ran up the steps and dropped the ball at his feet, so he grabbed it and stood. As he hurled it toward a running stream, he remembered the man's first name was Wesley.

Chapter 4

PACIFIC OCEAN. 60 MILES WEST OF VANCOUVER ISLAND, CANADA:

Mike Tanner stepped out from the bridge of the *Mystic* to the railing and stared down at the open deck on the stern. An hour ago, the ultrasound unit on the ship had located a large deposit of methane hydride, and he had sent his two-person submarine called the *Wizard* down to retrieve a sample.

He bent over and leaned his arms on the railing behind the bridge while listening to the quiet humming from the hydraulic pump. The extension arm on the hoist raised a fifteen-foot long white submarine from the ocean, and then water dribbled across the dull-gray deck as the submarine was swung around and placed into a storage bracket on the left side of the stern.

A moment later, the winch shut down and Mike straightened up from the railing to look at the slim Scandinavian man standing beside him. "They said it's a pretty big slab of methane."

Captain John Dieter grinned at his boss. He had waited years for an opportunity like this, but it was not just to be the Captain of the *Mystic* searching for methane. He had a far grander need for this ship and its submarine. For now, he would play the part as the dutiful Captain and friend. "It appears your new unit is working as promised, Mike," he said with a slight accent.

They walked down the outside stairs to the deck and across to the submarine, where the deckhand, Leroy Bartram, leaned a white fiberglass ladder against the side of the sub. Both men looked up at the sound of the hatch being opened and watched a young scientist, Lisa Harding, climb up through the opening on top of the submarine.

Lisa waved down at Mike and Dieter, waiting on the deck below. "It's what we expected, Mike," she hollered, and then turned around to climb backward down the ladder.

Mike smiled as he remembered meeting Lisa two months ago at the alternative fuels seminar in Las Vegas, Nevada. At the end of the seminar, the five-foot-four brunette had timidly followed him to the lounge and asked to sit at his table. Her hazel eyes had stared at him through thin steel-rimmed glasses, as she stated she was a chemical specialist and he needed her expertize. He liked her self-confidence about her ability and told her when and where she would start working for him on the *Mystic*.

When Lisa stepped down on the deck and turned around to face him, Mike noticed the concern in her eyes. "What's wrong?"

"I'm not sure. There's something else mixed in with the methane."

"Is it dangerous?" Dieter inquired.

Lisa shook her head no. "The methane has an odd color, but it's not dangerous."

They heard the hatch close and looked up at the physically fit operator standing on top of the sub. Francis Okawna ran his hand through his shaggy blond hair, then turned around and climbed down the ladder. When he stepped onto the deck, he turned and looked at Mike. "I have a recording you should see. We saw something strange going on with the methane, and we're not sure what is happening."

Mike stared up at the six-foot-one, solidly built thirty-five-year-old man from San Diego, California, and was even more curious about the methane. "Josh is waiting for us in the lounge. Let's go take a look."

They followed Mike across the fifty-foot wide by sixty-foot long open deck, then through the double-doors centered in the rear bulkhead of the ship. The doors opened into a long walkway that continued straight through the center of the main deck to Mike's office and personal living quarters at the bow. Just inside the doors, a set of stairs went up to the control bridge. On the left, across from the bridge stairs, another set went down to the individual cabins, bathroom facilities, and the engine room on the lower deck.

They went past the stairs into the large open lounge and dining area with smoke-tinted windows spaced along the far wall. On the right side of the room, a serving counter divided the open kitchen from the dining table and chairs, and on the left side of the table was the lounge area.

A big, burly man stood up from a desk in the corner near a window. "I hear you found the mother lode," Joshua Mason stated in his baritone voice.

Mike thought the six-foot-six gentle giant from the Midwest looked more like a lumberjack than the computer and electronics expert on the ship.

Joshua grinned at Mike. "I get stock options for this, don't I, boss?"

Mike grinned and pointed at Okawna. "He has a recording we need to see."

Joshua took the flash drive from Okawna and inserted it into the computer on his desk, and then a fifty-eight-inch flat screen television mounted to the forward wall came on. The picture from the recording appeared on the screen, and the brilliant lights from the submarine illuminated the gray-green frozen slab of methane on the ocean floor. The massive, oval-shaped slab was roughly three-hundred-feet long, two-hundred-feet wide, and close to twenty feet thick. Oddly, it appeared to be growing upward from a long, large crack in the ocean floor.

Lisa walked over to stand next to the television and pointed at the slab. "What has me concerned is the green color. It could be some type of algae, and maybe we've found a new species that lives in methane."

"Here it comes," said Okawna. "We saw this on our approach. Keep an eye on the area beyond the methane."

A mass of white bubbles wobbled up beyond the slab, and everyone looked at Lisa for an explanation, so she shrugged her shoulders. "I have no idea. At that temperature and pressure, the methane cannot be melting on its own." She held up a small silver tube. "I'll take this sample of the methane to my lab for analysis. Maybe the strange color is a new type of organism, and the bubbles are a waste product."

Mike followed Lisa out of the lounge and across the walkway into her laboratory. She sat in front of her worktable and screwed the end of the pressurized stainless steel cylinder into the mass spectrometer. When she entered a command into the computer, she saw the results.

Mike noticed her puzzled expression. "Is something wrong?"

"Yes. There is something wrong with the composition of the methane. It contains large amounts of carbon monoxide, carbon dioxide, fluorocarbons, and sulfur dioxide. Those elements are only found in the atmosphere, not underwater. I can't explain why they're in the methane."

Mike leaned back against the worktable as he looked at Lisa. "What do we do?"

"I really don't know. As far as using it for an alternative power source, it's too contaminated to be worth the trouble of retrieving."

"Okay, I can live with that. Still, I'd like to know more about those bubbles. You mentioned it might be a new life form."

"I think the bubbles were coming up through the methane and not from behind it."

"I'll talk to Okawna about going back down for a closer look, and we'll take the remote rover to explore the area. It can maneuver around the methane much faster than the sub can."

"You won't make any money that way, Mike."

"I don't really care about the money. I have more than I could ever spend. I just want to satisfy my curiosity and discover new things. If I can solve some of the world's problems while I'm doing it, that's great. Like you said, maybe it's a new life form, and the bubbles are part of its metabolism. If it attracts those chemical elements you mentioned from the atmosphere, maybe it could help clean up our mess."

"I agree. We'll need a sample from a bubble to learn more, and we should do an ultrasound with the new rover unit. The one here on the ship only found the methane for us, but it couldn't penetrate deep enough to tell us how far down it extends. Maybe the rest of the methane in the crack would be worth recovering. Give me a little more time, and I'll go back down with Okawna."

"Why should you have all the fun? It's my turn, so this time I'm going down."

Lisa smiled up at Mike. Sometimes her boss reminded her of a fifty-year-old boy. He wasn't what people would consider handsome, but decent looking. "You just want to play with your new toy."

He headed back toward the lounge and paused in the doorway to look over his shoulder to smile at her. "That's the best part of being the boss."

***

Okawna checked the gauges inside the submarine one last time, and then looked in the rear-view mirror mounted above the clear bubble window in the nose of the submarine. Mike was sitting directly behind him, with a wide grin and a sparkle in his eyes, so Okawna keyed his headset microphone. "Mystic, Wizard is headed down."

Mike felt the g-force as Okawna engaged the rear thruster and they were finally underway. He was excited about operating the new remote controlled rover; one of three carried on the *Mystic*. Each was designed by the ship's engineer for a specific purpose. Besides its telephoto lens, this rover was equipped with a miniature version of the new ultrasound unit. It would enable them to look through the slab of methane and determine what was beneath it.

Mike could see Okawna's reflection in the mirror. "You never told me what you did after you graduated from college. That was eight years ago, wasn't it?"

Okawna liked Mike, and wished he could tell him he had worked for the CIA, but it was classified. "Let's just say I traveled a lot. Places you probably never heard of."

Mike knew how tight-lipped Okawna was about his past. He had met the thirty-five-year-old at a beach-side bar in San Diego, California, when they were both smiling at two bikini-clad women who strolled in. Okawna had nodded to the women, and before he knew it, they were sitting at a table with the two lovely ladies. He said to call him Okawna, and later he learned the man had a degree in mechanical engineering and was currently unemployed. When Okawna signed the contract to work for him two months ago, he had put the letter '*F*' for a first name without an explanation and insisted everyone just called him Okawna. He still didn't know what the *F* stood for.

***

Twenty minutes later, at a depth of 3,900 feet, the greenish white slab of methane hydride appeared through the front window. Okawna maneuvered the sub to a level area and then set it down on the seafloor. "It's all yours, Mike."

Mike set the computer tablet on his lap and watched the video display from the rover on a small screen mounted to the back of Okawna's chair. He pressed the button to release the latches and then maneuvered the rover forward to the methane.

***

Lisa and Joshua were sitting in her laboratory, watching the wireless video transmissions from the sub and the rover. The new technology developed for the ultrasound allowed the transmissions to reach the *Mystic* with no degradation of the signal, so they did not need a long cable. Lisa keyed the microphone on her headsets. "We've got a good picture up here, Mike."

***

Mike maneuvered the rover down to the edge of the slab, and that's when they noticed a change in color. The methane was divided horizontally by a six inch thick layer of black material.

Lisa's voice came through his headset. "Could you zoom in a little closer, Mike?"

"Yes, hang on a second." Mike maneuvered the rover and adjusted the camera lens. "How's that?"

Lisa could see a clear picture of the black line. "That's good. We didn't see it last time, so it must have been covered by the algae."

Above the black line, the green-tinted ice was a mixture of methane and other gases they had sampled. Below the line, transparent ice disappeared down into the crack in the seabed.

Mike keyed his headset. "What do you make of that, Lisa?"

"I'd say the lower ice is made of purified water, but that's impossible. Maneuver over the center and we'll do an ultrasound."

"Understood."

Mike maneuvered the Rover to the center of the slab and slowly brought it down onto the surface. "How's that?"

"Perfect. Here we go, 3, 2, 1, on."

Brilliant pale blue light flashed in front of the sub for a fraction of a second. Okawna blinked several times, trying to remove the blue dot in his vision, but it seemed burnt into his retinas. Something slammed into the sub, tossing it around like a toy and bouncing it against the seafloor. Okawna struggled to regain control as the sub rolled over and over through the water away from the methane, but the disorientation made his efforts useless.

The spinning tossed Mike out of his seat and pinned him against the wall of the sub. The turbulent action made him nauseous, and he fought desperately to hold it down. The sub bounced end over end across the sea floor before finally slamming onto the seabed, then it slid through the muddy sediment for a few seconds before settling on the ocean floor.

Chapter 5

CHARS HELICOPTER. POLAR ICE SHEET:
"This is ridiculous, Sonja. I can't stand just sitting here waiting to freeze to death. If we had a deck of cards, at least we'd have something to do."

Brilliant blue light suddenly flashed inside the ice, as the air was ripped open by a bolt of blue lightning shooting up from behind the helicopter. Tom felt the aircraft slide on the surface, so he shoved the throttle forward as he pulled up on the collective, and his bird climbed into the air.

The blue light blinked off, and Tom swung the aircraft away from the ice, then looked over at Sonja and smiled, grateful they were free. When he turned the helicopter around to see what was going on, his jaw dropped open as he tried to comprehend what was happening to the ocean.

The water below the wall began to freeze, and the ice was spreading across the water at eighteen miles per second. The northern end of the elevated ice sheet began moving south across the ocean as the water froze and shoved against the original polar ice sheet.

Tom gained altitude to watch the expanding ice and noticed most of the freezing was extending south. He had to increase their altitude to see the far southern edge as it continued to expand for nearly fifty kilometers before it abruptly stopped.

The new sheet of clear ice began to rise out of the ocean, shoving the old, smaller block of ice higher into the air, like a pyramid of transparent ice. When the new ice sheet stopped rising, Tom rotated the helicopter three-hundred-sixty-degrees to see the extent of the freezing. The southern end of the Polar Ice Sheet was now one thousand square miles larger, extending south, deeper into the Beaufort and East Siberian Seas.

Tom looked over at Sonja. "Can you believe that just happened?"

"That is the problem, Tom. Nothing can freeze that volume of ocean so fast."

"I don't mean to argue, but something just did."

"It was not a natural occurrence. Did you notice the perfect ninety-degree angle of the top edge of the ice? Nothing in nature is naturally that precise."

Tom noticed a small silhouette of something red and white near the eastern edge of the ice sheet. "I think that's a ship. We'd better go see if they're okay."

Tom applied full power to the engine, and then the nose of the helicopter dipped down as their speed increased. As they closed the distance, they saw a large cargo ship trapped in the surface of the new ice sheet.

Sonja saw small, dark outlines moving around on the deck of the cargo freighter and leaned forward in her seat. "They are climbing out of the ship! Call them on the radio. Hurry and let them know not to get out of the ship or they will freeze to the ice!"

"The radio doesn't work, remember?"

"We are a long distance from the GPS unit now, so maybe it will work this time."

Tom reached down and changed the radio frequency. "This is the Chars research helicopter, calling the red and white ship trapped in the ice. Come in, please." No one answered. "I say again, this is the Chars helicopter calling the red and white ship trapped in the ice. Please come in." He looked over at Sonja. "The radio signal must still be jammed."

"Can we go faster?"

"We're already at full speed. Let's hope they realize what's happening."

Sonja could distinguish several people standing at the ship's railing. "We might be too late."

Tom pressed the button on his headset. "Calling the ship stranded on the ice. This is Chars research helicopter approaching your vessel. Please come in."

"I see you, Chars. What the hell just happened?"

"Do not step onto the ice because your feet will freeze to the surface." Tom waited for a response. "Did you hear me?"

"Yes, but it's too late. One of my men stepped onto the ice just after it froze around the ship. His boots froze to the surface and a few moments later, he was frozen solid. The strange part is once the ice stopped rising into the air, his boots came free and his body toppled over onto the ice sheet and shattered into pieces. My men are bringing his body parts back on board right now, and they are thawing. My men don't seem to have any problems walking around, so I guess once the ice stops rising, the surface isn't as cold."

"I'm sorry we weren't able to contact you sooner. Can you call for help?"

"We just did, and they're sending a helicopter to pick us up."

"Good luck." He looked over at Sonja. "What's next?"

"We go back and tell Peter what happened, because it will not sound believable over the radio."

"I wouldn't believe what just happened if I hadn't seen it."

As Tom swung the helicopter around on a northeast heading back to Cambridge Bay, Sonja stared out the side window at the two-layer pyramid racing past below them. "The world is in big trouble."

***

CHARS. CAMBRIDGE BAY, NUNAVUT:

Sonja sat across the desk from Peter Hendrix and explained what had happened. "Do you know anyone who could explain this?"

He indicated he didn't. "It's hard enough just to describe what happened, much less put a label on it. Who would we contact? You're the leading glaciologist, Sonja."

"Perhaps, but I do not know how sea water could freeze that fast. That question is for physicists, not glaciologists. Whatever caused this did it twice."

"I wonder what effect this will have on the atmosphere. Maybe the planet will cool down again."

Sonja stood and looked down at Hendrix. "It happened too quickly, so nothing good can come from this. I have a friend in the United States who is well connected to the scientific community. I will explain it to him and see what he says. He would know who to contact, and I will call you when I have answers."

Sonja walked out of the administrative building and across the compound to the research facilities. They included laboratories and living quarters for the research scientists from all parts of the world, now stationed at CHARS. The structures were originally built to study the ice cap, and the accommodations were designed against the cold, but now, because of the global warming and the reduction in the size of the ice sheet, it was comfortable with the windows open.

Sonja realized the new ice sheet was already influencing the temperature, so she zipped up her lightweight jacket against the sudden chill in the air. She thought perhaps Peter was correct, but it was happening too quickly. She also knew the planet was a living entity and had always reacted violently to sudden changes.

***

BOZEMAN MONTANA:

Alex's cellphone rang, and he recognized the ID as Sonja Hanspevin, in Northeast Canada. He had met the attractive blond Icelander at a conference three months ago, and they had enjoyed drinks at the hotel bar before he flew home the next morning.

"Hi, Sonja. This is a coincidence."

"Hallo, Alex. Good of you to take my call. It seems we have a serious problem with the polar ice sheet."

He loved her accent. "What kind of problem?"

"The elevation and size of the ice sheet has increased dramatically."

Alex stared at the world map on the wall. "How long ago?"

"It happened twice today. Once in the morning, and again two hours later. It is difficult to describe, and I wish I had a recording to show you. It froze one thousand kilometers of ocean to a depth of two hundred meters in only three minutes. What is even stranger, the ice is transparent"

Alex stood and paced in front of the map, staring at the polar region north of Canada. "Who have you contacted about this?"

"That is the problem, Alex. I do not know who to contact. I was hoping you would know someone."

Alex thought about it. "I don't know anyone, either, but I'll do what I can. I was trying to remember that man we met at the conference. The one that looked like a hermit. Wesley something"

"I remember him. He had strange looking hair and beard. I saved his information in my phone because he was such an interesting character. Here it is. His name is Wesley Patterson, and I just sent you the number."

"I'll keep you informed on what I discover."

"Thank you, Alex. Bye, love."

Alex entered Patterson's number and was asked to leave a message, so he did. A few seconds later, it rang, and he recognized Patterson's number. "Hello, Mister Patterson. Thanks for calling me back so soon."

"Hi, Alex. I remember you from the convention in Iceland, but I didn't know you were Robert's son until I got home. I live up the mountain from your Ranch. Don't you work for the government?"

"Not anymore. I'm an instructor at a college in Bozeman, Montana."

"Good. I don't work with the government anymore. What can I do for you?"

"I'm calling about that seismic event in Victoria. I was told it was not an earthquake and I've been asked to find out what happened, so I wanted to get your opinion about what might have caused it."

"Any chance you can fly out here to Washington? There's something you need to see."

Alex looked at his desk calendar. His students were leaving to study the Yellowstone volcano with his friend Jerry Mercer for the rest of the week, and with the state holiday next Monday, he had seven days until he was due back at the College. "I'll fly out today and call you when I reach Sparrow Valley."

"Good. I look forward to it."

Alex made a quick call to the dean of the college to let her know where he was headed. When he called the airport, he was lucky and got the last seat available on a jet to Seattle, Washington.

Chapter 6

THE SUB:

When the blue dot in his vision faded enough for him to see again, Okawna grabbed the steering arm and brought the sub upright on the sea floor. He looked in the rearview mirror, but didn't see his companion. "Mike! Are you injured?"

Mike pushed away from the wall and dropped into the chair. "I don't think so. Remind me to use my seat belt next time."

Even with the sub's powerful exterior lights, Okawna could not see through the roiling cloud of gray silt. He engaged the thrusters, and the sub rose above the swirling muck, drifting away from the slab of methane, and then keyed his headset. "Are you there, Lisa?"

"I'm here. What just happened? All we could see was bright blue light."

"Mike and I went for a rough ride. We're headed back to the ship so I can check for any damage."

"Are you guys okay?"

"We're fine. See you shortly."

When the sub passed over the slab of methane, Okawna noticed white bubbles rising from the fracture at the bottom of the ocean. When he didn't see their little machine, he looked in the mirror at Mike's reflection. "I can't locate the rover. Are you getting a picture on your screen?"

Mike saw the small screen in the back of the headrest was dark, so he felt around the floor until he found the computer tablet and entered a few commands. "No, and the remote control got banged up a little. I'll try sending it to the surface, and Harrison will pick it up in the motorboat."

Mike entered a command, and the rover climbed up out of the silt and began its return to the ship then Okawna keyed his headset. "I hope you got all that, Lisa."

"Yes. Can you get a sample of the bubbles?"

"Not this time. Something crazy is going on down here, and I want to get back to the surface before something in the sub breaks. I'll see you on the ship."

***

***MYSTIC*:**

Joshua was waiting on the stern, rocking from foot to foot while waiting for Harrison and Bartram to set the sub in the storage bracket. He leaned the ladder against the side of the Wizard and looked up as Mike climbed out of the hatch first. "I sure am glad you two didn't get hurt."

Mike turned around and climbed backward down the ladder, then stepped off and looked at Joshua. "I hope it was as good a recording as it was live."

"It wasn't that great for me, boss. We couldn't really see anything because of the silt."

Okawna closed the hatch and climbed down the ladder to join them. "We were hit by a tsunami, and the ultrasound should not have caused that to happen. Since Rita isn't here right now to diagnose her creation, let's go talk to Lisa. Maybe she knows something to explain what's going on."

***

They walked into Lisa's lab and she rewound the recording until she found the moment when the blue light appeared. When she enhanced the image from the ultrasound, she noticed something unexpected and pointed at the picture. "That clear ice under the methane is over a thousand-feet deep, and it looks like there's something at the bottom. Watch this."

Lisa used the mouse to zoom in until it was visible, but all she saw was an oblong object, like a torpedo. "That's the best picture I can get using the ultrasound. Whatever it is, it's been down there since the crack first opened."

Okawna was more worried about what he had felt. "When that blue light appeared, something down there created a pressure wave that slammed into the sub. Once I make sure the sub's okay, we should go back down and try to figure out what happened."

Chapter 7

SEATTLE, WASHINGTON:

Alex stared out the window at the Cascade Mountain Range as his commercial jet swung around on final approach to Seattle/Tacoma International Airport. The glaciers on Mount Rainier and Mount Baker looked much smaller because of the greenhouse effect, and the pilot announced the temperature in Seattle was eighty-nine-degrees 'F'. He tried to see the San Juan Islands and Victoria, but the elevation of the aircraft was too high to see any discernible features.

After landing, he rented a car and drove north on Interstate 5, and an hour later, he took the off ramp toward Mount Baker and across the Skagit River Valley. The two-lane highway began climbing a gradual grade up the side of the mountain and crossed a large stone bridge over the Skagit River. On the other side of the bridge, the highway continued up over a rocky ridgeline. When he drove over the top, he looked down into a vast expanse of flat land called Sparrow Valley, which was once the bottom of a massive lake on the side of Mount Baker.

The State Park was another twenty miles east of the valley, so he pulled over into a picnic area and selected Wesley's number. "I'm here, Mister Patterson."

"Good. I live up past the State Park, but there's a little mom and pop grocery store just up the road from the entrance. I'll meet you there."

"Yes, I remember it from when I was a kid. I'll be there in twenty minutes."

Alex tossed his phone onto the passenger seat and drove down into the valley. Once he reached the bottom, he drove along the two-lane highway, following the left side of a small river.

When he drove past the only grocery store in the valley, he noticed the large white sign on the side of the red brick wall. This year's high school track and field championship game was against their number one rival, Darrington High School. The games would be hosted by Sparrow Valley High this year, on Friday, at 4:00 PM.

He remembered how fierce the competition had been while he grew up in the valley. At least one hundred visitors would drive up the mountain from Darrington just to see all the sports events, and the

Sparrow Valley community went down the mountain when the games were in Darrington.

He drove onto the shoulder of the road, next to a forty-foot long stone bridge over the river. On the other side of the bridge, the asphalt road continued for two miles before becoming a dirt road, which ended at the Cave Appaloosa Ranch, his boyhood home.

Because of the strange circumstances of the death of his brother and sister-in-law, Ken and Doreen Cave, he thought perhaps his past was catching up with him. He would never consider going home again, were it not for his nephew and niece, who were living with his father, Robert, on the ranch.

While working for the CIA in Holland, the Russian mafia had tried to kill him, but only murdered his wife, Sevi. Losing his true love had driven him crazy, and he had gone on a killing spree against those responsible. That was five years ago, but the Russian mafia never forgets, so he suspected they took their vengeance out on his family.

Even though the police reported it as a vehicular accident, Robert suspected he was the reason they were killed. He also knew Robert would never forgive him for their deaths, so he did not even try to mend things between them.

He pulled back onto the road, and when he reached the other side of Sparrow Valley, the highway quickly gained elevation as he continued up Mount Baker. Twenty minutes later, drove into the parking area in front of the old grocery store, and the two orange gas pumps and the neon signs in the windows were just as he remembered as a young man.

He parked next to a dark green Humvee with a tall suspension package and wide tires, then climbed out and went into the store. He smiled at the pleasant aroma of bread, spices, and coffee, which had permeated the wood walls and ceiling over the past sixty years. Even the shelving looked the same, with updated versions of the same supplies.

Standing next to the old wooden counter was a big man, who turned to look at him. Wesley Patterson's long, shaggy brown hair protruded beneath a sweat-stained cowboy hat, just as he remembered from the seminar in Iceland. As he walked up and extended his hand, he could barely see the man's mouth behind the thick beard. "It's nice to see you again, Mister Patterson."

Patterson smiled as he accepted the handshake. "Wesley will do," he said in a slow, deep voice.

A slender, silver-haired woman came around the counter and looked up at Alex. "I haven't seen you in twenty years, but I recognize those blue eyes."

It took a moment before Alex recognized the store owner and then smiled at Carrie Sorenson. "It's nice to see you again, Ma'am. How are you doing?"

Carrie remembered the last time she had seen Alex was when he had stopped at the store to buy a six-pack of beer on his way up to the reservoir to go fishing with his brother and father. There were a few new scars on his tanned, ruggedly handsome face since then, but his shiny black hair and thick, dark eyebrows were what she remembered most. The difference was in his deep blue eyes. They expressed a sense of sorrow, unlike the sparkle of enthusiasm when he was a young man. "I'm doing just fine, Alex. The last I heard, you live in Montana. What brings you out this way?"

"I came to see Wesley."

Carrie looked up at Patterson. "I didn't know you knew Alex."

"We only met briefly three months ago, when I went to Iceland. Let's go to my place, Alex. There's something I want to show you."

"Is it very far? I still need to find a place to stay for the night."

Carrie stared up at Alex. "Aren't you going to stay at your home?"

"I'm not welcome anymore. Not since Ken died."

Carrie nodded. "We heard. I'm sorry, Alex."

"Listen, Alex. Once I show you what I've discovered, you won't want to leave right away. I have a guest room you can stay in, if you like?"

"I accept. It's nice seeing you again, Miss Sorenson."

Alex followed Wesley out of the grocery store and they climbed into their vehicles, then Alex followed the Hummer up a dirt road behind the store. The single lane road twisted up the mountain, through a thick forest of evergreens, and it was cool enough he lowered the windows, and took a deep sniff of pine-scented air. They turned onto a short side road and over a stream by using an interesting-looking bridge and then continued on a less used road.

Twenty minutes later, he followed Wesley into a large green meadow with a small lake. They parked in a graveled area between a modest cabin covered with cedar shake siding, and a matching barn a short distance from the edge of the water.

Wesley climbed out of his Hummer and tossed his hat through the open window onto the seat. The geese on the lake honked at them while he waited for Alex to climb out of his rental car. "What do you think of my little piece of heaven?"

Alex hadn't realized how high up the side of the mountain he was until he saw the Pacific Ocean through a gap between the fir trees. He also noticed how much cooler it was at this altitude. "This is fantastic."

"I know. You're one of the few people I let up here. What I want to show you is in the barn."

When Alex turned back, he noticed both roofs were covered in solar panels, but the barn had large skylights in the center. He strolled beside Wesley to the rear side of the building and waited while Wesley unlocked the door, and then followed him inside and abruptly stopped to look around.

Straight ahead, an array of modern electronic equipment was mounted in a metal frame, six-inches from the rear wall. Behind the rack of electronics, a bundle of cables went up to the open wood beams across the ceiling, where four satellite dishes were aimed in different directions through a section of clear panels in the roof.

In the large open space on his left was a trailer holding a fourteen-foot aluminum boat with a gas outboard motor. What drew his attention was the two-person yellow snow cat with black rubber tracks sitting on a trailer.

Wesley had continued over to a beat up desk, then sat in a brown leather swivel chair and entered several commands on a computer keyboard. The picture on the television was from a video camera focused on a seismographic sensor arm drawing a black line from top to bottom on the screen. A digital clock was displayed on the upper left corner, next to a straight black line, indicating no abnormal seismic activity.

"Alex, you'll find this interesting."

Alex hurried over to a chair at the end of the desk, sat down, and stared at the TV as the seconds scrolled across the clock. What am I looking at?"

"I'm going to rewind back to when I detected an unusual seismic event." Wesley studied the clock counting backward while the image remained the same. When the clock reached 9:00 AM, he hit pause. "Notice anything unusual?"

Alex studied the readout. "No, it looks like nothing happened."

"That's right. Now watch this."

Wesley moved the mouse pointer to a small area just past the seismometer needle and zoomed in. Now magnified, Alex could see a gap in the line, and looked over at Wesley. "What happened?"

Wesley leaned back in his chair and frowned at Alex. "It didn't vibrate like an earthquake. The needle just jumped off the paper for an instant."

Alex leaned back in his chair, surprised by the magnitude of what he had just seen. "Any idea what could have caused that needle to bounce?"

Wesley slowly shook his head no. "I have a theory, but nothing I can prove. If part of the North American tectonic plate rose up temporarily, that would allow the Pacific plate to move underneath it at the Cascadia fault line. The movement would not have been a jarring motion like an earthquake, because it was a smooth transition when the pressure was released. More like suddenly sliding a thin spatula under a large rock. It wouldn't cause a major earthquake, but it could change the elevation and shake things up pretty good."

"It shook things up, all right. Even so, it would take an enormous amount of energy to force a fault line to expand."

"I agree. Something might have occurred beneath the mantel, but my idea about what could have caused it to rise like that is only a theory."

They felt a small thud in the concrete floor, then heard a quiet beeping tone and stared at the television while Wesley quickly typed another command into the computer. The picture now showed two different seismograph pictures side by side, each with a wavy black line above the ink pens.

"What's going on, Wesley?"

"The one on the left is from my mountain, Baker, and the one on the right is from Mount Rainier. These are readings from my own sensors, and they're more sensitive than the ones the government uses. I can activate them remotely when I need to, so I don't drain the batteries. I turned them on after that first seismic event in Victoria. The problem is those smaller events should not have affected my volcanoes. That's the basis for my theory."

"How can you tell the difference?"

"Because that's what my sensors do best. The one I had at Mount Saint Helens indicated the eruption would happen in three days. I told the USGS, but they wouldn't listen to me because I was unknown to them. I was right, so to hell with them. I do my own research now."

"Are you saying we're going to have an eruption?"

"No. At least, not right away. If they continue, it will definitely increase the possibility. Especially if they get greater in magnitude. Whatever is causing this has to be sub-tectonic, and there's nothing we can do about it. I'll keep an eye on the activity, and hopefully, there won't be another seismic event."

"We have to figure out why this is happening, Wesley. If it only happened one time, I'd say it was odd. Two times is a different matter and indicates it could happen again."

Wesley swung his chair around and got up. "Not much more we can do right now. I set the alarm to beep at the cabin if anything happens, so let's go inside and you can fix us some dinner."

"Sounds good. Don't you cook?"

"Not if someone else can do it."

They walked out of the barn, and Alex stopped long enough to grab his bag from the trunk. He took one more look at the Puget Sound through the gap in the trees and then followed Wesley into the cabin.

Chapter 8

***MYSTIC*:**

Lisa looked up from the computer when she saw a reflection on the screen, so she spun her chair around and frowned up at Okawna standing in the doorway to her lab. "None of this makes any sense. I can't figure out how that could be pure ice below the methane."

Okawna leaned against the doorframe. "The ice is a problem, all right, but I'm more concerned about what hit us in the sub." He could see her frustration. "Dinner's ready. Let's get something to eat."

Lisa stood, and Okawna followed her across the walkway. When they entered the lounge, the aroma of hot spices filled the air. They saw the rest of the crew walking past the kitchen serving counter, so they continued across the room to join the others filling their plates.

Okawna stood beside Harrison, who was a crusty old sailor with a face made of leather from being on the water most of his life. "Smells like your kind of food. Hot and spicy."

Harrison smiled and exposed his yellowed teeth. "Since my taste buds ain't what they used to be, the hotter the better."

Joshua stepped back to let Lisa get close to the counter, then looked at the pile of food on the plate of the ship's deckhand, Leroy Bartram, a skinny twenty-four-year-old kid with remnants of a bad case of acne. Bartram did the routine maintenance and cleanup, and any small tasks needed on the ship.

Once everyone was seated, and well into their meal, Lisa decided to tell everyone her idea. "I think we caused a disturbance in the fracture under the methane when we fired the ultrasound. I believe the tsunami was caused by a metal object reflecting our signal back to us, so we need to drill down through the ice to find out what's at the bottom of the crack."

Okawna looked up from his food. "For the moment, I don't think we should do anything. If you're right and we caused this, I don't think we should try anything else until we have more information. I'm going to call a friend of mine about it. He's a geophysics teacher in Montana, but he has a lot of connections."

Mike brushed his white paper napkin across his lips and set it on the table as he looked at the group. "I agree with Okawna. We should check this out before we try anything drastic, like drilling. In the meantime, I'm going to have the *Discovery* leave port and start heading in our direction. I'm not saying we're going to drill down into the ice just yet, but since I'm paying for it anyway, I want to have it nearby, just in case."

Harrison reached over the table, grabbed the dish containing the spicy red sauce, and poured some over his chicken and pasta. "I was up on the bridge when that happened down below, and I saw something on the surface of the water a short distance from the ship."

"Can you describe it?" Okawna asked.

"It was just a large circle of neon blue light about thirty-feet in diameter on the surface of the water, and I could tell it was shining up from below. It only lasted a fraction of a second, and I was lucky to be looking in the right direction."

Okawna indicated he agreed Harrison was lucky to see it. "I was wondering if it could be seen on the surface."

"It would look pretty at night," Harrison added.

Okawna stood and picked up his plate and utensils. "I'm going outside to make my call."

***

Okawna strolled out onto the stern of the ship and leaned against the large white post near the back edge of the deck, then stared down into the clear water. He could tell Mike was more shaken up about being tossed around in the sub than he was showing, and realized he was a little unnerved, too. The energy released by that object during the ultrasound test seemed unreal, and he wondered where something like that could have come from.

He took a deep sniff of air to enjoy the scent of the ocean, but even this far out at sea, the odor of pollution was discernible. He slid his phone from his front pocket, selected the number for his friend, and was asked to leave a message. "Hey, Alex. It's Okawna. I need help with a seismic event, so call me."

He slid the phone back into his pocket and stared out across the water. The sun was slowly descending over the horizon, creating a light show of orange, yellow, and purple on the bottom of the clouds. When he turned and walked across the deck, a knot formed in his stomach at the magnitude of what they had discovered. Whatever was under the ice had been down there for a very long time, and the engineering needed to create such a powerful device was not even possible yet. At least, not on this planet.

Chapter 9

TUESDAY, 8:00 AM. MOUNT BAKER:

Alex walked out of the bedroom and down the short hallway to the living area of the cabin. The interior was nicely done in horizontal white pine boards, with a thick matching mantel above the gas log fireplace. He followed the aroma of fresh coffee into the kitchen and saw Wesley sitting at the small oval table in front of the bay window, intently studying something on his laptop computer. The spacious kitchen was also done in white pine for the walls and cabinets.

Wesley glanced up when Alex walked in. "The cups are in the cabinet above the coffee."

Alex walked to the coffeemaker on the granite counter and filled a white ceramic mug, then sat at the table. "What's going on?"

"I just found this on the internet. That quake we felt yesterday did some damage to the San Juan Islands west of here. FEMA is setting up operations in Anacortes, near the ferry dock and the marina. They're having logistical problems getting rescue workers and emergency supplies to the islands, since the only way to get there is by boat or aircraft."

"Why is this happening, Wesley? A natural seismic event would not be so precise where it caused the damage."

"According to the USGS website, they didn't notice the needle jump off the paper."

Alex sipped his coffee and stared through the window. "I'll call the USGS representative in Seattle and let her know about the jump. She's the one who asked for my help."

"Would that be Sharon Aniston?"

"That's right. Do you know her?"

"She was the only one who believed my warning about Saint Helens."

Alex stood and felt his empty pocket. "I must have left my phone in the car."

When Alex stepped outside, the cool morning air was laden with the aroma of evergreens, and he found it to be a paradise compared to the hot lowlands. He looked through the car window, saw the phone on the passenger seat, and opened the door to get it. When he slammed the door closed, three beautiful Canadian geese floating on the lake began honking as he walked into the cabin.

The instant he sat down, the phone beeped, so he entered a code to play the voice message, then stared out the window and sipped his coffee while he listened. He smiled when he recognized the voice of his friend from California, but his joy quickly faded when he heard the urgency in Okawna's voice and wondered if the disturbance had reached that far south. He entered the number, and it was answered on the fourth ring. "Hey, buddy. I got your message. What's going on?"

"It's been a long time, Alex. Did you hear of any unusual seismic activity in the Pacific Northwest yesterday?"

"Yeah, twice. Why do you ask?"

"I think I know what caused it."

Alex turned on the speaker and set the phone on the table. "I'm with a friend on Mount Baker. Did it originate in California?"

"Not that I'm aware of. What happened on the mainland?"

"They had some unusual seismic activity and I've been told they didn't register like major earthquakes. We're still trying to figure out what could have caused them. Where are you?"

"I'm on a research vessel sixty miles off the coast of Vancouver Island. We were searching for methane hydride and found some on the ocean floor, but during our test, we activated something deep in a fissure under the methane, and it created a tsunami on the ocean floor. The object appears to be some kind of metal reflecting the signal back to the ultrasound unit."

Alex looked over at Wesley, then down at the phone. "It wasn't a tsunami that caused the destruction. It was a seismic event. The first one did severe damage to Victoria, and the second one hit the San Juan Islands." The line was silent for a moment. "Okawna?"

"I'm here, Alex. We had no idea that happened."

"Whatever you do, don't activate that thing again."

"Now that I know what it did, I'll make sure we don't. My boss has a drilling rig on its way to meet us. We think that's the only way to determine what's at the bottom of that crack."

"Would you have room for me on the ship?"

"I think so. I'll check with my boss and call you back."

"Thanks. I look forward to seeing you again."

Alex turned off the phone and looked across the table at Wesley. "Do you remember Sonja from the conference in Iceland?"

Wesley grinned. "The sexy blond woman? Of course."

"She called me yesterday about a sudden increase in the size of the Polar Ice Sheet above Canada, and it happened around the same time as the seismic activity down here. I don't see how they could be connected, but nothing about this makes any sense, anyway."

"I agree. At least your friend on the ship knows what's causing the seismic activity. I'm glad it's not in the hands of some crackpot terrorist." He noticed Alex's grin. "Or should I be worried?"

"I trust my friend, but I don't know the other people on that ship." His phone rang, and he recognized Okawna's number and answered. "Should I rent a boat to meet you?"

"No, my boss wants to know where to send the helicopter."

"Pick me up at the Mount Vernon airport so I can drop off my rental car. What time?"

"Is an hour okay?"

Alex hesitated, wondering if he should stop at his father's ranch first to explain what was going on to his nephew and niece, but decided it was too soon. "An hour is fine. I'll see you on the ship."

Alex turned off the phone and slid it into his front pocket as he stood to get his bag. "I'll let you know what I find out."

"What about Sharon Aniston?"

"That's right. It was your discovery. Would you mind calling her for me?"

"I'll take care of it."

Alex retrieved his bag. "I'll call you once I know what's going on."

Wesley followed Alex out to the car and they shook hands, then Alex climbed in and drove away. He stared after the vehicle until it disappeared into the forest, wondering if his new friend could really discover what was disturbing his volcanoes.

He went back inside and sat in front of his laptop computer and brought up the images from his hidden cameras, with the last one showing the strange bridge over the stream. He got up and headed to the bathroom to take a shower, and as he passed through the living room, he glanced at the fireplace mantel and a picture of him and his high school sweetheart taken many years ago.

When he returned and looked at the images on the computer, the last one was flashing a still frame of Alex's rental car going over the bridge. When he entered a command into the computer, the camera showed the bridge sliding away from the main road, leaving no way to get across. He closed the screen and then carried the computer out the back door.

***

WASHINGTON. MOUNT VERNON AIRPORT:

Alex parked the rental car in front of the main building, and then climbed out and grabbed his small backpack from the back seat. He strolled inside and over to the rental desk of the small air terminal and handed the keys and the rental agreement to a young woman standing behind the counter, waiting while she entered the information into her computer.

A slender black man set a magazine down, stood from a chair in the waiting area, and moved over to the counter. "Are you Professor Alex Cave?"

"That's right."

"I'm Carl Gregory, your pilot."

Alex shook his hand. "Are you a commercial pilot?"

"No, I work for Mike Tanner on the *Discovery*."

Alex signed a piece of paper for the car rental girl and grabbed his pack. "Ready when you are."

Carl held the door open, and Alex walked with him to a white helicopter, with *DISCOVERY* painted in light blue letters on the side. When Carl took his pack and set it in a storage compartment, Alex climbed into the co-pilot's seat, closed the door, and then put on the headset.

Carl climbed in, started the engine, and contacted flight control for clearance to take off. When he received approval, he took the helicopter into the air and headed west to meet up with the *Mystic*.

Alex pointed through the front window. "Could you take me over the San Juan islands and Victoria so I can see the damage? A few of my friends live on Orcas Island."

"No problem. It's on our way."

A few minutes later, Carl dropped to a lower altitude while Alex stared out the window at the amount of destruction on the islands. A large resort on Orcas Island lay in ruin; its hotel accommodations built onto the steep hillside above the resort were now a pile of rubble clogging the harbor. Pleasure boats had been tossed onto the shore like toys, and bodies were being stacked on what remained of the docks.

On another island, million dollar mansions were now rubble in the cold water at the bottom of steep hillsides. Small resorts had collapsed buildings and torn up docking facilities, and several outbuildings were now piles of charred wood. Victoria was no longer the beautiful city he had visited years ago, and would probably never be the same again. He knew whatever was at the bottom of the fault line must be powerful.

***

Thirty minutes later, they approached a beautiful white and light-blue ship, alone on the vast Pacific Ocean. "Is that the *Discovery*?"

"No, that's the *Mystic*, Mike's personal research ship. Isn't she a beauty? The *Discovery* will join her later this morning."

Alex admired the *Mystic*'s graceful design and recognized it from a boating magazine. It was a tri-hull, designed and built by a company in Australia. When it was underway, the center hull was held above the water by the two outside pontoons, with the front ends curved vertical wedges designed to slice through the waves instead of going over them. The bow swept up and back over tinted viewing windows on the main deck and continued up to the bridge. Large tinted windows ran along both sides of the main deck, with smaller windows for the lower deck spaced evenly along the sides of the ship.

They approached from the stern, and on the left side was a fifteen-foot white submarine cradled in a blue steel support frame. On the right side, another set of brackets held a nineteen-foot white fiberglass motorboat with a blue canvas top. Straight ahead was the main body of the ship, with double doors in the rear bulkhead. Above the doors was a viewing deck behind the bridge.

Alex saw a man standing on the bridge as Carl gently set the helicopter down on the stern between the sub and the motorboat. When he left the engine running, Alex looked over at him. "You're not staying?"

"No, I'm going back to *Discovery*. That's where I work. Good luck, Mister Cave."

"Thanks for the ride."

Alex climbed out and grabbed his pack while his best friend stepped out through the double doors, then smiled as he walked over to join him. Okawna motioned Alex inside the ship, and once they were safely out of the downwash from the rotor blades, the helicopter took off and soared back toward the mainland.

Alex set his pack down and gave his friend a quick hug, then stepped back and smiled. "It's great to see you again."

"You too, Alex. Let's go meet the rest of the crew. We have coffee waiting, and we'll show you what we've discovered."

"Sounds good."

Alex grabbed his pack and followed Okawna through the double doors, turned right past the inside stairs up to the bridge, then into the lounge. "This is a nice ship."

"Everything is top of the line."

They stopped and Alex set his pack down again to shake hands, as Okawna introduced him to Mike, Joshua, and then Lisa. When he shook her hand, he noticed her face flush. "It's nice to meet you."

Lisa felt her heart rate increase as she shook Alex's hand. When Okawna said he was an old friend and a teacher, she had imagined a frumpy old bald man with horn-rimmed glasses, not the tall, good looking man who just shook her hand.

Okawna indicated the table. "Let's sit down and we'll show you the recordings."

Alex sat at the corner of the table and poured coffee from the thermos. Okawna, Mike, and Lisa sat around him at the table. He was surprised when the big man named Joshua sat at a desk near a window and entered commands into a computer. Because of his size, he had assumed he was a deckhand.

Okawna unrolled a map and pointed to the location of the ship. "This is where we found the methane."

Alex studied the map for a moment and then looked around at the group. "That's the Cascadia fault line. It starts north of Vancouver Island and follows the coastline down to northern California."

Lisa looked over at Joshua. "Play the recording, please."

Joshua pressed play, and across the room, the television screen showed the video recording from the rover. After a few moments of darkness, the slab of methane hydride was illuminated by the sub's brilliant lights, and Alex turned to look at Lisa. "I thought methane hydride was white."

"You're correct, but that's not pure methane. It's a mixture of chemical compounds found in our atmosphere, and they shouldn't even be down there."

On the television, the picture from the rover was circling the slab, and then the lens focused on the black material separating the methane from the clear ice. In her excitement, Lisa reached over and put her hand on Alex's forearm. "Pause that, Josh. Something happened between the formation of the methane and that black material. After what happened yesterday, I didn't want to send the rover down to get a sample until we learn what's at the bottom of the ice. Please continue, Josh."

The picture from the Rover tilted down above the methane, and they saw the discolorations creating a spiraled green band, getting smaller towards the middle. The rover stopped, and the view from the camera was magnified until the rover was on the surface of the methane. Three seconds later, the picture suddenly changed to blinding blue light for a fraction of a second, and then the picture showed silt billowing up from the seafloor before going dark.

Okawna looked over at Alex. "That's when Mike and I were tossed around in the sub, and the view from the camera doesn't do it justice. What Mike and I saw from inside the sub was translucent neon blue light shooting up through the water from the crack in the sea floor. It happened just before a pressure wave slammed into the sub and I lost control. Our first mate saw a neon blue circle of light on the surface, near the ship, and wondered what it would look like at night. This may sound strange, but I wonder what it would look like from outer space."

Lisa realized her hand was still holding Alex's arm, and she quickly pulled it away. When he turned and smiled, her heart raced. She gave him a quick, embarrassed smile, and then looked back at the television. "Could you put on the picture from the ultrasound, please?"

The television showed several still pictures of the dark cylindrical object deep beneath the ice and stopped, so Lisa looked over at Alex. "That's the best picture I have. The only way to get a better look is to drill and send an optical cable down into the ice."

Alex looked at the faces around the table. "I hope all of you realize the magnitude of what you've discovered. Whatever it is also disturbed the Mount Baker and Mount Rainier volcanoes. We're worried that besides the destruction it's already caused, if these events continue, there could be a major eruption." Alex decided not to mention the incident at the polar ice cap and leaned back in his chair, then looked over at Okawna. "You mentioned you know what caused this to happen."

"Yes, when we fired our experimental ultrasound. I'm sure that's what triggered whatever happened."

"So, you used it twice, and this happened each time?"

Mike spoke for the first time. "No, that was the only time we did the experiment, right, Lisa?"

"That's right."

Alex wondered what was going on. "We had two events yesterday. The first was around 9:00 AM, the other about eleven AM."

Okawna grinned and shook his head. "You're right, Alex. We did it twice. At nine yesterday morning, we got our first detection of the methane from the ultrasound unit here on the ship. The second time was about eleven, when Mike and I were hit by the tsunami."

Alex noticed Lisa's puzzled expression. "Is something wrong?"

"I'm not really sure. We used a powerful, wide beam frequency of our new ultrasound to locate the methane, and it's extremely powerful, but I didn't think the sound waves were strong enough to penetrate the methane and that much ice, and still reach what's at the bottom."

Now Alex wondered if there was a connection with the polar ice cap. "Could the sound waves from the ship's ultrasound reach the Arctic?"

Lisa wondered where this was leading. "Sure. It's the same way whales communicate over long distances. With the power our new transducer puts out, the sound waves could have easily reached the arctic. Why do you ask?"

"Yesterday, I received a call from my friend at the CHARS station near the Arctic Ocean, and it seems the water south of the polar ice sheet was suddenly frozen into transparent ice that floated on the surface. I'm not sure what to make of all this, but at least you stopped using the ultrasound, so we won't have another seismic event."

"The ice under the black material is transparent, too, Alex." Lisa told him. "The only thing left is my idea to drill down through the methane. Once we find out what that thing is at the bottom of the crack, we'll have a better idea of what's happening."

Mike stood from the table. "I say we should do it. If we don't use the ultrasound, we shouldn't have any problems."

Alex glanced around and everyone was staring at him for a yes or no, so he looked up at Mike. "You've got my vote. I'd like to know what's down there."

"All right. I'll tell *Discovery* to get started."

Chapter 10

SEATTLE FEDERAL BUILDING. USGS HEADQUARTERS:

Patrick tapped his knuckles on the window of Sharon's office, waiting until she looked up from reading the morning reports before speaking. "You're not going to believe this. Wesley Patterson is on line three, and said he will only talk to you."

Sharon waved Patrick into the room and pressed the button for the phone speaker. "Hello, Wesley."

"Was that Patrick who answered?"

"Yes. He's listening to us."

"Tell him to leave."

Sharon looked up at Patrick's stunned expression. "Can I ask why?"

"Mount Saint Helens."

Patrick leaned across the desk to the phone. "Okay, I made the wrong call, and I'm sorry. Haven't you ever made a wrong decision?"

"Not when people's lives are at stake. That's the only reason I'm calling. There is a research ship conducting an experiment sixty miles west of Vancouver Island, and they might know what happened. I'm working with Alex Cave, and he's on it right now."

Wesley explained about the seismometer jumping off the paper and his theory about the tectonic plate movement. "Baker and Rainier are showing some activity because of those events."

Patrick shook his head at Sharon and leaned across the desk again. "That's impossible, Patterson. Nothing can create that much force and we didn't detect any activity on the mountains. This Cave person. What's his background, and why should we trust him?"

"Good bye, Sharon."

Sharon turned off the phone. "You're an idiot, Patrick. I called Mister Cave and asked for his help. You said it yourself. You don't have any idea why these seismic events are so precise and do so much damage for their size."

"I know, but you can't believe a crazy theory like that could really be possible, do you?"

"Unless you can give me a better explanation, I'm not going to dismiss his idea. I just hope he calls me back after Mister Cave returns from the ship."

***

MYSTIC:

Okawna stood from the table and placed his hand on Alex's shoulder. "Let's go out on deck and reminisce."

Alex stood and followed Okawna out of the lounge and along the walkway to the stern, and then they stopped next to the hoist and stared out across the ocean. The cool breeze off the water felt nice, compared to the heat on the mainland when he had come down from the mountain.

Okawna leaned his shoulder against the hoist. "I'm sorry about your brother and his wife. Director Donner let me read the file."

"I just hope it's over. My nephew and niece are staying at my father's place, but it's registered under my mom's maiden name, Parker, so hopefully, the Russians don't know anything about it."

"Anything I can do to help?"

"After what I did in Russia, I've lost all my connections, but Donner promised to let me know if anything comes up."

"I still have contacts in the agency, so I'll check around."

"You've always had my back, Okawna. If there is anything I can do for you, just let me know."

"You could tell me what really happened during the Dead Energy operation."

Alex thought about what Menno Simons had told him that night in the Nevada desert. "I just had the craziest idea you could ever imagine. How long until you start drilling?"

"I don't know. Mike hired me two months ago, so I'm the newbie."

"What do you know about the crew?"

"I did some checking, and Mike seems to be all right. He doesn't care about money. He just likes the research his wealth gives him. Lisa comes from a modest background and doesn't have a criminal record. Joshua spent some time in therapy for anger management, but other than a few bar scuffles, he's never been in much trouble. Our first mate is just an old sea dog, and from what little records exist, he's spent most of his life on ships traveling the world. I couldn't find anything wrong with the deckhand's background, but I'm worried about our Captain. His background is too clean, so someone created it for him. So, what's this crazy idea of yours?"

Before he could answer, they heard Harrison's voice through the ship's public address system, announcing the arrival of the *Discovery's* helicopter. They hurried across the deck and through the doors in the rear bulkhead and then turned to look out through the windows in the doors. When Carl landed the helicopter on the deck, a single person climbed out and hurried toward them.

Alex opened the door for an attractive woman dressed in faded blue jean shorts with a tight fitting white tank top shirt. She was slender, with red hair hanging in natural wavy curls to her shoulders.

As the helicopter took off, she smiled warmly and reached out to shake Alex's hand. "I'm Rita Harrow, Mister Cave."

Alex accepted. "Just Alex, will do."

"I understand you study rocks."

Okawna chuckled. "Don't let her fool you, Alex. She has master's degrees in electronics and mechanical engineering."

"Well, Ms. Harrow. You're the prettiest grease monkey I've ever seen."

The trio smiled and headed into the lounge, then turned in unison when they heard footsteps coming their way. Lisa, Mike, and Dieter were walking in their direction and stopped in front of them.

Rita noticed the way little Lisa was looking at Alex. "I understand you're a college professor. Does it get boring being around children all the time?" She looked over at Lisa and grinned.

From the moment he met Lisa, Alex knew she was attracted to him, but he wasn't interested in her. He felt more comfortable with Rita, since she was older and more experienced with life. "The students are never boring, but I get tired of repeating myself every semester."

Mike noticed what was going on and interrupted. "Alex, this is our Captain, John Dieter."

Alex held out his hand, but when Dieter hesitated before accepting, he realized the Captain was not happy to have him on the ship. "Sorry to inconvenience you, Captain."

Mike noticed Dieter's reaction and wondered why, but let it drop. "The *Discovery* will be in position to set up in three hours. Once *Celeas* anchors the drill head above the methane, I'm going to send down our experimental high-pressure steam drill. It is like an ice core drill, but we send steam down to melt the ice for an optical lens. We'll be able to see the picture from the *Discovery* in Lisa's laboratory."

"Who is *Celeas*?" Alex asked.

Rita smiled at him. "She's our robotic workaholic on the *Discovery*. It's an unmanned prototype I designed for underwater research. She is like the rovers I designed for the *Mystic*, but she is much larger and more powerful, and we can attach a variety of tools for working deep underwater. She's remotely controlled from the ship using the new technology I developed for the ultrasound system, and doesn't need a long control cable."

Alex strolled over to the rear window and pointed out at the white submarine in the brackets on the left side of the stern. Two mechanical arms were folded back along its length, and four high-intensity lights were attached to the front above the clear bubble shaped window. "What's this one do?"

Okawna grinned. "That's my baby, the *Wizard*. She can hold two people, and we use it for observation, investigation, and to collect samples. Mike and I were in her when we were tossed along the ocean floor." He looked over at his boss. "Mind if I take Alex down with me to watch the drilling?"

Mike was not anxious to go down again. "Not at all. He should find it interesting."

Okawna looked at Alex and grinned. "You're going to enjoy this. We'll wait until *Celeas* has finished setting the drill head in place, then we'll go down to watch."

"I missed breakfast. Do you have a snack machine?"

"I can make you something," Lisa offered.

Alex looked at Rita, who smirked at him, and then he indicated to Lisa that would be great. He followed her across the lounge to the refrigerator in the kitchen and stood beside her as she searched the shelves.

Dieter looked over at Okawna. "Your friend sounds like an educated man. What is his profession?"

Okawna could sense Dieter was not happy about Alex joining the crew and was searching for information. "He teaches geology at a college."

Dieter locked stares with Okawna, who had never shown him the respect he deserved. He was the Captain on this ship, and Okawna was just another new employee who needed to be under his command. The moment dragged on, but when Okawna did not even blink, Dieter decided to learn more about this geology teacher from his contact on the mainland. He turned and hurried out of the lounge, then up the inside stairs to the bridge.

Mike thought this might happen, and from the little time he had spent with Okawna in San Diego, he was a man that would not be intimidated. He noticed Okawna still staring at Dieter's back. "Well, Okawna. In a little while, we'll be able to see what that mysterious object is at the bottom of the ice."

"What's up with Dieter?"

"He thinks he's in charge, but don't worry about it. Let's find out what's in the ice."

***

An hour later, Alex followed Okawna up the ladder to the top of the sub, and they climbed down inside. Alex closed the hatch, sat in the seat behind Okawna, and fastened his seat belt, and five minutes later, they were in the water. Alex felt the rear thruster pushing the sub forward, and for the moment, there was nothing to see as they followed a flexible, six-inch diameter orange hose down to the ocean floor.

***

CHARS HELICOPTER:

Tom was steering the helicopter toward the southern end of the ice sheet to collect a sample of the strange, clear ice and glanced over at Sonja in the copilot seat. "Is it my imagination, or has the pyramid moved farther south?"

Sonja stared into the distance, and the angle of the sun was shining down through the ice like a prism. She noticed a dark area deep beneath the surface and directly below the top of the pyramid. As they drew closer to the top, the angle changed and the dark area was gone. "What is our current GPS location compared to the last time we were here?"

Tom looked down at the instrument panel. "I was right. The pyramid is over three hundred miles farther south than the last time we were here. It must move when the ice on the northern end expands and forces it further south."

Tom continued flying south, past the red and white cargo ship still locked in the ice, and it appeared to be deserted. When they reached the end of the clear ice, he kept the helicopter hovering above the surface, two hundred feet above the water. "Are you sure about this?"

Sonja nodded through the front window. "Once the ice stopped rising out of the ocean, those people on the cargo ship did not freeze to the surface, so we should be okay to land without getting stuck again."

Tom hoped Sonja was right as he cautiously set down and brought the engine speed down to idle. When she grabbed the door handle, he grabbed her arm. "Be careful."

Sonja opened the door and felt the cold wind flowing across the surface, but it didn't feel nearly as cold as the first time she had stepped out onto the clear ice. She cautiously touched the surface with the tip of her shoe, quickly pulled it back, and smiled at Tom. "I will be fine."

She stepped out of the helicopter and continued across the ice to the edge. When she looked down, the sheer wall of ice dropped straight into the ocean, two-hundred-feet below. She stepped back and pulled a plastic jar from her pocket, then knelt down and tried to use the lid to scrape some ice into the container. The ice was so hard, the plastic lid just slid along the surface without leaving a scratch, so she stood, walked back to the helicopter, and opened the door. "The ice is exceptionally hard, so I need a knife."

Tom climbed out and opened one of the storage doors, and dug around in a small plastic toolbox and found a small hammer. He knelt down and banged it against the surface, but it bounced up without leaving a mark. "What is this stuff?"

"Try it again."

Tom raised the hammer above his head and grinned at Sonja. With all his strength, he slammed it down onto the surface.

Chapter 11

PACIFIC OCEAN. THE SUB:

"Nice job you have, Okawna. What's up with you and Rita?"

"Nothing. We flirt, but I learned it's not a good idea to have a relationship with someone you work with. Especially when living on a ship so much of the time." He glanced up at the rear-view mirror and saw the sad expression in Alex's eyes. "I'm sorry, Alex."

"That's okay. And you're right. Sevi would be alive and on some photographic assignment right now if we hadn't fallen in love."

"I'm just glad it was me who managed to extract you from Russia. Our orders were to stop you, period. Some of our people would have shot you on sight."

"In that case, I'm glad, too." He glanced around the inside at the exterior walls, and the coating appeared to be glazed on, not painted. "How deep does this thing go?"

"It's rated at ten-thousand-feet, but I sure as hell don't want to test it."

"I don't recognize this material on the walls. Some new metal alloy?"

"No, the pressure hull is ceramic."

"You're kidding?"

"Welcome to the New World, my friend."

Alex grinned and lightly shook his head in wonder. "Great. I'm diving to the bottom of the ocean in a clay pot."

Okawna looked at Alex's reflection in the mirror. "We're coming up on the drill head. Take a look."

Alex leaned forward and around Okawna's chair to stare through the front window. The lights illuminated a two-foot thick, by six-foot diameter stainless steel disk on top of the massive slab of methane. Four separate one-inch steel cables were attached to the outside of the metal disk and looked like long black spider legs disappearing into the darkness. The orange tube was attached to the hole in the middle of the heavy steel disc, and he noticed it swaying with the current, flattened in some areas. "Is the tube supposed to be flat?"

"The tube is just a guide for the steam drill and fiber optic cable. It's full of sea water, so the pressure is equal to the outside so the tube won't stay collapsed."

"Wizard, this is Lisa. How do you read?"

"Loud and clear. How is the picture up there on the surface?"

"Your camera is good. I can see the transmission from the fiber optic lens, so we're ready to melt the ice. Are you sure you want to stay down there? You won't be able to see the pictures from the lens."

Okawna looked in the mirror at Alex. "I'd like to stay down until I'm sure the drill head and optical lens are working properly."

"I'm fine. This is exciting compared to my usual workday."

"Lisa, we'll stay for a while to make sure everything goes as planned."

"Okay. We're starting the steam now."

From their point of view in the sub, the only noticeable changes were the white bubbles wobbling up out of the methane. The bright white light from the optical cable was reflecting through the methane ice like a prism, putting on a light show on the outer edges, similar to the illuminated end of a glass rod.

"What does it look like down there?" Lisa asked.

"Everything looks fine."

"Great. I'm going through that dark material."

Okawna noticed the light in the ice flicker, then tumbling red bubbles boiled out from the methane around the drill head. It lasted several minutes before the red bubbles stopped and the white bubbles reappeared. "What just happened, Lisa?"

"It just punched through and the black material in the ice and it is so clear I can see the object down at the bottom. It's a long cylinder, but I'll need to go deeper to determine the size. It appears to be gray, so probably some type of metal."

Alex thought about the devices he had heard of during the Dead Energy mission. "Remember that crazy idea I told you about? It may not be so crazy after all."

"Okay, I'm waiting. Tell me about it."

Blinding blue light suddenly flashed in front of the submarine for a fraction of a second, causing both men to blink furiously to clear their vision. When the pressure wave slammed into the sub, the front window became vertical before flipping upside down. The seat belts dug painfully into their waists, keeping them from smashing into the ceiling as the sub flipped end over end above the seafloor. Okawna struggled to regain control, but the thrusters could not overcome the power of the wave.

Alex grabbed the back of Okawna's seat with both hands as he was hurled forward against the back of it, then the sub hit the mud and his shoulder slammed against the wall. The sub began tumbling in every direction, and Alex was tossed from side to side, with only the seatbelt keeping him from being tossed out of the chair.

The front window suddenly slammed down onto the seabed, and the lights blinked off. Alex's head bounced off the video screen on the back of Okawna's chair, and then the sub slowly leaned over onto its side in a billowing cloud of silt.

***

THE CABIN:
Wesley was watching the news reports and footage from the rescue efforts in the islands when he felt his recliner rise up and down a fraction of an inch, then the alarm for the seismometers in the barn began beeping. "Oh, crap!"

He leapt out of the chair, ran through the kitchen and out the back door, then across to the barn. He yanked the door open, ran to his desk, and remained standing as he used the mouse to zoom in on the readout from the seismograph. The needle had jumped off the paper again, but this time the gap was nearly one-quarter-inch long. There were two separate beeps, so he changed the picture to his sensor from Mt. Rainier. The lines on the readout started as a small wavy line, which increased to two-inches wide before tapering back to zero. "Oh, crap," he whispered.

He reached into his pocket and grabbed his phone to call Alex, and after four rings, he was asked to leave a message. "This is Wesley. We just had a major event. Call me."

***

POLAR ICE SHEET:
Brilliant blue light suddenly filled the ice as a bolt of blue lightning shot up from the top of the pyramid. A thunderous boom echoed across the frozen expanse, as it suddenly rose beneath their feet, tossing Sonja into the air and driving Tom down against the surface.

Sonja slammed down onto the ice as the surface shifted in all directions, rolling her toward the edge. Her legs slid over the side and she clawed at the ice with the tips of her gloves to stop slipping over the edge. "Tom! Help me!"

Tom tried to stand to run over, but the movement tossed him back down. He rolled onto his hands and knees, desperate to grab one of her hands as she slid farther over the edge. Her face was a mask of terror, her eyes were wide and her mouth was open in a silent scream.

He drove his foot against the runner and shoved with all his might, sliding across the ice and curling his fingers over Sonja's gloved hand, just as she slipped over the edge. "No!" He roared and dug his fingertips into her glove. He pulled back with all his strength, but he slid across the ice with her until he felt his foot hit the crossbar on the runner. He curled his ankle around the bar, but their weight and motion threatened to tear his foot away. "AH!" he screamed against the pain, but kept his foot around the bar and both his hands on one of Sonja's hands.

Sonja saw the agony on Tom's face, bit the glove off her free hand, and ripped it away. She swung her arm around with all her strength and grabbed his coat sleeve, struggling to keep from falling into the freezing ocean.

The motion abruptly ceased and Sonja dragged herself over Tom's shoulder, back onto the surface. She scrambled onto her knees, shoving her shoes against the slick surface while trying to gain traction away from the edge, and then pushed herself up off the ice.

Tom released his foot and rolled onto his back, staring up at the sky while trying to catch his breath. Sonja dropped onto her knees beside Tom, taking deep gulps of air and trying to calm her frazzled nerves. "Are you all right?" she asked between deep breaths.

Tom stayed on the ice. "Yeah. I'm okay. And You?"

Sonja held his hand. "Yes. Thank you."

She remained kneeling next to Tom and stared out across the new ice sheet below, but the end of the new clear ice was difficult to distinguish from the sky on the horizon.

Tom noticed her staring into the distance with her mouth slightly open. "What is it?" She pointed south, and Tom rolled onto his knees and followed her gaze. "That's something you don't see every day. Remind me not to use a hammer next time."

Sonja looked at Tom. Now that her adrenaline level had returned to normal, she laughed.

Tom sat up and laughed with her, and after a few moments, he stood and grabbed her hand to help her up. "Let's get out of here."

Sonja turned to get into the helicopter and noticed her jar and lid on the ice. She bent down to pick them up, but stopped and turned to look at Tom, then pointed at the helicopter's runner. "Look."

Tom looked down at the small mound of ice crystals scraped from the surface when the helicopter had slid on the ice, and then he looked up and gave her a puzzled expression. "Did I do that?"

"I don't know."

She knelt down, scraped the ice into the jar and closed the lid, then stood. "You are right. We should leave."

Tom walked around the helicopter and climbed into the pilot's seat. Once Sonja was ready, he took off and pointed the helicopter toward the CHARS facility.

Chapter 12

CAVE RANCH, SPARROW VALLEY:

Robert Cave heard the thumping of small feet running across the wooden back porch and smiled. The kitchen screen door slammed shut, and then Kristy Cave ran into the living room.

"I felt an earthquake, grandpa!" Kristy said with the excited enthusiasm of a ten-year-old girl.

Robert smiled at her tousled blonde hair and the smudge of dirt on her face. "It was just a minor tremor, sweetie. Nothing to worry about."

Kristy flopped onto the light brown couch and frowned at the dirt under her fingernails. "That didn't feel like a tremor, and the horses are acting weird, too." She looked over at Robert in his recliner. "We should call Uncle Alex. He knows all about this stuff. How come he never comes around anymore? Is it because you hate him?"

Roberts's hands tightened on the armrests. "I don't want to talk about it right now."

Kristy stood and went over to put her arms around his neck. She loved the way he smelled and the feel of the stubble on his cheek, but when his salt and pepper hair tickled her nose, she let go to look into his dark blue eyes. "I love you, grandpa. That counts for something, right?"

Robert gave her a hug. "It sure does. I love you, too."

Robert frowned when he heard the roar of a motorcycle coming up the driveway. His grandson, Derek, was in turmoil over the loss of his parents, and being torn from his high school friends in the city to live with his grandfather on a ranch during his senior year only made it worse. He was having difficulty balancing guidance and discipline with sympathy when he dealt with Derek's belligerent attitude.

"Derek's home!" Kristy yelled as she ran across the living room and through the kitchen, letting the screen door slam shut behind her. She leapt over the two porch steps onto the ground and ran to Derek, as he stopped the motorcycle in front of the large covered porch. She adored her big brother, but he had changed since their parents were killed. He seemed angry with grandpa all the time and she didn't understand why.

"Did you feel that, Derek?" She yelled over the noise of the exhaust pipes.

Derek shut the engine off and smiled at his little sister while he removed his helmet. "Feel what?"

"I don't know for sure. Grandpa said it was a tremor, but I think it was an earthquake."

"I still don't know what you're talking about."

"Didn't you feel the ground move?"

"No, I was riding around, trying to figure out where all the back roads go."

Kristy grinned at him. "Who were you with?"

"I always ride alone. Except with you, anyway."

"Yeah, right. I saw the way Jessica Parker looked at you in the mall."

He grinned. "You see too much for your own good."

"I told grandpa we should call Uncle Alex. He knows about this stuff."

Derek frowned as he hung his helmet on the handlebars and set the kickstand. He was having a hard time deciding how he felt about his uncle. He had not seen him since the funeral in Arizona, and that was under stressful conditions. Robert would not even talk to Alex anymore, but wouldn't tell him why.

He swung his leg off the motorcycle and walked with Kristy up the two creaking steps into the shade of the porch. They sat down on a well-worn wooden porch swing hanging from rusty chains, and Derek gave them a push. "What did grandpa say?"

"It just made him sad. He still blames Uncle Alex for mom and dad getting killed."

"I know. The cops said it was an accident, so I'm not sure what to believe, and Robert won't even talk to me about it."

"If we call Uncle Alex and ask him about the earthquake, he might come out and visit, and we could ask him ourselves."

He stopped pushing the seat and looked over at Kristy. "Why are you getting so excited about an earthquake? In fact, how do you know what an earthquake feels like? We didn't have any in Arizona."

"I just know what they're supposed to be like. The ground shakes and everything falls down. Only this one fell up."

Derek laughed and leaned back in the swing. "How can something fall up?"

"The ground pushed me up, like when I'm in an elevator."

Derek stopped smiling and sat up. If Kristy was right, something was very wrong. "When did it happen?"

"I felt it just before you got here."

"Did you explain that to Robert?"

"He said it's just a tremor."

Derek stood and grabbed Kristy's hand. "I think we'd better explain it to him. If you're right, we should call Alex right away." He followed Christie through the screen door and let it slam closed behind him.

Robert frowned and pushed himself out of the recliner, frustrated with the kids constantly letting the screen door slam shut. Just because they had lived in the city was no excuse for not obeying his rules. He turned toward the kitchen and stared at his grandkids. "What did I tell you about that screen door?"

Derek and Kristy stopped to look at each other, realizing they had forgotten about the door in their excitement. "Sorry," they said simultaneously.

"Kristy just told me about the earthquake. Something isn't right about what she felt, and I really think we should call Alex. You must've felt it, too?"

Robert waved off the idea and turned back to the TV. "It was just a tremor. I'm not going to call Alex about it." He plopped down into the recliner. "He's a busy man, and we should leave him alone."

Derek walked around the recliner to look at him. "You may not want to talk to him, but I do. This is very important, and you shouldn't let your hatred make you blind about the danger."

"Fine! You talk to him. His number is in the address book on the kitchen counter."

Derek turned, stomped into the kitchen, grabbed the address book and cordless phone off the counter, and then stomped out onto the back porch. Kristy ran across the kitchen, barely managing to grab the edge of the screen door before it slammed shut. She let out a soft sigh of relief and walked outside, and saw Derek sitting in the porch swing, looking through the address book. She stood in front of him and leaned back against the wooden handrail, and could tell by his scowl and his bunched together eyebrows he was mad at grandpa. They didn't get along like they did before the accident.

Derek handed the address book to Kristy. "The old man's a dinosaur. No cellphone and no computer. Read the number for me so I can dial."

Kristy looked at the page for C's and saw the names of their parents in her grandmother's writing. They said she had bad cancer when she passed away two years ago. Now things were different here on the ranch without her. "Here it is. Ask him to come out here."

Derek punched in the numbers and put the phone against his ear. "He's in Montana, Kristy. He can't just stop everything he's doing and come out here. I just hope he knows about this."

Derek let it ring several times, and then was told to leave a message. "Alex, this is Derek. The ground is doing some weird things out here, so could you call me?"

He pressed the end button and looked at Kristy. "He's not at home. I don't know what the time difference is, so maybe he's still teaching."

"He'll come out to see us. You'll see."

Derek stood and handed the phone to Kristy. "Don't get your hopes up." He walked down the steps and grabbed his helmet from the handlebars. "There's nothing to do here, so I'm going for a ride."

Kristy sat on the porch swing and watched Derek drive away. "He'll come and see us," she whispered to herself. "I know he will."

Chapter 13

THE SUB.

Okawna lay sideways in the darkness, with his head and shoulder against the wall. He ran his fingers across the instrument panel, flipped the switch for the emergency lights, and the interior was bathed in red light. "Alex?"

"I'm okay. I'm glad this thing has seatbelts. Are you all right?"

"Yeah. There's a circuit breaker panel on the wall near your head. Try resetting them so we can find out what condition we're in."

Alex pushed his shoulder away from the wall and opened the panel, then flipped the breakers on, one at a time. The first one clicked into place and the main lights came on, the second one clicked on, and they could hear a quiet whirring sound, but the third one would not reset. The fourth one clicked, but nothing happened. "That's all of them."

"Let me try the thrusters."

Okawna wrapped his fingers around the control arm, twisted the handle, and felt the sub rising off the bottom. When he pressed the thumb throttle forward, the sub slowly became level in the water. "So far, so good."

Alex checked out the walls of the sub. "I expected this clay pot to shatter when we hit the ground."

Okawna reached up and touched the knot on his head, just back from the scalp line. He inspected his fingers, but didn't see any blood. He studied the instrument panel, and many of the indicator lights were off, so he looked at Alex in the mirror. "The carbon dioxide scrubbers aren't working, and only two of the batteries are still connected. We have an hour's worth of air left without the scrubbers, but the pressure is holding steady at six atmospheres."

Okawna slid his headset on and pressed the button. "Calling the *Mystic*. Anybody there?"

Alex listened for a voice from the speaker, but no one responded. "Can we get back to the ship?"

"Let's find out."

Okawna pushed the control arm forward, and they felt the sub moving, but he had to hold the arm slightly to the right to move in a straight line. "We've only got one thruster operating, but it should get us back to the surface. It's just going to take a little longer."

"Will we have enough air, or should I hold my breath?"

"Depends on how long you can hold it. It's going to be close, so let's keep the conversation to a minimum."

"Wake me when we get close to the surface."

***

THE *MYSTIC*:

Lisa paced across the stern deck while the hoist seemed to move in slow motion, bringing the submarine out of the water. It had been over an hour since they had lost contact with Okawna and Alex, but a few minutes ago, Harrison saw the white sub bobbing on the surface near the stern and notified everyone on the intercom. Everyone except Dieter and Harrison ran out onto the stern to watch the retrieval, grateful the sub had come back to the ship. Since the sub was programed to return on its own, if possible, they did not know if Alex and Okawna were still alive.

***

Down in her cabin, Rita raised the corner of her mattress to retrieve a satellite phone, then slid it into her pocket and left the room. She hurried along the central walkway and up the stairs to the lounge, pausing at the top to look around.

With everyone out on deck, she continued up the stairs and peered out through the window in the rear door. When she saw everyone out on the stern, she moved back into the lounge and brought out the phone, then chose a contact. It rang four times before it was answered.

***

While the sub swung around toward the storage bracket, Lisa stepped out of the way of a trail of water dribbling across the deck. She ran to the front of the sub and tried to see through the bubble window, but it was fogged over on the inside.

Joshua quickly set the ladder against the side, but before he could climb up, the hatch opened. He was surprised when Alex and Okawna casually climbed out as if nothing had happened. "You had us worried for a while."

Lisa released the breath she had been holding. "Oh, thank goodness you're still alive!"

After they climbed down, Lisa wanted to throw her arms around Alex's neck, but saw the dried blood down the side of his left eye and stopped. "Oh, my, gosh! What happened to your head?"

Alex reached up and wiped the back of his hand across his forehead. He felt a crusty substance and looked at the back of his hand. "I guess I bumped it against something."

Rita hurried out onto the rear deck and wrapped her arms around Alex's neck, pulling him close for a tight hug. "I was so worried I'd never see you again."

Lisa grabbed Alex's hand and tried to pull him across the deck. "I have to clean that wound before it gets infected."

Alex gently pulled his hand back. "I'm fine, Lisa."

Mike moved closer and smiled at Okawna. "You had us worried. What happened?"

"The same thing that happened to us, Mike. The blue light flashed and the pressure wave slammed into the sub. We lost one thruster and communication, and the scrubber failed, so we barely made it back to the surface."

***

Dieter stared down at the stern through the rear bridge window. "They are still alive, Harrison."

"At least we got the sub back in one piece."

"We may not even need the sub. I would rather they did not return at all. I will be in the lounge." He turned and walked down the inside stairs.

***

Out on deck, Joshua got Okawna's attention. "I have the recording set up and ready to go."

"Great. I'm eager to see it."

Everyone followed Joshua into the lounge, where Dieter was casually leaning against the wall. From his expression, Alex could tell Dieter was not happy about something, so he sat at the table where he could see him. Mike and Okawna joined him, but Lisa and Rita remained standing.

Lisa grabbed the first aid kit from the kitchen, and then stood next to Alex, holding a gauze pad out in front of him. "Bend over so I can clean your wound."

Alex shoved her hand away. "Not now."

Lisa sat down on a chair and stared up at Alex, wondering if she had done something wrong. She was beginning to realize with Rita going after him, she didn't stand a chance.

Rita remained standing, studying Dieter. Her gut was telling her he had something going on other than the research, and Alex was interfering with his plans. She just hoped it didn't interfere with hers.

Joshua held the remote control and waited until everyone was ready and pressed play. The television screen was dark for a moment before they saw the lens easily enter the discolored methane. A few moments later, the lens entered the thick black area. It was obvious the drill was having difficulty punching through, as the black material was slowly turning red.

Okawna turned to look at Lisa. "Alex and I saw red bubbles boiling out of the hole when that happened."

"That black material must be extremely hard. I got a sample to analyze."

After several minutes, the lens entered the clear ice, and they could see both sides of the crack in the seafloor as if magnified, just as Lisa mentioned. One-thousand-feet below the lens, a gray cylinder was lying horizontally across the bottom of the crack.

Joshua pressed pause. "I finished writing a new computer program to enhance that cylinder, and it's flat on one end and pointed at the other. The picture may not be perfect, but watch as I bring it up for a closer view."

The picture suddenly changed, and they were looking at a long pewter colored cylinder. Starting at the flat end, the exterior of the device was covered with hundreds of dark dots along the outside before reaching the pointed end.

Alex looked at Joshua. "Can you estimate the dimensions?"

"It's approximately twenty-feet long and perhaps a foot in diameter. Like I said, writing this program was a rush job."

No one spoke for a moment, and when Alex looked around the table, all eyes were on him. "I don't know any more about this than the rest of you. I'm just a geologist, remember?"

Dieter remained leaning against the wall and tried to conceal his excitement when he saw the device. He had seen one before, but not in the water, and knew it was time to get rid of Cave. "Well, Professor. Rumor has it you are not just a geology instructor. From what I have learned about you, it would seem you are more the tough, fighting type of geologist. Perhaps you would be more at home on dry land."

Alex was surprised and wondered how much Dieter knew about him. "Honestly, I don't have the answers you're looking for. Whatever that is, somehow it's forcing the Cascadia fault line apart." Alex looked at each one of them. "Did any of you turn on the ultrasound while we were down below?"

They all shook their heads no, and from their expressions, he had difficulty believing someone here would do it on purpose. He paid close attention to Dieter, who was looking directly back at him, lightly shaking his head no.

Alex did not like where this was leading. "If nobody turned on the ultrasound, what made it go off?"

Lisa had a few ideas. "Maybe it was the vibration from the drill? Or maybe the light from the optical lens?"

Mike stood and looked at the group. "I had them bring the optical cable out of the tube, and I'm taking the motorboat over to see what happened to that lens."

"I'm going with you," Lisa stated.

Alex noticed Lisa was still holding the gauze pad and disinfectant. "I'll take that offer now." He leaned over to her.

Lisa smiled, poured the liquid on the pad, and then patted the dried blood away. "It's not as bad as it looks. You might have a little scar above your eye, but I can see you're already used to that. Are you going with us to look at the lens?"

Alex had no desire to see what happened to it. That was for the engineers. Right now, his only concern was what to do about that device. "No, thanks."

He had left his jacket on the back of a lounge chair before going down in the sub, and heard his phone beeping from the pocket. He grabbed the jacket, walked out of the room, and continued out to the stern.

When he had a signal, he entered the code and listened to the urgent message from Wesley. Undoubtedly, Wesley had recorded the event, and he needed to see the information and find out how big it was. Now that he had seen the device, he needed to verify his suspicions. When he listened to a message from his nephew, a knot formed in his stomach.

Okawna strolled across the deck and studied his friend. "You have that faraway look in your eyes. What are you thinking about?"

"Can I get a ride back to shore?"

"I'm sure Mike will have the helicopter take you back. I think he's just as worried as we are."

"Thanks. What about you?"

"I'll do what I can from here and be your contact on the ship."

"Could you call your friends in the agency and find out more about Dieter? I want to know how he found out about my past."

"My thoughts exactly. I'll call Carl and let him know you're coming over for a ride to the mainland. Do you think Dieter turned on the ultrasound?"

"No, and that's what worries me. I doubt it was the drill, either. If that thing is going off by itself, we're in big trouble."

Alex walked into the ship to grab his bag and then returned to the stern. While Bartram and Harrison set the motorboat in the water, he stood off to the side and called Wesley. "What happened?"

"That last disturbance did some major damage, Alex. It shook Whidbey Island and caused a lot of landslides."

"Okay, I'll fill you in when I get to your cabin."

Alex turned off the phone and joined Okawna, waiting near the motorboat. "Make sure that thing doesn't go off again."

"I know. I have a feeling you'll be back."

Alex shook Okawna's hand and climbed into the boat. Mike was sitting behind the steering wheel, and Lisa and Rita were sitting behind him, so Alex sat in the empty seat next to Mike. "I need a ride back to shore. I hope you don't mind?"

Mike indicated it was fine and started the engine. "Let me know what you find out."

"I will."

***

When they reached the stern of the *Discovery*, Alex stepped onto the deck where Carl was waiting, and then reached down and helped Lisa and Rita out of the boat. "It was nice meeting all of you."

Lisa stared up at Alex. "Will you be coming back?"

"I'm not sure."

Rita gave Alex a hug. "Let us know when you have more information."

'I'll let all of you know. It was nice meeting you, Rita. Perhaps we'll meet again someday."

Lisa's hands were clinched into fists at her sides as she watched Rita hugging Alex. They opened as she watched Alex and Carl climb the stairs to the top deck and disappear, and then Mike was suddenly standing beside her, so she looked at him. "Do you think he'll come back?"

"It's hard to say. Let's go see what happened to that lens."

***

Alex and Carl walked up to the helicopter on the top deck, where Alex noticed the rows of orange hose stacked on the other side of a twenty-foot hole, just forward of the landing pad. They climbed into the helicopter and Carl immediately began flipping switches. The turbine engine whined to life, and a few moments later, the helicopter leapt off the deck.

"I appreciate this, Carl. Can we detour down to Whidbey Island on the way?"

"Mike's instructions were to take wherever you need to go, so let's take a look."

Thirty minutes later, Alex stared out the window and shook his head at the destruction of Whidbey Island. Several large portions of the bluffs had slid into the water, and dozens of crumpled homes, furniture, and belongings now clogged the waterways, hindering shipping traffic in or out of Seattle. He also saw several people clinging to anything that would float while waiting for the rescue boats to work their way through the debris.

"I've seen enough, Carl. Thanks."

"Do you think it will reach Seattle next time?"

Alex stared out the front window as the mainland swept by beneath them. "The events are working their way east, so, with any luck, it won't reach that far south. I think the biggest concern right now is what will happen with the volcanoes. If they erupt because of the earthquakes, they will kill thousands of people here in Washington and affect millions of lives across the United States, just like Mount Saint Helens did back in 1980."

"That stinks. Maybe we'll get lucky and it won't happen again."

"I hope you're right."

***

Okawna knew he had to be discreet with his inquiries about Dieter and looked around to make sure he was alone before he called his contact at the CIA. For now, Lisa and Mike were the only ones on the ship he could trust, so he gave his contact the fax number for Lisa's laboratory, then turned off the phone and slipped it into his pocket. When he turned to walk back inside, he noticed Dieter standing at the railing up behind the bridge, and for some unknown reason, he looked happy. Whatever his agenda, Dieter did not like having Alex on board.

Chapter 14

MOUNT VERNON AIRPORT:
On the flight back from the *Mystic*, Alex had decided his problem with his father was no excuse for not stopping at the ranch to see his nephew and niece. He could have died in that submarine, and if there were such a thing as heaven, his spirit would never rest in peace if his stubbornness kept him from seeing them when he had the chance. For now, he would not tell them the magnitude of what was happening, and hoped Robert had not turned them against him. Especially Derek.

***

Forty minutes later, he drove over the crest, down into Sparrow Valley, then turned right off the highway and over a bridge to the ranch. He drove past a row of large fir trees on his left, and white wooden fences and six Appaloosa horses grazing in the pasture on his right. The asphalt road changed to gravel, and a few minutes later, he saw the tan-colored corral and barn, and the four bedroom rambler-style house where he grew up. He turned onto the circular driveway, stopped in front of the porch, and recognized Kristy sitting in the porch swing.

Kristy did not recognize the vehicle, but knew the man who climbed out and smiled. "Uncle Alex!" She leapt out of the chair, ran across the porch, and then leapt over the two steps to the ground. "You're here! I knew you would come." She reached up and Alex bent down, and they hugged each other warmly.

Kristy released him and grabbed his hand as he straightened up. "Did you feel the earthquakes in Montana?"

"No, but I'm doing some work here in Washington, so I thought I'd stop by." He turned as a motorcycle approached.

"Derek's home, Uncle Alex. I told him you would come out and see us, but he didn't believe me."

Derek was surprised to see his uncle standing in front of the house as he parked. He wondered what to say as he shut off the engine and climbed off the motorcycle, then hung his helmet on the handlebars and walked over to him. "Hi, Alex. I'm glad you're here."

Alex wasn't sure what to expect and reached out to shake his hand. "It's good to see you again." When Derek accepted, he knew things might still be okay between them.

"I told you he would come." Kristy blurted. "The earthquakes must be really bad if you came all the way out here to see us."

Derek noticed the change in his uncle's expression. "This is bad, isn't it?"

"I have some people working on it, and we're fine for now."

Kristy squeezed his hand. "Grandpa's in the house watching television. He's going to be surprised that you're here. I'll get him."

Kristy turned and ran up the steps and into the kitchen, but forgot about the screen door until it slammed shut behind her. "Sorry, grandpa," she yelled as she ran into the living room. "Uncle Alex is here!"

When Robert remained seated and stared at the television, she moved around in front of him. "What's wrong, grandpa? Don't you want to see him?"

Robert thought about it. It had been two months since the funeral and he wondered how he'd feel when he looked at him. He pushed himself out of the recliner and followed Kristy through the kitchen and out onto the porch, where he and Alex stared at each other for a long moment. "What do you want?"

Alex did not expect a warm welcome, but hello would have been nice. "I only came because of the kids. I'm on my way to see a friend monitoring the seismic activity."

Looking at Alex caused a knot to form in Robert's stomach. The resemblance to his older brother was too much, so he turned away and hurried back into the house.

Derek could tell there would never be peace between Alex and Robert, but things had changed since the accident, and they should at least try to get along. He noticed Alex was still staring at the screen door. "Is there anything we should do?"

Alex turned to look at him, realizing he was as tall as he was. "Not really. I'll call if I think it's necessary."

Kristy could tell her uncle was more worried than he was telling them. "Does that mean you're not going to stay here with us, Uncle Alex? What if we need your help?"

Alex glanced at the screen door, then back at Kristy. "I'm sorry, but I can't stay here. Mister Patterson offered to let me stay at his cabin for the night, and he lives way up near the State Park."

Derek turned and headed toward his motorcycle. "I'm going with you."

"I'm sorry, Derek, but Mister Patterson only has one spare room, and it's a school night. Just stay here."

"I can sleep on the couch." He could see the hesitation in his uncle's eyes. "This is important to me, Alex. I really want to go with you."

"I don't want to impose on Mister Patterson. It's better if you just stay here."

Derek glared at his uncle. "Fine!" he snarled and stormed up the steps into the house, slamming the screen door shut behind him.

Alex stared after Derek and felt bad he had upset him, and then looked down at Kristy. "I'd better go."

Kristy grabbed his hand. "You just got here, Uncle Alex. Can't you stay a little while longer?"

"I can't. I'm not going back to Montana right away, so I'll see you again tomorrow."

"You promise?"

"I promise." Kristy held out her arms, so he bent down to give her a hug. "I'll see you tomorrow." He stood, climbed into his car, and drove away.

Kristy was disappointed Alex was not staying at the house, and stared at his car until it disappeared down the road. She turned and headed toward the barn to see the new ponies, knowing she always felt better when she petted their noses.

***

Back in the house, Robert stood at the sink and turned on the water. He knew Alex was not telling him everything, and just the fact he came all the way from Montana meant he was worried about the earthquakes. He leaned over the sink and began peeling potatoes.

***

Derek carefully closed the door to his bedroom and crept across the living room. When he saw Robert had his back to the screen door, he quietly walked through the kitchen and eased the door closed behind him.

Robert thought he heard the screen door close and turned around, but no one was there. "Kristy?"

She didn't reply, so continued with the potatoes. A moment later, he heard the motorcycle and listened to the sound fading away down the driveway.

"Damn, fool kid," he grumbled. "Where is he off to now?"

Chapter 15

MYSTIC:

Okawna walked into Lisa's laboratory, noticing her frowning at the magnified image of the lens from the fiber optic drill. "Any idea what happened?"

Lisa spun her chair around and folded her arms across her chest. "No, darn it. Something made it so hot it melted the glass lens. Because of the freezing temperature at that depth, I didn't think that could happen."

"That is strange. How well do you know Captain Dieter?"

Lisa uncrossed her arms. "Not very well, really. The first time I met him was here on the *Mystic*, when I started working for Mike. Why?"

"I don't trust him, and neither does Alex."

"Do you think he turned on the ultrasound?"

Okawna sat in a chair in front of her. "No. Listen, a friend of mine is going to be faxing you some information here in your lab. For now, you're the only one I can trust, so please don't tell anyone else about this, and be discreet when the fax comes in. If I'm not here, hide it someplace safe until you contact me."

Lisa smiled. Her life was uneventful most of the time, yet since she started working for Mike, it had become a little more exciting. Ever since Alex came on board, she felt as though she was on a great adventure. "You can trust me. I've never liked the captain, anyway."

Okawna reached over and gently squeezed her arm. "Thanks."

Lisa looked into his eyes. "What's the deal with Alex?"

Okawna leaned back in his chair. "What do you mean?"

"For a geology instructor, he must have a lot of important friends to take over this project."

"He's not taking over anything, Lisa, but you're right. He has a lot of connections."

Lisa gave him a conspiratorial grin. "You guys sound like spies to me. Were the two of you in the CIA or something?"

Okawna leaned forward. "You really don't want me to answer that."

"You mean, if you tell me, you have to kill me?"

Okawna laughed. "No, nothing like that. You would disappear." He winked at her. "I'm waiting for a call from Alex, so I'll be up in the lounge if you need me."

When Okawna walked out of her lab, Lisa smiled as she thought about Alex and swiveled back and forth in her chair. The idea Alex and Okawna might have worked for the CIA was fascinating.

She spun her chair around and continued examining the recordings from the optical lens, one frame at a time. The last five frames showed the device for a fraction of a second before the brilliant blue flash and the screen went blank, then she noticed something strange happen to the ice during the flash.

She heard a beep as the printer ejected two sheets of paper, so she rolled her chair over to her desk and looked at the cover page. It was for Okawna, and she felt an adrenaline rush. She wanted to look at the second page in the worst way, but thought if it was CIA related, she might be breaking some law. "Oh, crud," she whispered. She shoved them into an envelope and then slid it between two folders in the bottom drawer.

She rolled across the floor back to the images and transferred the first three and the last five onto a flash drive, hoping Okawna and Joshua could help her figure out what was going on. When the transfer was complete, she stood and slipped the drive into the front pocket of her white nylon jacket, then walked out of her lab and across the walkway to the lounge.

When she saw Okawna and Joshua playing table shuffleboard near the windows, she continued across the room as Joshua shoved a puck down the table. She stood at one end and followed it with her eyes as it slid toward her and the other pucks.

Joshua felt his heart rate increase as he watched his puck slowly approaching Okawna's puck and held his breath when it connected. The light touch was just enough to send Okawna's puck over the edge. "Yes!" He looked over at his opponent. "That's game, Okawna."

Okawna looked over at Lisa. "I'll get him the next time."

Lisa removed the disk from her pocket. "Something happened to the ice that I can't figure out, and I'm going to need your opinions."

Joshua came around the end of the table, and she handed him the recording. He strolled over to his desk, sat down, and inserted the flash drive into his laptop. As he opened each file, he put the pictures side by side on the large television screen. In each picture, they could see the device at the bottom of the fracture, except in picture number four. "What do you need, Lisa?"

"Enlarge number four, and I'll show you what I'm trying to figure out." The picture suddenly filled the entire screen, and the device was blurry. "The ice appears to be fractured. Can you enlarge that area?"

Joshua did, and millions of small fractures in the ice suddenly filled the screen. "That's good. Now locate the same area on the third and fifth picture for a comparison."

With the pictures side by side, it was easy to see the change in the ice, from clear to fractured, and back to clear. "I have an idea about what caused the seismic event, so tell me what you think. When water re-freezes, it expands with incredible force. Enough to shatter rock, and in this case, force the crack in the sea floor apart, creating an instant seismic event."

Joshua leaned back in his chair. "That's a lot of force, but wouldn't it go up through the crack?"

"Not if it happened that fast."

Okawna stepped closer to the television. "So, each time that device was activated, it froze the water?"

"Not exactly. It melted the lens on the optical cable. That means it melts the ice first and instantly re-freezes it to expand and force the crack open. That would also explain why we saw the bubbles. They were created when the water was flash boiled into steam for an instant before re-freezing. That expansion would also cause the pressure wave that hit the sub and nearly killed you guys."

Okawna turned away from the television to look at Lisa. "Twice for me. The freezing idea makes sense. I'd better call Alex about this."

Lisa made sure she had Okawna's attention, and then cocked her head to one side as she stared at him. "I should get back to the lab."

Okawna understood her meaning. "I'll go with you and call Alex from the stern."

They stepped out of the room, and Okawna followed her into the laboratory, then she opened the bottom drawer and handed him the envelope. "This came for you a few minutes ago."

Okawna sat in one of the chairs and removed the pages, then set the cover page aside and began reading page two. When he was done, he looked over at Lisa. "Did you read this?"

"No, but my curiosity is driving me crazy."

"It seems Dieter has a German relative who was the captain of a U-boat during world war two. His relative was using his sub to transport confiscated gems to a secret location, but the ship and its crew was never heard from again."

"Is that why you have suspicions about Dieter?"

"I know there is something going on with Dieter, and I'll bet it has something to do with that lost submarine."

"So what? Maybe he's on a treasure hunt. What's that got to do with us?"

Okawna leaned back in his chair. "He would need a submarine to find a submarine, but why be so mysterious about it? I'm sure Mike would be interested in a new adventure." He stood up. "I'm going to call Alex and tell him what we discovered about the freezing. Thanks for the help."

Chapter 16

CAVE RANCH:
Derek drove the motorcycle across the bridge and stopped at the highway. He had paid little attention to the car Alex was driving, but the vehicle in the parking lot at the grocery store looked familiar. He drove around the corner of the building; out of sight, but still able to see the car. He did not have to wait long and watched Alex put two plastic bags of groceries into the trunk before climbing into the driver's seat. He waited until it pulled out of the parking lot and then followed Alex up the highway.

***

Alex parked next to the cabin and carried the grocery bags into the kitchen. "Are you in here, Wesley?"

Wesley turned off the television, pushed himself off the sofa, and walked into the kitchen. "That latest movement was big, Alex. It's headline news across the country, and people are scared about the next one hitting Seattle."

Alex set the bags on the counter and put some of the food in the refrigerator, then closed the door and looked at Wesley. "We might be in big trouble, my friend."

Alex told him everything that had happened on the *Mystic*. "The captain is up to something, but I don't think he set off the device. For now, I can only wait for something else to happen. If that thing goes off again, it's doing it by itself, and we had better stop it before it tears the continent apart."

"The volcanoes will kill us first."

Alex felt his phone vibrate in his pocket, but ignored it. "How bad?"

"Baker was the worst and measured three point one on the Richter scale. Rainier registered a two point zero, but I think that will change if we have another event."

Alex slid his phone out of his pocket and looked at the ID. "It's my friend on the *Mystic*." He pressed the speaker button. "What's up?"

Okawna explained about the ice melting and freezing and the information on Dieter. "My friend is still trying to chase down a connection between him and you."

"I have a friend who can do research on Dieter's relative, and we'll see where that leads us. What was his name?"

"It's Eric Dieter, and he went missing near the end of world war two. That's all I have on him. How bad was the last event?"

"They're becoming greater in magnitude. Nothing has happened since we returned to the surface, but we still need to get that thing out of the ice so it won't happen again. I think there could be another device in the Arctic, and we need to locate that one, too."

"Do you want me to talk to Mike about it?"

"Yes. Find out if we can take the *Mystic* to the arctic, but don't tell him about Dieter and the missing treasure just yet."

"Got it. I'll call you tomorrow, either way."

"Thanks, Okawna."

Wesley waited until Alex turned off the phone. "Let's go to the barn and I'll show you the recording." He opened the cabin door and stopped. "Who are you?"

Alex looked past Wesley's shoulder. "That's my nephew." He followed Wesley through the doorway and looked at Derek. "How long have you been listening?"

Derek folded his arms across his chest as he stared into his uncle's eyes. "Long enough. I'm eighteen, Alex, so stop treating me like a boy. I want to know how bad this is. I'm the one who will have to take care of Kristy and Robert, not you."

Alex thought about it for a moment. "You're right, and I'm sorry. It could get bad."

Wesley was glad the issue was settled. "Let's all go to the barn."

Derek followed them across the parking area and through the doorway. Once inside, he strolled around Wesley's toys. "Neat place, Mister Patterson."

"Thanks, and call me Wesley."

Alex sat in the wooden chair, with Derek sitting on the edge of the desk while Wesley sat in his own chair. Wesley played the recordings from all three events and explained the differences for Derek's benefit. "These recordings are from my own seismometers on Mt. Baker and Mt. Rainier. They're more sensitive than the ones the government uses. You can see the difference in magnitude by the width of the line. This last one here, on Baker, was a magnitude three point one."

Derek remembered something from school. "Okay, but those lines are from side to side, like a regular earthquake. What Kristy felt today was straight up."

Wesley looked at Alex and grinned. "Have you been teaching this young man too, professor?"

Alex looked at Derek. "Pretty good."

Derek thought his chest would burst with pride. "I'm a quick learner."

"That's right," Wesley continued, as he brought up the recording of the latest event and magnified the break in the line. "The needle jumped off the paper."

Alex suddenly leaned forward when he saw the picture. "Is that the latest one?"

"I'm afraid so."

Alex looked at Derek. "The distance of the break in the line tells us how high the ground jumped. The first two were barely measurable, but this last one indicates an increase in magnitude."

"Is that a lot?"

"Yes, that's a lot. Especially if it's not supposed to happen at all." When his phone rang, he recognized the number and put it on speaker. "Hi, Sonja."

"I am so glad you answered, Alex. The ice sheet went into another expansion five hours ago, and it is freezing hundreds of square kilometers each time it happens. I was on the ice sheet when it happened and saw a flash of blue light just before the expansion. What have you learned?"

His suspicions were confirmed, so Alex explained everything he knew, except where he suspected the devices came from. "Now that I know it's not a natural disturbance, I'm going to call a friend of mine for help with this. His name is Martin Donner."

"He is your Director of National Security, correct?"

"That's right. I'll do what I can from my end, so let me know about anything new."

"I will. Bye, Love."

Derek was stunned by what he had just heard, and stood up from the desk. "Which ice sheet is she talking about?"

"The one up north. The Arctic Ice sheet."

"Isn't that a good sign? That means the atmosphere is cooling down again, right?"

"It doesn't happen this fast."

Wesley leaned back in his chair and looked at Alex. "The Director of National Security, Alex? You have some powerful friends."

Alex picked up his phone. "Yes, and it's time to use them."

***

OFFICE OF THE DIRECTOR OF NATIONAL SECURITY. WASHINGTON D.C.:

Martin Donner picked up the phone. "I'm glad you called, Alex. I'm getting reports from FEMA about what's happening in Puget Sound, and the USGS doesn't know a thing. I called Marcia at the College, and she said you were in the Pacific Northwest to check it out. Do you know what's going on?"

"I do now. It's bad, Martin."

Donner listened to Alex explain everything he knew and was not sure how to reply. "I had no idea they were artificial. How much time do we have until the next activation?"

"Impossible to say, at the moment. They could activate on their own. I'll coordinate everything out here with Mike Tanner to use his ship, the *Discovery*. It's off the coast of Vancouver, and we can use it as a research and recovery platform. From what I've learned about it, they have everything needed to retrieve that device. If we're lucky, it won't go off again. Even so, we need to retrieve the one from under that Arctic ice, too."

"It might take some time to set things in motion, but I'll stress the urgency and do what I can."

"I know you will. Just one more thing. Set things up so I can talk to Lewis Norton. I'm thinking this is one of the devices I told you about from the Dead Energy operation."

"I'll make some calls right now. I know a couple of people with the right security clearance, too, so I'll send them to the Discovery and put Doctor Heinz in charge of the recovery operation. Is this a good number to reach you?"

"Yes, and thanks, Martin."

Donner hung up and entered a number into the phone, then waited for an answer. "Things are never dull around you, Alex Cave," he whispered.

***

THE CABIN:

Derek had no idea Alex knew so many important people. He had assumed he was just a geology teacher, but now he knew this must be really bad.

Wesley noticed Derek's troubled expression. "I want to tell you what might happen, Derek. I've studied this mountain all my life, and if it becomes active, it won't be like St. Helens. That one blew because of the tremendous pressure from the steam and gasses released from the magma that was trapped inside the mountain. Our seismic activity is artificial and very recent, so hopefully, the mountain will fracture, release any new pressure, and not explode. Even if it doesn't erupt, there will be an increase in temperature from the rising magma, which will cause the rapid melting of the glaciers. The water level in the reservoir above Sparrow Valley could rise so fast the dam won't be able to hold it back. Have you ever heard of a lahar?"

"No."

"It's a mixture of water, mud, rocks, and debris, and if the dam breaks loose, it will all rush down the mountain and bury everything in Sparrow Valley. If things go to hell, you need to make your way up here. I picked this location to build my cabin because it's the safest place on my mountain. I don't want anyone else to know, son. You and your family are welcome, but I'll shoot the first stranger who thinks this place is a safe haven. I don't want hundreds of people camped in my front yard. Is that clear?"

"Yes, Sir. I understand."

Alex was surprised by Wesley's offer, and it was appreciated. He looked up at his nephew. "I don't think you should tell anyone what you've learned today."

"What about Robert?"

"Okay, just him. Don't tell Kristy, either. I could tell she's scared enough, so she doesn't need to know. This may be the end of it, so we don't want to start a panic."

Derek indicated he agreed. "It's going to be hard not telling Kristy. She has a way of tricking someone into a confession."

Wesley pushed himself out of his chair. "It's going to be dark soon."

Derek understood his meaning. "I'd better head home. Thanks for telling me the truth, Alex. You too, Wesley."

Wesley headed toward the door, and Alex and Derek followed. When they reached the motorcycle, Wesley shook Derek's hand. "Nice to meet you, son. Just remember what I said about the lahar. It could happen with no warning, and I'll do my best to let you know if it's imminent."

"I will."

Alex and Wesley waited until Derek rode away, and then walked into the cabin. Alex grabbed his groceries from the refrigerator and set them on the counter. "I hope you like Italian."

"I don't care what it is, as long as someone else is cooking."

***

CAVE RANCH:

It was dark when Derek parked the motorcycle in one of the garage stalls near the barn and carried his helmet toward the porch. On the ride back, he had thought about what to tell Kristy, knowing she would hound him for information when he walked into the house. The boards creaked as he climbed the steps, then Kristy suddenly stood from the porch swing and folded her arms across her chest.

"It's about time, Derek Cave. Where have you been?"

Derek grinned and shook his head in wonder, thinking he should have realized she would be waiting outside. "I followed Alex, and he showed me all the neat equipment Mister Patterson has in his barn."

"I learned that Mount Baker is really a volcano. It was on the news with the stuff about Witchy Island. Are we going to have an eruption like Mount Saint Helens?"

He sighed with relief he would not have to lie to his sister. "No, it's not going to explode like Saint Helens. And it's Whidbey Island. Are there any leftovers?"

"I wrapped it in foil and left it on the counter so it would stay warm."

Derek put his arm around Kristy's shoulder. "You're the best sister a brother could have. I'm hungry. Let's go inside."

***

ARCTIC ICE SHEET:

A brilliant bolt of blue lightning burst up out of the top of the ice pyramid, as a thunderous crack raced across the frozen wasteland for a fraction of a second, then the light blinked out. No one was around to see the frantic thrashing of the humpback whales partially trapped in ice. The ocean froze another one hundred miles south, dragging the pyramid with it. A moment later, the entire new ice sheet rose one-hundred-feet out of the water.

Chapter 17

8:00 AM. CAVE RANCH:

Kristy was sitting at the kitchen table with her grandpa and brother when she heard the horn from the school bus coming up the driveway. She got up and grabbed her bright yellow backpack off a chair, slinging it over her shoulders as she looked at Derek. "Aren't you going to school today?"

"In a minute."

"Is something wrong?"

Derek glanced over at Robert, reading a magazine article, and then back to Kristy. "No. I'll see you this afternoon."

Kristi studied her brother's body language. "Uncle Alex told you something bad is going to happen, didn't he?"

Derek stared at his sister, wondering what to say without lying. For a ten-year-old, she was very perceptive. "Nothing you need to worry about right now." The look in her eyes told him she didn't believe him, and it tore at his heart. "I'm sorry, Kristy, but I made a promise to Alex, and he said there's nothing to worry about right now."

Kristy opened the screen door and then turned to look at Derek. "All right. I know Uncle Alex would never tell a lie. Bye, Grandpa." She walked out onto the porch and eased the screen door closed.

Derek watched her jump over the steps to the ground and run down the driveway to the bus, with her little yellow backpack bouncing on her shoulders. He knew without her, he would be a mental mess.

Robert saw the distress in his grandson's eyes. "What's going on, Derek?"

Derek explained what he had learned last night. "Did you know Alex is a friend of the National Security Director?"

Robert leaned back in his chair, wondering if he should tell his grandson what he suspected about why his parents were killed. "Alex used to work for the government." He stood, carried Derek's bowl to the sink, and turned on the water.

Derek stood and moved to Robert's side. "You're holding something back. What is it?"

Robert continued rinsing the dishes. "That's up to Alex. Ask him yourself."

Derek stared at Robert for a long moment, wanting more information. When Robert did not respond, he stomped across the room and out through the screen door, slamming it closed behind him, wondering why Robert hated Alex so much.

Robert turned off the water and dried his hands with a small towel, as he turned around and leaned back against the counter. He heard the roar of the motorcycle and watched a cloud of dust rising into the air down the road. He only suspected Alex was responsible for the death of Ken and Doreen, and it would not do any good to tell that to Derek right now. That would be up to Alex.

He walked across the kitchen, grabbed the keys for his truck, and continued out onto the porch and across the driveway to the garage. If what Derek had told him was possible, he needed to get some supplies in case they were stranded on the ranch for a while. The river had flooded three times over the past thirty years, but the ranch had always survived. Only the pastures ended up under water, and his only worry was having enough food to last until the water level dropped and they could leave.

***

THE CABIN:

Alex lay in bed, staring at the ceiling. With so much at stake, the night had passed slowly, and he was eager to get started. When he heard Wesley walk out of the bathroom, he swung off of bed to start the day. After a quick shower, he poured a cup of coffee and joined Wesley, sitting at the kitchen table. "Good morning."

"Is it?"

Alex sat down. "What's going on?"

"I hope your friend Donner has some brilliant engineers. I was one ten years ago, and I can't imagine an easy way to retrieve that device at that depth. Especially through all that ice."

"Donner and I have some mutual friends that can figure it out. At least it hasn't activated since I was down there yesterday. Or has it?"

Wesley took a sip of coffee and grinned. "No. I wasn't going to say anything to jinx the situation."

Alex felt his phone vibrate and stood to pull it out of his front pocket. He recognized Sonja's ID, turned on the speaker, and set it on the table. "I'm here, Sonja."

"The Polar ice sheet had another expansion last night, Alex. It froze another one hundred square kilometers of the Bering and East Siberian seas, and it is already causing an effect on the weather in the northern hemisphere. Many of my colleagues are frustrated trying to find out why this is happening, and I do not know what to tell them. Only disastrous events will come from this sudden change in the ice sheet, so we are all very anxious to find out why and stop it."

Alex and Wesley exchanged puzzled expressions, since none of their alarms had activated. "We're just as frustrated as you are, Sonja. Nothing happened here, so I don't understand why it would activate on its own."

"A few of us have created a computer model to track each event."

"If you can determine a location for me to search, it would be a big help."

"I noticed a dark area in the ice the last time I flew over the pyramid. It could be that device you are looking for, but I am not positive."

"Once I talk to a friend in Nevada, I might have some information that could help us with our search."

"Thank you, Alex. Bye, love."

Alex turned off the phone and stared out the window while he sipped his coffee. "I hope my friend in Nevada can give me a better idea of what I'm dealing with."

Wesley stood up from the table. "I'll go check the equipment in the barn just to make sure."

Alex looked at his watch. "I'll see if Okawna is up yet."

Wesley got up and walked outside, closing the cabin door behind him. Alex entered Okawna's number, and it was answered immediately. "I guess I didn't wake you up."

"Hey, Alex. No, I've been up for an hour. Any new information?"

"Did anyone activate the ultrasound last night?"

"Not that I'm aware of."

"There was another increase to the ice sheet. Are you sure nothing happened?"

"Positive. Rita locked the system down after what happened to us. There's no way we could have caused it."

"That means the one up north activated on its own. Did you talk to Mike about using the Mystic to search for it?"

"Yes. Whenever you're ready, we'll send the helicopter to pick you up."

"Great. I have to go to Nevada first, so I'll call you when I'm back."

"You're never going to tell me what's down there, are you?"

"There is one thing I can tell you. Once this is over, you'll have a much better appreciation for our little blue planet. I'll call you later."

Wesley walked in and poured another cup of coffee. "Nothing happened around here. What did he say?"

"They didn't do it, but at least I have a boat ride to the Arctic when I need it. Mike is an interesting man. He's trying to solve our global warming problem, and has the money to do whatever he wants. I'm sure when he heard about another device in the Arctic, he wanted to help."

"What's next on your list?"

"A call to a friend of mine at the college, and hopefully, a trip to Nevada."

While Alex talked on the phone, Wesley opened the refrigerator door, took a few items out, and set them on the counter. As he closed the door, he heard Alex end his call. "Let's eat breakfast. You cook while I watch the news."

Alex stood from the table. "Are you really that bad a cook?"

"Hell, no. I just like being pampered."

***

When they finished eating, Alex set the last of the dishes on the counter for Wesley to wash, then poured another cup of coffee and sat at the table. Just sitting around with so much going wrong was frustrating, and he needed something to do.

His phone rang, and it was the Dean of his college in Montana. "Good morning, Marcia. I was going to give it another hour before I called you."

"David is with me, and we've been watching the news. It sounds very bad. What have you found out?"

Alex explained what he knew. "I need a favor. Could you do a background check for me? The name is Eric Dieter. All I have on him is he was a German U-boat captain near the end of World War II. He supposedly smuggled confiscated jewelry with the U-boat and was never heard from again. He has a relative that might help with your search. A fifty-year-old male of Scandinavian descent named John Dieter. I want to know about him, too. He's the captain of the Mystic, and I'm getting a bad vibe from him."

"I'll start on the background immediately and call you when I have something. George wanted me to thank you for recommending he be placed in a minimal security prison."

"How's he holding up?"

"He's being treated for PTSD from his time as a prisoner in North Vietnam, and it seems to be working. His nightmares are less frequent now."

"He didn't strike me as your type of man, Marcia."

"People can change. He was just bent, not broken."

"Hi, Alex, this is David. Maybe I can help your chemist, Lisa. She sounds like she knows what she's doing."

"I think you'd like her. I'll give her your number."

"Cool."

"Good pun, David."

"Thanks. What can we expect to happen next?"

"I'm not sure. We've found the cause of the events out here, and it shouldn't happen again. My main concern now is the expansion of the Arctic Ice Sheet. I'll call you if anything changes."

"Thanks, Alex."

"I'll call you soon," Marcia added.

Alex turned off the phone and looked away from the window as Wesley sat down across from him. "Donner is usually an early riser, and he's probably busy getting things started for me. That's the end of my list until he calls."

Wesley's phone rang, and he answered. "Hi, Jamie. I thought you might be calling." He covered the phone and looked over at Alex. "It's a young woman who just started working in the park as a Ranger." He removed his hand. "It was not a prelude, and it's over now. Yes, I'll call if anything changes."

Wesley turned off the phone. "She's one of the Parker kids from Sparrow Valley and just transferred from Eastern Washington. Let's go for a ride. I want to show you my mountain."

"I'd like that."

***

MOUNT BAKER STATE PARK, MARMOT CAMPGROUND:
Jamie Parker turned her phone off and felt intimidated by so many questioning eyes from the occupants. When she drove into the campground ten minutes ago, seven of the campers approached her Park Service SUV, expecting her to have all the answers about the earthquakes yesterday afternoon. She hadn't realized how many people used this park

until her new supervisor said it was always packed with people escaping the higher temperatures below.

She climbed out of her SUV to satisfy the campers. "We don't know what happened to the islands, but it's over now, so enjoy your time in the park."

She felt relieved when most of them walked away, but one woman with a little girl and a young boy remained. She saw the fear in the children's eyes, so she knelt down and smiled at them. "It's all right. It's all over now."

The kids wrapped their arms around their mother's legs, so Jamie stood. The woman's smile was troubled as she turned away and held her children's hands to lead them back to their campsite. She looked at her watch and realized if this happened every time she stopped, checking all the campgrounds this morning was going to take a while.

She climbed into the SUV and drove out of Marmot Campground. "One down, twenty-three to go."

***

SPARROW VALLEY:

Robert Cave parked in front of the only restaurant in the little town, climbed out of his truck, and noticed a piece of paper taped to the inside of the window. The District high school track and field championship games would take place this Friday, here in the valley.

He grinned as he thought about the high school rivalry between Darrington and Sparrow Valley. It had been going on for generations, and he was a student at Darrington High School thirty years ago. Going to Sparrow Valley to compete in sports was how he had met his wife, Shannon Parker, one of the locals.

It was Sparrow Valley's turn to host the games, and over one hundred students, parents, and faculty would drive up to the valley from Darrington to watch the competition. Last fall, during the football playoffs, over twenty motorhomes, trailers, and campers came up early and stayed in the school parking lot. After listening to Derek, he wondered if he should ask them to cancel the event, but knew if he told them why and nothing happened, he would look like a fool.

He walked into the restaurant, and a small silver bell above the door tinkled. All conversations suddenly stopped as he continued to the counter, aware that all eyes were on him as he sat down.

Molly Moran, the server and part owner, walked up with a pot of coffee and set a tan mug on the counter in front of Cave. "How are you doing, Robert? I hear your son's in town. Does it have to do with the destruction of the islands?"

Robert watched her fill the mug. "That's right."

"Carrie Sorenson said he's been staying with Wesley. Does it have something to do with those tremors yesterday?"

Robert turned his head and looked around the room, and everyone was listening to his conversation. He agreed with what Derek told him about starting a panic, so he turned back and took a sip of coffee. "We don't talk much since the funeral."

"Bob called from the grocery store and said you bought a bunch of supplies. Should we be worried?"

Robert heard the doorbell tinkle and didn't answer the question. While he sipped his coffee, he saw Molly look over his head, and then heard a familiar voice behind him.

"Hey, Cave?"

Robert knew it was Arnie Parker calling his name and refused to turn and look at him. He and Arnie had been fighting since their high school years, when he started dating his sister. When Arnie had called his sister a traitor for dating a Darrington student, Robert had knocked him to the ground with one punch, and they've been fighting ever since then.

Arnie hooked his thumbs over his utility belt and holster and then smirked at the people in the restaurant. He was the sheriff, and this was his town, because no one ever ran against him in the elections. Something about Cave had rubbed him the wrong way since they had first met, and was the only person who refused to call him sheriff.

Arnie walked up next to Robert and leaned back against the counter so he could look at the other people watching his every move. "I have thirty bucks says we'll kick the snot out of Darrington on Friday."

Robert set his cup on the counter, swiveled his stool around, and then stood and looked into Arnie's eyes. "Make it one hundred and you've got a bet." He watched the smirk slipped from Arnie's face. "Is it a bet? Or is that too much money for you, Parker?"

Arnie stood up straight and glanced around the room, then looked at Cave and forced a grin at everyone watching. "You've got a bet."

When Robert grinned and walked out of the restaurant, Arnie heard a few chuckles from the patrons as he stared out the window and watched Robert drive away. "You're a real ass, Cave," he whispered.

Chapter 18

NEVADA. GROOM LAKE:

Alex looked out the window of the private Gulfstream jet as it taxied to a small air terminal. The plane rolled to a gentle stop, and then the engines shut down, and since he was the only passenger, he opened the door himself and walked down the steps. At the bottom, he recognized a small, gray-haired man smiling up at him. Doctor Henry Heinz had been working at top the secret facility since he had emigrated from Germany as a young man in 1958, and had helped him during the Dead Energy operation.

"Alex, my friend. It is so good to see you again," he said with a slight accent.

Alex smiled and shook his hand. "You look like you're having fun, Doc."

"It has been so exciting since your discovery. Lewis is waiting for us inside. Come, come."

Alex followed Henry into a small office and watched Lewis Norton stand from behind an oak desk and clasped his hands behind his back without smiling. He had forgotten about Lewis's no nonsense behavior, but noticed one change in the man's physical appearance. He had let his hair grow into a short ponytail, which was a sign he was loosening up a little from his normally stoic demeanor. Not that he was un-friendly, only that he had never shown any type of emotion to anyone.

"Hello, Professor Cave. I understand you have an issue that needs my attention."

"Yes, your brother told me about some type of device that can clean our atmosphere. What does it look like?"

Norton stared into space. "Cylindrical. Gray. Perforated around the exterior. Twenty-feet long. Twelve-inch circumference. Weight: Four-thousand-six-hundred and twenty-seven pounds."

That was the estimated size of the device in the Pacific, so Alex had his confirmation. "Do you mind if I sit down?"

"Of course not."

Alex sat in front of the desk next to Henry while Lewis sat down across from them. "We've discovered one of those devices in the

Northwestern Pacific Ocean, and there is probably another one somewhere in the Arctic." Alex explained everything that had happened. "The urgent problem right now is the one in the Arctic. It appears to be activating on its own."

"That is a problem. Once they are activated, they are programmed to sample the environment and act appropriately."

Alex stared at him. "What do you mean, appropriately?"

"The device will continue to activate on a predetermined schedule that depends on the chemical elements it sampled. Once you expose the device to a different environment, you will have approximately twenty-four hours before the next activation. If you manage to get the device out of the water, it will sample the new environment and determine which frequency will attract the specified elements from the atmosphere. When the device activates, the exterior surface will be minus four hundred and seventy-three-degrees Celsius, so do not touch it."

"There is an operation underway to retrieve the device in the Pacific Ocean. If we manage to get it to the surface, can we open it up and disconnect something?"

"No. You need the original spacecraft that deployed the device to turn it off."

Henry leaned forward. "You did not mention this device before, Lewis."

"It was not pertinent to our mission."

Alex also leaned forward in his chair. "It's pertinent now, so how does it work?"

"Every atomic element resonates at a specific frequency. The device can be programed to attract a specific atomic structure from the environment. It does this by creating a complex combination of resonant frequencies, which alter the atomic structure to create a physical mass in a solid state that can be recovered."

"Okay, but why does it freeze?"

"The atmospheric pressure allows many elements to remain in a gaseous state, and when the molecular resonance stops, those become solid and do not produce energy, so they become ultra-cold."

Alex leaned back and sighed in frustration. His only option was to retrieve the devices somehow, and keep them out of the water, and the task seemed insurmountable.

Lewis noticed the disappointment in Alex's eyes. "However, if you manage to retrieve one of the devices, we could identify the control frequency and broadcast the deactivation code through the orbiting satellite system."

With a new sense of hope, Alex sat up straight in his chair. "That's more like it. How soon can you arrange for my return to Washington State?"

Henry reached across the desk for the base's private telephone system. "I will find out."

"Have you located the other two devices?" Lewis asked.

Alex stared across the desk with his mouth slightly open. "There are four of them?"

"Apparently not. In order to perform efficiently, one device must be positioned in the atmosphere above the northern axis of a planet, one at the southern axis, and two equilaterally on opposite sides of the planet."

"As far as I know, only the two devices were activated. The others must be out of range for that ultrasound they used to activate them."

Henry set the phone down and stood up. "Your plane is refueled and waiting."

Alex stood. "Thanks. I need a favor before I leave."

***

MOUNT VERNON MUNICIPAL AIRPORT:
Alex looked through the side window of the Gulfstream as it taxied to the small air terminal. When the jet engines shut down, he opened the door and walked down the steps, noticing the helicopter and pilot were different this time. The blue letters on the white copter said *Mystic*, and the small pilot standing outside the air terminal was a tough-looking young woman with short blond hair.

He noticed her jaw busily chewing a piece of gum as he walked over to introduce himself. "I'm Alex Cave."

The woman turned her head, spit out the gum, then reached out to shake his hand. "Betty Mason, but everybody calls me Bett."

The woman spoke as if on speed, and Alex grinned. "I need to see some people before we leave. Can you wait for me?"

"Yeah, but ya better hurry. The Mystic is already underway."

"I will."

Alex's car was where he had left it, so he climbed in and headed toward the mountain. He figured this late in the afternoon, school would be out, and the kids would be at the ranch.

***

CAVE RANCH:

Kristy climbed onto the parked motorcycle in front of the porch, and then crossed her arms over her chest as she glared up at her brother in the swing. "You are not leaving this ranch, Derek Cave! Uncle Alex promised to see us today, and you are not going anywhere until he does."

Derek frowned and tried to look upset, but it was hard not to laugh at the smudge of dirt on her determined little face. They both turned to look at a red mustang leaving a cloud of dust in its wake as it approached.

Kristy waited until the car stopped in the circular driveway, then grinned at Derek. "Your girlfriend's here."

Derek gave her a stern look. "She's not my girlfriend, okay?"

He thought Jessica Parker was a snob, and tried to ignore her advances, but she was relentless. He thought maybe it was because he wasn't interested in her, like the jocks that vied for her attention.

Jessica shut off the engine and climbed out of the mustang then lightly shook her shoulder-length brown hair as she smiled at Derek, hoping for a response. Since his first day at school, when he was in one of her classes, she found his bad boy appearance and attitude irresistible.

Derek remained sitting on the porch swing, and thought Jessica was attractive in her slim blue jeans and tight fitting red tank top, but he could not stand her attitude. Her father was wealthy, and she was attractive, so she always got what she wanted.

Kristy climbed off the motorcycle and ran up to Jessica, smiling. "Can I sit in your car?"

Jessica had never been to the ranch before, but had seen Derek with his sister a few times in the Mount Vernon mall. "What's your name?"

"I'm Kristy. Derek's my brother."

"No, you can't sit in my car. Your clothes are filthy."

Kristy crossed her arms and stared up at her. "Is it because you're a snob?"

Jessica looked down, her mouth slightly open. "What? How dare you call me a snob! You don't even know me!"

Derek stood and looked at his sister. "That's enough, Kristy," he said in a nice tone of voice before looking at Jessica. "What brings you out this way?"

Jessica shook her hair as she regained her composure. "Everyone's talking about the strange earthquakes. I know your uncle is a geologist, and everybody in town knows he's here now, so we're all wondering what he said about them."

Derek sat back down on the porch swing. "I'm sure he'll tell everyone when he's ready."

Jessica waited for Derek to say more, but he did not. She crossed her arms over her chest and gave him a stern look. "I bet you think I'm a snob, too." When he grinned, it was all she could take. "Go to hell!" she snarled, then stomped back to the mustang and climbed in. She slammed the door closed and started the engine. When she looked over at Derek, he and Kristi were both grinning. She stomped on the gas pedal and a rear tire spun, throwing dirt and fine gravel into the air as the mustang raced down the driveway.

Kristy walked up the porch steps and sat beside her brother. "I bet you'd like to drive that car of hers. Her dad's rich, you know. If you hook up with her, he might buy you a new car, too."

Derek grinned, thinking how much he loved his brazen little sister. "You talk too much."

They both heard another car coming up the driveway, and Kristy jumped off the porch swing. "I told you he would keep his promise."

She waited until Alex stopped in front of the porch, then leapt over the steps, ran to the car door, and yanked it open. "I knew you'd come back."

Alex climbed out and grabbed the small cardboard box from the passenger seat before he closed the door. Kristy grabbed his hand and pulled him onto the porch, where he held the box out to Derek.

Derek opened the box and then looked up at his uncle. "This is a satellite phone."

"That's right. It even has GPS capability. I'm going on a boat ride when I leave here, and it's important you can reach me, or I can reach you. I have that number on my satellite phone, so I'll know it's you calling. My number is speed dial one, and Wesley's is two."

***

Robert heard another car door close and wondered who was here, and then he heard Alex talking. He pushed himself out of the recliner, walked through the kitchen, and stopped to look through the screen door to listen to the conversation.

***

Kristy sat next to Derek on the porch swing. "Why are you leaving so soon, Uncle Alex? You just got here."

"I'm meeting some people, and we're going to the North Pole. It's a kind of treasure hunt."

Derek stood from the swing. "When will you be back?"

"I'm not sure. I have a helicopter pilot waiting for me, so I'd better go."

Derek gave Alex a quick hug so he could whisper in his ear. "I'll take care of Kristy and Robert, so don't worry about us."

"I know you will. Thanks."

Alex looked down at Kristy. "Listen to your brother, and do what he says, okay?"

Kristy stood from the swing. "Why? Is something going to happen?"

Alex understood what Derek had meant about Kristy getting information from people. She was very perceptive, so he knelt in front of her. "Right now, he's smarter than you, but that will change in a year or two."

Kristy wrapped her arms around her uncle's neck and hugged him. "Probably sooner."

When Kristy let go, Alex stood up. "I'd better get going or I'll miss my boat ride."

He walked back to the car, climbed in, and started the engine. As the car started to move, he thought he saw a shadow on the other side of the kitchen screen door, and then it was gone. He waved out the window as he drove away.

***

Robert stayed behind the screen door while he watched the car disappear down the road and then returned to his recliner to watch the updated National News reports.

"Our weather specialist explained the increased expansion of the Arctic Ice Sheet has changed the climatic conditions across the northwestern United States and Canada. So far, officials do not know the reason for the increase in size and speculate on what effect this will have on the planet. Some of our unofficial contacts think this change could be a benefit by reducing the temperature of the atmosphere, while others believe it will create worse problems. Our affiliate station in Oklahoma

reports the colder winds now circulating from the north will increase the chance of tornados sweeping up the central plains of North America. Another earthquake shook the Pacific Northwest yesterday, and after the recent disastrous seismic activity, they fear if these earthquakes continue, Seattle will be next."

***

NEVADA:

"Please stop pacing, Doctor Heinz."

Henry stood still in front of the desk and stared at Lewis. "When the Director of National Security asks a favor, you do not say no."

"I am not the one saying no. I was not asked to supervise the recovery operation in the Pacific Ocean."

"I did not say no, exactly. The only reason Director Donner asked me is because I have the necessary security clearance, but I need your help with that device in the ocean. You must come with me."

"You are a competent scientist. You will have twenty-four-hour communication capability with me and I will assist you from here."

"But I will not know any of those people when I get to that ship. I have always been in charge here, because I have worked with these people since they were hired. Now, I will be starting over again. I am your friend and I am asking for a favor."

"Doctor Heinz." A slight grin formed on Norton's lips; possibly for the first time. "Henry, my friend. You have my full endorsement. You will do very well in your new position."

Henry realized he had never seen Louis smile. That meant a lot to him, and he smiled back. "Thank you. I will do the best I can. I must call Director Donner to make the arrangements for my trip to Washington State."

Chapter 19

MOUNT BAKER STATE PARK:
Jamie Parker was glad the day was finally ending, since her daily routine included stopping at each campground in the morning and then again on the way back to the ranger station before going home. At each campground, she was confronted by people wanting answers about the earthquakes, and she was tired of repeating the same statement.

She drove into Marmot Campground, where she had met the woman with the two children. She did not think the woman would have been that scared if there was a man in her camp, and thought she should stop to make sure they were okay.

She parked in front of the woman's campsite, next to an old green sedan, and climbed out, but there was no one at the table or in the blue nylon tent. She heard a splash of water and the laughing of a high-pitched voice, but there were no ponds or streams near the campground, so she followed the sound a short distance into the woods.

The woman was sitting next to a ten-foot pool of shallow water, which was obviously new, and her toddlers were playing in it. "It sounds like everyone is having fun," she said to get their attention.

The woman stood and smiled. "I know. I didn't notice the pond when we arrived."

Jamie looked at the small stream filling it and realized it was coming from a small gap below the base of a large boulder, which should not be happening. "When did you first see it?"

"My son found it about an hour ago and showed us." She looked at her children. "Time to get out of the water. We need to fix dinner." The kids jumped out, and then she turned and smiled at the ranger. "The brochure didn't say anything about a hot spring."

Jamie gave her a half smile. "Enjoy your evening, ma'am."

When the woman and kids moved away, Jamie walked over to the boulder, knelt down to feel the water rippling out from the base, and frowned when it felt very warm. "This is not good."

She stood and went back to the SUV, and out of curiosity, slowly drove through the rest of the campsites. When she didn't see any other water, she drove out of the campground.

***

The Ranger Station was near the entrance to the park, and when Jamie arrived, hers was the only personal vehicle in the parking lot. She looked at her watch and realized her supervisor, Larry Cobb, and the longtime Park Assistant Ranger, Frank Olson, had gone home for the night, so she would have to tell Larry about the water in the morning.

She locked the SUV, climbed into a brand new black Mustang, and began her drive to her father's house in Sparrow Valley. She could not stop thinking about the new hot spring, and even though she was not a geologist, knew it was a bad sign. Something was happening since the earthquake, and she needed to tell her friend Wesley about it when she got home.

Chapter 20

MOUNT VERNON AIRPORT:

Bett did the pre-flight check of her helicopter and warmed up the engine, while Alex returned the rental car, and when he climbed into the co-pilot seat, she took off immediately. "I radioed the *Mystic* to stop so they won't get outta my range."

Alex noticed she was busily chewing again. "The other helicopter didn't have any problem."

"I know, but this here's my baby, and she's good, but she ain't got the range. The Mystic, with her twin turbine engines and water jet pumps, can cruise at seventy-eight knots, and was already sixty miles from shore when Mike called."

"I didn't see you the last time I was on board. Are you usually on the Mystic?"

"Yeah, I'm usually there because it's my home. Once I'm back on board, I can refuel, but we still need to get there on a tank of gas. They didn't need me for two weeks, so I've been visiting friends up in Northern Canada, and then Mike called this morning and asked me back to work. Said I was supposed to pick up a professor. You ain't what I expected."

Alex could not quite pinpoint her accent. Somewhere from the southwest, he thought. "I'm sorry for keeping you waiting, but it was important."

"Not a problem. This time of day, the fish are biting, and I'll bet Joshua and Okawna have lines in the water by now."

They flew past the Islands, and the air flowing into the helicopter smelled better than the smog from Seattle hanging in the Skagit Valley. "How long have you been with the crew?"

"I came aboard just after she passed her sea trials six months ago and got to know everybody soon as they was hired."

Alex turned and looked back between the front seats into the rear section of the helicopter, where an open area separated the rear seat from the cockpit. There were attachment points in the floor, indicating another seat could be installed if needed, for a total capacity of six people, including the pilot. As he turned to look forward again, he noticed Bett was still rapidly chewing away, and was glad she wasn't popping the gum.

Dieter still bothered him, and he needed information. "So, where did Mike find all those people?"

"Dieter and the skinny kid were already on board when Mike hired Josh and me. Don't know a lot about them, except they came from Sweden, or Switzerland, or something." She smiled and looked at Alex. "Mike got a two for one when he found out I could fly a helicopter. Hell, me and Josh have been together since high school. Old man Harrison came aboard a week later in Seattle, and then two months ago, Okawna and Lisa came aboard together. They seem all right. That Okawna's a hunk. You ain't bad yourself, professor. The next day, Rita showed up, and man, did she take a liking to Okawna. Now, Mike's a city-raised good old boy, and don't care about money. Last year, he spent thirty million on some kind of research with seaweed. Supposed to kill cancer or something."

He liked Bett just as he liked Joshua from the moment he had met him and found them an interesting couple. In the distance, he saw the outline of the *Mystic* glistening in the evening sun on the horizon. He scanned the surrounding waters, and she was alone on the vast Pacific Ocean.

A few minutes later, Alex saw Okawna standing outside the bridge, awaiting his arrival. Bett set down lightly on the stern and shut down the engines, then they climbed out as Okawna and Joshua came down the outside stairs from the bridge. She jumped into Joshua's waiting arms, giving him a passionate kiss, while Alex grabbed his backpack from the storage compartment.

Alex closed the side door and strolled beside his friend across the deck. "That was a great ride."

"Glad you enjoyed it. The others are waiting for us in the lounge."

***

Dieter folded his arms across his chest as he stared down at Cave through the rear window of the bridge. He knew dealing with Okawna later would be hard enough. Now that Cave would be on this trip, things could get ugly when the time came.

He watched Bartram climb up the side of the helicopter and fold the blades back along the tail, while Harrison pushed a U-shaped type of pallet lift under the helicopter. Bartram jumped down, and together they jacked the helicopter up an inch above the deck, pulled it forward eight feet, and then set it back down.

Within moments, the helicopter was secured to the deck with tie down straps, and then Harrison ran up the stairs and onto the bridge, and Dieter turned to face him. "Let's get underway."

***

Rita was smiling at Alex as he entered the lounge, and then she stepped forward to wrap her arms around him, holding him close. "I'm glad you came back. It will be nice having someone new on board."

Alex dropped his pack and wrapped his arms around her waist. When he felt her pelvis gently moving across his crotch, he grinned and let go before he got too excited. "Yeah, I'm looking forward to getting to know you better, too."

Lisa folded her arms across her chest and moved closer to Okawna. "It's hard to compete with someone like her. Is it something I did wrong?"

"Not wrong. Just bad timing. You're looking for romance, and Alex isn't ready for that right now. He knows Rita isn't the settling down type, and neither is he, so he wants to be with her for a while. That's all."

Mike was listening while watching the interaction between Alex and Rita. It appeared Okawna was okay with it, but he wondered if it might be a problem for Lisa.

Alex noticed Okawna's smirk. "Why don't you show me where I'll be sleeping?"

Okawna put his hand on his friend's shoulder and tilted his head close to his ear. "I was wondering the same thing."

Alex followed Okawna down the steps to the lowest level, leaving his pack at the bottom of the stairs as they continued along a hallway in the center of the ship. Several doors on both sides were labeled with numbers for the cabins, then Okawna showed him the two co-bathrooms, but only one had a shower.

Walking back the way they came, Okawna stopped to open the last cabin door on the right, near the bottom of the stairs. "This is yours."

Alex heard the soft whine of the turbine engines increase and felt the *Mystic* gaining speed. He stared at Okawna, his eyebrows forming an unasked question.

Okawna shrugged his shoulders. "I know it's a little noisy, but it's the only one left. Besides, the way things are going between you and Rita, I doubt you'll be sleeping in here very often."

Alex was immensely grateful he was not alone on this quest. Okawna was the only person he trusted right now, and he knew his best friend would have his back if something went wrong. "I'm glad you don't mind."

"Well, hell, she's not really my type anyway, and it's good to see you getting on with your life."

Alex grabbed his pack from the floor and stepped into the cabin, where light coming through the two foot wide window glistened on the varnished paneling. On his left was a four drawer dresser with a mirror, next to a matching double door closet. The bed had sheets, pillows, and blankets stacked on one end of the mattress, so he tossed his pack onto the other end, then stepped out and closed the door.

They climbed the stairs to the main deck, turning left past the low wall at the top. No one was in the lounge, so Alex looked around while Okawna went to the refrigerator. Joshua had explained his computer station on his desk in the corner was connected to the entire ship. When the *Mystic* was built, Mike had spared no expense for the state-of-the-art electronic control system.

The large open room had windows on the right side, starting at the kitchen near the stern, and along the dining and recreation area on the far side of the shuffleboard table. The entertainment center was mounted on the forward wall, separating Mike's office and living quarters in the bow.

Alex turned when Okawna walked up and handed him a cool brown bottle. He looked at the label before opening the cap and then took a small sip. "Mike has good taste."

"Hey, I brought the beer."

Alex looked at the shuffleboard table for a moment, then walked over and picked up the chromed steel disk with a colored plastic top. It resembled something he had seen before and held it out for Okawna to see. "Remember this shape, and let's go outside, so we can talk without interruption."

***

Outside on the stern, Alex told Okawna about the Dead Energy operation, and what he had learned from Lewis at Groom Lake. "These devices were never meant to be in the water, so I just hope we can retrieve them before it's too late."

"Mike talked to Donner and learned his experts should arrive on the *Discovery* late this morning, so they're probably there by now. Do you know any of them?"

"Yes, Doctor Henry Heinz, the director of Area 51 research, is a friend of mine. He should be a big help with the recovery."

Alex looked out over the water, admiring the setting sun painting the clouds in beautiful pastel colors. "Do you know how many stops we'll make along the way?"

"No. I didn't think about it, but I can find out easy enough."

Alex turned away from the water. "I smell food."

"Josh is making something special for his wife. Let's go inside and we can ask Mike about where we'll stop for supplies."

Alex thought about how much he should tell everyone. "We need to play dumb about where the devices came from. For now, all anyone needs to know is that they need to be recovered."

"I'm with you."

***

Alex and Okawna entered the lounge, where the only person missing was Harrison, who was on the bridge monitoring the automated controls. Bartram piled a mountain of food on a plate before leaving with it to relieve Harrison.

Alex sat next to Rita, finding her easy to be with as they talked about their interests. He discovered they had a lot in common, so he was looking forward to being with her for the rest of the adventure. The rest of the dinner conversations were lighthearted, and after the delicious meal and clean up, Bett and Joshua disappeared, an Alex and Okawna returned to the table with Mike, Lisa, Dieter, and Rita to discuss the trip.

Alex explained his plan. "I have a contact at the CHARS station in Northeast Canada, trying to give me a location for the search. That's why I asked for your help, Mike. We may need your sub to look under the ice."

"Ah, shit!" Harrison exclaimed as he carried a plate of food to the table and sat down. "I hate the cold."

Mike looked around the table. "Then our first stop is Seward, Alaska. I need you to come ashore so I can buy you some cold weather gear." He looked at Dieter. "What do you think, John?"

"We should stop in Prince Rupert, Canada, instead. Seward will take us too far north, and we could be in Rupert early tomorrow morning. We will top off our fuel and supplies, and from there, we can make it through the Aleutian Islands and the Bering Sea. We can top off the fuel in again in Burrow, Alaska."

"You're the Captain, so whatever you think is best."

Alex stood. "I appreciate this, Mike. I need to make a few calls."

Alex left the room and descended the stairs to his cabin. This far from shore, his cellphone would be useless, so he grabbed the satellite phone from his bag and carried it up to the stern of the ship.

His first call was to retrieve messages from his voice mail, and the only one was from Wesley, who was worried about something. He entered the speed dial number, and Wesley answered on the second ring.

"Who is this?"

"Hey, Wesley. This is Alex."

"I didn't recognize the number, but I figured it was you. I'm glad you called. That lady from the park called a little while ago, and my mountain is showing more activity."

"How bad?"

"A hot spring suddenly appeared at one of the campgrounds, so I'll go look around tomorrow."

"Okay. I'll be out of cell phone service, so you'll have to use this number for a while."

"Any chance you can get me some current satellite images of Mount Baker?"

"I'll see what I can do."

"Thanks. How'd it go in Nevada?"

"It's not good. There are four devices, but so far, only two have been activated that we know about. The only way to stop them is to get one to the surface, and hopefully, the one in the Pacific will remain dormant until they recover it."

"What about the one in the Arctic?"

"It will be impossible to find unless Sonja and her team can get a more precise location."

"I see. Until tomorrow then."

Alex made a call to a friend at NASA and had current satellite images of Mount Baker faxed to Wesley. He turned off the phone and put it in his pocket, then stared across the water, speeding past at seventy-eight knots.

He was worried about Derek and Kristy, and his father, of course. Derek was a smart young man, and he was confident he would take care of his family. Still, he hoped the activity on the mountain would not get any worse and put Derek in a precarious situation. He felt exhausted, deciding to call it a night.

***

Dieter stared down at Cave from the bridge and waited until he walked inside, then grabbed the satellite phone they kept on the bridge and entered a number. He was alone on watch and listened carefully for someone coming up the inside stairs. A moment later, someone answered the phone.

"This is Dieter. I had to change the plan. We will be in Prince Rupert tomorrow morning, so find out where Blacktooth would like to meet. I will meet you at your shop first, so have the money ready." He set the phone in its storage bracket and stared through the front window. "You are making things very complicated for me, Professor."

Chapter 21

9:00 AM. PRINCE RUPERT CANADA:

Alex stood at the open railing behind the bridge, watching Harrison and Bartram setting the motorboat into the water. The morning air was cool as he stared across the harbor at the fishing wharf. The warmer temperature of the water was affecting the fish populations, and if something didn't change, the industry would collapse. Breeding farms for different species were still experimental, and only certain types were hearty enough to live in captivity.

They had topped off the *Mystic*'s fuel tanks two hours ago, and then Captain Dieter had moved her away from the fuel pier into the harbor. The stores were opening, so they would go ashore when the motorboat was ready.

Alex turned when he heard someone approaching, then Lisa walked up to the railing beside him. "Good morning."

Lisa handed Alex a cup of coffee. "I thought you might like something warm."

He took a sip, grinned, and lightly shook his head no as he gave it back to her. "Thanks anyway."

Lisa frowned. "Okawna said you like four spoons of sugar in your coffee."

"I like it black."

Lisa laughed at the joke. "I'll get you another one."

"I'm fine, thanks."

When Alex turned back to the view, Lisa thought about last evening. When she finally went to bed in her cabin, she heard a soft moaning coming from Rita's, which was next to hers. "You left early last night."

"It was a long day."

"And night," she whispered.

Alex turned from the railing. "What was that?"

"When I was on the *Discovery* yesterday, I recovered some dark material flushed out from the drill. I'm not sure what to make of it, and since you're the geologist, I thought you might know what it is. As far as

I can determine, it's some type of carbon, and incredibly hard. Under the microscope, it looks like tiny black diamonds." She noticed his expression suddenly change. "Is something wrong?"

"Did you say diamonds?"

"Yes. I could break it down into smaller elements if I had a mass spectrum analyzer. I didn't think we needed one on the ship for the type of research we do, but now I wish I had one."

Alex thought about David. "A friend of mine has one of those. His name is David Conway, one of the students at my College. I'm sure he would love to have a sample of that carbon for his analyzer."

"I'll get a sample ready and we can send it to him when we go ashore."

"I wish you could meet him. You have a lot in common."

"I thought he was a student."

"He's more like a faculty member and actually instructs some classes. They won't grant him a fellowship because of his age. He's only twenty-six."

"I guess that is a little young. I'll go down and get the sample ready."

When Lisa walked away, Alex looked down at the motorboat tied against the rubber cushion on the back edge of the deck. Okawna, Mike, Dieter, and Rita suddenly appeared from the doorway below, but he had asked Bett and Joshua to stay on board as a precaution. He headed over to the outside stairs and then went down to join them.

***

Bartram sat behind the steering wheel of the motorboat, thinking while waiting for everyone to arrive. The captain was upset when Cave changed their plans, but said he had another way to get what they wanted. They were going to take the *Mystic* while everyone was ashore, but that plan was ruined, because Cave insisted on leaving Josh and Bett on the ship. He should have just let him shoot the professor and toss him over the side. It wouldn't be the first time the captain had asked him to get rid of someone.

The other thing that bothered him was why the captain had hired Harrison. The old man was just a mercenary, and worked for money, not friendship and loyalty, like him.

He waited until everyone but Harrison, Joshua, and Bett had climbed into the motorboat, then started the engine and backed away from the stern. After a slow, short ride, he maneuvered the boat against the floating dock.

After everyone had climbed out, he tied off the motorboat while waiting for the first load of supplies being wheeled down the ramp by a man with a hand dolly. When the person stopped, he stepped into the boat and grabbed the boxes of supplies from the man and began stacking them between the bench seats. Once loaded, he started the engine and headed back to Harrison, waiting on the *Mystic*.

***

Alex held Rita's hand while they walked along the street, past various stores selling items for the tourists, with Mike and Lisa leading the way and Dieter last in line behind Okawna. The women wanted to stop at each one, but Mike insisted they purchase the new clothing first.

Mike entered a store with winter sports equipment on display in the window, and they followed him inside to the racks of winter clothing. The girls grabbed several styles and headed for the fitting rooms, while the men first studied the equipment.

Okawna noticed Dieter didn't follow them into the store and touched Alex on the shoulder. "I'm going to follow the captain. You know my size."

"Okay. I'll meet you back on the ship."

When Okawna looked out the doorway, Dieter was nearly a block away. He glanced in the opposite direction to make sure no one was watching, and then hurried out to follow him.

***

Dieter was nervous about his unscheduled meeting, and since Cave had joined the crew, he had to change all his carefully laid plans for the *Mystic*. He thought maybe he was being paranoid, but he had a feeling someone was watching him, and as a precaution, he suddenly turned right onto a side street and stopped to look back around the corner. He waited several moments, but did not see any unusual activity, so he continued down the side street.

He stopped at store advertising nautical equipment and then rang the patina covered brass bell hanging from a black wrought iron bracket. A moment later, the door was opened by a short bald man, looking through bifocal glasses.

The man stepped out of the way, and Dieter walked inside and waited for him to close the door. "Do you have my package?"

The man moved to the sales counter and reached into a small safe, then grabbed a thick envelope and held it out to his customer. "Here is what you wanted, Captain Dieter."

Dieter opened the envelope and saw the bundles of US one-hundred-dollar bills, then closed it and slid it into his inside coat pocket. "Did you contact Blacktooth?"

The man handed him a small scrap of paper. "Yes. He will meet you at this address. It's a warehouse up the street. Go right when you step outside."

"All right."

"He is not happy with this sudden change in plans."

"Neither was I." He turned and hurried out of the store.

* * *

Okawna waited in a recessed doorway until Dieter had gone inside and then looked through the window of the nautical shop. He saw Dieter looking into a thick white envelope before putting it into his pocket, but when Dieter suddenly turned and walked out the door, he barely had time to duck around the corner of the building.

He thought Dieter would return to the ship, but he turned right and continued up the narrow street. Okawna felt fortunate there were several openings between the buildings on both sides, and he had no trouble staying out of sight.

He followed Dieter for several blocks until he entered a small warehouse, where the only window was a small opening in the front door. He glanced around and then looked inside. Dieter appeared to be arguing with a big, mean looking man until he brought the envelope from his pocket and held it up, and then exchanged it for what appeared to be a plastic CD case.

When Dieter slipped it into his coat pocket and turned to leave, the big man was hollering after him in a deep baritone voice, but Okawna could not distinguish the words, so he ducked behind the corner of the building. He waited until Dieter was a good distance away before walking back out onto the street to follow him. When Dieter turned the corner at the nautical supply store, he knew he was returning to the ship, so did not need to keep up with him.

He was wondering why a CD would be worth an envelope of money when he suddenly felt an object press against the back of his spine. He heard someone say 'stop' with a Russian accent, so did as asked and raised his arms. From the tone of his voice, he knew it was the big man from the warehouse.

"Why are you following Dieter?"

Although Okawna knew he could easily disarm the person, information was a weapon, and he wanted to know what this man's interest was with Dieter. "We had a deal, and he backed out."

"Turn around."

When Okawna slowly did as instructed, he could tell the man was a brawler by his physical size and facial scars. The black 9mm semi-automatic in his hand showed he meant business.

The stranger grinned, exposing his blackened teeth. "That is because I already have a deal with him. I have never known Dieter to back out, so why did he not take yours?"

"I have no idea. That's why I followed him."

"My deal is not over until I get the rest of my money. I am Blacktooth. You ask around, and they will tell you not to get in my way."

Naturally, Okawna thought, and tried not to grin. "Not a problem."

"What is your name?"

"Jamison."

The stranger laughed and put the pistol away. "Like the whiskey."

Okawna laughed with him, hoping for more information. He stopped smiling and stared at Blacktooth. "I wish you good luck with Dieter." Blacktooth's expression became serious, just as he had hoped.

"Why do you say that?"

Okawna shrugged his shoulders. "He backed out of a very lucrative deal with me. What makes you think he will keep your deal?"

"Because I know that ship he is on does not have weapons. Only scientists. He would be a fool to cross me."

Okawna decided not to take any chances by pushing harder. "He's your problem now. I'm going to get some whiskey. Care to join me?"

"No."

When Blacktooth turned and walked away, Okawna continued down the street. He figured Dieter must have information about his long-lost relative on that disk, and somehow, he had to get a look at it.

When he reached the main street, he continued down to the sporting goods store and looked through the window, but there was no sign of Dieter. The floating dock was only a few blocks farther down the street, where he saw Dieter standing next to a stack of supplies, waiting for the next ride back to the ship.

He walked into the store and realized everyone had found what they wanted to wear. Mike and the women were playing with the sports equipment and didn't notice him come in, so he moved over to Alex, who grabbed a dark blue winter coat and pants off the rack and handed it to him.

Alex smiled at his friend. "Try these on. They should be close to your size."

Okawna quickly looked around. "Thanks. I think Dieter's after the stash from the U-boat. I followed him to a meeting in a warehouse, where he paid a lot of money for what looked like a CD in a case. I was on my way back when the man who made the trade shoved a 9mm against my back. His name is Blacktooth, and he knows the Mystic is unarmed."

Alex grinned. "Blacktooth? Really?"

"Yeah, I know, but it's true."

"Okay, but why the Mystic?"

"It takes a submarine to find one. The Mystic's perfect for the job and only has a small crew and untrained scientists on board. At least, that was the original plan until you showed up."

"I had a talk with Bett in the helicopter, and I think Bartram and Harrison are with Dieter."

"I suspected as much. I think he's going to hijack the Mystic from Mike and use it to find the U-boat. What did you bring for a weapon?"

"A .38 caliber pistol."

"Good. I have my .45 and two shotguns stashed on the ship. I had Bett pick them up before she came back. She's an Army Vet, Alex. She flew helicopters in Afghanistan."

"I should have guessed. Does that mean she and Josh are on our side if Dieter tries to take over the ship?"

"I believe their loyalty is to Mike."

"Good. How do you feel about Rita?"

"You're getting to know her better than I ever did. What do you think?"

"I know she loves her job, so I doubt she would betray Mike."

Okawna looked around again. "It looks like the women are ready to leave. I'd better go try these on."

Ten minutes later, they all walked out of the store and down the street to the pier, then down the ramp to join Dieter at the end of the floating dock. A moment later, the motorboat pulled alongside, and they handed their packages to Bartram. Mike and Dieter climbed in for the ride back to the *Mystic*, but Alex and Okawna were hijacked by Lisa and Rita, who wanted to walk around town before returning to the ship. Bartram told them they had another load of supplies on the way, so they had some time before leaving the harbor.

The four of them went back up the ramp to the main street, with Alex walking arm in arm with Rita. After walking out of the third store, Okawna demanded they stop for iced coffee at a rustic dockside restaurant and bar next door.

The place was crowded, so they waited a few moments for people to leave a table near the front window, and then sat down. The server hurried over to grab the tip and wipe it clean before taking their orders. It only took a few moments for the server to return with their drinks.

Alex paid for them, and then raised his mug to the group, casually watching Rita's reaction. "To fair winds and following seas, and the treasure at the end of a successful quest." After smiling and a round of toasts, she remained impassive about the mention of a treasure.

Okawna tapped Alex's foot under the table and tried to hide his face as he nodded to the window. "That's him."

Alex casually looked at the large man standing outside. When the man turned and walked through the doorway, Alex stood to block the man's view of Okawna. Once he passed by, Okawna stood and left the restaurant.

Lisa stared after Okawna. "Where's he going?"

Alex sat down. "He forgot something for the trip."

He kept an eye on the big man, now standing at the end of the bar. He was talking with a short man wearing a dirty white Skipper's hat with something embroidered on the front, but he could not read the words from this distance.

The two men suddenly decided to leave, so Alex stood just in time to bump into the short man and smile. "I'm sorry about that. I didn't see you."

The man ignored him and followed the big man out of the tavern, and then Alex sat down. The embroidered name on the hat was CONDOR.

Lisa gave him a concerned expression. "Is something wrong, Alex?"

"No. What makes you think that?"

"That's the second time you jumped out of your chair, so you tell me."

"I'm just eager to get underway, I guess."

Lisa smiled at him. "I know what you mean. Me too. My life is so boring most of the time, but since you joined us, I finally have some excitement in my life."

Rita reached over under the table and placed her hand on Alex's thigh. "I'm ready to go."

They stood and walked out of the tavern, then down to the dock, and found Okawna sitting behind the steering wheel of the boat. Harrison was in the passenger seat, but the rest of the seats were empty.

Okawna looked up at the group. "Last run of the day, folks."

Alex helped the women into the boat, and a moment later, they were cruising smoothly across the water to the *Mystic*. He studied Harrison's expression, and he seemed to be enjoying the ride while chatting with Okawna, and thought perhaps he was wrong about the man's loyalty.

***

Alex hung his new white cold weather clothing in the closet with the other clothes he had unpacked last night. He silently cursed that there was no lock on the door as he left his cabin and climbed the stairs to the main deck.

There was no one in the lounge, but he heard the hoist growling through the open doors at the end of the walkway, so strolled out to the stern to watch the activity. Harrison was controlling the hoist using a small remote control pad, while Bartram was guiding the motorboat into the storage brackets.

When the hoist suddenly shut down, Alex heard voices, so turned to look up behind the bridge. Okawna was leaning back against the railing, talking with Mike, Joshua, and the three women. He noticed Lisa holding a tall glass of Champaign while laughing and felt sorry for her. This may become more exciting than she could ever imagine.

***

Dieter and Mike were on the bridge, leaning over a chart of the Aleutian Islands while discussing the various routes into the Bering Sea. Dieter pointed to a narrow gap between two large islands. "We will save time if we detour through this area."

Mike frowned as he studied the chart. "Are you sure? According to this, it appears to be shallow at low tide."

"I checked the computer for our estimated time of arrival, and even at low tide, we will have plenty of water beneath us."

"All right. You're the Captain."

Dieter waited until Mike walked down the stairs and then leaned back in the chair. Last night, he had received a call from his information source at the Pentagon, who was related to a member of the Russian Mafia. Now he knew Cave's history with the CIA and his relationship with the Director of National Security. "Your Director Donner cannot help you this time, Professor."

Chapter 22

60 MILES WEST OF VANCOUVER ISLAND:
It was his first time in a helicopter, and Henry found it exhilarating as he approached a large white ship, alone in the vast expanse of ocean. From above, the *Discovery* was sleek in design, with a square stern and two decks above the waterline, but he thought the ship was very odd looking. It had a twenty-foot diameter hole down through the center of the ship, near the stern, and the top of the ship was a florescent orange color.

As the helicopter approached, he admired the large, swept back, tinted windows for the bridge, which wrapped around the bow and continued along both sides of the four hundred foot long main deck. Carl Gregory brought the helicopter over the top of the ship to land, and Henry saw the reason it was orange. They were long rows of flat orange hose stacked twenty feet high, starting at the bow above the bridge, and ending at the edge of the open hole.

Past the hole near the stern was a large flat area with a black 'H' painted on the grey deck. Henry's hands tightened on the armrests as Carl gently set the helicopter down on the H and waited for Carl to tell him what to do next.

Carl shut everything down and took off his headset, then got out and opened the rear door for his passenger. "I'll take you down to meet everyone, Doctor. Follow me."

When Henry stepped down onto the ship, he stopped and looked out over the water. The air smelled so clean compared to the mainland in Bellingham, he thought it was amazing. Now that he was actually here, the enormity of his task became real. He felt his heart rate increase, knowing he was responsible for the success of this mission.

Carl stepped past Henry, retrieved his suitcase from between the back seats, and then grinned at Henry's expression. "Is this your first time on a ship, Doctor?"

"Yes, as a matter of fact. I live in Nevada."

Carl grinned and moved away. "This way, Doctor."

Henry followed Carl across the platform to the handrail rising out of the deck, then down the stairs to the main deck. When he saw a huge open area, he stopped to look around. This section of the ship was enclosed on three sides, with the stern open to the sea. Only a removable chain railing keep someone from falling into the water.

Straight ahead was an odd-looking fifteen foot submarine without windows. Two massive mechanical arms were folded back along its sides and a row of lights curved around one end. He looked up at the round opening in the roof he had seen when they landed, then over at the handrail around the matching opening in the deck, down into the water, where he saw the open connection on the end of another orange hose disappearing into the depths of the ocean.

Carl was kind enough to wait while he looked around, then Henry followed him past the right side of the hole in the deck and a large glass window in the forward wall. Just past the window, they turned right, through white double doors into the middle of the ship. They continued through a long hallway with doors on both sides labeled with numbers and nameplates.

Carl held up the suitcase and indicated an open doorway labeled CONFERENCE ROOM.

"I'll make sure this gets to your cabin, Doctor."

"Thank you, Carl. It was a very enjoyable ride."

Henry looked into the room, where a number of people had gathered already. As he entered, the ship's Captain, a burly man with curly white hair, smiled and walked over to shake his hand.

"Welcome aboard, Doctor Heinz. I'm Captain Paul Jordon. Let me introduce your fellow scientists. This is Doctor Victor Hugo, a marine engineer from the California Institute of Technology."

Henry looked up at a slender man with a gray goatee and no hair, and reached out to shake his hand. However, Victor did not smile and his handshake was limp and brief.

Victor crossed his arms and looked down at the little man Director Donner had sent to help him with the recovery. "I have a laboratory waiting, Doctor Heinz, so when you're through with the pleasantries, we have to get started."

Henry wasn't sure what to make of Victor, and then a small woman with gray hair tied back in a bun smiled and held out her hand.

"Welcome aboard, Dr. Heinz. I'm Janice Shepard." When her hand touched Henry's, Janice suddenly felt flushed and sensed her heart rate increase. She had never cared for tall men, and Henry was only five foot six, an inch taller than she was. He looked to be about the same age as she was, too, somewhere in his mid-sixties.

"Please, call me Henry, and it is nice to meet you too, Janice."

Victor turned and walked toward the door. "Time to go to work," he barked over his shoulder.

Henry followed Janice and Victor back along the hallway toward the stern, and Victor went through the last door on the left, where he had seen the large window. Janice grabbed his arm and pulled him through the white double doors to the stern deck instead, and over to the railing to look down into the hole.

"This is where they lower the equipment to the ocean floor. Look up behind us." She turned and pointed at the opening in the roof, and the flat rows of orange tubing curved back onto the top deck.

"I noticed those tubes when we made our approach."

"Victor and I arrived earlier this morning, and the Captain gave us a grand tour and explained what the Discovery does in Mister Mike's research company."

"And what is the purpose of the orange hose?"

"It's a flexible tube rolled around something similar to a giant conveyor belt. They have enough tubing to reach a depth of five thousand feet. They use it as a guide for the drilling and optical cables, and the other end is attached to a large steel base anchored on the seafloor. We better get going. Victor isn't a patient man."

Henry turned and could see Victor staring at them through the thick glass window on the right side of the doors. He was confused about Victor being in charge, since the man did not have a clue what he is dealing with. The most important thing about this operation was to be cautious. He decided that for now, he would just see how things would go, but if Victor tried to rush things, he would talk to Director Donner about it.

He followed Janice through the double doors and stopped at the first door on the right, where the nameplate read, OBSERVATION, not laboratory. Inside the room were several computers, monitors, and video screens with numbers for specific cameras.

Victor uncrossed his arms when Henry and Janice finally walked in. He had no idea who this Heinz person was or his specialty, and he did not like it. "Are you done with the tour, Janice?"

"Bite me, Victor."

Henry's mouth opened slightly. *Janice appears so innocent,* he thought.

Janice smiled at Henry's expression and took his arm. "Come over here and have a seat, Henry. I'll show you the recordings of what we're up against."

"Of course."

Henry sat in a swivel chair in front of a video screen, and Janice and Victor rolled their chairs over to sit on either side of him. "You did not tell me your occupation, Janice."

"I work for the Environmental Protection Agency as a chemical specialist, but I tinker with resonate frequencies as a hobby. From what little Director Donner told me, I guess both my skills are needed. My priority is the safe removal of the methane and the pollutants mixed in with it. Once we start melting the ice beneath it, all that material will rise, expand into a gas, and enter the atmosphere within twenty minutes, and the environmental consequences will be significant. Our current global warming situation is bad enough, but if we allow this amount of pollutants to reach the surface, it could be enough to put us past the point of no return, and the air is foul enough already."

Henry watched the recordings while Janice explained what he was seeing. "Have you determined the composition of that dark material?"

"Nothing definitive. We do know it resembles tiny carbon crystals similar to diamonds."

When the magnified view of the grey cylinder appeared on the screen, Victor pressed pause. "We know that device melts and freezes the water very quickly, but nothing else. Director Donner told me you would tell us why it's doing that."

Henry told them about how they operate. "What ideas have you discussed so far?"

Janice leaned back and crossed her arms. "None that will work."

Henry noticed something missing in the recordings. "Does that dark area cover the entire under surface of the methane hydride?"

Janice glanced over at Victor and back to Henry. "We don't know yet. We'll have to wait for *Celeas* to go down and take a closer look. What's on your mind?"

Henry swiveled his chair to face her. "Who is Celeas?"

"She's that un-manned underwater robot out there on the stern. You probably saw her when you arrived."

"Yes. Un-manned, you say? That is incredible. I was thinking that dark material could indicate a place to sever the two types of ice."

"Maybe. We know it was difficult to drill through. It's an interesting idea."

Victor stood and leaned back against the thick window. "The pressure at that depth is enough to keep it frozen, and we know it's the extreme cold of the clear ice that's keeping them together so it doesn't drift away."

Janice stood. "That's all we know for now. Let's get you settled into your cabin and we'll talk more about how to recover this device over dinner."

Henry stood and held his elbow out. "After you, Janice."

Chapter 23

ALASKA. THE ALEUTIAN ISLANDS:

It was dawn on the *Mystic*, with Harrison sitting on a chair in front of the control console on the bridge. He was staring through the front window at the islands on both sides of a narrow strait of water, which was the route suggested by the captain. In twenty minutes, they would be in the Bering Sea.

The turbines suddenly shut down as the ship's speed quickly fell away. He stood and checked the control console, but the only noticeable problem were the RPM indicators for the turbines, now showing zero.

***

When the whine of turbines next to Alex's cabin suddenly became completely quiet, he looked up at Rita, lying naked on top of him. "We're not scheduled to stop. Let's find out what's going on."

She rolled to the side, got off of the bed, then quickly put on her clothes. "You go topside while I check the engine room."

Alex sat on the edge of the bed while he pulled on his pants and shoes and then stood to put on his shirt. "I'll call you on the intercom."

Alex hurried out into the walkway, surprised there was no sign of the rest of the crew. He ran up both sets of inside stairs onto the bridge, where he was alone with Harrison. "What happened?"

"I don't know. The turbines just suddenly stopped."

"Where's the main power supply?"

"Just inside the engine room, but that's not the problem. All the electronics are working, but the turbines are offline."

Alex grabbed the microphone for the ship's intercom system from its overhead bracket and selected the button for the engine room. "Rita, we still have power up here, but no engines." He clipped the microphone into its bracket and then studied Harrison's expression. "Tell me what happened."

"I was keeping an eye on things, and then the engines just stopped." He could see the skepticism in Alex's eyes and knew he had better think of something in case this didn't work. "Look, we still have thrusters. Let me get us back underway."

"How fast can we go?"

Harrison flipped four switches on the master control panel. "Only fifteen knots, but it's better than nothing. We need to get through these islands."

Alex watched Harrison enter the command in to the computer, and then the maneuvering thrusters began pushing the *Mystic* through the water toward the other side of the two islands. He was tempted to call Rita for an update, but knew she was probably busy.

Alex heard the roar of a ship's horn and saw a large black ship speeding in their direction, so he grabbed the microphone and selected all the stations. "We've got company, and it's not the coast guard. We won't be able to outrun them, so I'll stay up here. Okawna, you know what to do."

Alex kept the microphone in his hand as he waited to see what would happen. After the incident with Okawna in Prince Rupert, he always carried his .38 caliber Air-weight pistol in the front pocket of his jeans.

The black ship was approaching at an angle to block the way, and Alex knew without the turbines, they could not outrun it. "Turn us around."

Harrison spun to face Alex. "What good would that do? We should stop and find out what they want."

"I saw the way they worked in port, and we can stop faster than they can, and we might keep some distance between us for a while. Use the damn thrusters to spin us around!"

Alex watched Harrison hold his hand above the control panel, hesitant to follow his order. "What's the problem? Are they friends of yours?"

"Honestly, Alex, I've never seen that ship before."

"Then do what I say and get us out of here, damn it!"

Harrison pulled back on the joystick and it was like hitting the brakes, as the thrusters rotated one-hundred-eighty-degrees at full power. Anything loose was hurled forward and the ship nearly stopped, then he twisted the joystick so that the *Mystic* spun around then they were moving away from the black ship.

***

In the engine room, Rita checked the circuit breakers, but nothing was tripped. She knew it had to be something to stop both engines at once, and it took several minutes to identify the problem. Someone had cut the electrical wires for the master fuel solenoid. She realized whoever it was knew what they were doing, since they cut the wires too short to splice them back together. A workbench with tool drawers was bolted to the wall, so she grabbed the wire strippers. Now all she needed was a short piece of electrical wire.

***

Alex stared through the rear window and kept his eyes on the black ship as it corrected its course, then it was quickly closing the distance. Dieter and Mike ran up the stairs, and Alex pointed behind them. "Friends of yours, Captain?"

Dieter took his time responding as he studied the black ship. "I have never seen that ship before." He could sense Cave staring at him, and wondered how much he knew. "Piracy happens in all parts of the world, Professor. What makes you think I would know them?"

Alex didn't answer and looked at Mike. "Who chose this route?"

"John and I agreed it was the fastest way through the islands."

Alex let the matter drop for now and was counting on Okawna to organize a plan if they were forced to stop. "They're gaining fast, so we'd better hope Rita fixes the problem with the turbines before it's too late."

***

Okawna waited near the top of the stairs from the lowest deck and grabbed Lisa's hand as she reached the top. "You should wait in your cabin until I know what's going on."

"What about Alex?"

"He knows what he's doing, and doesn't need to worry about you right now, so please go below."

Lisa stepped out of the way as Bett and Joshua ran up the stairs carrying three shotguns.

Okawna found it interesting that Joshua and Bett looked eager for a fight. "We need to control the high ground," he told them. "You two will be on the bridge and try to keep out of sight until something happens. Everything forward is too high from the water for a fast assault, so if they try to board this ship, it will be from the stern. They may think we're unarmed, so don't give them a reason to shoot."

"What about you and Alex?" Bett asked.

"We'll let Alex take the lead from the bridge, so just wait for him to resolve this without a fight. He has a way of doing that. I'll be the rover and take care of this deck and the stern."

Joshua grinned. "I might have a hard time hiding." A thought suddenly occurred to him. "Hey, Rita can shoot. She's pretty good, too."

"If she can get the turbines running, none of us will have to shoot. Let's go."

***

Dieter jumped back when Bett suddenly came up the stairs onto the bridge, carrying a shotgun. He watched her crouch down behind the bulkhead near the left door, and then Joshua ran past him with a shotgun and tried to hide near the right door.

Alex watched Dieter's expression, and it was obvious he was surprised they were armed. Mike surprised all of them when he opened his coat to show his pearl handled .45 caliber revolver in a shoulder holster.

When Alex looked at Harrison, he was completely at ease, as if dealing with this kind of thing every day. Or he might already know what was going to happen. In order to get on board, the black ship had to make the *Mystic* stop, so as long as the thrusters kept working, it would be difficult. That's when he heard a cannon fire, and then the water near the stern erupted like a geyser with a muffled thud, causing everyone to turn to see what happened.

Alex grabbed Harrison's arm and spun him around. "What do you know about this?"

Harrison raised his hands. "Hey, don't get mad at me, Alex. This is my sixth time dealing with pirates, and it's usually in the same way."

"Explain!"

"They threaten to shoot you full of holes, so you stop. Then they send a boat over and rob what they can. If no one tries to stop them, they just take what they want and leave. No big deal. That's why I always carry a quarter ounce of gold in my pocket."

Harrison slowly reached into his front pocket, brought out a small leather pouch, and held it up. "This has saved my ass several times."

Alex wondered if he might be wrong about a high-jacking, but that black ship was after something, and it had to be big to be worth trying to rob them. The cannon exploded again as the whine of a projectile passed over the bridge, and then water soared into the air off the starboard bow.

***

Rita heard the thud through the hull and knew things were getting bad topside. She knew she had a roll of wire somewhere and had already dug through the drawers, frustrated when she didn't find it. She could not think of another place in the engine room she might have put it then had an idea and ran out of the engine room and into Alex's cabin.

***

"Shut it down, Harrison," Mike ordered.

Alex snapped his head around to look at Mike. "What are you doing?"

"I'm not going to let anyone get hurt. We'll do like Harrison says and give them what they want."

Alex thought about Okawna's encounter with Blacktooth. "No, Mike. We don't know what they'll do if we let them on board. As long as we keep moving, we're harder to hit."

Mike was still undecided. "What do you think, John?"

Dieter knew with so many weapons on board, the chances of Blacktooth taking over the ship had dropped immensely, and so far, he could get away with acting innocent. "I agree with Alex. We need to keep moving." He looked at Harrison. "Use the thrusters to move us from side to side. We may lose some speed, but we will be harder to hit."

When Harrison twisted the joystick, the *Mystic* was suddenly sliding diagonally through the water. The next roar from the cannon was louder as the black ship drew closer to the stern, but the round hit two-hundred-feet ahead and slightly off the port side.

The turbines suddenly came online, so Harrison quickly switched the joystick from thrusters to turbines and engaged the jet pumps. He shoved the throttle to full power, and the *Mystic* lurched forward with incredible power as she got up onto the pontoons, slicing through the surface of the water.

Alex stared through the rear window as the black ship quickly fell away in the distance. Now that the engines were running, he wanted answers. "Stop us here, Harrison."

Mike was surprised by Alex's order and looked at him. "What are you doing?"

"We're out of range and can stay that way, but we still need to get to the arctic. Let's find out what happened to the engines before we try it again." He looked up at Joshua. "Mind staying up here with Harrison?"

Bett slung her shotgun over one shoulder and leaned back against the rear window. "I can handle it, Alex."

"All right, let's find Rita."

***

Okawna was waiting in the walkway just inside the doors out to the stern when he heard someone running up the stairs from below and looked around the corner. He expected to see Lisa, but it was Bartram, who went to the side window in the lounge, instead of stopping to ask what was going on.

Alex came down the stairs with Joshua, Mike, and Dieter, and while they continued into the lounge, he saw Lisa hesitate to come up the stairs from below. "It's all clear. You can come up now."

Once Lisa came up and entered the lounge, Mike stepped around Alex. "Rita's still down in the engine room, so I'll get her."

***

Rita was still checking the engine room, wondering if something else had been sabotaged, and looked up when Mike walked in. "Are we still under attack?"

"No, we're fine for now. Everyone is waiting for you in the lounge."

She tossed the pliers onto the workbench. "Good. This was intentional."

Rita followed Mike up the stairs and stood next to Okawna. "Someone sabotaged the fuel system in a way that was difficult to fix, so I had to run a new wire to get them working again."

Okawna noticed a faint grin from Bartram and moved over in front of him. "This is the first time I've seen you since we left port. What were *you* doing when the turbines stopped?"

"I was in my cabin, reading and sleeping."

"You didn't notice the cannon fire?"

"I looked in the hallway and saw Bett and Joshua with shotguns, so I just stayed in my cabin until it was over."

Alex realized it might be difficult to discover the culprit right away, and they had to continue to the Arctic. He looked at Rita. "Are the engines able to operate safely?"

"They're fine for now. I'll do a permanent job at our next port when I get some wire. Someone must have thrown mine overboard. Oh, and you're going to be without a reading light for a while, Alex."

"That's fine. Okay. For now, we take another route through the islands and continue to our destination. We'll play the blame game underway."

Chapter 24

THE CABIN:

Wesley stared at the television, but it might as well have been off. After the call from Jamie last night, he knew the incident at the campground was a warning that things could get much worse. He heard a beep from his computer and walked to his desk as the printer shoved out four large colored photographs of his mountain. He smiled and grabbed them from the tray. "Thanks, Alex."

He spread them out on the desktop, matching two sides on each to form one large image of his mountain. Someone had circled two large orange areas, indicating significant heat. "Oh, crap." he said softly.

He grabbed his personal map of the mountain and matched the locations of the heat blooms in the photographs. He was familiar with one area and knew he could use his modified Humvee to get there without disturbing the ecological system. The eighteen-inch wide tires were gentle on the vegetation and the high-rise suspension allowed him to travel over small trees with little damage to the foliage.

He grabbed his map and the photographs, went into the kitchen to put on his hiking boots, then walked out the door and climbed into his Hummer. The engine roared to life, and he backed up to the front of the barn and climbed out. He opened the padlock between the two large doors, ignoring the complaining squeal of the overhead rollers as he shoved one side open.

He entered the barn and went over to the metal shelving attached to the wall. He had worked for the Hughes Corporation as an electronic engineer, designing specialized seismic sensors for twenty years. He just happened to have acquired a few test models before retiring.

Each custom made sensor was twenty inches square by eight inches thick, with a flip up antenna on the side, and each unit could sense motion and temperature and transmitting the information to his receivers in the barn. He hefted a pair of them, and the thirty-pound weight in each hand attested to the large capacity of the self-contained batteries.

He carried two units over to the Hummer and set them in back behind the rear seats. After closing the barn door, he climbed into the cab and drove away, following an old logging road behind his cabin up the side of Mount Baker.

Twenty minutes later, he followed another abandoned dirt logging road for another half hour before turning off the road and continuing through virgin forest. Fifteen minutes later, he recognized the exposed thirty foot area of flat granite protruding from the ground, but something was wrong. Wisps of yellow vapor swirled across the grey granite surface before vanishing into the air.

He shut off the engine and climbed down from the Hummer, walking over for a closer look. A yellow liquid substance was boiling up through a fresh fracture in the granite and he knew it was a new fumarole; a place where magma was close to the surface. "Oh, crap."

He pulled a pocketknife from his front pocket and knelt down beside the fracture, and the stench of rotten eggs assaulted his nostrils. He scrapped the thick yellow sulfur from the granite and saw it had not yet begun to harden, which meant the fracture was only a day old.

He stood and looked around for more fumaroles, but the rest of the area was clear, so he walked to the Hummer, grabbed one of the sensors, and returned to the fracture. He placed it on a level area of bare granite and flipped up the antenna. When he turned it on, a small red light indicated it was working. "One down."

He returned to the Hummer and studied the photograph and his map, and the next location would be too steep for his Hummer and he would have to carry the other sensor for nearly three miles through steep terrain.

He tossed the maps inside the Hummer and climbed in, then drove onto the bare granite to turn around before retracing his route back down the dirt road. Even in extreme circumstances, he was careful not to disturb natural vegetation any more than necessary, and he was not about to change old habits.

***

MOUNT BAKER STATE PARK:
Jamie recognized the little boy standing outside the restrooms as she drove into the last campground to complete the morning inspections. She parked the SUV and climbed out, and he ran up to her, tears streaming down his cheeks.

She knelt in front of him. "What's wrong?"

"The water burnt my sister," he sobbed.

Jamie stood, grabbed the boy's hand, and led him into the woman's side of the building. The little girl was sitting on the beige changing table and the woman was wrapping wet paper towels around her little feet. "What happened, ma'am?"

The woman spun around. "This is your fault!" she snapped. "You people should not have put a campground so close to that hot spring! She went to the pond this morning, and I heard her scream. When I got there, the water was steaming, and she was lying on the ground, screaming in pain. What's wrong with you people?"

Jamie felt terrible about what happened, but knew trying to explain it was not the Park's fault would not comfort the woman. "I'm very sorry for what happened, ma'am. The water seemed fine yesterday. I'll block off the area so no one else gets hurt."

"You're right. I'm sorry I yelled at you. It's just that I'm hiding from my ex-husband, and now this happens."

"I have some medical training. Mind if I look at her feet?"

The woman moved out of the way, and Jamie stepped in front of the little girl and smiled, but the trails of tears down the girl's dirt smudged cheeks and the sad frown broke her heart. She carefully unwrapped the wet paper towels from her tiny feet. "They're not blistered, so that's a good sign. They might be painful for a little while, but she should be all right. I'll get my first aid kit and wrap them for you, but you should see a doctor as soon as you get a chance. Would you like me to help you move to a different campsite?"

The woman shook her head no. "Thanks, but now that I know it's dangerous, I'll be more careful."

"I'll be right back. I just need to get my first aid kit."

Jamie returned and wrapped the tiny pink feet in gauze, then grabbed a small spiral notepad from her shirt pocket and wrote down her phone number, which she held it out to the woman. "Call me if you need anything."

The little girl grabbed the paper, and the woman picked her up, nodded her thanks, and left the restroom. Jamie left the building and went to the back of her SUV, and dug through a large green plastic storage container until she found a new bundle of yellow nylon rope. She walked through the campground and into the forest until she was standing next to the new pond. White steam was rising from the surface, and she realized there was more going on in the park than was obvious.

She began stringing the yellow rope around the trees to make a temporary barricade and made a mental note to call Patterson after she told her boss what had happened. They might need to shut down the park before anything else went wrong.

***

MOUNT BAKER:

"Oh, crap." Wesley mumbled and set the sensor on a bed of pine needles next to a large grey boulder. He pulled a handkerchief from his coat pocket to wipe his brow, and then plopped down on the boulder, frustrated he would have to carry the sensor back down the mountain. The banks of a small stream had washed away, allowing the water to flood a large area of the small valley, too deep to cross. Out of curiosity, he leaned forward and put his hand in the water, then yanked it back to blow on his fingertips. "Oh, crap!"

His worst fears were coming true. The glaciers were melting fast and the runoff water was flowing deep underground through fractures in the rock until super-heated by magma and forced back to the surface. He made a mental note to check the glaciers and find out how fast they were melting. If it was slow and steady, the water would flood the streams and not rush down the mountain like a lahar. He stood, hoisted the sensor onto one shoulder, and then began walking back down the mountain.

***

MONTANA COLLEGE, BOZEMAN:

David Conway felt his cellphone vibrate in his front pants pocket and pulled it out to look at the caller ID. The text message was short and simple. Come to my office. Marcia. He ran down the hallway and burst into her office. "Did Alex call?"

Marcia held out a small package. "No, but he sent this by special courier."

David tore at the padded envelope, but it refused to yield its contents. "Why do they have to make it so difficult to open?" He glanced over at Marcia, and she was holding the scissors. He grinned and took them from her hand. "Thanks."

He cut the end of the envelope, looked inside, then reached in and brought out a small plastic vial and a handwritten note. He tossed the envelope into the trash, set the vial on Marcia's desk, and looked at the note.

He looked over at Marcia. "This isn't from Alex. It's from that girl he was talking about. Listen to this. My name is Lisa Harding, and I'm working with our friend Alex Cave on board the research vessel, Mystic. He told me you have a laser spectrum analyzer and you could determine the composition of the material in the vial. It was collected during our attempt to drill down to a cylindrical object of unknown origin. We know the black material is a type of carbon, but my equipment on the Mystic cannot break it down into a smaller atomic structure. We would appreciate your help, and here is Alex's satellite phone number. Please call us with your findings. Thank you. Lisa Harding."

He picked up the vial and studied the contents in the light from the window. When he rolled it around, the material inside appeared to be a fine black powder.

Marcia noticed that David appeared apprehensive as he studied the material. "Is there something wrong, David?"

David looked down at her. "The last time we did a test for Alex, it was during the Dead Energy situation. That was an unknown material, too. You remember the results of that test. It nearly destroyed part of the science building."

"I remember. Just be careful."

"Right." He turned and walked out of Marcia's office with the sample.

Chapter 25

NORTHERN BERING SEA:

Mark Hess, the captain of a Canadian cargo freighter, set the engines to stop and walked out of the bridge to join his crew. He shoved his hands deep into his thick coat pockets as he stared at the massive wall of transparent ice blocking their passage across the north Beaufort Sea. He turned to look at his first mate, who had an imploring look in his eyes. "I know what you're thinking, and we'll just have to accept the fact we'll lose some money on this trip. We'll have to go further south until we can go around this thing."

"I know, but how can a glacier reach this far south? Something's not right about all this."

Brilliant blue light suddenly filled the ice, and then a soft crackling sound disturbed the air. A crewman standing at the railing looked over the side of the ship, and then his mouth opened slightly before his eyes went wide. He spun around and ran across the deck to the opposite railing, and in numbed fascination, watched as the water turned to ice, with the far edge of it racing away from the ship.

Everyone ran to the opposite side and stared at the ice sheet as it disappeared over the horizon, then Captain Hess heard a cracking sound and turned to look at the ice wall. Thin fracture lines began forming on the surface, racing toward the top, then the ship shook so hard it tossed him off his feet and he crashed onto the deck, his head slamming against the steel. He rolled onto his hands and knees and stared at the wall as massive slabs of transparent ice crashed onto the ship.

The shaking continued as he crawled across to the railing, while watching his men jumping from the ship onto the ice sheet, hoping they could get far enough away. He was just about to jump over the side when he noticed something odd. His men suddenly stopped running and stared down at their shoes.

They all started screaming, and he watched one man grab his leg with both hands, but when he pulled, his foot broke away at the ankle and he toppled over onto the ice. When he tried to get up, his hand stuck to the surface and his arm suddenly turned frosty white. When he pulled, it shattered into a thousand colored pieces that bounced off the surface, like chunks of pink metal.

Hess noticed frost climbing up onto another man's legs, and when it reached his chest, he started gasping for air. In an instant, his mouth became frozen into a permanent scream of agony. He couldn't keep watching and turned away from the grisly scene as massive slabs of ice continued battering his ship. Half of the bridge suddenly crumpled, and when he looked up, the slab rising out of his ship looked like a clear obelisk.

His entire ship felt like it was rising into the air, and then abruptly stopped. The sound of crashing ice slowly subsided, and the air grew deathly quiet. He grabbed the railing and slowly pulled himself up off the deck, then stood to look around. His ship was now a crumpled pile of twisted steel and massive blocks of ice.

He slowly turned back to the railing, dreading what he would see. When he saw the frozen red shards of his men scattered across the ice sheet, he felt nauseated and spun away from the rail, retching violently onto the deck. He stayed bent over, spitting out remnants of the foul bile and catching his breath, and could not get the image out of his mind. He leaned back against the railing, and then slowly slid down onto the deck as tears rolled down his cheeks.

Chapter 26

MOUNT BAKER:

Wesley stopped his Hummer in the parking lot of the Ranger Station, shut off the engine, and then climbed out and walked around his trailer with the yellow snow cat. He heard the door of the station close and turned around while a smiling young woman strolled over to him.

Jamie stared up at the machine. "Is this yours?"

"That's right."

"I saw it through the window. Why did you bring it up here?"

"I'm going up to inspect the glaciers. I just stopped to let you folks know where I'm going. If I'm not back in four hours, send someone to look for me."

"I've never been in a snow cat. Can I go with you?"

"You're in uniform, so you must be working right now." He could see the disappointment in her eyes. "I'll take you for a ride when we get some snow."

Jamie grabbed his arm, pulling him toward the station. "You need a permit, right?"

"No, I don't."

"I know they always let you slide because this is your mountain, but there *are* rules."

"Why are you calling it *my* mountain?"

"On my first day, Larry told me I needed to learn how this park operated. He thinks since I'm only thirty-four, I don't know what I'm doing, so he gave me a list to memorize. Fourth item on the list of do's and don'ts? This mountain belongs to Wesley Patterson, so leave him alone."

Wesley didn't know what to say until she smiled. "I get it. You're pulling my leg, right?"

"We need to talk to Larry."

He followed her into the building and past the front wooden counter, then through the open doorway into the office of his friend, Larry Cobb, the park supervisor. "How you doing, Larry?"

"I'm fine, but Jamie showed me the hot spring at the campground. What's going on?"

Wesley explained what he knew. "I'm on my way up to check the damage to the glaciers, and this ranger lady says I need a permit."

Larry looked at Jamie. "Rule four, remember?"

"I know, but I thought if he doesn't have a permit, I have to go with him as a representative for the park."

Larry stared at her. "Say what?"

"Come on, Larry. I really want to go with Wesley. This way, I'm still doing my job."

Larry shrugged his shoulders and looked at Wesley. "Are you sure you want to take her with you?"

Wesley hesitated. "I didn't invite her in the first place." He watched her mouth open slightly as she stared at him. "Get your hiking gear, Miss park representative."

Jamie smiled. "I'll be right back."

Wesley turned to his friend. "You should start moving people out of the park."

"Is it that bad?"

"It's not an emergency yet, but if the melting continues, they need to go home before the streams rise and the roads wash out. I'll have a better timeframe once I see how bad the glaciers are melting."

Jamie stepped into the office, wearing jeans and her ranger shirt, and carrying a light blue backpack. "I'm all set. Let's go."

When she spun around and rushed out of the office, Wesley looked through the window and saw her climbing onto the trailer and snow cat, then turned to Larry. "I'll bring her back and let you know what we find."

***

When Jamie saw Wesley stroll out from the station, she opened the side door on the snow cat, tossed her backpack inside, then jumped down onto the asphalt and smiled at him. "Ready when you are."

"Jump in and I'll show you my mountain."

Once they were in the Hummer, he drove out of the parking lot and headed around the building to a back road used only by park personnel, and pulled the trailer along the old logging roads for nearly two hours before he was forced to stop. A swollen stream had washed out the road across the bottom of a canyon, and there was no other road up to the glaciers.

Jamie stared through the front window at the river. "Can you turn around?"

"I'm afraid not. Let's find out how deep it is."

Jamie climbed out of the Hummer and walked to the edge of the rushing water, then looked up at Wesley standing beside her. "Is this because of the melting glaciers?"

"That's right."

"How much farther until we reach them?"

"An hour's drive, if we had a road. Maybe forty-five minutes if we follow this stream up the mountain."

"All right. Let me get my backpack."

"I saw you put it in the snow cat."

"I know."

"Help me with the ramps so I can back it off the trailer."

"Ah, you're kidding, right? You're going to cross the stream in the snow cat?"

"No, we're going to drive it up the stream."

"I can see why they call this your mountain, Wesley. I never realized you could travel in a snow cat without snow. By the way, I really want to thank you for bringing me along. I've seen some beautiful areas that no tourist will see."

"My pleasure. There's more to come, so let's get started."

Fifteen minutes later, Jamie's hands tightened on the padded armrests as the front of the snow cat dipped into the water, looking as though it would rush in through the front window. When the cat leveled out and began crawling upstream, she grinned at Wesley. "That was the most exciting thing I've ever done."

"That was the easy part."

For the next forty minutes, Jamie thought it was like being on a weird rollercoaster while continuing to hold tight to the armrests. The rubber seals around the doors stopped the water from flooding into the cab, but she thought they might start leaking at any moment.

While climbing up over a small waterfall, the front of the snow cat became nearly vertical. Wesley thought her fingers might leave permanent indentations in the armrests, but she had not stopped grinning since they had left the Hummer.

The front of the cat flopped down over the top and crawled across a wide-open expanse of smooth, round stones brought down by the glacier.

Jamie pointed through the window at the wide vertical face of light blue ice one mile away. "There it is. It's beautiful."

A knot formed in Wesley's stomach when he saw how far the glacier had receded since his last visit. "Let's go take a closer look."

Wesley continued driving up the wide, shallow stream, and then stopped twenty feet from the face of the glacier. "Oh, crap."

Jamie looked over and saw his worried expression. "What's wrong?"

"Let's get out and I'll show you."

They climbed down from the cat, finding the air outside pleasantly warm, as they walked along the wide stream of water flowing from beneath the ice. They stopped in front of the opening into a massive ice cave, while Wesley made a quick assessment of the twelve foot tall, by thirty foot wide entrance.

"This is worse than I thought, Jamie. The glacier has been melted by heat radiating from the ground. Let's see how far back this goes."

"Do you think it's safe?"

"I believe so. It's melted, not fractured. Come on."

She pointed up at the translucent blue ice inside the cave. "It's raining in there and you've got a hat. I don't."

"Stay out from the center and you'll be fine."

"I'm not buying it."

"You can stay here, if you like."

"Are you kidding? Where you go, I go. You first."

Wesley admired her fearless attitude as he entered the ice cave. Jamie strolled beside him and he felt the drops of water hit his hat. When he looked down at Jamie, the drops were hitting her head, but she was still grinning.

Chapter 27

MYSTIC:

While Mike and Dieter remained on the bridge to determine a new course through the islands, everyone else gathered in the lounge, waiting for answers. Alex indicated for Okawna to follow him away from the group and stepped out onto the walkway, then stopped and stared back into the lounge to make sure no one else joined them. "Do you know where everybody was when the engines died?"

"Yeah, I was already up and getting ready to go on watch when the turbines stopped. I saw you go up to the bridge, so figured I'd wait until you found out what happened. No one came up until you talked on the intercom, and then Mike came from his quarters. Everyone else was below, so I can't be sure. I know Bartram didn't show up until just before all of you came down from the bridge."

"We need to know who did this. Let's use Mike's Office and start with Bartram."

They turned and walked back to the group, where Alex looked at Joshua, Lisa, and Rita standing together and stared at Bartram sitting on the edge of the table. "I need to find out what's going on, so I'll start with you."

Bartram stood. "Who made you chief prosecutor? You're just a visitor on the ship, and it's up to Captain Dieter to decide what to do."

Alex leaned forward and down, his face only inches from Bartram's, as he looked him in the eyes. "I don't know what your problem is, but you don't want a problem with me."

Bartram felt a knot in his throat just before he looked away to the others for sympathy, but no one backed him up. "Sure. Let's go talk."

Alex led Bartram out to the walkway toward the bow, then through the doorway into Mike's office and living quarters. He continued around the desk and sat in the comfortable tan leather chair, while Bartram sat in a chair across from him. When the *Mystic* gained speed, he noticed Bartram glancing around the interior to avoid making eye contact. "What did you do before you came on board?"

"I mostly worked on tramp ships. You know, just sailed from here to there."

"I understand you came aboard with Dieter. Where did you meet him?"

Bartram crossed his arms over his chest as he stared across the desk into his opponent's eyes. "I met him at a bar in North Dakota."

Alex realized this would not work without evidence. "Mind if Okawna searches your cabin?"

The corner of Bartram's mouth curled up in a wry smile. "Go right ahead. You've got nothing on me, Professor Cave."

Alex stared back and Bartram's attitude told him he was the saboteur, but without evidence, there was nothing more he could do. He stood, leaned across the desk, and stared into Bartram's eyes. "You can go now, Lee-Roy."

Bartram tried to maintain a casual demeanor, but the look in the man's eyes gave him a chill. Cave did not act like a teacher, but like someone who knew how to kill in cold blood. He slowly stood and stepped back from the desk, then turned and hurried out of the office.

Alex got up and followed Bartram back along the walkway until he went down the stairs to the cabins. He saw Rita and Okana playing table shuffleboard, and was about to join them when he was stopped near the bottom of the stairs up to the bridge by Bett and Joshua.

The couple pulled Alex around the corner to the doors out onto the stern. Joshua was a few inches taller than Alex, so leaned over to whisper. "We've got your back, Alex."

Alex looked down at little Bett, then up at Joshua. "I know. Thanks"

When they walked away, Alex saw Lisa standing near the door to her lab, with a pleading expression in her eyes, so he went over to her. "What can I do for you?"

"When we stopped, I peeked out from my cabin and saw Bartram coming out of the engine room."

"Did he have anything with him? Wire, tools, anything like that?"

"Not that I noticed. He went straight to his cabin."

"All right. Thanks."

When he turned to leave, Lisa grabbed his arm. "Aren't you going to arrest him or something?"

"I'm just a geology instructor, not the sheriff. No offense, but all I have is your word, and we need evidence."

When Lisa let go of his arm, Alex walked out onto the stern and stared out across the water. He knew Dieter would talk his way out of any wrongdoing, so it was a waste of time to try. Harrison had been with him on the bridge when it happened, and even though he was certain Bartram was the saboteur, there was no proof.

***

When Mike looked out the rear window of the bridge, he saw Alex standing alone on the stern deck. He opened the side door and went outside, then down the stairs and across to join him. "Hey, Alex. What are you thinking?"

Alex looked around, and they were alone. "I can't prove anything right now. Tell me about Dieter."

"I found him on the internet. His credentials checked out, so I arranged a meeting with him and we got along fine. He's never acted suspiciously, so why do you ask?"

Alex told him what Okawna had discovered. "He's not who he claims, and I'm waiting for a background check. A real one."

Mike felt grateful Alex was with them. "So, what do we do?"

"Nothing until we can recover that device. No one's been injured yet, so let's keep it that way."

"That works for me."

"Do you have a lock we can put on the engine room door?"

"I'll ask Rita. Those pirates can't catch us, so we shouldn't have any more problems until we try to locate the device."

They felt the *Mystic* suddenly slow down and then heard Dieter holler their names. They turned to look up behind the bridge and saw him standing at the railing.

"Mike? Professor? You should come up here. We have just received a call from the U.S. Coast Guard, and they have discovered unusual ice floes in the Bering Sea."

Mike looked at Alex. "I guess I jinxed us."

"You're the second person to tell me that. Let's find out what's going on."

Alex followed Mike across the deck and up the outside stairs onto the bridge. Dieter waved them over to a computer monitor, and they crowded around the screen, waiting for the *Mystic's* logo to change.

Dieter started the recording. "They transmitted this digital video recording of the ice flows."

The view was from a helicopter as it approached assorted sized slabs of clear ice scattered across the ocean; some at least twenty feet square.

They were not high above the water, like a white iceberg, just large flat slabs of transparent ice bobbing on the surface. They would be impossible for a ship's crew to see until it was too late to avoid a collision.

Alex looked over at Dieter. "How long until we arrive in that area?"

"I checked the charts, and we will encounter the ice in another hour."

"All right. When we get close, we should have Bett guide us through from the helicopter."

Mike was silent for a moment, thinking. "We still don't know where that device might be located, Alex. I think we should avoid those ice floes until we have a definite location to start our search."

Alex knew he was correct. "Okay. I'd better make some phone calls."

Alex walked out from the bridge and stood at the railing, and even at the slower speed, the breeze gave him a chill as he unzipped his thin jacket to retrieve the sat phone. When he entered his code for his voice mail, a message from Sonja stated it was urgent he call her back. He touched the number, and she answered on the second ring.

"I am so glad you called Alex. Our computer model is predicting that within twenty-four hours, the water will freeze all the way down into the Aleutian Islands."

"Have you found a location to start my search?"

"Yes. After the last expansion, we have narrowed the location to a sixty-mile area of the ice, one hundred miles north of the southern end, but we cannot narrow it down to a smaller area. I am sorry, Alex, but that is the best I can do for you. Here are the GPS coordinates."

"All right. I appreciate your help with this. We've been informed large pieces of transparent ice will make our trip very hazardous, so it may take us a while to get there."

"I know. We discovered the ice blocks in the ocean are breaking off from the ice sheet as it rises out of the water. I collected a sample of the ice, and it did not contain a single trace of minerals. It is pure H20."

"Okay, thanks for getting me close. I'll call when I find the device."

He shoved the phone into his coat pocket and zipped the front closed, and knew it was time to put on his new white coat. He turned and walked back into the ship to tell the others what he had learned about the ice cap, then headed down the inside stairs.

When Alex entered the lounge, everyone but Joshua was sitting at the table, so he continued over and stood at the end. "There are some interesting events happening because of these devices." He told them what he had learned from Sonja. "I have GPS location to start the search, but it could be within a sixty-mile radius."

"My baby can do that." Bett informed him.

"I'm sure it could, but the GPS location might already be more than a hundred miles from the edge by now. We can't risk hitting one of those big slabs of ice, so it's going to take some time to reach the southern end of the ice pyramid, as they are calling it."

He looked at every face around the table, and then stopped when his eyes settled on Bartram. "With the number of guns on board this ship, only a fool would try to sabotage the mission again." He looked around the table again. "That's all I have for now."

Bett slid her chair from the table and stood. "I could use something to eat."

Okawna remained sitting at the table while everyone stood and went to the kitchen. He stared at Dieter, who had separated from the group and was walking down the stairs to the cabins. He waited until Alex sat down, then leaned close to him. "While everyone is still up here, I'll try to find that CD case. I overheard Dieter mention needing a shower."

Okawna slid his chair away from the table and gave Alex a mischievous grin as he stood. "Hell of a thing, not having any locks on the doors."

Okawna continued across the room to look down the stairs and heard water running in one of the showers. He slowly walked down to the bottom and noticed Dieter had left his cabin door open, so he tiptoed past the shower, down the hallway to Dieter's cabin, and slowly peered around the corner of the doorway. He glanced down the hall toward the running water and then stepped into the room.

He quickly glanced around the interior, but did not see the plastic case. He looked through the doorway and could still hear the running water, so he opened the top dresser drawer and slid his fingers under the flat rows of blue socks, but it was not there. He quickly did the same with the remaining three drawers, with no luck. He raised the side of the mattress just enough to look underneath, but the plastic case wasn't there, so he turned around and opened the double doors on the closet.

The disk was not on the top shelf, so he moved the clothes out of the way to look at the floor and saw the edge of a portable DVD player protruding from beneath a pile of dirty clothes. "Got it." He reached down for the player to check inside for the disk and then saw movement in his peripheral vision.

Dieter stopped in the doorway of his cabin. "What do you think you are doing, Okawna?"

Okawna slowly stood and turned to face Dieter. It was only then he noticed the corner of the plastic case protruding from his folded towel, so he crossed his arms and leaned against the side of the cabinet. "Why don't you tell me what's on that disk?"

Dieter wondered how he knew about it and stepped back into the hallway. "Get out."

Okawna uncrossed his arms, casually strolled out of the room, and once in the hallway, turned and glared at Dieter. "This is a small ship, Captain. It's hard to keep things hidden."

"It is password protected, so you need not bother, Okawna."

Okawna searched Dieter's eyes for a hint he was lying, but they remained impassive, so he turned and headed down the hallway, then up the stairs. Dieter waited until Okawna was out of sight and released the breath he had been holding, and then his lips formed into a sly grin.

Chapter 28

MOUNT BAKER:

Jamie grabbed a lock of wet hair dangling across her face and shoved it out of the way. "Stay out from the center, Wesley? This whole place is the center, and it's raining on me no matter where I walk."

"Do you want to go back?"

"No. I'm already drenched, so what's the point? It's amazing walking under a glacier. I would never have known about this place if you hadn't brought me along."

The ground suddenly moved up for a fraction of a second. When he heard a loud crack, he spun her around toward the entrance! "Run!"

The left side of the ceiling crashed to the ground, but when Jamie tried to move out of the way, the wet gravel shifted under her feet and she fell. Wesley grabbed the back of her coat as she toppled over, hauling her onto her feet as they ran for the entrance.

He heard the rumble of massive chunks of ice smashing onto the rocks, and when he looked back over his shoulder, the cave was collapsing behind him. "*Faster!*" he hollered as he pushed her across the gravel toward the shrinking exit.

The crashing sound was right behind him, so he shoved her through the narrow opening. Chunks of ice smashed onto his head and shoulders, but he saw her clear the entrance just as a massive block of ice drove him to the ground.

***

Jamie staggered to a stop outside the cave and then dropped onto her hands and knees while taking deep breaths. "That was close."

She rolled over and sat on the gravel to look around, then realized he wasn't there. She scrambled to her feet and ran back to a crack in the collapsed entrance, staring through the narrow opening, but didn't see him. "Wesley!"

She clawed at the blocks of ice, desperately trying to get back inside, then one large chunk fell onto the ground and she stared through the opening. Wesley's arm protruded from a pile of shattered ice, but it appeared the collapse was over. She grabbed another block and pulled, but it wouldn't budge, so she placed one foot against another block, clenching her teeth as she pulled with all her strength.

The block broke loose, and she crashed back onto the gravel. She looked at the narrow opening and scrambled back onto her feet, then ran into the cave. He wasn't moving, so she knelt down to shove a large block off his back, then the smaller pieces off of his head and shoulders. She tried to feel for a pulse, but only heard her own racing heartbeats, so stopped. "Wesley!" She screamed near his ear.

Wesley groaned and slowly rolled onto his back, then saw the relief etched in Jamie's face. "I thought I threw you out of here."

"You did. Can you get up?"

"Hell, yeah!"

Wesley grunted against the pain in his ribs as he pushed himself up from the gravel. Jamie helped him climb over shattered blocks of ice and out through the opening, and then he bent over, clutching his right ribs while taking shallow breaths.

Jamie noticed the bloody water dribbling down the side of Wesley's face, then parted his blood-soaked hair above his ear. "You have a nasty cut, and you're going to need stitches."

"I lost my hat."

"What?" Jamie thought she heard wrong and stepped back. "We were almost killed, there's a possibility you've got broken ribs, and you're worried about your hat? Really, Wesley?"

"I'll be fine once we get down the mountain."

She saw the pain in his eyes. "Can you tell if any are broken?"

"I think one might be bruised, but I'm okay."

"Listen, Wesley. That was a rough ride getting up here in the snow cat, and I don't think you can take that kind of punishment in your condition. Not without aggravating your injuries."

"I'm not staying here." He slowly stood up straight. "I'll be all right. I just need to wrap my ribs before we get into the cat. Let's go."

"I've got a radio in my backpack. Let me call for a helicopter."

"I'll be fine, Jamie."

She crossed her arms and stared at him. "Raise your hands above your head."

"What?"

"If you can raise your hands above your head, we'll take the cat. If not, I call the helicopter."

"Fine."

Wesley brought his left arm up, but when he tried to raise his right arm, a searing pain in his ribs caused him to wince, so he brought them down. "Okay, no snow cat, but let's not wait for a helicopter. They might have a real emergency, and it would be a waste of time for them to come all the way up here. We can hike down to my truck a lot faster."

Jamie didn't care for the idea, but knew Wesley was determined to leave. She ran to the cat and climbed into the cab, then tossed both backpacks out the door and climbed down. When he grabbed his pack with his left arm and slung it over the same shoulder, she noticed him trying to hide his discomfort, but decided to not say anything to him unless it got worse.

Wesley looked around to get his bearings and then began walking across the loose gravel down to the tree line. "That game trail is headed in the right direction."

Jamie slung her backpack over her shoulders and then followed him toward the thin forest. "What do you think caused it to collapse?"

Wesley did not think someone would be stupid enough to activate that device again, but Alex was not around to stop them. "I'll find out when I get to my truck."

"I guess you won't have your snow cat for a while."

"Just give me a couple of days to recuperate, and I'll come back and get it."

Chapter 29

MYSTIC:

Alex heard his satellite phone beeping and pulled it from his coat pocket. He recognized the ID and looked at Okana. "It's my friend, David Conway, from the College."

He and Okana were the only ones left in the lounge, so he pressed the green button to answer. "Hi, David."

Alex listened to David explain what he had discovered about the black material. "That's great, David. Hang on a second." He looked down at Okana. "What's the fax number here on the ship?"

Okana told him the number for Lisa's lab, and Alex read the numbers to David. "Thanks for the help. I know it's getting colder, and I'm doing my best to stop. Okay."

Alex turned off the phone and slipped it into his pocket. "It's about that black material we found in the methane. I'm going to Lisa's lab and fax a copy to the *Discovery*. It should help with the retrieval of the device."

***

DISCOVERY:

Henry set his cup of coffee on the table in the dining room and leaned back in his chair, then crossed his arms and stared out the window at nothing in particular. Retrieving the device was his responsibility, and so far, none of their ideas would work without releasing the methane into the atmosphere.

"Doctor Heinz, you have a call from Alex Cave."

The announcement did not come from the intercom, and Henry recognized Janice's voice from the doorway behind him. He stood and turned around to greet her. "Good news, I hope."

"I don't know yet. The call has been routed to the conference room. The Captain and Victor are waiting for us."

Janice took his arm, and they strolled down the hall and into the room, and Captain Jordan and Victor were sitting near the end of the table, near the phone. Henry sat down and pushed the button for the speaker. "Hello, Alex. I am sorry, but it appears there is no way to retrieve the device without releasing the methane."

"This will help. Remember David Conway?"

"Yes, a brilliant young man."

"He analyzed that dark material for me, and it's a unique formation of hydrocarbon molecules. It reacts to a specific frequency in the microwave range and becomes gelatinous until the frequency changes."

"Will the water temperature affect the gelatinous state?"

"He couldn't tell from the sample he had to work with. He did say it's a onetime attempt. If it becomes solid again, it will remain that way forever."

"What is the specific frequency?"

"Give me a fax number and I'll send you his report."

"In a moment. I do not know the number. How are things up north?"

"I had a few bumps along the way, but nothing you need to worry about. I hope this information helps."

"Thank you, my friend. We will do what we can. Here is the number."

"You should receive it in a moment. Call if you need anything."

Chapter 30

***MYSTIC*. THE BERING SEA:**

Alex hurried up the outside stairs to the bridge, grateful Mike had bought him the thick, white winter coat he was now wearing. The new ice sheet was already affecting the weather in the northern latitudes, and the thin jacket he had brought was useless against the frigid temperatures they were now encountering.

He walked onto the bridge and found Okawna alone, guiding the *Mystic* slowly through the scattered ice flows, and for the moment, it was easy. "What a cushy job you have."

Okawna grinned up at Alex. "It has its moments. You look like a man with a question."

"Which side do you think Harrison is on? Bett told me he joined the crew after Dieter and Bartram."

"Hard to say. I think he's just a sailor working for whoever pays him."

Joshua suddenly came up the stairs, wearing a thick, black winter coat. He was carrying a red plastic toolbox and a square fiberglass object. "Your friend David is a genius, Alex. Lisa read his report, and discovered he's isolated a particular type of radiation emanating from the black hydrocarbons."

Joshua held up the fiberglass object attached to a square base with clamps on the bottom. "I modified this radar unit to detect that particular type of radiation, and I'm going to mount it above us to see how it works. I could use your help, Alex."

When Alex indicated he agreed, Joshua stepped out of the bridge onto the lookout station and set the equipment down. He climbed up a narrow stainless steel ladder bolted to the back corner of the bridge, then looked down while he waited for Alex to come out of the bridge.

Alex went outside and looked over the railing at the twenty-foot slab of clear ice gently sliding past the side of the ship. It was the fifth one in the past two hours, even though they had not reached the end of the ice pyramid. At this slow speed, they could see the ice with plenty of time to move out of the way, and once Joshua was down from the roof of the bridge, they could increase the *Mystic*'s speed a little more.

"Hey, Alex? I'm ready for your help up here."

Alex turned and looked up at Joshua squatting on the roof. "Be right up."

"Hand up my toolbox and the radar first."

Alex did as asked, then climbed onto the roof and knelt beside Joshua as he bolted the radar unit to the railing around the roof. "What can I do?"

Joshua reached into his coat pocket and held out a small plastic tube filled with black hydrocarbons. "Hold this sample I got from Lisa and walk to both sides of the roof when I say. I'm going down inside to make sure that black material shows up on the radar scope."

"All right. Tell me when to walk."

Joshua climbed down the ladder onto the deck, then went around to the left side door of the bridge and latched it open. When he went inside and turned on the radar unit, the LCD screen had located the radiation emitted by the sample in Alex's hand, so he leaned out through the doorway. "Walk over to the starboard side, Alex."

Joshua went back inside and watched the flashing red dot move to the right, then stuck his head out through the doorway again. "Now move to the port side."

Joshua ducked back into the bridge, watched the red dot move to the other side of the screen, then smiled as he walked back through the doorway out onto the deck and looked up at Alex. "You can come down now."

When Alex moved to the top of the ladder, Joshua was reaching out to the edge of the roof.

"Hand me my tool box, would you, Alex?"

"Sure."

Alex slipped the plastic tube into the chest pocket of his coat, then grabbed the red plastic tool box and set it close to the edge, near the big man's hand. When Joshua stepped away, he climbed down and followed him back onto the bridge.

Joshua pointed at the red dot on the screen and then smiled at Alex and Okawna. "I just converted a radar unit into a radiation sensor capable of detecting the source from miles away."

"Are we ready to go, Josh?" Okawna asked.

"All set."

Okawna eased the throttle forward, and the *Mystic* slowly sped up while they all kept watch for the floating ice. The fronts of the pontoons were strong enough to move them out of the way at slow speeds, but if the Mystic went too fast, they could be damaged and lose their effectiveness at high speed.

***

Three hours later, the entire crew was dressed in their heavy winter coats outside the bridge, while staring at the one-hundred-foot high wall of transparent ice, two hundred yards in front of the *Mystic*. When Lisa saw dozens of gray seals frozen in the wall of ice, she turned away and buried her head against Mike's chest.

They had received a satellite image from NASA showing the extent of the expanding ice sheet, and compared it to a previous photo showing the normal size of the ice in summer. The new ice cap was shaped like a gigantic egg, with the large round end reaching deep down into the Bering Sea. One hundred miles inland from their location, the picture showed concentrically smaller circles of the pyramid, forming a target on the vast expanse of the ice sheet.

According to Joshua's radiation detector, the device should be at the center of the target north of their current position, which was close to the GPS coordinates Sonja had given Alex. Joshua stipulated it was only an estimate because of a strange anomaly appearing on the radar screen, which he thought might be caused by a much larger deposit of the hydrocarbons.

Alex heard his satellite phone ring, slipped it out of his coat pocket, and recognized the ID. "Hey, Sonja."

"Alex, we have a major problem in the Atlantic Ocean. The salinity of the water flowing down from the north has increased significantly. The water is so laden with salt it is rapidly sinking and flowing south into the Atlantic Ocean much faster than normal, which is affecting the ocean currents. It is driving warm water from the Gulf into the northern Atlantic at a much faster rate, and the atmospheric conditions over northern Europe are changing. This is a very dangerous condition, Alex. It will affect the weather patterns in the northern hemisphere and the storms will be massive."

"We have located the device near the southern end of the ice cap, and I'm about to leave to discover what I'm up against. I'll call you when I know something."

"I know you are doing your best. Call me with good news. Bye, love."

Okawna noticed Alex's grim expression. "Not good?"

Alex explained the call. "With a little luck, we'll find the device."

"I'll make sure the ship is still here when you return."

When they heard the jet engine from the helicopter rising in pitch, everyone turned around and looked down at Harrison and Bartram moving out of the way on the stern. Alex, Mike, and Lisa walked down the steps to the helicopter, and then Mike and Lisa climbed into the back seat, with Alex in front with Bett, leaving Okawna, Rita, and Joshua behind to guard the *Mystic*, in case Dieter and his friends tried to steal it.

When the blades rotated, the others moved onto the bridge to avoid the downwash when the helicopter took off. A moment later, Bett's baby leapt into the air.

***

As the helicopter gained altitude up over the wall of clear ice, everyone stared in rapt fascination at the scene, which was something they could never have imagined. Fifty miles ahead, another wall of ice stood above the vast expanse of ice. Two hundred miles farther inland was another transparent wall, and another beyond that one, creating an oblong pyramid of transparent ice.

Bett kept increasing their elevation as the ice raced past beneath them, and then the top of the pyramid appeared. Alex doubted the device would be above the water level, but did not voice his opinion. The pyramid was a spectacular sight, and he wanted a closer look.

When they were within five-hundred-feet from the top, the angle of the sun was such that the ice acted like a prism, sending small beams of rainbow-colored lights bouncing around the inside the top layer of the pyramid.

Lisa moved forward for a better view and held her phone out at arm's length, then began recording. "Oh my, that is fantastic. Everyone's going to want to see this when we get back."

No one spoke as they admired the light show, then Bett dropped the helicopter down on the flat surface and set the engine speed to idle. Lisa opened the side door and leapt out onto the ice, but her feet slid out from beneath her and she plopped onto her butt.

Lisa put her hands on the ice to push up, but abruptly stopped when she looked down. "I see it!"

The others carefully climbed down from the helicopter and knelt beside her. Deep beneath the surface, the device was visible, looking small and innocent in the fantastically clear ice.

Alex lowered his head in frustration and then looked at the others. "We won't be able to retrieve it from up here, but now that we know its exact location, we might be able to remove it from below with the submarine."

When Alex stood and reached down to help her stand up, Lisa took his hand and got off the ice. "Just imagine what this recording will be like on the cover of National Geographic Magazine." She began recording as she turned in a circle.

Once Mike and Bett were standing, everyone climbed back into the helicopter for the return trip, and then Bett touched the button on her headset. "Mystic, this is Bett." No one answered, so she tried again with no response. She noticed Alex listening. "It must be because of the interference Josh mentioned. I'll try again when we get closer to the Mystic."

***

Okawna was sitting in a bridge chair, with only the radio for company. He had volunteered to stand watch over the thrusters to occupy his time, but the computer was keeping the *Mystic* stationary in the field of ice slabs, so he had nothing to do but think. Dieter informed him the disk would stay in his pocket for the duration of the trip, but now his curiosity was driving him crazy over what could be so important. Trying to take over the *Mystic* was a stupid idea, so why was he still being so secretive about it?

"Mystic, this is Bett."

Okawna grabbed the microphone from its overhead bracket. "Hey, Bett. Okawna, here. Any luck?"

"In a matter of speaking, I suppose. We're going to need the sub ready when we get back."

"How long do I have?"

"We'll be there in fifteen minutes. I would have given you more warning, but the radio didn't work until now."

"I'll be ready."

Okawna snapped the radio microphone back into its bracket, then grabbed the microphone for the intercom system. "I just got a call from the helicopter, and we need to prep the sub and have it ready to go in fifteen minutes."

***

Dieter looked around for bystanders as he walked out onto the stern with Harrison and Bartram. "Okawna will not trust you, so do it quickly, before he comes down."

***

Rita went up the inside stairs onto the bridge, then leaned against the control console to face Okawna. "Did they tell you what they discovered?"

"Not exactly, but I'm guessing they think it's underneath the ice."

"One of these days, you'll have to take me down with you in the Wizard."

"It's a different world down there. According to the sonar, the ice is only six-hundred feet beneath the surface, and vertical like that wall in front of us. That should make for an easy dive. Could you take over for me up here? I don't trust Bartram or Harrison to prep the sub, and I would hate to get under the ice and have something go wrong."

"I don't think you have to worry about Harrison. He was on the bridge when the engines stopped. My money is on Bartram."

"Maybe." He stood from the chair. "I'll see you on deck later." He didn't tell her the only person he trusted right now was Alex.

Okawna stepped out through the starboard door, but as he approached the stairs, saw Dieter glance up at him. He continued down to the bottom and over to face the captain. "Last-minute instructions?"

Dieter looked over at Harrison releasing the tie down straps on the sub. "Do not worry, Okawna. No one will sabotage your precious submarine."

When Dieter hurried into the ship, Okawna continued across to the sub, wondering why the captain would refer to it as precious. He was about to climb the ladder to go down inside, when Bartram suddenly came out of the top hatch. He studied Leroy's expression for a hint that he did something to the Wizard, but it remained impassive as he stepped off the ladder to face him.

"The batteries are fully charged, Okawna."

Okawna hesitated to climb up, until Bartram had joined Harrison, who was getting the hoist ready to move the sub, and neither looked his way. A knot formed in his stomach as he climbed the ladder and dropped into the sub to do his pre-launch inspection.

***

Alex stared through the window as Bett brought the helicopter over the stern and saw Okawna, Rita, Joshua, and Dieter waiting up in the bridge. The helicopter set down, and then everyone climbed out while Harrison and Bartram walked over to secure it to the deck.

Lisa hurried up the stairs to the bridge. "You have to see this."

She held her phone out facing everyone, so they could watch her recording. When they were crowded together in front of the small screen, she pressed play. Okawna was the closest, and a few moments later, he looked at Lisa. "You recorded snow?"

Lisa stopped smiling as she brought the phone back and stared at the screen. "That's not right. Let me rewind it."

Joshua could see her frustration. "It might be because of that anomalous reading on my radiation sensor. I still don't know what's causing it."

Lisa's shoulders sagged as she slipped the phone into her coat pocket. "It was this beautiful glass pyramid. When we were close to the top, the light was shining into the ice, creating this beautiful rainbow inside." She turned when Alex stepped up beside her. "It's all gone, Alex. The recording is just snow."

"At least you have the memory." He looked over at Okawna. "Are we ready to go?"

"I'm all set. We can be in the water in less than five minutes."

Lisa reached into her coat pocket and held out a folded piece of paper to Okawna. "You're going to need this. It's the direction and approximate distance to the device. I figured it out on the way back."

Okawna took the paper, then turned and went with Alex down the stairs to the sub. "Could you tell how deep the device is?"

"We could barely see it down through the ice, but it's definitely at the bottom."

"I wish Lisa's recording would have survived. It sounds interesting."

Alex followed Okawna up the ladder and down into the sub, then secured the hatch while Okawna slid into the front seat and informed Harrison they were ready. When the sub was lifted off the support bracket, Alex looked over Okawna's shoulder through the front window. As it slowly spun around, he saw the rest of the crew standing behind the bridge, watching the launch. "I forgot to ask how deep we're going."

"Six-hundred-feet to the bottom edge of the ice, so add another ten for good measure."

"That shouldn't be too hard. What attachment did you bring?"

"One circular saw and a pincher-spreader combination tool. It shouldn't take too long."

The sub continued to swing around until they were facing the sea, then slowly dropped into the water. The ice was acting like a prism, transferring the light from the surface to illuminate the massive block as they slowly descended along the strange-looking wall.

Chapter 31

DISCOVERY:

Henry pressed the end button on the telephone keypad and looked around the table. "Yesterday, Alex mentioned that the *Mystic* used an ultrasound frequency to locate the methane. Do you have such a device on this ship, Captain?"

"We have one of the prototypes on a rover."

Janice shook her head no. "you cannot use that again. That's what activated the device in the first place."

The fax machine beeped, and Jordon stood and walked over to get the report. He looked at the rows of numbers and gave it to Janice. "It's Greek to me."

Janice quickly read the report and then looked up at Jordon. "Do you have a specialist for the rover on the ship?"

"We have a couple of people that can operate it."

"No, I mean an electronic engineer."

Jordon shook his head no. "Not specifically for that transmitter. He takes care of the ship's systems. What's on your mind?"

"It's a good thing I'm here. If I can recalibrate the transmitter to send only *this* frequency, we may be able to separate the methane from the clear ice."

"You know how to do that?"

"It's a hobby of mine. I'll need all the engineering specifications and drawings, and a place to open the rover and make the changes."

Jordon sat down and slid the phone closer so he could enter a number. "I'll have everything you need faxed from the main office in Seattle."

Henry gently put his hand on Janice's forearm. "Both your skills *are* needed. How do you know when the device activates?"

Janice could see the concern in his eyes. "They had a submarine near the methane two of the times. Why?"

"It should have activated again. Do you have a submarine down there all the time?"

"No, *Celeas* stays on board unless we need her to do something."

"So we do not know if it actually activated when we assumed it would."

"You're right."

"Alex was working with someone on the mainland who recorded the effect. I should try to contact him right away and find out if he noticed any new seismic activity." He reached into his shirt pocket and brought out a notebook. "Alex gave me his number when he came to see me in Nevada."

"A notebook, Henry? Don't you have a smart phone with the numbers?"

He lightly shook his head. "I do not make many personal calls, so I did not see the need to have one."

Jordon hung up the phone and stood. "The information is on its way, so let's get you set up in the electronics laboratory, Janice. My crew is getting one of the rovers down from the storage rack as we speak."

Henry remained seated when the others stood and left the conference room. He entered Wesley's number and waited for the connection.

"Hello."

"Mister Patterson, I am a friend of Alex Cave. My name is Henry Heinz."

"I remember hearing your name. What can I do for you?"

"I was wondering if you had detected another event in the past twenty-four hours."

"Nothing that affected me. Why?"

"I had reason to expect the device to activate twenty-four hours after the last event. This is good news. It seems the device is no longer activating on its own."

"I hope you're right. Any news from Alex?"

"Yes. Apparently, he had a few problems, but they are still sailing to the Arctic Ocean."

"Is this a good number to reach you?"

"Yes, while I am on this ship."

"Ship? I thought you lived in Nevada."

"I am temporarily on board a ship named *Discovery*, near Vancouver Island, in Canada. I am trying to recover that device in the Pacific Ocean. It is a daunting task. We cannot tell if the device will activate while on board this ship. Could you call me if another event should occur?"

"I will. Good luck."

"Thank you." He stood from the table. *One less issue to worry about,* he thought as he left the conference room and entered the hallway. He looked in both directions, but had no idea where everyone had gone. He turned and walked toward the stern, looking through every open doorway to find his friends.

Chapter 32

MOUNT BAKER:

Jamie wondered where Wesley was going as they continued across another logging road back into the trees. Every time he had to step over a fallen tree trunk, she saw him wince in pain. It would be much easier on his ribs if they stayed on a road, but he ignored her suggestion, and she gave up trying.

Twenty minutes later, they stepped out of the trees, and the Hummer and trailer were right in front of them. "This really is your mountain, Wesley." She looked over at him, and he was grinning. "I don't know why you're so happy. You're going to have to back that trailer a long way to get out of here."

"That's not a problem. I just realized if you weren't along, I might have been trapped in that ice cave."

"I'm glad you asked me to go with you."

"I didn't. You invited yourself, remember?"

She gave him a quick grin. "How old are you, Wesley?"

He was surprised and hesitated to answer, wondering why she wanted to know. "I'll be fifty in April. Why?"

"Have you ever thought about shaving and getting a haircut?"

"Now listen, Miss Representative. We may be friends, but don't try to change me."

Jamie put her hands on her hips. "You don't have to get all huffy about it. I didn't mean you had to do it."

"Damn straight, I don't."

"I bet you're not bad looking under all that hair."

He turned away to study his situation. "Help me get the trailer off the road."

Jamie opened the rear door of the Hummer and tossed her backpack inside. When Wesley stepped up beside her, she slipped the strap of his pack off his shoulder. As she tossed it in with hers, she heard him sigh with relief. "I bet that feels better."

When he didn't reply, she looked over and saw him staring at the river and turned to see why. "It looks like we can cross it now."

"This shouldn't be happening, Jamie. The water level is dropping because something is holding it back."

"What? How?"

He walked around the front of the Hummer and gently climbed into the cab. "That's a good question, and we need to find out why. Guide me back into that wide area so I can leave the trailer here."

Chapter 33

SPARROW VALLEY HIGH SCHOOL:

Derek closed his locker door and tried to avoid the other students looking at him. Word had gotten around that his uncle was a geology instructor, and during an earlier class, the students stared at him when the ground moved. He tried to avoid any groups of people wanting to know what happened, since if they knew the whole story, they might panic, and it was better to play ignorant.

He hurried down the hallway to the exit doors, where he saw Jessica waiting on the other side of the glass. He was sure she would hound him for answers, and as he stepped out through the doorway, she stepped in his way.

"Where have you been, Derek? I've wanted to talk to you all afternoon, and looked everywhere for you."

"I was hiding."

"From Me?"

"From everyone."

When Derek turned and began making his way toward the parking lot, Jessica stared after him for a moment, and then hurried to walk beside him. "Derek?"

He glanced over at her. "What do you want me to say?"

"My older sister works for the park service, and last night she said there are some strange things happening up there."

Derek abruptly stopped and looked at her. "What kind of things?"

"A little girl was scalded by a hot spring near a campground."

"Is that all?"

"No. The hot spring was never there before the earthquakes. My sister is a friend of Wesley Patterson, and he's worried, too."

Derek thought about what Wesley had told him about the flooding. "I'm going for a ride."

Jessica crossed her arms and stared at him. "Why won't you talk to me, Derek? Do you really believe I'm a snob?"

"I didn't say you were a snob. That was my sister."

She uncrossed her arms. "I know, but you smiled when I asked you."

"I smiled because you're cute when you're angry."

"Where are you going? We still have classes this afternoon"

"I've got an hour until my next class and I want to see if the streams are rising." He turned and mounted his motorcycle, started the engine, then put on his helmet and headed out of the parking lot, leaving Jessica staring after him.

***

Derek drove west, over the crest of the valley, and followed the highway down the mountain toward Mount Vernon. Three miles farther, he arrived at the main bridge over the river coming down from Sparrow Valley. He found a small area to park next to the massive stone abutment and then climbed off to get a better view of the water level. He could tell by the watermarks on the bridge support, the water was above normal, and knew it was a bad sign.

He climbed back onto the motorcycle and rode back up the mountain, then parked at the school. The rest of the students were in class, and as he ran into the building, he stopped and grabbed the sat phone from his locker. He pressed button two and held it to his ear while it rang, but Wesley did not answer, so he left a message.

Chapter 34

MYSTIC:

Okawna turned on the submarine's exterior lights as he steered underneath the *Mystic*, and then stopped fifty-feet from the wall as they slowly began their descent to the bottom of the ice. A few minutes later, Okawna looked into the rearview mirror at Alex. "Do you believe that?"

When Alex leaned forward around Okawna to see out the window, the bottom of the ice wall turned ninety-degrees at a sharp edge back under itself. The flat bottom of the ice acted as a lens, bringing light down from the surface and illuminating the water as if in daylight. "That is amazing."

The bottom of the ice continued to be flat for another fifteen minutes, and then Okawna slowed down and stopped. "This should be directly underneath the device. I'm going to bring the nose up so we can see what's above us."

Okawna maneuvered the submarine until it was pointing up and hovered directly below a dark object, high up in the ice. "There it is."

Alex grabbed the back of Okawna's chair to pull himself out of his seat and got closer to the window. When he saw the device was nearly the same size as it had appeared from the surface, he let go and dropped back into his chair in frustration.

Okawna saw his friend's disappointed expression in the mirror. "I'm sorry, Alex. There's no way we can get it."

"I know. We might as well go back."

Okawna noticed a clear liquid dribbling down between his feet and reached under the instrument console for the main hydraulic manifold. One of the high-pressure hose fittings felt slippery, and the connecting nut turned easily in his fingers. He tightened it as best he could, then leveled the sub and set a course back to the *Mystic*.

***

Bett was on the bridge with Dieter and saw the rage in his eyes when he heard the *Wizard* was nearing the ship. When he spun around and stomped out the door to the stairs, she grabbed the microphone for the intercom. "The sub's here."

***

When Dieter reached the bottom of the stairs, he looked around to make sure no one else was on the stern as he stomped across the deck to Bartram, who was sitting on the sub's storage bracket. "They are coming back. Did you do what I told you?"

Bartram jumped down onto the deck. "I did just like you said, Captain. I don't know what went wrong."

Dieter heard footsteps approaching and saw it was Harrison. "Just keep your mouth shut. I will take care of this."

***

Ten minutes later, the sub was in its bracket, and then Alex climbed down first and moved out of the way. He watched Okawna climbed down the ladder, noticing his hands clenching into fists as he moved past him. "What's going on?"

Okawna didn't answer, just drove his fist into Bartram's jaw, driving him over backward onto the deck. He stood over him, staring down into his eyes. "You mess with my sub again, and I'll kill you!"

Okawna turned and glared at Dieter. "Did you really think you could get away with this?"

Alex wasn't sure what was going on. "Okawna?"

"They tried to kill us, Alex. Bartram loosened one of the hydraulic fittings. If I hadn't found it, we would have lost all the hydraulic controls and we wouldn't get back."

Bartram got back on his feet. "I didn't do anything, Okawna. You should take better care of your equipment."

Alex grabbed Okawna's shoulder when his arm reached back to swing at Bartram again. "Not yet, my friend." He stepped past Okawna and stared at Dieter. "He was just following orders. Isn't that right, Captain?"

"You are a suspicious man, Professor. It was a simple maintenance issue."

Mike knew without proof, nothing would be resolved, and he walked up to Alex. "What would you like us to do next? We still need to shut down the devices."

"I'm not sure. If you wouldn't mind, I'd like to stick around until I talk to a few people."

"No problem. We'll stay here until you're ready to go."

Alex turned and walked away, then up the stairs to the bridge deck. He leaned forward with his arms against the railing as he stared across the bow at the wall of ice, and was not looking forward to telling the bad news to all the people counting on him.

He looked back over his shoulder at the sound of footsteps, and then turned from the railing as Okawna approached. "I fear we are too late, my friend."

Okawna turned up his collar and shoved his hands into the pockets of his thick, dark blue coat as he stared at the wall. "Maybe the *Discovery* is making some progress."

Dieter stepped onto the bridge deck from the outside stairs. "What would it be worth if I knew the location of one of those devices that is not in the water?"

Okawna spun around, fire in his eyes as he grabbed the front of Dieter's coat. "What's it worth for me not to throw you over this railing?"

Alex put his hand on Okawna's arm. "Let's hear the man out. Then we'll decide whether to throw him overboard."

Okawna gave Dieter a shove as he let go, then took a step back, but continued to glare at him. "You're lucky Alex is here to stop me."

Dieter remained calm and stuck his hands in to his coat pockets. "It appears your journey has ended, Professor. I was not talking about you paying me. I was talking about what percentage of a large stash of treasure you would want in exchange for using this ship to find it."

Alex leaned back against the railing and folded his arms over his chest. "This isn't my ship, but I'm listening."

Dieter looked over at Okawna. "I will tell you what is on that disk you are so interested in. It is a digital copy of a motion picture made in 1945, at the end of World War II." He turned back to Cave. "There are two items in the movie that no one has identified until you showed up, Professor."

Alex stood from the railing. "I'm interested. Show me."

***

DISCOVERY:

Henry, Carl, Janice, and Victor were set up in the observation room. With the information from Alex, they had strategized a plan of action for when *Celeas* finished anchoring four steel cables into the slab of methane. Once the hydrocarbons turned to jelly, the sub would grab one cable and pull the methane away. When it let go, the slab should float until the cables stopped it from rising to the surface.

Carl Gregory was lying back on a small reclining chair, wearing a head mounted binocular display screen. Two cameras on *Celeas*, which was already on the sea floor, gave him depth perception while his hands held two handles with raised plastic buttons built into the armrests of the recliner for maneuvering the thrusters and robotic arms.

Under the thin padding of the recliner, electric actuators would apply a small amount of pressure under his butt and against two points behind his shoulders. It would give him the sensation of *Celeas*'s motions, up and down, forward and reverse, and side-to-side. For Carl, *Celeas* was an extension of his body, and the bands around his wrists let him sense of the amount of pressure being applied by the massive arms and tools.

Carl finished attaching the last cables to the four anchor points in the methane. "Ready when you are."

Janice was operating the rover with the ultrasound using a video feed and would turn on the transducer to melt the hydrocarbon layer. She looked up at the expectant faces. "Firing the frequency, now."

When brilliant blue light flashed on the screens, Carl gasped and let go of the controls, yanking the headset from his eyes. "I can't see!"

***

Bright blue light suddenly radiated from the wall of ice, and then high-pitched cracking sounds echoed off the face of the ice wall. When Okawna ran into the bridge and engaged the thrusters, Alex moved along the railing to keep an eye on the ice blocks, as the *Mystic* spun one-hundred-eighty-degrees in the water. The turbine engines increased to a high-pitched whine as the jet pumps moved her forward, but the broken slabs of ice scattered across the open water created a formidable maze ahead of the ship. There was no way to go around, and the only option was to nudge the slabs out of the way while hoping the water did not suddenly freeze.

Alex glanced into the bridge through the rear window, where Okawna was doing the best he could to steer through the blocks of ice. Dieter walked over and stood beside him at the railing, feeling the heavy thuds against the hull of the ship.

When Okawna looked out the rear window, his jaw dropped open. The water at the bottom of the wall suddenly froze, quickly expanding in his direction. He turned back to the controls and shoved the throttle further forward, causing the number of thuds against the hull to increase.

Alex's fingers tightened on the railing as the new ice continued to close the distance from the Stern. He spun around and ran to the front railing to see what was ahead of them, and fortunately, the floating slabs were thinning. He turned around and ran to the rear railing, but the ice was now less than one hundred feet from the stern. He looked down, and the rest of the crew was huddled together on the stern deck, staring behind the *Mystic* at the approaching ice.

The *Mystic* was gaining speed as the number of slabs decreased, and Okawna stared out the rear window at the ice, still closing the distance. He shoved the throttle forward, desperate to reach open sea, then the *Mystic* leapt onto the surface, her pontoons slicing through the water and riding up over the smaller slabs of ice.

***

The unexpected surge from the twin engines tossed those on the deck below off their feet, sending them tumbling across the surface. Bett, Joshua, and Bartram grabbed onto the helicopter, and Rita managed to grab the bracket for the sub with one hand. She reached out for Mike's hand as he tumbled toward the stern, but she was too late, and he tumbled out of range. She was surprised when Lisa suddenly grabbed her arm, so she pulled her closer so she could grab the bracket.

Mike saw the world spinning around him for a moment, and then his eyes locked onto the back edge of the ship. He clawed at the flat surface, but he was helpless to stop sliding into the freezing water. Harrison nearly went over the stern himself, but managed to wrap his arm around the hoist post before sliding over the edge into the water. He grabbed Mike's hand as he slid past, but the body continued moving until the lower half of Mike's torso was hanging over the stern.

Harrison could not pull Mike back aboard with just one hand. "I can't hold on much longer. Grab my arm with your other hand and pull yourself up!"

Rita jumped up and ran to Mike, grabbed his free wrist, and was nearly dragged over the stern when Harrison lost his grip on Mike's other hand. Lisa was suddenly kneeling next to her, pulling on Mike's coat collar, and together they dragged him up over the edge onto the deck. The *Mystic* stopped accelerating, and Mike rolled onto his back and stared up at Rita and Lisa's ashen faces. "Thanks."

***

Alex looked up from his friends below to stare at the sheet of ice, still closing the distance to the stern. He was amazed by the speed of the freezing water, still gaining, if only by a few feet at a time. The ice pyramid shrank into the background, as the *Mystic* and the new ice raced across the water at nearly the same speed, with only fifty-feet of separation. When he looked into the bridge, Okawna was staring back, so he knew the *Mystic* was at full speed. If something didn't change, in a few moments, the Mystic would be caught in the ice and destroyed.

Okawna thought about turning the *Mystic* on a different heading, but the width of the approaching ice was miles across, and they would lose the race if he tried. He felt a sudden lurch in her speed, but it was nothing he had done. Alex felt the *Mystic* lunge forward, and thought the reflection of the sun was causing an illusion, but the distance was widening between the stern and the ice.

Everyone watched the receding ice sheet, now one thousand feet behind them, as the *Mystic* continued to increase the distance, then the freezing abruptly stopped. Outside the bridge, Alex felt their speed decrease rapidly, and then Okawna stepped out to join him and Dieter. They heard loud cracking sounds as they stared at the new ice wall to rising out of the water, forcing the old wall of ice higher into the air to increase the size of the pyramid.

Dieter moved across behind the bridge to join Alex and Okawna, looking back over the railing. "You do not see that every day."

Alex turned to Okawna. "I felt our speed increase. What did you do?"

"It wasn't me."

"Hey, Alex?"

Alex looked down at the main deck, and Rita was smiling up at him. "Yeah?"

"I bypassed the governor for the turbines, so don't increase our speed until I can reset them, or they'll fly apart."

"How did you know they would hold together?"

"I didn't. I figured we didn't have much choice, so I had to try it."

Alex blew her a kiss. "You have my undying thanks."

Okawna stepped onto the bridge, switched the controls from turbines to thrusters, and set them to hover. When he went back outside, he grabbed Dieter's arm. "Let's watch a movie, Captain."

Dieter jerked his arm free and glared up at him. "There is more to this than just the movie Okawna. If you want my help, you had better show me a little courtesy, or you will never find that device."

Mike was still on the stern with Lisa and Harrison when he heard Okawna yelling behind the bridge, then he ran up the outside stairs to join him, Alex, and Dieter. "What happened?"

Okawna indicated Dieter. "The captain has been holding out on us. He nearly got us killed trying to recover the device from the ice sheet when he knew there is another device already out of the water. He was just explaining he wants to show it to us. Isn't that right?"

Dieter knew he had little choice. "That is correct. If you will follow me down to the lounge, I will play the movie for you."

Everyone went into the bridge, but when Dieter headed for the stairs, Okawna shoved his palm against the man's chest to stop him. "Where are we headed to find it?"

"Set a course back to the Aleutian islands."

Okawna checked the radar for other ships, but there was nothing in their area. He entered the coordinates into the computer and then set the thruster speed to slow ahead. He grabbed the microphone for the intercom and informed everyone to meet in the lounge, then headed down the stairs.

Chapter 36

DISCOVERY:

Victor knelt beside Carl, watching him blink to clear his vision. "You should be fine in a few moments. The same thing happened to the crew on the *Mystic*."

Henry noticed something very odd on the video feed from *Celeas*. The camera appeared to be rolling in and out of a cloud of silt, and the massive slab was bouncing along the seabed. "Janice, look!"

Janice took control of the rover and swept the camera around until she saw the slab. It bounced up through the silt and began rising toward the surface, but one side was rising higher than the other one. She maneuvered the rover above the silt and saw that only two of the cables were still attached to the methane. "Oh, no!" She spun around to Carl. "Can you see anything yet?"

"Yes. I mean, I see a bright blue light in the center of my vision, but it's fading."

"The methane tore loose and two of the cables have been yanked from the slab, and it's about to tear loose from the other two cables. *Celeas* is still hidden under the silt, so you need to take control and try to anchor that slab down before it breaks free and floats to the surface."

"I'll try. Give me the headset, Victor."

Victor bent over, grabbed the headset from the floor, and helped him put it on. "How's that?"

"Okay, I can see the silt. I'll bring her up and get my bearings."

Everyone turned back to the video screens, showing the images from both underwater vehicles. Janice swung the rover around to look for *Celeas*, and a moment later, they watched her rising out of the cloud of silt. On the other display, the view from *Celeas's* cameras focused on the slab.

"Okay, I see it," Carl informed them. "What do you want me to do?"

Henry spun around to face him. "The eyebolts are not holding, so try to bring the other cables over the slab to hold it down."

"How? The other cables are buried in the silt. I can't grab what I can't see."

Janice had an idea. "Use *Celeas* to push against the side of the slab and force it back down with the thrusters. At least enough to take the strain off the other cables."

"I'll try."

Everyone sat on the edge of their chairs, staring at the displays. The view from the rover showed *Celeas* maneuver up around the slab and settle on the upper edge. "Here we go," Carl said softly.

Small bubbles appeared behind the two large thrusters as the propellers began cavitating, creating a vacuum that forced the water to vaporize. No one dared breathe for several long moments until the slab slowly began to lean over. Everyone gasped as *Celeas* suddenly slid sideways along the edge and the slab began to rise again.

"Damn! Okay, I've got it," Carl informed them.

The video from *Celeas* jerked as it bumped against the slab, and once again, it slowly leaned over. They dare not breathe while time seemed to advance in slow motion as the slab continued to lean over. When it was nearly horizontal, Carl gradually moved *Celeas* back from the edge and forced it down to the seabed. The view from the rover showed only the top of *Celeas* protruding above the swirling cloud of silt, and everyone released a collective sigh.

Carl continued to hold *Celeas* steady against the slab. "Okay. Now that it's down, what are we going to do?"

They looked at each other with puzzled expressions. Henry leaned back in his chair. "How long will the batteries last under that load, Carl?"

Carl looked at the upper corner of his headset display. The reading for the power consumption was near the yellow line. "At this rate, we have less than an hour before the batteries are too depleted to hold it down. Take this visor off for me, would you, Victor?"

Victor removed the visor, and Carl continued to hold the control handles as he looked around the room. "You guys are the brainiacs, but it appeared to me that the device activated again. You said that wouldn't happen. I bet that's what tore the cables loose."

"That's not our immediate problem," Victor announced. "We need a solution within the next forty-five minutes."

Carl looked up at the two video screens mounted on the wall. "The silt is drifting away with the tide. We should use the rover to locate the cables and drag one over the methane."

Janice shook her head no. "It won't work unless we can anchor the other end."

Henry had an idea. "Janice, would you guide the rover to the areas on the slab where the cables tore loose?"

"Sure. What have you got in mind?"

"We should compare them to the anchor points that are still attached to the slab and see how well they are connected. We may be able to simply control the rate of rise of the slab until it is floating and held in place by the other two cables."

"I wouldn't call that slab of methane simple to control," Carl informed them. "You saw how hard it was to bring that monster down."

"Yes, but you are already on top of the slab, so you will not be fighting to push it back down. Just let it up slowly."

"Easy for you to say."

Janice swung her chair around to face the video screen. "Let's check it out."

Henry and Victor stood and stared over Janice's shoulders at the video screen from the rover. A moment later, the little craft moved cautiously along the outer edge of the slab. After several minutes, it was possible to discern a large, ragged, pie-shaped area missing from the top of the methane.

Victor pointed at the screen. "That's amazing. The mass of the methane must be incredibly heavy. Once it was moving, the anchor couldn't hold it back."

"It's not just the methane," Janice added. "Add all the heavy pollutants they discovered in the methane, plus it's all held together by frozen water molecules. Let's move to the next one."

Janice carefully maneuvered the rover around the outside edge to the second anchor point, now a large ragged hole ripped out of the ice. The rover continued to the third anchor point, still firmly embedded in the methane, with a taut steel cable stretching away into the darkness.

Henry placed his hand on her shoulder. "If the last one is like this, we should not have any problem."

Several minutes later, the rover stopped three feet away from the fourth anchor point, where they could see a small crack in the ice across the anchor bolt. Otherwise, it looked solid, with a slack cable snaking away across the seafloor into darkness.

Janice spun her chair around to face everyone. "This could work."

Victor shook his head no. "We don't know if they will hold."

"Hey!" Carl hollered from his chair. "The clock is ticking over here, so is there another option?" He could tell by their blank stares that they had none. "Okay. Give me a higher angle from the rover so I can see what I'm trying to do."

Janice brought the rover around the outside edge until she could see *Celeas* pushing on the slab fifty feet below. "How's that?"

"Very good. Okay, I'm backing down the power to the thrusters, so let's see what it does."

Small amounts of brown silt swirled off the grey-green surface as the slab slowly started to rise, with *Celeas* riding piggyback near the outer edge.

As the angle increased, *Celeas* began sliding across the surface. "I don't know how much longer I can control the rate of rise, Doctors."

The others could see what was happening on the display, feeling helpless as *Celeas* continued to slide from side to side across the surface.

"I'm losing it!" Carl warned them. He could see the image from the rover as *Celeas* suddenly shot forward over the edge of the slab. "Shit!"

The slab was suddenly rushing up toward the rover's camera. Janice tried to swing it out of the way, but it was too late. The picture shuddered for a long moment, as the rover slid across the surface, then it was clear of the slab. When she brought the rover back around, they saw the edge of the slab pointed up toward the surface. It slowly moved sideways through the water, held down on one side by the taut cable. The snaking cable suddenly snapped taut as the slab stopped moving, then everyone released their breaths as the massive, green-tinted formation floated vertically in the water.

Carl brought *Celeas* around to look at the cables. "Hey guys. That second cable is not going to hold. It's that crack we saw. When the cable snapped tight, it must have yanked on the anchor point."

The crack suddenly raced across the surface, through the anchor point. "Back up, Carl!" Janice hollered. "It's tearing free!"

Carl applied full power to the elevation thrusters, forcing *Celeas* up away from the slab. The cable tore loose and sliced through the water only inches below sub.

Janice flinched and yanked her hands from the controls as the cable slammed into the camera lens of the rover and the screen went dark. "Shit!" She spun her chair around to see the video from *Celeas*.

Carl made a tight U-turn and focused on the slab. It was rising at an angle, still anchored to the last cable. Moments dragged by as it continued to rise, now nearly vertical. A small bubble escaped and everyone flinched, but the slab remained anchored to the seafloor by the single cable.

"We did it," Henry whispered.

Janice leapt out of her chair and threw her arms around Henry's waist, pulling him close. "That was brilliant," she whispered into his ear.

Henry gently put his arms around her waist. "It was a team effort."

They parted and smiled into each other's eyes for a moment, then let go and looked at Victor and Carl, both grinning back at them.

Carl swung *Celeas* around the slab, looking for any anomalies, and focused on the anchor point and it appeared solidly anchored in the slab. He entered the auto pilot command for *Celeas* to stay focused there and released the controls.

He stood to stretch and relax. "That was exciting," he told them while opening and closing his hands to relieve the stress.

Henry approached Carl and smiled. "Magnificent job, young man."

"Thanks, Doc. I damn near got hit by that cable."

"You did better than I did," Janice told him. "That rover is history."

One problem solved, Victor thought. "Now that this problem is temporarily resolved, we need to start our next phase of this operation immediately."

Carl stared at him. "You need to lighten up a little, Victor. Give us a break, for crying out loud!"

"You people have no idea how long this will take! We don't have time to just sit around."

Henry stood to look sternly at Victor. "Please do not rush into this. We need to be cautious at this stage. We must determine why the device activated again before we move forward with the recovery."

Victor's shoulders sagged. "You're right, Henry. Let's take a break and talk about this over coffee."

Chapter 37

RANGER STATION:

When Larry heard a vehicle drive into the parking lot, he stood from his desk to stare out through the window. He recognized Jamie in the passenger seat of Wesley's Hummer and went outside to find out what happened to the snow cat.

Wesley did his best to hide his pain as he climbed out. "Hey, Larry. What's the extent of the damage from that last seismic event?"

"A little worse than the last one, so I decided to evacuate the park and campgrounds. Frank is informing them right now. You look like you're hurting, and you have blood in your hair. What happened?"

"I'm okay. Nothing to worry about."

Jamie put her hands on her hips in frustration. "He *is* hurt and not just the cut on his head. He's being delusional, Larry. We were nearly killed in an ice cave, and he has a possible cracked rib."

"I'm fine. We have more important things to worry about right now."

Jamie and Wesley followed Larry into the station and looked at the large plastic covered map of the park mounted to the wall, and then Larry indicated four areas circled in red. "Those are the campgrounds we've cleared so far. We couldn't reach Marmot Campground, because the creek flooded and washed out the road."

"There were a woman and two kids staying there," Jamie told him. "They're the ones who found the hot spring where the little girl got burned. They were hiding from her ex-husband, and only had a beat-up car, so they could not have made it out."

Wesley indicated an area on the map. "There's an old logging road that drops behind the campground." He looked at Jamie. "It's near that canyon where we left the trailer, and I want to find out what's holding back that water. We can go down into the campground from there and see if they got out."

"I'll call my sister and let her know what happened."

When Jamie moved to one side of the room, Larry looked at his friend. "Are you sure you feel up to bouncing around?"

"I'll be fine."

Jamie turned off her phone and then grabbed a portable radio from the charging rack. "We'll be on channel two."

Wesley knew it was going to be a painful ride, but had to go. "We'll let you know what we find out."

"Be careful in the woods, you two. I don't want to see you get hurt again."

***

The number of old logging roads Wesley had taken was like following a maze, before he finally parked his Hummer at the bottom of a low ridge. "If I remember right, the canyon should be just over that rise."

They climbed out of the Hummer and hiked up the steep slope, but were surprised when they reached the top. Water had backed up into a deep valley.

"You were right, Wesley. That's a new lake, isn't it?"

"Yeah, and this is very bad. Now we know why that stream was so low."

They stared down at a massive pile of logs, branches, and brush of a forty-foot high logjam across the canyon, holding back thousands of gallons of water for over a mile up the gorge. A fast-moving stream gushed from under the tree trunks at the bottom, dragging more debris down the canyon and creating smaller dams, all collecting water, and at the bottom end of the canyon was the reservoir for the old logging dam.

Jamie had an idea and turned to Wesley. "What if we open one side of the blockage to let the water out?"

"It won't work. The entire logjam could tear loose."

"How far are we from the campground?"

"Fifteen minutes, if we take that logging road we passed a moment ago. It follows the canyon on the other side of that hill and drops into the campground."

Jamie could tell he was trying to hide his discomfort, but knew not to say anything. At least the ride was not too bad, although sometimes she could not see any road at all. "What do you want me to tell Larry?"

"To be honest, I don't know what to say. It could tear loose at any moment or not break at all. That concrete dam is so old it won't handle the load, and when it breaks, the lahar will destroy anything in its path, starting with the track field behind the high school."

"Won't it just follow the river and miss the valley?"

"Nope. The water from the reservoir didn't originally flow in its current direction, because the loggers diverted it around the valley. The best thing to do is open the dam right now and drain the reservoir. The river will flood downstream, but the damage to Sparrow Valley will be minimal compared to what will happen if we don't open it."

Jamie stared at him for a moment. "Okay. So, what do I tell Larry?"

"Just let him know he did the right thing by evacuating the park."

Jamie called Larry on the radio and told him what they found and then noticed Wesley checking his pockets. "Did you lose something?"

"Yeah, my cellphone. If Larry opens the dam, the Cave ranch will flood, and I told Derek I would let him know when it was time to leave the ranch."

"It probably fell out in your Hummer."

"Maybe. Let's get going."

They walked back down to the vehicle and searched for the phone, but could not find it.

"Do you know Derek's number? You could use my cellphone."

"No, it's one of those satellite phones. I'll call him after we check the campground and talk to Larry to decide what to do."

Jamie climbed into the passenger seat and watched Wesley try to hide his pain as he climbed in and closed the door. As he drove along the side of the mountain toward the campground, she looked over at him, and he appeared to be more comfortable. "Did you know about the track meet tomorrow?"

Wesley jerked his head around to Jamie. "What? That's Tomorrow?"

"It starts at four in the afternoon."

"Oh, crap!"

***

SPARROW VALLEY HIGH SCHOOL:

Derek walked out of the classroom and saw Jessica waiting near his locker, and could tell from her expression something was bothering her. "What's going on?"

"Jamie and Wesley were in an accident, and Wesley has a fractured rib."

"Is Jamie okay?"

"She's fine."

"What happened?"

"They used Wesley's snow cat to go up to the glaciers, and they were in an ice cave when we had that earthquake. It collapsed and nearly killed them."

Derek opened his locker, grabbed the sat phone, and pressed speed dial number two. He held it to his ear, but it just kept ringing, so he slipped it into his backpack. "Wesley's not answering, so I'm going up to his cabin."

"Just wait a minute. Let me call my sister and find out if Wesley is with her in the park."

Jessica dug through her purse for her phone, then selected a contact and put it on speaker. "Jamie? Where are you?"

"In the park with Wesley. The glaciers are melting too fast, so we're evacuating the park. Listen, you need to find Derek Cave."

"I'm with him now, and he's listening."

"Derek, it's Wesley. Do you remember when we talked about that lahar? There's a good chance it will happen to the valley."

"What can I do to help?"

"Find the Sheriff and tell him to cancel the track meet tomorrow."

"What makes you think he'll listen to me?"

"Your grandfather and Arnie have a history. If he won't listen to you, tell Robert. As excited as Arnie is about the games, Robert could be the only person he'll pay attention to and call it off."

"Got it."

"Jamie? Be careful and call me if you need anything. Bye, sis."

Jessica slid the phone into her purse as Derek turn and continued along the hallway and hurried up beside him. "Let's try the restaurant first. It's on the way. What's a lahar?"

"I can take care of it, Jessica."

"I know you can. Let's take my car. So, what's a lahar?"

"A lahar is a massive mud slide. If that dam breaks, it will wash everything away."

When they reached Jessica's mustang, she opened the driver's door and stared across the roof at Derek, still standing on the other side. "Get in, and I'll drive us to the restaurant."

"I'll take my motorcycle and meet you there."

Jessica didn't climb inside and watched him walk across the parking lot to his motorcycle, wondering why he was treating her that way. When the motorcycle engine roared, she climbed into the mustang and followed him down the street.

A few blocks farther, she saw the sheriff's patrol car parked in front of the restaurant, so she parked beside Derek's motorcycle, climbed out, and grinned at him. "I told you."

They noticed the advertisement for the track meet in the window as they entered, then the doorbell tinkled, and the three people inside turned to look at them. The sheriff was sitting at a table with the town's Mayor, Warren Magnuson, and Molly Moran, the restaurant owner.

Molly stood from the table. "What can I get for you two?"

Derek started to speak, but Jessica cut him off. "I'm here to talk to you, Uncle Arnie. You need to cancel the track meet. In fact, you should evacuate the valley."

Arnie and the Mayor laughed. "Are you insane, Jessica? What for?"

"The dam is going to break and flood the valley."

Derek watched the Sheriff and the Mayor grin at each other and knew they were not taking her seriously. "If that dam breaks, it could kill everyone at the track meet."

Arnie studied Derek's demeanor, and he seemed sincere. "What do you know about it?"

"I'm a friend of Wesley Patterson. He said the glaciers are melting, and the dam may not hold it back."

Arnie looked up at Jessica. "I can't just cancel the games without some major repercussions. Not on the word of a crazy old man."

Derek's hands clenched into fists. "He knows what he's talking about, Sheriff. He's working with my Uncle Alex."

Arnie slouched in his chair. "Did he say when it would happen?"

Derek knew where this was leading. "Just an estimate. Maybe tomorrow?"

"Could it happen today? Next week? A month from now? Do you see where I'm going?"

"Okay, but at least you're aware of it now, so if you don't do anything, it's your fault!"

Arnie sat up and turned his back to Derek. "I'll see you at the games."

Derek felt his fingernails digging into his palms as he fought hard to keep his anger in check. "Don't just dismiss what I'm telling you, Sheriff. Haven't you felt the earthquakes? You could put people's lives in danger."

Jessica could tell Derek was not going to back down. "You should get your head out of your butt, Uncle Arnie, and cancel the track meet."

Arnie and the Mayor laughed, and then Arnie turned back to Derek. "I'm not canceling the games on the word of that crackpot hermit."

Jessica saw the look in Derek's eyes, and it scared her a little. "Let's go, Derek." She grabbed his arm to guide him out into the parking lot, but he jerked it away.

"He's not a crackpot. He's a volcanologist, so he knows what he's talking about. Haven't you been listening to the news? Mount Baker is becoming active because of the earthquakes, you idiot! He's trying to stop it from happening, not sitting around in a restaurant, acting like a pompous jerk."

Arnie stopped grinning and leapt up from the table, glaring at Derek.

Derek saw the anger in the sheriff's eyes, but wasn't about to be intimidated. He glared back as he pulled his shoulders back and forced his chest out toward the sheriff.

Arnie had seen that look before from the only person who defied his authority, and his face flushed in anger. "You had better leave before I lose my temper!"

Jessica put her hand on Derek's shoulder. "Let's go. We're going to be late for our next class."

Molly could tell this was not going to end well without some intervention, so she stepped between them, facing the sheriff. "Your burger is ready, Sheriff. Have a seat, and I'll bring it right out."

Arnie gave her a nod and sat down, but his jaw clenched in anger at the defiance from another member of the Cave family.

Jessica grabbed Derek's hand. "That's all we can do for now. Let's go."

Derek slowly turned, glaring back at the sheriff until Jessica pulled on his hand, then looked away and followed her out of the restaurant.

Jessica stopped next to her car. "We're going to be late. I'll follow you back to the school."

"You go ahead. I need to go for a ride to clear my head. I'll see you later."

Jessica knew it was useless to argue with him right now. "All right. I'll talk to the principal about it. He married into our family, too, so maybe he'll listen to me. I'll see you back at the school."

Derek climbed onto his motorcycle and started the engine, then backed out of the parking spot. He gunned the engine several times, then slipped the clutch and squealed the rear tire defiantly as he drove away.

Jessica watched him race down the road, and was worried about the ramifications of his confrontation with Arnie. The only other person who acted that way toward the sheriff was his grandfather, but he was an adult and had lived here most of his life. Derek was a newcomer to the valley, and now uncle Arnie had a reason to harass him whenever he wanted. Sure, uncle Arnie was conceited, but he was still the sheriff.

Chapter 38

MYSTIC:

In the lounge, Alex watched Lisa, Harrison, and Bartram stroll in from the stern, while Rita came up from the engine room, but none of them knew what was going on. Rita moved up beside him, so he took her hand in his, and then spoke to the others. "It seems the captain had a secret. He knows where there is a device already out of the water, and he's about to explain why he risked our lives to keep it."

Mike stared at Dieter for a few moments. "Why didn't you tell us sooner, John? We barely escaped that ice sheet, and I was almost killed. What were you thinking?"

"I did not know that would happen, Mike. We were not supposed to make it past the islands, but the professor ruined my plans by saving us from the pirates. If anyone is to blame, it is him."

Okawna's face flushed with rage as he stomped across the room, and he would have driven his fist into Dieter's face if Alex hadn't stepped in his way. "You heard him, Alex. Let's take his movie and I'll throw him over the stern."

"Not yet. Let's find out what he's *not* telling us first."

Dieter looked around at the expectant faces and indicated for them to sit down. "Last year, I was working in the Netherlands and discovered information about my grandfather. He was a Nazi opportunist and captain of a German U-boat. Evidently, he had smuggled large amounts of precious metals and gems out of the Netherlands before the end of the war, and was never heard from again. I paid a very large sum of money to get this movie, and it will show us the location where he hid his plunder."

Rita was intrigued by the story. "What has that got to do with finding the device?"

Dieter reached into his coat pocket and brought out the plastic case. "In this movie, you can see one of the devices on the same island where he hid his treasure."

When Okawna reached out to take the plastic case, Dieter gave him a wry grin and then slowly held it out to Joshua. Joshua yanked the case from Dieter's hand, glaring at him before walking to his desk and inserting the disk into the player. He turned on the television, and then pressed play.

The television screen was white for a few seconds, then the movie began, and it was like watching a director cut from a major motion picture. The camera was focused on a small island protruding above the surface in a vast expanse of ocean. The screen turned white again, and the camera zoomed in on a large 'V' at the top of the island, fifty feet in front of a ship. The white screen appeared, and the sound came on as the movie showed two men standing at the railing of a ship, with the island in the background. A slender man was wearing a dark brown leather jacket and a white captain's hat, and the other man wore a German officer's uniform.

1944

Captain Jim Burk was facing the German Officer. "Damn it, Colonel. Do you have to film everything?"

Colonel Eric Dieter smiled as he continued staring at the island. "When Hitler loses this war, we are going to be very wealthy men. The new economic system will be driven by science, where new inventions and discoveries will make a few men into millionaires, and I will be one of them. That is why I need documentation about my discovery."

"How did you find this place?"

"You are not the first man with, shall we say, a questionable reputation I have worked with. This was a smuggler's hideout, but he does not use it anymore. He had a small accident just after he showed this island to me. This is where I have hidden my plunder, but what is more important is what I have found in the crater."

"The war isn't over yet. If Hitler has one of those atomic bombs I've been hearing rumors about, things will change in his favor."

"Not to worry, Captain. It is only a theory. No one could build such a device. When we recover this cylinder, we will keep it secret until the allies win then we will show it to the new scientific community, and they will throw money at me for research. You will see."

Burk turned away from the railing when one of his men walked up to him. "What is it?"

"The tide is as high as it will get, Captain."

"All right, take us in." He turned to face Dieter. "You had better make this fast. This extreme high tide will only last another hour. If we don't get my ship out before then, we will be trapped inside that volcano for an eternity."

"You worry too much, Captain."

"This is my ship, and it's my job to worry. You have half an hour to load that thing. If you're not done, I'm leaving without you. Get my meaning?"

"I do not respond to threats, Captain."

Burk stared at him, a venomous look in his eyes. "It's not a threat. It's a promise."

"You Americans are a bunch of cowboys."

When Dieter turned and went down the steps to the main deck, Burk concentrated on the narrow opening. The rock walls of the V-shaped gap in the side of the crater slowly slid past the sides of the ship, with only two-feet of clearance on each side, and then he looked through the open doorway at the man minding the helm. "What's our depth?"

"Thirteen-feet, Captain."

"Damn, this is close."

"That it is, Captain. That only leaves three-feet of clearance under the hull."

"You're doing good, son. Nice and slow."

Burk moved along the outside of the wheelhouse to the rear railing until the stern slowly cleared the opening, and then his ship was inside the crater. He walked back to the wheelhouse and looked inside. "How much water is under us in here?"

"We've got twenty-feet, Captain, so as long as we get out before . . . What is that?"

Burk spun around and his mouth opened slightly. Directly in front of the ship, on the far side of the crater, a massive mirrored object was protruding from the lava rock wall. A short distance to the left was a large cave with a gray torpedo looking object on the ground partway inside.

"As soon as the skiff is in the water, get us turned around and ready to leave."

"Damn right, Captain."

Burk turned and glared at the German soldier. "Get that damn camera out of my face."

***

Present day.

The movie suddenly ended, and Dieter looked around the room, stopping at Cave. "We all know what that is, Professor. Your device. What do you know about it?"

"I'm not at liberty to say. On which one of the Aleutian Islands is that device located?"

"That is the problem, Professor. It is not in the chain of islands, but somewhere near them. Only those pirates know exactly where it is. I was going to steal this ship and meet them in Prince Rupert to get the disk and a map. I managed to get this motion picture, but my contact would not give me the map until I took over this ship."

Mike jumped out of his chair and glared at Dieter. "I trusted you! If you would have told me what you were doing, I would have helped you."

"I could not take that chance, Mike. You may not care about money, but I do, and it is on that island." He glanced around the room at the hostile expressions. "I was not going to kill you. I was going to wait until all of you went ashore, then Harrison, Bartram, and I were going to disappear with the Mystic."

"I would have told the authorities."

"You would not even know where to search. You know how fast this ship is, so you would never have found us."

When Joshua stood up, Alex saw the rage in his eyes and his clenched fists, so he stood to stop him. "Just wait a minute, Josh. He's not going anywhere." He could tell Joshua did not even hear him.

Bett suddenly jumped up in front of Joshua. "Anger management, Josh. Do you remember the therapy? Just calm down." She turned her head and glared at Dieter. "The therapy doesn't always work, and I wouldn't mind watching him beat the crap out of you, so you'd better go outside until my man calms down."

Dieter knew he had better leave and kept his distance from Joshua as he quickly moved across the room and out of the lounge. Okawna glared at Harrison before moving over to help Bett and Alex with Joshua.

Harrison stood and raised his hands. "Hey, I'm just the hired help. I wouldn't have hurt anyone. Honest." He saw the warning in Okawna's eyes and walked out of the room.

Alex got Mike's attention. "That device could solve all our problems if we can get it back to Nevada."

"I know, but how are we going to get it?"

Alex gave everyone staring at him a wry smile. "We become pirates. I'll have Dieter call them and set up a meeting."

***

Dieter finished his negotiations with the pirates over the radio, clipped the microphone into the overhead bracket, and then looked over at Alex and Mike. "See how you have complicated things, Professor? Now we are forced to deal with the pirates on their terms."

"I think we have sufficient firepower to take care of ourselves. We can do this if we're careful and have a contingency plan. Since we will arrive first, we have time to see what we're dealing with and find an advantage."

Dieter turned and gave a nod to Bartram, who engaged the jet pumps and set a course for a GPS location he heard from the man on the radio. Dieter waited until Cave and Mike went down the stairs to the lounge and leaned close to Bartram. "I'll tell Harrison what's going on and give you a break when we are close so you can get your weapon. Cave will assign someone to stay on the ship when we go ashore, and I want you to stay, too. For now, we are allies, but that could change."

"What about the treasure?"

"Mike does not care about the money, and Cave only wants to stop the freezing, so there will be plenty for us. Use the intercom when we are close." He turned and walked down the stairs.

***

An hour later, everyone gathered outside the bridge and shared the binoculars as the *Mystic* approached a small, barren brown island rising thirty-feet above the water. If it had not been for the V in the nearly vertical cliff, it would look like an ordinary large rock and if you did not know the island was there, you would never have seen it from a boat until you were close.

They felt the ship suddenly lose speed and everything was quiet, but they were still five miles away when Bartram stepped out of the bridge. "Hey, everything shut down and the radar and radios aren't working."

Joshua walked into the bridge and did a few checks and then stepped back out. "I'm getting interference on every frequency, and it's jamming the electronics. It must be interference from the device on the island." He looked at Bett. "That means your helicopter won't work, either."

Mike handed his portable radio to Joshua. "I guess I won't need this."

Joshua shoved the radio into his coat pocket. "The regular electrical system is still working, so Rita and I will try to create some type of bypass so we can control the turbines, but it's going to take some time. Fortunately, we'll still be able to use the thrusters to continue to the island and maneuver once we get there."

***

It took the *Mystic* another twenty minutes to reach the island using the thrusters, and now they were floating forty feet from the only landing area. When they stepped out from the bridge, the wind coming from the north was forty-degrees F.

Up close, the island was larger than it had appeared from a distance, at two hundred feet in diameter and twenty feet high. The bottom of the V was seven-feet above the narrow strip of rocky beach.

Alex turned to the group. "I'll go with Mike and the Captain in the motorboat, while the rest of you stay on board in case the pirates try to board us. We don't know how long until their ship arrives, so let's get ready."

Okawna didn't like being left out of the action, but knew he had to stay on board. "I'll sound the horn when we see the ship."

"Works for me. All right, let's get moving."

Okawna and Harrison followed Alex, Mike, and Dieter down onto the stern, then used the hoist to set the motorboat into the water. A moment later, Mike climbed in, and then Dieter sat behind the steering wheel and started the engine. Alex untied the bowline from the deck cleat, then stepped down into the boat and pushed them away from the ship.

Chapter 39

MOUNT BAKER:

Wesley stopped the Hummer at a small river rushing across a low section of the dirt road, put it into neutral, and turned to look at Jamie. "That's the way we need to go to get to the campground."

Jamie stared through the front window at the thirty foot wide river, then at the bank on the far side. "It looks deep. Are you sure?"

He grinned. "You said it yourself. This is my mountain."

Wesley put the hummer into four-wheel drive and eased down into the water. He wasn't too worried about the depth, because of another adaptation he had made to his vehicle.

Jamie leaned out the window, watching the water level rise on the side of the door. When it continued up, she looked over at Wesley, who was grinning.

She leaned back out until the level was near the bottom of the window, and then closed it just before the water lapped at the bottom edge of the glass. When she looked at the water rippling over the hood, her stomach tightened into a knot. "Wesley? Won't it drown the engine?"

"That large black tube behind my seat is called a snorkel, and supplies the air into the carburetor. We're almost through."

When the Hummer drifted sideways with the current, Jamie grabbed the dash. She felt the tires thump against the ground, and the Hummer slowly climbed out of the water. She leaned back in her seat, sighing with relief as they continued over the embankment.

Wesley drove over the newly formed bank of the river and continued along the dirt road. "Nearly as good as Disneyland."

"Oh no, Wesley. That was real life or death."

***

Ten minutes later, the road dropped into the backside of the campground. As they drove around the campsites, Jamie scanned through the trees for the green car, but the place was deserted, so she relaxed. "The woman must have got out, okay?"

Wesley continued toward the normal exit. "Let's see how bad the road is from this side."

A woman suddenly ran out of the restroom in front of his vehicle, waving her arms. He slammed on the brakes, barely stopping before hitting her.

Jamie recognized the woman with the children and threw open the door to get out. "What happened?"

The woman ran back into the building and brought out her children, then wrapped her arms around Jamie's neck while sobbing against her shoulder. "I was so scared no one would come. We tried to leave, but the car slid into the mud and we couldn't get out. We were all alone, and I heard your car."

"It's all right. You're safe now."

Wesley climbed out and looked around the area, then gritted his teeth against the pain as he knelt in front of the two kids and smiled. "I'm Wesley, and I'm going to take you and your mom out of here, okay?"

When the woman let go and stepped back, Jamie looked down at the kids hugging Wesley. She realized his gruff manner hid the softer side of his personality.

Wesley slowly stood back up and looked at Jamie. "Stay here while I check out the road."

Jamie stepped out of the way as he climbed into the Hummer and drove out of the campground, then looked at the woman. "I didn't get your name?"

"I'm Serra Billingsley. This is Gail and William."

"Wesley has four-wheel drive, so he can get us out of here."

A few moments later, Wesley drove the Hummer into the campground and stopped in front of the building. He waved Jamie over to his window, and she joined him. "We won't be able to get out that way. We'll have to go back across that river."

"I don't know, Wesley. We started floating away the last time."

"We'll have more weight to hold us down. Tell them to get in, and we'll get out of here."

Serra heard what they were saying and moved up to the window. "I need to get my purse. It's still in the car."

Wesley shook his head no. "It's not going anywhere. We need to leave before things get worse."

"I'll be right back."

When Serra ran down the road before they could stop her, Jamie looked through the window at Wesley. "I'd better go with her." She turned and ran after Serra.

"Wait! We can drive to her car."

When the women disappeared into the trees, Wesley caught movement in his peripheral vision and saw the young boy was suddenly standing on his toes, looking up at him through the open window. He leaned out to look down at him and smiled. "What is it with women and their purses?"

"Can we get in?"

"You bet. Stand back now."

Wesley slowly opened the door and climbed out, then moved to the rear door and opened it. When he bent over to lift William onto the seat, he felt a sharp stab in his side and stopped.

William noticed Wesley seemed to be hurting, so he helped his little sister up onto the floor, then onto the seat. He did the same and smiled at the big man. With all the hair on his head, the man looked like a bear.

Wesley closed the rear door and climbed into the front seat. He tapped his fingers on the steering wheel for a few minutes, then looked around and checked the rear-view mirror, but there was no sign of the women. When he heard a loud cracking sound of a falling tree echo through the forest, he knew the water was tearing up the vegetation around the campground, and looked back between the seats at the kids. "I wish they would hurry."

The girl smiled. "You look like a bear."

The boy growled. "A big grizzly bear."

Wesley growled back, and they laughed, then he heard the women running up the road. He looked into the mirror, and saw Serra trying to keep control of the very large green canvas bag bouncing behind her shoulder, and Jamie carrying two suitcases. He climbed out as they ran up to the Hummer. "Things are getting worse, so get in."

Serra suddenly ran back along the road toward the trees. "I have more stuff in the car."

Wesley stared at Jamie. "Can you talk some sense into that woman?"

"She's running away from her ex-husband, Wesley. Give her a break."

Wesley released a long sigh of frustration. "All right. Get in and we'll drive down to her car."

Wesley and Jamie climbed in and he followed her directions down the road and stopped at a muddy campsite. The car was over the embankment, so they didn't see it the first time through.

Jamie got out and went over the side to the car to help, and Wesley tried to be patient while Jamie and Serra filled the back part of his

Hummer with Serra's belongings. The woods echoed with the crackling of another falling tree, and his patience was wearing thin. When they finally slammed the rear hatch closed and climbed inside, he drove to the back of the campground and onto the logging road.

They drove over the small rise down to the river, but he was forced to stop. A large fir tree lay at an angle across the water, blocking their way.

Wesley shut off the engine and climbed out, while Jamie did the same, then they walked down to the rushing water to assess the situation. He looked downriver at the base of the tree, with its roots tangled in a ball of dirt pulled from the bank. "I'll drag a cable across and attach it to the top, and then you can pull it out of the way with my winch."

Jamie stared up at him. "You want me to drive?"

"I'll already be on the other side. When the tree floats downstream, I won't be able to get back across, so you have to do it."

Jamie glanced back at the kids in the Hummer and then looked at Wesley. "You'll be lucky just to make it across. How about I go across and you drive?"

"You'll be fine. I'll show you how to use the winch."

Jamie watched him plug in the cable and unlock the reel, and then waited while he walked along the bank to the tree trunk, dragging the cable behind him. "Be careful, Wesley."

Wesley gave her a nod as he waded out to the tree, then held on to the branches while working his way forward, checking the depth. The water was much deeper than he thought, with the mud underneath slick. The current dragged against his legs, threatening to pull him under the tree as he made his way to the middle of the river.

The sound of clattering rocks made him turn around as the ball of tree roots suddenly rolled down the bank, but he could not hang on as the water dragged him under the tree. With nothing to grab, he tumbled over and over down the river. Water rushed down his throat as he gasped for air, with no control over where the water was taking him.

***

"Wesley!" Jamie screamed, watching him tumble away until he was swept around the corner and out of sight. She stared down the river, but Wesley was gone. She stared at the ground as she walked in a circle, trying to accept what had just happened, then stopped and stared down the river as tears blurred her vision. "Wesley?" she whispered.

She jumped back when the roots tore loose from the bank, dragging the rest of the tree downriver. She wiped her eyes, went to the Hummer, and then leaned back against the front, not really seeing anything in particular.

Serra stared through the windshield, watching the events. She opened the door and climbed out, then went around and stood in front of Jamie, but she didn't seem to notice. "Jamie?"

Jamie looked up and wiped her eyes. "I'm not sure if we can make it across without Wesley."

"I heard what he said. He thought you could do it."

Jamie straightened up from the Hummer. "You're right. I can do this."

She walked around to get in and noticed the cord for the winch and the loose cable. "I can do this."

She followed Wesley's instructions and reeled in the cable, then unplugged the power and climbed into the Hummer. She tossed it onto the floor and started the engine, and when Serra climbed in front and closed the door, she looked over at her. "Here we go."

Jamie eased the Hummer into the water, and then suddenly remembered it coming up the side of the doors. "Serra? Roll your window up."

While Serra did as asked, Jamie continued forward, her knuckles turning white on the steering wheel as the Hummer crawled across the river for what seemed forever. The water rushed off the hood as they crawled up the other side, and she released her breath and looked at her passengers. "We did it!"

She continued forward until they were on flat ground, then shut off the engine and climbed out. They were higher on this side, and she shaded her eyes as she stared down river, but there was no sign of Wesley. She reached inside to grab a radio, but it was no longer on the seat and she looked across at Serra. "Did you see a portable radio anywhere?"

Serra reached down to the floor and felt around in a pool of water, then grabbed the rubber antenna on the radio and held it up as water drained out the bottom. "I guess my door wasn't closed all the way."

Jamie looked over the hood, trying to maintain her cool. "That's just great!" She told her, then climbed inside and drove up the dirt road.

Chapter 40

THE ISLAND:

While Dieter drove the motorboat slowly across from the stern of the *Mystic* to the island, Alex remained standing, enjoying the feel of the breeze through his hair. A few moments later, Dieter nudged the bow against the narrow strip of rock-strewn beach, where Alex tossed the anchor onto the gravel, then jumped off to pull the boat farther onto shore. He held it in place while Mike and Dieter climbed out, then they strolled across the beach to the V-shaped notch in the side of the volcanic crater.

Steps had been carved into the rock face leading up through the opening, and Alex climbed up first. When he reached the top, he stopped on a wide flat area and looked down into the two hundred fifty foot wide crater. Directly below him was a small pool of water, where the ship from the movie was now a rusted hulk leaning against the wall, with a decrepit-looking gangway across to the beach.

He looked across at the open cave, where the device was plainly visible on the ground halfway out of the entrance. A short distance from the cave, blackberry vines nearly concealed a mirror surface protruding from the solid basalt rock.

Alex turned as Mike and Dieter stopped beside him. "It appears Colonel Dieter wasn't fast enough. The tide must have dropped before they could get what they came for."

Dieter's adrenalin level spiked when he saw the ship. "The jewels must be in that cave."

When Dieter stepped around him, Alex tried to grab his arm to stop him, but missed as the captain climbed down the rock steps onto the rusty main deck of the ship. "Wait! That deck has been deteriorating for a long time, so the steel could be thin from all the rust."

Dieter stopped and looked up at Cave. "I am not one of your students, Professor. I know what I am doing."

Dieter turned and continued across the deck, then down the remains of the gangway onto the beach. Alex and Mike continued down the stone steps onto the deck, as Dieter ran up the beach and into the cave. When they reached the gangway, it was in better shape than it appeared, so they continued across to join him.

Mike ignored the cave and walked up to the massive silver object buried partway in the side of the crater. "How about an explanation, Alex? I saw your expression when it appeared on the television."

Alex could not believe they found the spaceship that had brought the devices to this planet. If it was not too severely damaged, they could use it to shut them down. "Well, Mike. It all started one hundred and eighty million years ago."

Mike looked into his eyes. "You're joking."

Alex grinned at him. "I won't start that far back."

He told Mike the story of the Dead Energy operation. "They were the first race of human inhabitants on this planet, and were advanced enough to travel in these spaceships, and they were forced to leave the earth when a super volcanic eruption killed all life on the surface. It's one of the few planets capable of supporting complex life, so they sent a ship back with these devices to clean the atmosphere. Unfortunately, they lost contact with it. Now that we've found it, all we have to do is deal with the pirates and I can call my friends for help."

"Do you think it still flies?"

"I doubt it. I'll be grateful if my friends can activate the shutdown code." They both turned when Dieter ran out of the cave.

"There is nothing in there but a big mirror!" Dieter yelled.

Alex was not surprised. "Did you really think those pirates would leave anything behind?"

Dieter clenched his fists. "Damn you, Cave! You knew this would happen!"

"I'm surprised you didn't think about it."

Alex and Mike walked over to the cave entrance, where Alex knelt down next to one end of the twenty-foot long, gray cylinder, like the one off Vancouver Island. The rusted remains of a chain hoist, and three splintered four by four posts lay on the ground. He touched the rusted chain wrapped around the one-foot diameter device, and then stood up. "They tried to move it, but the wood posts broke under the strain. It must be incredibly heavy."

Mike waved his hand across the beach to the rusted hulk of the ship. "The radio on Burk's ship would not have worked, just like with us, so they didn't have any way to call for a rescue. I don't see their skiff, so they must have used it to leave the island with that movie."

Alex walked back over to the berry vines and gently spread them apart while getting poked by the thorns. He reached through and placed his palm against the cool smooth side of the spaceship, then carefully pulled his arm back. A deep roar from the *Mystic*'s horn echoed off the walls in the crater, and he turned to the others. "It's time to go."

The trio hurried down the beach to the gangway, where Dieter ran up first. Alex allowed Mike to go next, while he looked along the side of the ship. Something about the double doors for the cargo hold was out of place, but he didn't see anything obvious, so he continued behind Mike.

Alex heard Dieter scream for help and they hurried up the gangway, and saw Dieter struggling to pull his left leg out of the rusted steel plating and grabbed Mike's arm before he made it to the captain. "Let me go first and we'll follow our original tracks."

When Dieter saw Alex and Mike suddenly slow down, he stopped struggling. "Get me out of here!"

Alex led the way across the deck, testing the areas near Dieter's footprints. Most of the deck was firm, but it was Dieter's luck to find a soft spot.

Alex stopped and grabbed Dieter's left arm. "Easy now. Nice and slow."

When Mike grabbed the captain's right arm, they eased him up out of the hole, and Alex bent over to check the damage to his leg. "You have a few deep abrasions, but you'll be fine. Can you climb the stairs?"

The roar of several screaming outboard engines echoed around the crater, and they looked up at the top of the V, then Dieter pushed Alex's hand away. "Go up and tell me what is happening!"

The roar of the engines idled down, as Alex climbed the steps and slowly peeked over the edge. Three large inflatable black boats were drifting around the front of the *Mystic*, and in each were four tough-looking men holding rifles across their waists.

Alex eased back from the edge and looked down at Dieter. "I believe they want their money."

Dieter grabbed Mike's coat. "I do not have any cash! I was going to pay them with the treasure."

Mike shoved Dieter's hand away. "How much do they want?"

"Two hundred and fifty thousand."

"I don't suppose they'll take a check." He noticed Alex suddenly stand up and look down at him. "What's happening?"

"One of the boats is coming this way, so you might as well come up." He reached down, grabbed Dieter's hand, and helped him over the top. "Can you make it down?"

Dieter looked up at Cave. "Yes. Probably to my own burial at sea." He turned and carefully eased his way down the steps to the beach.

Alex and Mike followed him down, as one rubber boat nudged against the shoreline, and Alex recognized the big man standing at the bow. "This should be interesting."

Dieter hobbled over to the boat and stared up at Blacktooth. "I did not find the treasure, but I promise I will pay you when we get back to port."

Blacktooth gave a hearty laugh. "I cannot believe you are so stupid. Did you really believe you would find a treasure?" He stopped laughing. "Where will you get the money? You are only a Captain."

Mike walked up to the boat. "I'll pay you."

Blacktooth studied Mike. "I do not know you, so how can I trust you?"

"That's my ship. I can give you fifty thousand in U. S. cash right now if you leave us alone."

Blacktooth laughed while he looked at his men, then stopped laughing and turned back to Mike. "That is too far from one-quarter million. No deal. I want what I was promised."

"I can get you more when we get to a port."

"No. I will leave you here and take your boat. I saw how fast it can go. I will take it to Russia and get much more than one-quarter million."

Mike stared back evenly. "How much do you want?"

A sly grin slowly formed around his black teeth. "One million, US."

"I can do that. Follow us to Seward, and I'll get you the money."

Blacktooth stared at Mike for a long moment. "I go with you. Three of my men, too."

"Deal."

"Get in."

Alex stepped up to the rubber boat and stared up at Blacktooth. "We'll take our boat back to our ship."

"You will go nowhere. You are a hostage."

Mike and Dieter were hauled over the edge into the Pirates' boat, and then Blacktooth smirked down at Alex. "No worry. I will leave your small boat and one of my men to keep you company. Dieter says you are a teacher. You can teach my man to speak English, yes?" He laughed with his men, and then turned to Alex. "Push us off."

Alex pushed on the hard rubber bow until it was floating away, then climbed the steps up to the V and sat on the edge to see what would happen next. A few minutes later, one of the other rubber boats eased against the shore, and then a hard-looking man with a short machinegun jumped off the bow onto the beach. Alex remained sitting on the edge of the crater, staring down at his new companion. "This should be interesting."

***

Okawna set the binoculars on the control console in the bridge and looked at Rita. "I'm not sure what's going on, but they left Alex on the island with one of their men, and they're bringing Mike and Dieter this way. As long as they have hostages, we don't jeopardize them."

"What about Lisa? I gave her a small pistol, but she's still in her cabin."

"I don't think she should hide. If the pirates find her, it would only make them lustful. Take her to the lounge and wait for us to make a move. We'll just have to wait and see what happens." He turned and looked at Harrison and Bartram. "What about you two?"

Bartram crossed his arms. "I'll wait and see what the captain has to say."

Harrison looked at the motorboat approaching the stern. "I'm on the side that doesn't get me killed, Okawna, so I'm with you."

"All right, I'll meet them at the stern with Bett and Joshua."

Okawna turned and walked out of the bridge, then down the outside stairs to the stern. As the boat drew near, he kept the shotgun over one shoulder and his pistol tucked visibly into his belt. While watching the approaching visitors, he continued over to Bett and Joshua. "The Pirates left Alex on the island with one of their men, and they're bringing Dieter and Mike to our ship. I'm not sure what's going on yet, so let's stay cool until we see what happens."

When the black inflatable boat pulled up to the stern, Okawna recognized the big man standing at the bow. "This may be complicated, so follow my lead."

One of the pirates held the boat against the stern as three men climbed out. Mike helped Dieter up onto the deck, then stepped up behind him and looked at Okawna. "We have an arrangement, and we will travel with these fine men."

Blacktooth stepped onto the deck, recognized the man in front of him, and grinned. "Jamison. So, you made a deal with Dieter. Did he say he would find a treasure?"

"Yeah, and I want my cut."

"There is no treasure, so no cut. He is a stupid man, thinking there is anything of value on the island."

Okawna turned and grabbed Dieter's coat collar. "You lying bastard! You owe me and my guys here ten thousand bucks!"

Blacktooth laughed. "No worry, Jamison. This man over here made a deal to pay me. He is very generous, so ask him for your money."

Mike realized what Okawna was up to, so stepped up to him. "I'll give you whatever you want, Mister Jamison. Just tell your men not to hurt me or my wife and daughter."

Bett stepped up to Mike. "Do as you're told, and no one gets hurt." She turned and smiled at Blacktooth, then spit out her gum. Blacktooth stopped grinning, looked down at the gray glob, then back at the smiling blond woman, not sure what to make of her.

Dieter was confused by what had just happened, but whatever Okawna was up to appeared to be working. He looked up when Harrison and Bartram stepped up to the railing behind the bridge, and shook his head no.

Blacktooth noticed. "Those are your men, Dieter?"

"That's right."

"Tell them to come down."

Dieter looked up at the bridge. "Come down here."

Harrison had a bad feeling about this, but turned and walked down the stairs, with Bartram right behind him, then continued over and stood next to Dieter. "What's going on?"

"I do not know."

Blacktooth pointed at his boat. "Too many to guard here, so you both go with my men."

Bartram stepped back. "Captain?"

"Just do what he says, Bartram. He will not harm you."

Harrison put his hand on Bartram's shoulder. "Let's do what he wants. Once he gets his money, he'll let us go."

Bartram reluctantly followed Harrison to the rubber boat, and they climbed in. He looked back at Dieter with an imploring stare, but Dieter turned away.

Blacktooth shoved Dieter toward the stairs up to the bridge. "Start the engines."

Dieter stopped and turned to face his captor. "Have you noticed a problem with your electronics?"

"Yes, our radios do not work."

"We have the same problem, and it's also affecting our engines." He looked over at Joshua. "Can we leave?"

"Yes. Use the thrusters until we get far enough away to use the turbines."

When Dieter turned and hobbled across the deck, Blacktooth sent one of his men with him. He had difficulty climbing the outside stairs, but made it into the bridge and engaged the thrusters.

Okawna watched the island shrinking into the distance behind the *Mystic*, and the three black boats following behind them. He wasn't worried about Alex dealing with the Russian, but knew the motorboat could never reach another island, much less the mainland. Right now, his only concern was regaining control of the Mystic. He turned to look at Joshua, while subtly indicating the bridge.

Joshua gave Okawna a look he understood his meaning. He knew when Okawna made his move Dieter would be useless against Blacktooth's man, so he walked across the deck and up the stairs to the bridge, while Okawna led Blacktooth and his two men into the ship, with Mike and Bett following close behind.

***

Alex watched the *Mystic* and the three rubber boats leave the island, and then looked out across the water at the top of the ice pyramid on the horizon. When he looked down at his new companion, he was checking out the motorboat. He had studied the charts when they had set a course for the island, and knew he would never make it to a populated area. If something went wrong on the *Mystic*, he would be stranded on this rock.

"Hey, teacher."

Alex saw the Russian motioning him down to the beach with his small machinegun, so he smiled and waved, and then went down the steps to the beach. "Did you bring any vodka? We should celebrate."

The Russian grinned through yellowed teeth. "You are a funny man. I speak a little English, teacher. Move to the water."

"Are we going for a swim?"

"Blacktooth say get rid of you and take your boat."

Alex hooked his thumbs into the front pockets of his blue jeans and felt the butt of his pistol. He knew he would meet up with the Russians eventually, so he had taken it with him to the island. "I didn't bring my swimsuit, and I don't want to ruin my new jeans."

The Russian was not sure he understood the teacher correctly. "What do you mean? You will not go swimming. You will be dead."

"Tell you what." He slipped his hand into his pocket. "Let's both get naked and swim together. I hear you Russian boys like to play with each other in the water, where no one can see what you're doing."

When the Russian cocked his head, trying to understand the meaning, Alex slipped the gun out of his pocket and pointed it at him. The Russian's eyes went wide, and he tried to bring up his machine gun, but Alex calmly aimed and fired. The Russian flew back onto the beach, and Alex strolled over and stared down at the red hole in the center of his forehead. "Das vi Dania, comrade."

He looked across the empty ocean and thought about his options. For now, the only one was to wait for Okawna and the *Mystic* to return.

Chapter 41

DISCOVERY:
Carl had been sitting in the recliner for over an hour as he concentrated on the image in his visor, showing the two mechanical arms illuminated by the lights on *Celeas*. He woke up early, knowing he would have to bring new cables down to anchor the drill head and it would be very time consuming.

He attached the orange hose to the drill head, above the clear ice, and was done. He loved his robotic girlfriend and smiled proudly as he set her on automatic hover. He pulled his hands free of the controls and reached up to remove his visor, then looked up at his three teammates. "Ready when you are, Doctors."

The four of them stood and walked out to the stern deck, then stopped to look over the railing into the hole. Ten feet below, two people stood on a three foot wide walkway around the inside of the opening. They disconnected the nearest coupling on the orange hose, attached it to a guide cable, and then climbed out of the hole. The supervisor standing at the railing pressed the control button and a thick metal iris slowly closed around the hose connection.

The supervisor looked over at Carl, waiting for instructions, and when Carl indicated to proceed, he began inserting the optical cable and the steam line down through the hose.

Carl looked at the three doctors. "The lens and the steamer are on the way, and we should see the ice in about fifteen minutes. I missed breakfast, so I'm going to grab something to eat." He turned and walked back into the ship.

Janice slipped her arm around Henry's. "Let's get some coffee before we go back to work."

Henry smiled and put his hand over hers. "Very kind of you."

Victor slowly shook his head as he watched them walk through the doors. *They don't have any concept of discipline,* he thought.

***

Twenty minutes later, Carl, Henry, and Janice returned to the observation room and found Victor leaning against the window with his arms crossed and a scowl on his face.

"None of you have any concept of the time restraints we're under," Victor snarled. He stood and pointed at the recliner. "Get in that chair and do your job, Mister Gregory."

Janice and Henry were stunned by Victor's outburst and looked over at Carl.

Carl glanced over at Janice and Henry before staring at Victor. "You're going to give yourself a heart attack, Victor. You need to learn to chill out once in a while."

Victor's shoulders sagged, and he indicated he understood. "I'm sorry, Carl. You just don't understand the pressure I'm under for the success of this mission."

Carl nodded, sat down in the recliner, then put on the visor, then slipped his hands around the controls. "Here we go."

Carl felt pressure from the recliner against his shoulders and the image from *Celeas* on his headset showed he was backing away from the drill head. "You can start the steam."

The three doctors stared at the two video screens in the observation room. One screen was the picture from *Celeas*, showing the progress of the melting ice being ejected into the ocean, and they could see the difference in salinity as the clear water began mixing with the salt water. The other picture was from the optical lens next to the steam nozzle at the bottom of the orange hose.

Victor was controlling the depth of the steam and the lens with a joystick type handle and could move them in any direction as the steam melted the ice.

Both video screens suddenly changed. The one from *Celeas* showed large white bubbles boiling up around the bottom of the drill head, and the one from the optical lens showed fast moving clear liquid rushing past the lens as the ice began to melt.

Victor slowly increased the depth and watched the readout on the upper right edge of the video screen. When the display showed three feet in depth, he rotated the lens to check the progress. A three-foot diameter bowl had been melted into the ice.

Janice grabbed Henry's hand. "It's working just like we planned. At this rate, we should reach the device in six hours."

"I hope you two are watching how I do this," Victor told them. "One of you will need to trade with me in a little while."

Janice looked over at him. "You make it sound so difficult. You're always so serious, Victor. Take Carl's advice and lighten up a little."

Victor looked up from his video screen. "I have to be serious, since neither of you realize the scope of what we need to accomplish."

"Everything looks good from here," Carl informed them. "I don't know if you can see it, but the anchor block is floating up from the water pressure from the steam and the melting ice. The cables appear to be holding it in place without any problems."

Victor looked up from the video screen. "This is going to take some time. The rest of you might as well go relax and relieve me in a couple of hours."

Carl set *Celeas* on automatic and removed his visor. "I'll keep you company, Victor. Let me know when you need a break."

"I appreciate it."

Janice slid her arm around Henry's. "You haven't seen the view from the top of the ship yet. Let's leave this to these young people and go for a walk."

"I saw the view when Carl brought me here, but I did not take the time to enjoy it. That would be nice."

****

Two hours later, when Henry and Janice walked into the observation room, Victor was still holding the control handle for the steam line. Carl had offered to relieve him an hour ago, but he had refused, stating he didn't trust anyone else to do it correctly.

Janice turned her head close to Henry's ear. "I think he's enjoying himself."

Victor could see their reflections on the video screen. "I heard that. I'm almost down to the device. Take a look."

Henry sat in front of the video screen with Janice looking over his shoulder, and could see the device another two hundred feet below the lens.

Janice went over to the recliner. "How are you holding up, Carl?"

Carl was watching the two video screens on the wall straight ahead, in case he needed to take control of *Celeas*. He smiled up at Janice and accepted the fresh cup of coffee she offered. "Everything looks good." He indicated at the picture from *Celeas*. "Victor is doing a great job. The hole down through the ice is thirty feet wide. That leaves plenty of room to bring the device to the surface."

Henry was getting a strange intuition about what might happen and swung his chair around. "Excuse me, everyone. I think we should stop for a while. We have made great progress, but we need to step back and think about this before we do something wrong."

Victor looked at Henry and shook his head no. "We can't stop now. We're almost there. If the water starts to freeze again, we'll have to start over."

"I'm sorry, Victor, but I must insist that we stop."

"You're not in charge, Henry. I am. We keep going."

Henry stood up next to Victor. "Mister Donner assigned this task to me, Victor. I *am* in charge. I insist that you stop."

When Victor jerked his head around and was about to argue the point, Henry put his hand on Victor's shoulder. "You have been at this a long time, Victor. We know how to melt the ice again. I think you need a break."

Victor sighed and leaned back in his chair. "You're right. I'm just worried that we might not get it out in time."

"I know. I will call Alex and tell him about our progress. Maybe he has some good news."

Victor moved the optical lens to the center of the hole and pointed it down at the device so the steam would keep the water melted until his return, then stood and stretched for a moment. "I'm going to the kitchen to get something to eat."

Carl did not know how long it would be before they would start again, so he instructed *Celeas* to come home and followed the group out of the room. Halfway along the corridor, Victor turned into the dining area and Carl continued with Henry and Janice to the conference room.

Henry sat at the end of the table and looked in his notebook for Alex's number, then pressed the buttons and turned on the speaker. After ten rings, he pressed the end button and looked over at Janice and Carl. "That was his satellite phone number, so he must be out of range on the ice cap."

Carl knew he was wrong. "No, the satellites can reach anywhere on the planet. There has to be another reason. I'm sure he checks his cellphone voice messages, so tell him to call you."

"Good idea." Henry left the message, and then stood. "Let us join Victor and discuss our options." When Janice and Carl stood, he led them out of the room and down the hallway to the dining room.

Chapter 42

MYSTIC:

Joshua took over the bridge for Dieter just as the electronics came on. He started the turbines and switched from thrusters to the jet pumps, then eased the throttle forward. The Mystic quickly got up to speed, and he headed for the large black boat three miles away.

***

When Mike entered the lounge, he saw Rita and Lisa standing on the other side of the table. He held his arms out as he hurried across the room, and then wrapped them around Rita so he could whisper in her ear. "Just go along with this." He let go and gave Lisa a hug. "Trust me."

Mike turned around to look at Blacktooth. "I'll give you what you want, so please don't hurt my wife or daughter."

Blacktooth stared at the women as if appraising their value. "You go in the helicopter and get my money. If all goes well, your ship will be fine." One corner of his mouth rose up, exposing half his black teeth. "If you do not come back, there is a market for your daughter."

"I'll get your money. Just don't do anything to them."

Dieter came down the stairs from the bridge and heard what was going on. "I should go with them in the helicopter."

Blacktooth held his finger up to Dieter, indicating for him to shut up, then looked over at Okawna. "What do you think, Jamison? Will he come back?"

Okawna smirked at him. "Oh yeah, he'll get our money. If he doesn't, I might even bid on his daughter myself."

Blacktooth gave a hearty laugh. "I like you, Jamison. Who flies the helicopter?"

Bett brought her shotgun up over one shoulder as stepped forward, rapidly chewing on another piece of gum. "That would be me," she answered, and continue chewing.

Blacktooth was momentarily distracted by the rapid movement of her jaw, then looked over at Mike. "My bad manners. I do not know your name."

Okawna stepped forward. "This here is Mister Allen, and this lovely lady is his wife, Betsy. That shy one over there is his daughter, Peggy. She's my favorite."

Blacktooth turned to Bett. "Okay. You fly Allen and one of my men to Seward and come back with my money."

Okawna looked over at Bett, who indicated she agreed, before winking at him. "I guess it's settled. My pilot will take Mister Allen and your man to get our money."

When the Mystic suddenly slowed down, Blacktooth went to the bottom of the stairs up to the bridge, where his man hollered down in Russian, then turned back to the group. "We have arrived at my ship." He looked at Bett and put his hand on the shoulder of one of his men. "This is Ivan. He speaks good English, so he will go with you. Go get your helicopter ready."

Bett turned around and looked at the dark-haired man with two parallel scars along his lower left jawline, sizing him up as an opponent. She turned around and grinned at Okawna. "Not a problem."

Bett turned and hurried out of the lounge, so Blacktooth indicated for Ivan to follow her, then looked at Mike. "Go."

When Mike hurried from the room, Okawna studied the last man, and the look in his eyes and stocky build showed he could be dangerous. He stepped past Blacktooth and hurried up the steps to the bridge, then continued outside to check things out. The black ship chasing them through the islands was now floating thirty-feet off the starboard bow, with four armed men standing at the railing.

Blacktooth walked up beside Okawna. "Now that I have this ship, when we get our money, I will upgrade to a fleet of boats."

Okawna did not like Blacktooth's insinuation. "I thought about taking this ship myself, but I know eventually the authorities will find my location with satellites."

Blacktooth grunted. "You are right. I will sell it for parts. I know a place no one can see."

Okawna looked down when the whine from the helicopter's turbine engine climbed in pitch, and Bett nodded up at him through the window. Mike was in the co-pilot seat, and Ivan was in the back, leaning forward between the seats. "We better step inside or the down wash will blow us overboard."

Blacktooth slapped his hand down on Okawna's shoulder and then walked onto the bridge. Okawna gritted his teeth against the urge to rip his hand off and shove it down his throat. He waited inside with

Blacktooth until the helicopter had departed, then noticed Blacktooth's strange expression as he stared out the rear window. "Is something wrong?"

"I am waiting for my boats to return with the rest of my men."

Okawna smiled, but it was not for Blacktooth's benefit. He needed to make his move and retake the ship before the rest of his crew in the rubber boats arrived. Right now, it was only Blacktooth and two men, so he gave Joshua the signal before placing his hand on Blacktooth's shoulder. "Let's go down and have that beer I promised you."

When Blacktooth turned around and headed down the stairs to the lounge, Okawna drove his foot between the man's shoulder blades, driving him face first down the steps. Joshua spun around and drove his fist into the guard's face, then grabbed the man's jacket with one hand and drove his fist into the man's stomach, over and over, until the guard crumpled to the floor.

***

Dieter was at the bottom of the stairs to the bridge when Blacktooth smashed into him like a sledgehammer, driving him to the floor. The stench of Blacktooth's breath rushed across his face, and he felt like vomiting. He desperately tried to push Blacktooth's stinking, thrashing body off his chest, but he was pinned like a wrestler.

When the guard stared at Blacktooth flopping down the stairs, Rita drove her elbow into his nose. When he dropped the rifle, she kicked him in the gut and drove him back onto the floor, then grabbed the machinegun and ran over to Dieter.

Dieter looked up at the rage in Rita's eyes as she brought a rifle butt down against Blacktooth's skull. When she hit him a second time, Blacktooth stopped moving, but now all that weight was on his chest, making it difficult to breathe.

Lisa felt frozen in place as everything became crazy in the lounge. She flinched when she saw the blood dribbling down the side of Blacktooth's head, then flinched again and jumped back as the guard on the floor stood up, his face a mask of rage as he yanked a pistol from his belt. She backed against the wall, feeling the pistol Rita gave her in the small of her back, but then it was all a slow motion dream.

When the guard aimed his gun at Rita, she reached back, grabbed her pistol, and swung it around to point at the guard. The gun was still moving when she closed her eyes and pulled the trigger, then a deafening explosion tore the gun from her hand. She opened her eyes and watched the guard topple back onto the floor, but she could not take her eyes off the jerking body and the blood pooling around him. She felt the bile rising and wanted to throw up, but her throat felt too tight to let it out.

Rita heard a gunshot and spun around. She saw Lisa staring down at the guard with a hole in his chest and rushed over, putting her arm around Lisa's shoulder to turn her away from the bloody body.

Lisa slowly looked up at Rita. "He was going to shoot you."

"I know. It's over now."

Dieter looked around Blacktooth's head and saw Okawna running down the stairs. "Get this stinking bastard off of me!"

Okawna reached down, grabbed Blacktooth's belt, and rolled him off Dieter's chest. When Dieter reached up for his hand, Okawna ignored him and ran back up the stairs to check on Joshua.

***

Joshua turned from the window as Okawna reached the last step onto the bridge. "Is everything okay down there?"

"Yes, we have the ship."

"Then we had better get out of here. Those rubber boats are coming up fast, and I don't know if they heard the gunshot over on that ship."

Okawna turned to look at the three rubber boats racing across the water in their direction. "Yeah, go." He looked down the stairs to holler. "Hang on down there. We are leaving."

Joshua shoved the throttle forward and twisted the joystick away from the black ship and the *Mystic* nearly leapt out of the water, as though sensing newfound freedom. The black ship and rubber boats quickly shrank away behind them, and he smiled at Okawna. "Where are we going? Back for Alex?"

"Not yet, or we'll lose radio contact with Bett. Head away from the islands for now and let them watch so they think we're headed to the mainland."

"What about Harrison and Bartram?"

Even though he detested Bartram, Okawna felt bad about leaving Harrison behind. "Maybe they'll make friends and take over Blacktooth's crew. I'm going down to get rid of some deadweight."

Joshua shook his head no. "Let me take care of it. I'll start with him."

When Okawna took over the controls, Joshua grabbed the man by the feet and dragged him out of the bridge, then hurled him over the railing. He went back inside and ran down the stairs, then stepped over Blacktooth's body as he looked around the room. Dieter was sitting on the floor, and the two women were standing near the table.

The shocked expression in Lisa's eyes only fueled Joshua's rage. He yanked Blacktooth off the floor by the belt and collar and tossed him into the walkway, not caring if he was alive or dead. He stomped across the lounge and picked the guard up around the waist with one arm and carried him out of the room. He stopped long enough to grab Blacktooth's leg and then continued out to the stern while dragging the big man's limp body across the deck.

He hurled the first body into the water and then kicked Blacktooth over the edge. When the bodies sank, he turned and looked up at Okawna, looking down at him, and then entered and went back into the ship. He strolled into the lounge and indicated to Rita it was okay to leave, and after she and Lisa passed him on their way to the stern, he looked at the blood on floor and then went to get a mop and bucket.

***

Okawna looked down at the women on the stern through the rear window of the bridge, intrigued Rita had reacted so fast, and the grizzly scene did not seem to bother her. Joshua said she could shoot, so he realized there was more to Rita than he imagined. He turned when Joshua came up the stairs. "How bad is the mess?"

"I cleaned up the blood."

"Thanks. I think I'll check on Lisa. It's a shame she had to be part of all that ugliness."

"I know. I wonder how Bett is doing with Ivan."

"She let me know she could handle him."

"Yeah, that's my gal."

"See you in a few minutes."

***

SEWARD, ALASKA:
Bett received clearance from the Seward airport control tower and set the helicopter down a short distance from the air terminal. She pushed the

radio frequency selection button, and then the stench of Ivan's breath blew past her face.

Ivan leaned forward between the seats to look at Bett. "What are you doing?"

"I'm just letting your boss know we landed safely." When he leaned back, she pressed the activation button on her headset. "*Mystic*, this is Bett. Come in, please?"

"Josh here."

"Just letting you know we made it to Seward."

"I'm glad you called. Our guests are being well taken care of, so I'll wait for you to call when you're heading back."

Bett smiled over at Mike and grinned before replying to Joshua. "Good to hear. Over and out." She took off her headset and turned to look at Ivan. "Let's go get our money."

They all climbed out of the helicopter, but Bett stopped in front of Ivan as she furiously chewed her gum. "You can't take that pistol into the bank."

"Okay. You stay with me and wait for him to come back."

Bett grinned. "Whatever works, sweet cheeks." She turned her head and looked for any bystanders, then spit out her gum. When Ivan's eyes followed the gray glob to the asphalt, she drove the heel of her hand into his nose and watched him stagger back. When he collapsed onto the ground, she spun around to mike. "Hurry and help me get him back into the helicopter!"

Mike grabbed Ivan under the shoulders while Bett grabbed his legs, then they hoisted him inside and he closed the door. "Now what?"

"We go back to the ship."

"What about Blacktooth and his men?"

"I imagine he's sinking to the bottom of the ocean by now. The *Mystic* is ours again. Get in."

Bett climbed into the pilot's seat and put on her headset. "Are you still there, sweetie?"

"I am. How'd it go?"

"Mike and I are on our way. Which direction?" She listened to the GPS coordinates. "All right. We need to dump some extra cargo on the way, so see you in about thirty minutes."

***

MYSTIC:

Out on the stern deck, a frigid breeze from the north blew across the water, and Rita wrapped her arms around Lisa. She could feel her shaking, but it was not from the cold. "It's over now."

Okawna walked over to the women. "You can go back inside." When Lisa looked up, he saw the tears on her cheeks and was heartbroken she had been forced to kill someone. "It was not your fault, Lisa. You saved Rita's life. The rest of us, too."

Lisa finally stopped shivering. "I suppose so. I've never seen a dead person before." Her lips formed a humorless smile. "That was the first time I've fired a gun. I guess it was a lucky shot, because I had my eyes closed when I pulled the trigger."

Joshua stepped out of the bridge and looked down over the railing at the group. "Bett is on her way back and should be here in half an hour. They're also missing a passenger."

Okawna looked at the women. "Let's go back inside, where it's warm."

Okawna led Rita and Lisa into the ship, where he found Dieter sitting at the table with a bottle of vodka in front of him. "When we get Alex, you better hope he's in a good mood."

Dieter picked up the bottle and held it out to the group. "Here's to you, Okawna. Our savior."

When Rita noticed the flames in Okawna's eyes, she grabbed his arm. "Not now."

Okawna jerked his arm free and stomped across to the table, and then stood over Dieter, glaring down at him, but when the man looked up and grinned, it was all he could stand. He grabbed Dieter's jacket and slammed him back against the wall. "None of this would have happened if it wasn't for you, you greedy bastard! I should toss you over the side!"

Dieter stared up into the savage eyes. "You are not a murderer, Okawna. Do not start now."

Okawna shoved him back one last time and let go. "Don't push it, Dieter. I've always enjoyed trying something new."

Lisa moved over to Okawna and held his hand while looking up into his eyes. "I've seen enough violence today. Please leave him alone for now?"

Okawna eased his hand from Lisa, then turned and headed out of the room. He stopped at the bottom of the stairs up to the bridge to glare at Dieter one last time and then headed up to join Joshua.

***

THE ISLAND:

Alex used his foot to roll the Russian's body into the ocean, then walked over and climbed the steps up to the rim of the crater. He continued down the other side, then across the rusted deck to the gangway. When he looked over the side, he saw the hatch covers were farther forward, so he studied the deck and remnants of the handrails.

He eased his way along the ship until he was directly above the hatches and looked over the side. Five-feet below the doors, water filled the six-foot gap between the ship and the beach, so without a ladder, there was no way to look inside.

He climbed down the gangway and hiked up the beach and into the cave. Ten-feet inside the opening, he found a skeleton wearing a German Officer's uniform, so he stopped. He heard the tinkling of running water from inside and moved past the bones to the back of the cave.

His eyes slowly adjusted, and he saw water trickling from a crack in the rock. He moved closer, and the liquid was streaming down into a handmade bowl carved into the solid rock on the ground. He reached out and let the water flow through his fingers, brought some up to his tongue, and smiled. It was fresh water from deep underground, which explained how the blackberry vines could take over the inside of the crater.

He knelt down and scooped two handfuls into his mouth, then saw the light from the entrance reflected in a small area of silver surface on the side of the cave. There was a section of the volcanic rock on the ground beneath it, but when he pulled on the ragged edge around the silver surface, the stone was hard, so he stopped before he tore up his fingers.

It gave him an idea, so he hurried out of the cave and grabbed the longest piece of the busted four by four, then carried it over to where the berry bushes met the side of the rock. He used it to pry the brush away from the spaceship protruding from the side of the crater, while suffering through pokes and scratches until he could see most of the ship.

He went back into the cave to drink and wash the blood off his hands and face. When he strolled back outside, he saw his white coat had several small tares, but it had protected his arms. When he looked at the area he had cleared, he saw the spaceship was tilted at a slight angle toward the beach. Only eleven-feet of the silver surface was exposed above the ground, with the rest was buried in the solid rock he was standing on. He knew for this ship to have survived the temperature of molten rock was a testament to the genius of that long ago race of humans.

He felt the frigid air swirling down from the top of the crater, while his breath left wispy white clouds in the air. Even if he had matches, the only wood was the splintered four by fours, but they would only last a short time. If the *Mystic* did not return, he would freeze to death on this chunk of rock.

He flipped the coat hood over his head and shoved his hands deep into the pockets, thinking about what to do next regarding the spaceship. He would need Lewis to take over this operation, but convincing him to leave Groom Lake would be difficult.

He suddenly thought about Wesley and the kids, and wondered what was going on with Mount Baker. For the moment, he was helpless to do anything for anyone. "Damn you, Dieter!" he yelled.

He reached down, grabbed a piece of wood, and hurled it across the beach at the rusted ship. It bounced off the side with a hollow thud and splashed into the water, and then he sat on the gravel. "Don't let me down, Okawna."

Chapter 43

MOUNT BAKER:

Jamie stared through the windshield of the Hummer, grateful the children were being quiet on the drive down the mountain. At one point, Serra had tried to reassure her Wesley would be okay, but she knew the rough ride down the river could have driven his fractured rib into his lungs. She fought hard to hold back her tears, thinking all they would find was Wesley's limp body.

There were no other cars in the lot when she parked in front of the ranger station and shut down the engine. She leaned her arms over the steering wheel while staring at the station door, hoping by some miracle Wesley would walk out of the building.

Serra felt bad about Wesley but had her own problems. "What are we supposed to do now?"

Jamie leaned back to look over at her. "Let's go inside and you can call someone to come and get you."

"I don't have anyone to call."

Jamie's frustration reached the breaking point. "What do you expect me to do about it? Wesley is dead because you had to get your precious junk!"

Serra opened the door but did not get out. "That *junk* is all we have. What would you have done?"

Jamie stared over the steering wheel at the building and then released a sigh of frustration. "I'll take you down to the store. Misses Sorenson knows a lot of people who could help you."

Serra closed the door. "Thanks."

Jamie started the engine and backed away from the building. When she stopped to put the vehicle into reverse, she looked at the station door one last time and drove out of the park.

***

When Jamie returned from the grocery store, she saw Larry's SUV parked in front of the station. She stopped and shut off the engine, then threw open the door and ran into the building and found Larry staring at the map on the wall, but did not see Wesley. "Did you find him?"

Larry noticed the desperation in Jamie's eyes. "Are you okay?"

Jamie tried to hold back her tears. "Not at all. We had an accident and Wesley was washed downstream. I couldn't follow him, so I don't know what happened to him."

"I've been driving around the park checking the damage, and I didn't see anyone." He watched Jamie's desperate look change to determination as she grabbed the doorknob. "Where are you going?"

"To find him."

"Just hang on for a second. I'll call Frank and we'll do a proper search. Wesley is a resourceful man, so I'm sure he'll be okay."

Jamie let go of the doorknob and stepped over to the map. "Show me an area, and I'll get started."

Larry grabbed a red erasable marker and divided the map into three sections. "Where did he get washed downstream?"

Jamie grabbed a blue marker and circled a spot on the map. "This is where the water tore out the road above the campground, and he was going in this direction before he disappeared."

"All right. You search that area below the campground, and I'll take this area to the east. Frank can search the area to the west."

"Got it." Jamie grabbed a fresh radio from the charger and walked out the door.

Chapter 44

DISCOVERY:

Henry knew Alex was having difficulties in the Arctic, and when he did not answer his satellite phone, he assumed something had gone terribly wrong. Now he felt even more pressure for the success of his mission to retrieve the device. He, Carl, and Janice had joined Victor in the cafeteria to discuss the next phase of the operation. After much debate, they had reached a consensus and returned to the observation room.

The device had not activated during the previous operation, and Victor insisted on finishing his task. Now the device was resting in liquid water at the bottom of the fault line. Carl had taken *Celeas* down to disconnect the orange tube, and they were watching her detaching the cables for the drill head. Carl brought *Celeas* around to one side of the thirty foot wide hole in the ice and dropped the heavy metal drill head onto the seafloor.

A scissor type grapple had been flown out to *Discovery* by a logging company on the mainland, and was attached to the end of a thick steel cable hanging from a hydraulic reel above the hole in the deck. Carl swung *Celeas* around the steel cable, wrapped the mechanical fingers around the grapple, then carried it over to the hole above the device and let it go. He backed her away, and the camera showed the cable slowly slipping through the water into the hole.

Carl set *Celeas* on automatic, grabbed the visor off his head, and then stood. "Now comes the tricky part. If the ship moves around while *Celeas* is down in the hole, the cable could snag and pin her against the side. She's not indestructible." He flexed his fingers and tried to relax.

Henry could see that Carl was worried. "Could you use a different submersible so you do not have to put your *Celeas* in such peril?"

"No, nothing with enough power."

Victor swung his chair around to Carl. "The Captain has his best men operating the thrusters. I checked and the water on the surface is calm."

"Thanks for making so much room to maneuver, Victor. That helps."

They heard a click from the intercom speaker. "The grapple has reached the device, Carl. You're free to take her down."

Carl nodded at the group. "Here we go."

He sat in the recliner and put on the visor, then slid his hands around the controls.

Captain Jordon walked into the room and closed the door. "I want to see this. She's quite a piece of machinery."

Carl heard him. "Don't be badmouthing my girl, Captain. She doesn't know she's mechanical."

"Sorry, Carl. Or should I say, *Celeas*?"

"You're a funny man, Captain. Okay, here we go."

Carl felt a trickle of sweat slide along his cheek. He had never taken *Celeas* this deep and the fathometer on the heads up display continued to climb. From his point of view from the visor, one camera was looking across the top of *Celeas* at the sides of the ice, slowly rising out of sight. The other camera was staring at the device and cable below. He would need to attach the grapple to the device manually, or he would not have taken her down this deep.

A bright blue light flashed in his eyes and he reached up and yanked the visor from his head. The others flinched at the bright blue light on the video screen before it went dark.

"Oh, no," Janice whispered. She spun her chair around and hurried over to Carl, who was blinking furiously.

Carl felt a hand on his shoulder and turned his head to look up, although the figure was hidden by the blue haze clouding his vision. "The device activated, didn't it?"

"I'm sorry, Carl." Janice said softly.

A knot formed in Carl's stomach when he realized why Janice was sorry. *Celeas* had just been crushed by the ice. "Listen, uh." He tried to be stoic about what happened, but it was difficult. "We should send down a rover and see how bad she is."

Janice gave Carl's shoulder a light squeeze. "Of course. I'll get started right away."

Victor stood and walked over to Carl. "Maybe the ice didn't reach her."

Carl swung off the recliner and stood. "The light wasn't as intense this time and my vision is starting to clear. I want to see the recording."

Henry swung his chair back to the video monitor and rewound the recording. "I have it ready, Carl."

The group huddled above Henry and stared at the screen as he pressed play. Everything looked fine for a few moments, then the light flashed and everything appeared to fracture before the screen went black. No one even whispered for a moment.

Carl stepped back. "She's gone."

Janice wrapped her arms around his neck. "I'm so sorry. I know what she meant to you."

Victor looked at the sad expressions on their faces and shook his head in disgust. "I can't believe you're all getting so emotional about a machine. You should feel lucky you weren't down there, too."

Henry stood and looked up at Victor. "Did you have a pet when you were a boy, Victor?"

"No. My parents considered all animals a nuisance and filthy. All they do is consume food and defecate on the floor."

Henry nodded in understanding. "I feel sorry for you, Victor."

Carl turned and walked toward the door. "I need some fresh air," he told them over his shoulder.

***

THE ISLAND:

Alex was inside the cave when he heard the crack of a lightning bolt as neon blue light flashed past the entrance. He jumped up and ran through the opening, but it was gone. A soft crackling sound echoed inside the crater, and he realized he had heard it before.

He ran across the beach and up the gangway then around the hole in the deck and up the steps to the V. When he reached the top, he slowly put his hands in his coat pockets, as he stared at an ice pyramid rising out of the water on the northern horizon. "Damn."

A soft, high-pitched whine suddenly echoed around the walls inside the crater. He spun around to locate the source, thinking it was emanating from the spaceship, then looked at the cave and saw the device was nearly transparent. A breeze suddenly blew over his head into the crater, and a small tornado formed over the tip of the device.

He ducked below the ridge out of the wind, then stared across the crater at a dark, shell-like coating forming over the outside of the piece of alien technology. He suddenly remembered what Lewis had told him. The devices were designed to attract the harmful molecules in the atmosphere.

It really works, he thought. The wind increased, and the dark material was slowly getting thicker around the device. "Time to leave."

He kept low as he crawled over the ridge and eased his way down the steps and then noticed the slight breeze from the whirlwind was driving the boat sideways against the shore. He grabbed the anchor off the beach and tossed it into the boat, then pushed the bow out into the wind. When the stern spun around, he jumped over the transom into the boat, and then stood as it drifted past the island into open water.

He hurried to the driver's seat and looked at the compass as he sat down, but the needle was slowly moving around the dial. When he looked out the window, he realized the boat was caught in the light whirlwind around the island.

He turned the key, and the engine roared to life, so he shoved the throttle forward and turned the boat away from the island on a course for the eastern horizon. According to the chart, the nearest land would be in that direction, although he knew he could never reach it, and was counting on Okawna to know what to do when the *Mystic* returned. When he doesn't find him on the island, he will search toward the nearest land to rescue him.

***

THE MYSTIC:

Joshua was still on watch on the bridge when Okawna suddenly jogged up the stairs and stared out the window. "What's going on?"

Okawna turned from the window and sat down in front of the control console. "Dieter is getting on my nerves. Too bad Blacktooth didn't get rid of him."

"I'm more worried about Alex. I'm sure the man who stayed with him was armed."

"That Russian is dead."

"How can you be so sure? You said Alex is just a teacher at a college."

"Before our current careers, we were operatives in the CIA together. Lisa's still a little shaken up. I thought maybe watching the television might take her mind off recent events."

"I'll go down and try to pick up a satellite signal for a news report. This has to be affecting the mainland."

"Good idea. I'll take over."

***

When Joshua entered the lounge, Dieter was still sitting at the table with his bottle of vodka. The girls were in the recliners, with Lisa's head leaning against Rita's shoulder, while they stared at the dark television screen. He continued over to his desk, sat in front of his computer, then turned on the television while selecting the satellite dish. A moment later, he had the signal of a news broadcast.

A woman reporter was seated at a desk, with global weather patterns swirling across the planet on a large screen in the background. In the upper corner of the television screen, a red sign read *Special Report*. The background changed, showing the central United States, so Joshua turned up the volume.

"This incredible change in the size of the polar ice cap has authorities baffled. The temperature in the northern latitudes around the world is dropping dramatically. Extremely cold air flowing down from Canada through the central plains is meeting an increased temperature flowing up from the Gulf of Mexico, creating a steady cycle of new tornadoes ripping through the heartland of North America. In France and England, that same warm water from the gulf is flowing north and meeting the frigid arctic air, creating massive hurricanes along the western shores of Europe, devastating coastal towns, and reaching inland to Germany."

Joshua stood and went to the table, then sat across from Dieter. "I forgot to ask. Did Alex find what he wanted on that island?"

"You heard what Blacktooth said. What do you think?"

"I'm talking about a way to stop the freezing, you greedy bastard."

"He seemed happy before he was marooned."

The intercom speaker clicked. "The helicopter is back."

Joshua stood and glared down at Dieter, desperately wanting to drag him out to the stern and throw him off the ship. He gritted his teeth, then hurried to the doors out onto the stern and stared through the window as Bett made her approach.

Once she set down and shut off the engine, he shoved the doors open and hurried outside as they climbed out of the helicopter. He wrapped his arms around Bett's waist and pulled her up for a passionate kiss.

Mike saw Okawna coming down the stairs from the bridge and met him at the bottom. "I owe you big time."

"Not a problem. I'm glad Bett was with you."

"Yes, me too. What happened to Blacktooth and his men?"

Okawna smirked at him. "They're fish food. Listen, Mike. Lisa is still pretty shaken up, so maybe you should talk to her."

"I will. What's our plan? Go back for Alex?"

"That's right. I'll go up and set course for the island."

When Okawna headed up the stairs to the bridge, Mike turned to Josh and Bett. "Would you mind securing the helicopter while I go talk to Lisa?"

When they nodded they would, Mike looked up at Okawna and gave him the signal to proceed. As they slowly gained speed, he went through the doors into the ship.

***

When Mike entered the lounge, he saw Lisa leaning her head against Rita's shoulder while watching the news broadcast, and Dieter sitting at the table. He took off his coat and tossed it onto a recliner as he walked over and sat across from him.

Dieter slid the bottle of vodka across the table. "Have a drink."

Mike stared at him for a long moment, and then slowly slid the bottle back. "Why didn't you trust me?"

Dieter stared at the label on the bottle. "It had nothing to do with trust." He looked up. "It had to do with money. You do not care enough about it, and I do." He turned and stared out the window.

"Like you said. I don't care about money. The adventure of the search would have been motive enough for me."

Dieter turned to face him. "I know that now, and I am very sorry I caused this."

Mike stood. "As soon as we reach a port, pack your things and get off my ship."

Mike went to the recliners and sat next to Lisa, but she didn't seem to notice and kept her head on Rita's shoulder. Rita was looking at him and moved so Lisa would sit up.

Lisa turned her head when she noticed Mike. "I'm glad you're back." She pointed at the television. "The weather is getting bad all over the world."

The picture only lasted a few minutes before they lost the signal. When Bett and Joshua strolled into the lounge, the Mystic quickly got up top full speed.

***

THE MOTORBOAT:

Alex was sitting behind the steering wheel when the outboard motor coughed and sputtered, then was quiet. He looked at the fuel gauge and saw the needle was below the red line, then he realized since they were only going to the island, no one had bothered to fill the gas tank. He stood and clung to the windshield for balance, while looking for land or a ship, but there was only the horizon in all directions.

He raised the aluminum frame to stretch out the canvas over the top and then fastened the clear plastic sides of the cover. After fastening the straps and snaps on the clear rear panel, he sat on one of the bench seats and stared out through the plastic windows. He remembered Mike giving the portable radio to Joshua before they went to the island, and now he didn't even have his satellite phone.

He shoved his hands deep into his coat pockets as he stared at the whitecaps on the water and knew this could get bad. With the wind driving the boat south, he would be too far off course when the *Mystic* tried to find him. He leaned his head back and closed his eyes, wondering if he would die out here, then the corners of his lips moved up into a skeptical grin. *Not for a while,* he thought, and would just have to see where the rest of the day would take him.

Chapter 45

MOUNT BAKER RANGER STATION:

The sun was dropping over the horizon when Larry had radioed to Jamie to call off the search. If he had not ordered her to return to the station, she knew she would have continued all night. She Parked next to Larry's SUV, climbed out of the Hummer, and hurried inside. "We still have an hour of daylight left, Larry. Why are we stopping?"

Larry looked at Frank. "I'll see you in the morning." He waited until Frank had left, then leaned back against the counter and looked at Jamie. "It's been a long day, and the one thing I've learned since I've been in the park service is tired minds make mistakes. Wesley knows this mountain better than anyone does. If he's still alive, I'm sure he's found shelter for the night."

"I know, and I'm hoping he is, but he's injured."

Larry knew she was frustrated and worried, but also knew they were doing the right thing by calling off the search. "Why don't you stay at his place tonight? There's a chance he might try to make it home."

Her shoulders sagged in acceptance. "I suppose you're right."

"I'll see you back here in the morning, okay?"

She gave Larry a nod that she agreed and then traded her portable radio with one in the charging stand. She looked up at the markings on the map and then left the building.

***

In the parking lot, she looked at her black Mustang, but climbed into the hummer and headed away from the station. As she drove out of the park, she realized she did not even know where Wesley lived, only that it was north of the park entrance. She stopped at the store to get directions from Carrie Sorenson, who was reluctant, until Jamie pleaded her case about his injuries and the accident, and then she told her how to get to Wesley's cabin.

Upon entering the meadow in the last of the remaining daylight, Jamie's senses were stimulated by the sheer beauty of the lake, and surrounding evergreen canopy reflected on the surface of the water. She followed the edge of the lake and parked next to Wesley's cabin, and as she shut off the engine and climbed out of the vehicle, a gaggle of geese near water began honking.

She used a key attached to the ring to unlock the door to the cabin, then strolled around the inside. She noticed the pictures on the fireplace mantel and went over for a closer look, then smiled when she saw a picture of a beardless Wesley and the pretty woman in his arms. She thought he was a very good-looking man without the beard and scraggly hair, and wondered if he was divorced or widowed.

She continued through the cabin and found his bedroom, then sat on the bed. When tears blurred her vision, she laid her head on his pillow and cried.

Chapter 46

THE ISLAND:

Everyone, including Dieter, was standing outside the bridge, staring at something they never expected to see. A slow spinning whirlwind was extending one-hundred-feet into the air above the crater.

Using the thrusters, Okawna steered the Mystic around the island until he saw the small beach, but the motorboat was gone. He set the controls to stationary and stepped outside. "He must have left the area to get radio reception."

Mike remembered giving his radio to Joshua and turned to him. "Did you give mine back to Alex before we left?"

Joshua brought a radio out of his pocket. "I guess not. What if the boat was blown away by the wind? Maybe he's in the cave trying to keep warm."

Okawna stepped back inside and pressed a button on the control console and the deep roar of the horn echoed back from the island. Everyone watched the V for Alex to walk over the top, but after fifteen minutes, they knew he wasn't coming.

Dieter felt light-headed and grabbed the handrail for balance. "Maybe the Russian killed him and took the boat."

Okawna heard the slur in Dieter's voice and felt like hitting him, but resisted. "There is no way the Russian could have overpowered him. I suspect Alex killed him and had to leave because of the whirlwind."

When Dieter began to speak again, Mike saw the rage building in Okawna's eyes, so moved between them before there was trouble. "I studied the chart with Alex before we arrived, and he would head east, toward the nearest land. He would never reach it, of course, and he knew it. The wind would have forced him southeast, but even using the helicopter, there is no way we could cover that much territory. As much as I hate to say it, we might never find him."

Okawna had another idea. "I'm not giving up. We'll do the same thing the wind would do to his boat. If we head in a southeast direction, we'll find him."

"I hope so. He's a good man."

When everyone went down the stairs to the lounge, Okawna engaged the thrusters and moved the *Mystic* away from the island. When they were five miles away, the electronics came on, so he switched to turbines. He entered a southeast course into the guidance system and the computer took over control, then the *Mystic* quickly got up to speed.

***

Lisa could not stop thinking she had murdered another human being today and wanted to be alone. She left the others and walked into her laboratory, then sat in front of the computer monitor. When she pressed a button to bring it out of sleep mode, a picture of the dark material appeared, and she glanced over at the worktable, noticing that one of the small tubes was also missing. She slid the keyboard to one side, put her elbows on the table, and then clasped her hands to support her chin, while staring at the dark material on the monitor.

It seemed she had just sat down when she felt the speed of the *Mystic* decrease, and opened her eyes. She leaned back and stretched her arms, then noticed the time on the bottom of the monitor showed 4:00 PM. She stood and stretched before making her way back to the lounge, but the room was empty, so she climbed the stairs to the bridge.

***

Lisa saw everyone standing outside and opened the door to join them, but the sudden blast of frigid air was like a slap in the face, and her grogginess vanished as she walked over to the group. "What's going on?"

Rita turned from the railing when she heard Lisa's voice. "We can't find him anywhere, so we're discussing what to do before it gets too dark."

"We can't give up. He needs our help."

"I know, and we're not giving up. We just need a new plan."

Lisa looked up at Joshua. "Do you still have my sample of black material?"

Joshua gave her a blank look. "I gave it to Alex for the test."

"Do you think he still has it?"

"I don't know."

"Can you track the radiation, like you did with the stuff up north?"

"I'm not sure if I can detect a sample that small from a long distance, but it's certainly worth a try."

Joshua hurried into the bridge to turn on the sensor and saw a small dot flashing only twenty miles due south. He smiled and spun to the open door. "I've found him!"

Joshua entered the direction into the computer and pressed start, and the *Mystic* immediately turned south and slowly increased speed. No one wanted to leave, so the crowd on deck moved back into the bridge and lined the walls, where they could have a good view of the operation.

***

THE MOTORBOAT:

Alex opened his eyes at the sound of a horn in the distance. He heard it once again, slightly louder, and a smile spread across his face as he recognized the sound. He stood and moved to the stern to unzip the clear rear cover, then stepped outside and waved his arms at the *Mystic,* quickly approaching the rear of the boat.

Joshua stopped the *Mystic* thirty-feet away from the motorboat and spun in a stationary circle, then backed up slowly to block the wind while Okawna hurried down the stairs to the stern.

Alex saw the smiles from the crew on the bridge as Joshua eased back against the motorboat, then looked up at Okawna. "What took you so long?"

"The pirates didn't take the hint. You know how hard it is to get rid of party crashers. What happened to your new coat?"

"I wanted to see the spaceship, but the berry vines were in the way."

Alex heard a mechanical growl and looked across at Mike operating the hoist, which stopped with the straps directly over the rear of the motorboat. Alex dropped the plastic side curtains and canvas top and then helped Okawna attach the straps to the boat. Okawna signaled Mike they were ready, and they both stepped onto the deck while Mike brought the motorboat out of the water and swung it around to the storage bracket.

While Mike put away the control box, Alex helped Okawna strap the boat in place. "What happened after you left with the pirates?"

Okawna told the story. "I hope Harrison and Bartram make friends easily."

"How is Lisa holding up?"

"She was really worried about you."

Mike moved over to join them. "That helped to distract her from what she went through today. She's the reason we found you, by the way. She wanted her sample of the black material back from Josh, and he said you had it."

Alex frowned, checked all his pockets, and found the small plastic tube in the chest pocket of his coat. He held it up so the others could see it. "I'll give it to her later." He turned to Mike. "What's the latest news about the freezing?"

"It's getting bad, Alex. The weather is worsening all around the world."

"We should go back to the island and find out what we'll need to stop it."

"It won't be easy. We saw a small cyclone spiraling up out of the crater."

"I thought that might happen. That's why I got away from there. I know a few smart people who might help us."

Okawna looked at the stairs up to the bridge. "I'll go relieve Josh."

"All right. I'll get my phone and join you."

***

When Alex went into the ship, Rita and Bett were waiting just inside the walkway. After receiving a hug from Bett, he wrapped his arms around Rita's waist and smiled. "I was hoping I'd see you again."

Rita Wrapped her arms around his neck and gave him a warm kiss on the lips. "Me, too."

Alex looked over Rita's shoulder. "Where's Lisa?"

"We told her to wait for you in the lounge."

"All right. I'll go talk to her."

When Alex tried to move away from her, Rita made him stop and looked up into his eyes. "You know she has a crush on you, don't you?"

"Still? I thought after knowing you and I are together, she would have stopped."

Rita let go of him. "Just be gentle with her."

When Alex walked into the lounge, the sad, pleading expression in Lisa's eyes broke his heart, so he went over to her and held out the sample. "I believe this is yours."

Lisa burst into tears and threw her arms around Alex's neck. "I was so worried about you. After everything that happened, I thought I might never see you again."

Alex wrapped his arms around her waist to hold her close and felt her body jerk with deep sobs. After a few moments, she let go and wiped the tears from her cheeks, so he smiled at her. "Thanks for rescuing me. I understand it was your idea."

She gave him a small smile. "You're welcome. What happened to your coat?"

"I tangled with a blackberry bush and it almost won. I need to make a few calls, so I'll see you in a little while."

"Okay."

He turned and hurried over to the stairs, and then down to his cabin, feeling relieved to be back. He grabbed the satellite phone from the charger on the dresser and then went up both sets of stairs to the bridge.

***

Okawna looked up at Alex and pointed at the radar screen. "That wall of ice is still moving south. I hope we can shut that device off before it reaches the island."

"I know. This is going to be hard enough just dealing with the whirlwind. It seems I have a few messages." He entered his code and turned on the speaker.

"Alex, this is Henry. Somehow, the device near Vancouver activated on its own again. Please call me."

Alex pressed the speed dial number, and a woman answered. "This is Alex Cave. I'd like to talk to Doctor Henry Heinz." He was put on hold and looked at Okawna. "You had my back again. Thanks."

"You should have seen the way Blacktooth acted like we were best friends."

Henry's voice came from the phone. "Alex?"

"I'm here, Doc. I found the original spaceship and one of the devices, so we might be able to shut them all down. I need you to convince Lewis to join me in the Aleutian Islands."

"I will try, but it is doubtful he will leave Nevada. You should contact that young man, David Conway. He knows the systems on those ships as well as any of us, and he was most helpful here at the base."

"It would be nice if you could join him. You two are our best hope of shutting down all the devices from one location." The phone was quiet for a moment. "Doc?"

"Of course. And I will bring the crystals to power the ship."

"I'll meet you in Prince Rupert, Canada tonight."

"I will leave right away."

Alex disconnected the call. "Sonja is next." He played her message.

"Hallo, Alex. The weather is becoming increasingly unstable over Western Europe. You must call me."

Okawna noticed his puzzled expression. "It was on the news earlier, and it looked pretty nasty over on that side of the planet. Something to do with a convergence zone, I think"

Alex selected her number, and a few moments later, she answered. "Sorry it took so long to return your call, but I've been busy."

"I am so glad you called Alex. The weather is getting very bad, but that is not our most serious concern. The weight of all that ice on only one side of the planet is causing the earth to wobble. If we do not stop it soon, the axis of our planet will change and everything on the surface will suffer."

"I might have a way to shut down the devices."

"How long will it be?"

"I'm getting everything in motion as we speak, but I don't know how long it will take. I have to be honest with you. I don't even know if we can get the shutdown command working."

"I appreciate your honesty, Alex. I will tell our friends what you are doing. Good luck."

Okawna grinned at Alex. "Man, this is the craziest situation I've ever been in. I don't even know what I can do to help."

"You already have by saving my life. Now it's up to me." Alex entered David's number, and he answered on the second ring. "How's the weather?"

"Hey, Alex. I was thinking you forgot about us. It's snowing here, and Marcia's worried about the change in the weather. Have you been watching the news?"

"No, but I was told what's happening. Pack your cold weather gear. I need your help."

"What's going on?"

"I found the crashed spaceship, and you need to get it working."

"Heck yeah, I'll help. We'll need at least one crystal."

"Doc is getting them and meeting us tonight."

"Where is the ship?"

"North of the Aleutian Islands."

"That's where the ice is headed, Alex."

"I know, and that's why we need to hurry. I'll arrange for a plane to pick you up at the Bozeman Airport to take you to Prince Rupert, Canada. I'll meet you there and bring you to the Mystic."

"Okay. What should I tell Marcia?"

"Just tell her I need your help to fix the weather problem."

"Right. See you soon."

When Alex entered Donner's number, his receptionist answered. "Tell him it's Alex Cave." A moment later, Donner came on the line.

"Alex? I was hoping you'd call. No one has informed me of your progress, and I was getting worried. The news about the ice sheet is causing a lot of panic around the world, and the President is hounding me for an update."

"I had a couple of problems, but I've located the spaceship and one of the devices that's not in the water. Henry has agreed to join us, and we should be able to give you an update sometime tomorrow. I need a jet to fly my friend David Conway from Bozeman, Montana, to Prince Rupert, Canada."

"I'll take care of it. Good luck, Alex."

Okawna looked at the monitor and saw the blue dot indicating their current position. "I'll set a course for Rupert."

"No, we need to see how bad the conditions are getting on the island first. That way, if we need specialized equipment, we won't have to make two trips. I can make arrangements once we know how to proceed, and have what we need waiting for us."

"The timing should be about right for filling our tanks with fuel, too. We're down to one quarter now."

"How did you know the motorboat would run out of gasoline?"

"I knew it would, eventually. I just didn't think it would be that soon."

"No one bothered to top it off. I smell food."

"No one felt like eating until we found you, but I guess they're ready now."

Alex gave him a nod. "Me, too."

When Alex walked down the stairs, Okawna adjusted the gain on the radar. They would reach the island in twenty minutes.

***

DISCOVERY:

Henry pressed the end button on the speakerphone and looked up. He had not even noticed his friends standing in the doorway. "I must leave soon." He looked over at Carl. "I am so very sorry about your *Celeas*. Perhaps if we succeed, you will be able to bring her home again. Now, if you would not mind leaving the room, I would like to place a personal call."

After everyone had filed out of the conference room, Henry opened his notebook. He entered a number and leaned back in his chair. A moment later, a voice came from the phone speaker.

"Hello. I do not recognize this number. Please state your name and the purpose for this call."

Henry grinned and lightly shook his head. "Louis, my friend. We have located the crashed spaceship."

"That is exceptional news, Doctor. How will you proceed?"

"Alex said it has no power. How do we get inside?"

"That will be the easy part. Getting the ship to function properly could be quite difficult. We have received images from the space station and the ice is continuing south across the Bering Sea. Time is of the essence."

"I know. Please send the plane to Bellingham, Washington. I will be there within the hour."

"Very good. Good bye."

Henry pressed end, then stood and walked down the hallway. He looked into the dining room and saw his friends sitting around a table, so he went over to join them. "Whenever you are ready, Carl, they will pick me up in Bellingham."

Carl stood. "Go pack your bags, Doc. I'll meet you at the helicopter."

After Carl had left, Henry looked at Janice and Victor. "It has been a pleasure working with you both."

Janice stood and came around the table to face him. "You make that sound so final, Henry. You'll be back to help with the recovery, won't you?"

"Perhaps. You should continue with the melting process and we shall see what develops."

Janice threw her arms around him. "Keep us informed about what will happen." She kissed him on the cheek and let go.

Victor stood and held out his hand. "Good luck, Henry."

Henry smiled and accepted. "I will call when I can." He turned and walked out of the room, and continued to his cabin.

Chapter 47

THE CABIN:

When Jamie rolled over, Wesley's familiar aroma escaped from the pillow. She smiled as she opened her eyes, but it slipped away when she discovered he was not lying beside her. She sat up and rolled onto the edge of the bed, seeing 8:12 AM on the clock on the nightstand.

After a quick stop at the bathroom, she grabbed Wesley's cellphone off the coffee table on her way to the kitchen, and then grabbed her coat off the chair on her way out of the cabin. She climbed into the Hummer, and a moment later, drove away.

***

Jamie drove into the parking lot of the ranger station, and Larry's SUV was already in front of the building. She stopped and leapt out, then hurried inside and saw him studying the wall map. "Anything from Wesley?"

"Sorry, no."

When she thought Wesley might be dead, she fought hard to hold back more tears. There was still a chance he was alive, and she would not give up hope until she saw his body.

She knew he would want her to continue what they had started and vowed not to stop until she saved the valley. "We should go check that logjam. It was getting close to collapsing yesterday, and we might need to warn everyone."

"I'll have Frank mind the station and we'll take my truck. Let's get started."

***

As they headed up a dirt road, Larry realized he wasn't sure where they were headed. "Which way?"

"Wesley and I found the logjam in the same canyon where he was washed downstream, so he could still be in the area."

"I doubt it. If he could walk, he would probably continue downstream until he found help."

Larry followed Jamie's directions to the area where they had found the blockage and parked his truck at the bottom of the ridge. They climbed out and hiked to the crest, then gazed down at the logjam.

Jamie saw the water was another three-hundred-foot further up the canyon. "It's getting worse, Larry."

"Your description didn't do it justice. I can see why you and Wesley are so worried."

"Wesley said the old dam for the reservoir will fail when this much water breaks loose. He said we should open the floodgates now and drain the reservoir before that happens."

"That will flood the river all the way to Mount Vernon."

"He thought it would do less damage than a complete failure, and the lahar wouldn't follow the river. It will take the original route down the mountain and destroy everything in the valley, starting with the high school."

"He's probably right. Okay. I'll call Frank and let him know what we are about to do, so he can warn the authorities downstream."

Larry grabbed a portable radio from the clip on his belt as he and Jamie hiked down to the truck, then he explained what needed to be done to Frank. They climbed in and drove down the mountain to the old concrete dam and reservoir, then parked and climbed out to stare at the torrent of churning water gushing from the overflowing spillway.

"This is bad, Jamie."

Larry walked over to a ten-foot by twenty-foot gray concrete building and unlocked the rust coated iron door. "I don't think anyone's been in here for twenty years. I hope it still works."

Jamie followed him into the building and grinned as Larry brushed the thick layers of spider webs from his head, arms, and chest. She took a few steps into the building and understood what Larry meant about not working.

Sunlight dulled by thick layers of grime on the two windows illuminated a six-foot cast iron wheel. Remnants of gloss black paint clung to flakes of rust on the floor, and a thick, rusted chain was wrapped around a sprocket on the end of a four-inch iron shaft. The other end of the shaft went through the center of the spokes of the massive wheel, which was supported by a heavy cast-iron base.

Jamie studied the old equipment. "When was this thing built?"

"That plaque outside said 1906. They did a lot of logging in this area back then and needed the water for a trough to float the logs down to the rail cars. I've seen pictures of men riding the logs like a roller coaster."

Jamie suddenly remembered Wesley's warning. "Crap. Wesley said the Cave ranch would flood if we opened the dam, so I need to warn them. My sister goes to high school with his grandson, so I'll call her."

When she pressed the speed dial, she was told to leave a message. "Jessica, it's me. When you get this message, find Derek Cave and tell him the ranch is going to flood soon, and it's going to be very bad. He needs to get his grandfather out of there right away. Call me when you can."

Larry could tell Jamie was hesitant to open the dam. "We can't wait just for him, Jamie. Too many other lives are at stake."

"I know, but I promised Wesley I'd warn them before we opened it. I just wish there was another way to reach him. Okay, so what do we do? Just turn the wheel?"

"That's right."

He grabbed one side of the heavy wheel and pulled, but it did not move. He tried rocking it, but it didn't budge.

Jamie studied the rusted letters around the face of the wheel. "I can see two arrows, and you're pulling the correct way for it to open. I'll push from this side."

When that did not work, they tried rocking it, but the wheel would not turn. They continued to push and pull in both directions, but it did not make any difference, so they finally gave up.

Jamie stepped back and stared at the chain. "Do you have any grease in your truck?"

"No, and we'd need a gallon of the stuff. We must be doing something wrong."

"Or it's just busted. Do you know how this thing works?"

"No, not really." He heard a click from his portable radio.

"Larry? This is Frank. Come in."

He grabbed it out of the clip. "Yeah, Frank."

"I told the Skagit River Valley Sheriff's Department what's going to happen, and they'll let everyone know."

"Okay. Thanks."

Larry looked at the iron wheel, then at Jamie. "We might as well go back to the station. Maybe Wesley will show up, and I'm sure he knows how to open this thing."

Chapter 48

MYSTIC:

After a quick meal, Alex climbed the stairs to bridge to relieve Okawna. "Josh is waiting for you. He said you have to eat it while it's hot."

Okawna grinned. "Now, why does that worry me a little?"

"It's fantastic. I'll take over."

When Okawna stood from the chair and went down the stairs, Alex took his place in front of the control console. A moment later, Mike came up and sat beside him to stare at the open water.

"Hey, Alex. I can't imagine what you were thinking while floating alone on the ocean. It's a miracle we found you."

"I thanked Joshua for that stroke of genius."

"Lisa had a little to do with that idea. She was looking forward to a great adventure, but who would have guessed little Lisa would save the crew?"

"Calling *Mystic*. Calling *Mystic*. This is the Canadian Coast Guard. Please come in."

Alex indicated the radio. "It's still your ship."

Mike reached up and grabbed the microphone from its clip. "This is the *Mystic*. Go ahead."

"We understand you have a Mister Okawna Jamison on board. He is being charged with murder on the high seas, and we want you to bring him to Prince Rupert as soon as possible."

"Who's filing the charges?"

"Captain Montego, of the merchant ship, *Condor*."

Alex looked at Mike. "I saw him in Prince Rupert. One of Blacktooth's men must have told him about the botched hijacking."

"We can't turn Okawna over to them. He'll be stuck in jail until they straighten things out with our government."

Alex smirked. "Getting there as soon as possible is a relative term. Just agree to do it."

Mike grinned. "Canadian Coast Guard, this is *Mystic*. I understand, and we'll be there as soon as we can. *Mystic* out."

"Copy that, *Mystic*."

"I hope your friend Director Donner sent jets to pick up our passengers."

"I'm sure he did. We should approach the island any time now. Are the turbines still disconnected from the computer?"

"Yes, and we'll keep them that way, so we will only lose communications."

"Who's your best pilot?"

"Dieter, but he's drunk in his cabin. Joshua can handle it."

"If we can manage to get close, I'll take Okawna in the motorboat so we can see what's going on inside the crater."

"I'm not sure that's a good idea. When we were there earlier, the whirlwind coming from inside the crater looked powerful."

"I'll have to chance it. We need to see what we're up against to know what to do."

Mike pointed through the front window. "There it is. The whirlwind looks the same as last time, so I suppose that's a good sign."

"All right. Take over and I'll send Joshua up."

***

Alex went into the lounge and sat at the table next to Okawna, then looked across at Joshua. "We're getting close. Okawna and I will take the motorboat over, so we need you to take over control of the ship. Stay a safe distance from shore unless we run into problems."

Okawna took another bite of food. "I'm ready. This is great, Josh."

Alex frowned at Okawna. "I'm sorry to tell you this, but you're a wanted man, Mister Okawna Jamison. According to the Canadian Coast Guard, you're wanted for murder on the high seas."

Okawna stopped chewing and stared at him. "You're kidding, right?"

"Nope. We are supposed to turn you over in Prince Rupert."

"Mike wouldn't do that. Would he?"

Alex shrugged. "He's a law-abiding citizen. As soon as we reach Prince Rupert, we have to escort you off the ship into the hands of the law." He winked at the rest of the crew.

Okawna grinned and continued eating. "You're a funny man."

Alex became serious. "I'm sure people in Prince Rupert will remember the *Mystic*. After you left the tavern, Blacktooth was speaking with the captain of a merchant ship named Condor, and he's the one who told the coast guard about the murder of Blacktooth and his men."

"I'll stay on the ship, but let's worry about that later. Right now, we have to get on that island."

As they felt the ship lose momentum, Okawna scraped the last bits of food from his plate into his mouth and stood. "I'll do my dishes later."

***

When everyone except Dieter came up the stairs onto the bridge, Mike stepped aside so Joshua could take over and gave him instructions. "The whirlwind is only affecting the inside of the crater, but the water level has dropped dramatically because so much of it is trapped in the ice. Just make sure we don't bottom out."

"Okay. I've got her now, Mike." Joshua looked over at Alex. "How do you want to do this?"

"The safety of the Mystic comes first, so once we're in the water, move a safe distance from shore."

Okawna turned and headed outside, with Mike and Alex following him down to the stern. Alex and Okawna climbed up onto the motorboat and took the canvas down to eliminate drag. After a few moments to fill the gas tank, they were ready. Mike retrieved the hoist control pad from its storage locker, brought the motorboat out of the brackets, and lowered it over the stern.

When Alex and Okawna climbed in to undo the straps, Mike looked down at them. "Be careful. I want my motorboat back," he said with a grin.

Okawna moved to the steering wheel to start the engine as Alex shoved the boat away from the stern. "See you in a few minutes."

Joshua surprised them by bringing the *Mystic* across the wind with her bow twenty-feet from the shore, making it an easy short ride to the beach. With the water level so low, the front edge of the beach was now a solid rock wall protruding two-feet above the waterline. The top edge tapered up across the gravel beach and stopped below the V in the crater.

Alex climbed onto the bow and waited as Okawna bumped the motorboat against the rock, then he leapt onto the shore, kicking the motorboat away, then quickly climbed the steps to the V and peeked over the edge. The device was covered in a thick black material, with a tornado spinning off the tip, but they were in luck. The tornado did not expand into a whirlwind until thirty-feet above the ground in the crater. He felt a small amount of wind being sucked into the crater above his head, but other than the rusted ship to deal with, they should be able to work on the spaceship with no problems.

Alex went back down the steps, and Okawna drove over to pick him up. He grabbed the front of the boat and leapt onto the bow, and then Okawna reversed from the shoreline as he climbed inside. "We are lucky, my friend. Now all we have to do is keep you from getting arrested in Prince Rupert. Let's go back. I need a shower before we pick up David and the Doc."

Joshua and Bett stared through the side window of the bridge, watching the motorboat back away from the beach. Joshua brought the *Mystic* around, bow into the wind, and when the motorboat was safely stored, he engaged the jet pumps. Once the *Mystic* was far enough away from the island for the electronics to work, he entered a course for Prince Rupert at full speed.

Chapter 49

MARMOT CAMPGROUND:

Sunlight was streaming through the window as Wesley opened his eyes and felt the cold concrete floor beneath him. Nothing looked familiar, and for a moment, he wondered where he was. When he turned his head, he saw the bases of two porcelain toilets under brown swinging doors, and remembered what had happened.

The river had been freezing cold, and daylight had been fading fast when he found the campground last night. He remembered the hot spring Jamie had mentioned and found the yellow rope around the trees, then followed the running water down to the river where they mixed. After sitting down in the warm liquid, it took several minutes before he stopped shivering, and even though it was comfortable, he knew he could not sleep in the open, and had returned to the campground, where the only available shelter was the bathrooms.

As he sat up, his wet clothes stuck to his skin, and then he gritted his teeth against the pain in his ribs as he grabbed the edge of the changing table to stand up. He realized he was in the woman's restroom and strolled outside.

A quick look around told him the campground was now an island in the river, which meant the logjam would be under even more pressure. He needed to get up to the dam, or at least find out if Jamie managed to get it open.

He was much closer to the dam than the ranger station, so he looked for a way out of the campground then remembered Serra's sedan had gotten stuck in the mud, not the river. He went down to check it out, but even from a distance, it was obvious the car would be useless. He looked upstream, where the water was barely moving, and headed up to check it out.

On the opposite side was a gully, too steep for a vehicle, but not for someone walking. He waded into the water and it was only three-feet deep, so he continued across to the opposite bank and walked uphill. He knew if he continued west through the forest, he would find an old logging road, and that would take him to the dam. The problem was, on foot, it would take him at least an hour to reach it, and he could only hope it would not be too late. He noticed his ribs felt better than yesterday and quickened his pace.

Half an hour later, he walked out of the woods and noticed the fresh tire tracks on the logging road. He knelt down for a closer look, and the pattern suggested an SUV had driven up and down the road recently.

He stood and followed the road, which eventually followed the side of the reservoir. He could tell it was at full capacity, which meant the dam was still closed. With the reservoir this full, a break in the logjam would easily overwhelm the system.

He continued down the road and stopped next to the concrete building, then stepped up to the door. When he turned the knob and pulled, it opened, so he stepped inside. He brushed a few strands of spider web out of his hair and saw overlapping footprints had recently moved around the room. He strolled around the wheel and it was obvious the giant mechanisms had not been moved in many years, but then he noticed a smaller set of footprints on one side, and wondered if they belonged to Jamie.

He grabbed the wheel for balance and kicked the rust off a flat cast iron rod sticking out from the base, just an inch above the floor. He stepped down on the rod, but it barely moved, so he stomped on it until he heard the thump of thick metal. He grabbed the wheel on one side and pulled down, and the screeching of grinding steel was almost painful as the wheel slowly moved.

The strain of pulling down set his ribs on fire, but he gritted his teeth and kept turning. Two more pulls were all he could take, and he had to let go, and as the wheel rolled backward, he raised his foot off the rod, and then heard the thud when the wheel locked into place.

"Oh, crap," he whispered between breaths, as he bent over to cradle his ribs.

He slowly straightened up and headed outside, then around the building to the wide, flat surface of the concrete dam. Fresh flakes of rusty steel lay on the concrete under the twenty-foot long, six-inch diameter iron rod. It was supported on two sets of concrete blocks, with chains to raise the massive slabs of concrete hanging down in the water.

The top of the blocks had moved up five-feet by his turning the wheel, and water dribbled from thick green algae clinging to the side of the concrete slab, now above the waterline. He walked over to the chain-link fence along the top of the dam and looked over the edge at the river below, and saw a ten-foot wide stream of water gushing out, one-hundred-feet below. The river was quickly rising up the banks, and he hoped the people downstream were ready for the flooding coming their way.

He went over to one of the concrete blocks, then sat down and wished he had the strength to continue opening the dam. At this slow rate of flow, the reservoir would take a long time to release enough water to make a difference.

He released a long, slow breath, hoping the fire in his ribs would ease up a little and he could open it a little more, but for the moment, there was nothing he could do. He wondered if Jessica had convinced her uncle to postpone the track meet, because if he could not get the dam open, a lot of people could die. He just needed a short break, and then he would try again.

Chapter 50

6:00 AM. PRINCE RUPERT:

The fog was still thick as a flatbed truck backed up to the *Mystic*'s stern and stopped. Okawna extended the arm of the hoist over the top of the load, so the driver could attach the straps to a twenty-foot long by ten-foot wide wooden platform. Okawna swung the load from the truck around to the stern and eased it down onto the deck. Once he locked the platform in place with pressure from the hoist, Alex's project was ready.

He stared along the pier until the truck vanished into the fog, finding being a wanted man stressful, and wondered how long it would be before Alex and Mike would return and they could leave.

He set the control pad into the storage locker and then froze when he heard footsteps approaching from behind him. He slowly closed the door and tightened the latches, then placed his hand on the pistol tucked into the front of his belt.

The footsteps stopped, and the air was still, and he heard someone breathing behind him. The far off ringing of a bell was muffled by the thick fog, and a dog barked somewhere on shore. He pulled the pistol, spun around, and aimed it directly at Dieter's head. "Going somewhere?"

Dieter set his suitcase on the deck. "I was asked to leave the ship once we reach port."

Okawna slipped the pistol back into his belt. "Don't you mean *ordered*?"

"Whatever you wish, Okawna. I just want to get off."

"Not until Alex and Mike return. It's just a precaution."

"You are a suspicious man. Mike could easily have me arrested, so why would I aggravate the situation? I only want to leave."

Dieter saw red and blue flashing lights approaching through the fog. "Maybe he is going to have me arrested after all."

Okawna spun around to look at the approaching vehicle. "It's not you they're after. Some of your friends filed a murder charge against me."

Dieter grinned. "A turn of the page, Okawna."

Okawna crossed his arms and glared at him. "You owe me, Dieter."

Dieter turned serious. "You are right. Blacktooth would have used me as bait. Find someplace to hide and I will cover for you." Okawna didn't move. "Go, before it is too late!"

While Okawna sprinted across the deck, Dieter concealed his suitcase in a locker. The door in the side of the ship was open, with a blue fiberglass gangway across the gap to the pier, so he went over. A moment later, a Prince Rupert Police car emerged from the fog and stopped alongside the *Mystic*. He watched two officers climb out, inserting their black clubs into their utility belts as they moved in front of him.

"Sir, is this your ship?"

"I am the Captain. What can I do for you?"

"We are here to take custody of one of your crew. A Mister Okawna Jamison."

"He left the ship hours ago."

"When will he return?"

"I had to fire him for insubordination, so he will not be returning. You are welcome to come aboard and see for yourself."

He stepped back from the gangway while one officer stared at him. The moment seemed to last forever, and then the other officer spoke.

"Did he mention where he was going?"

"No. Back to the States, I would imagine."

The officer looked at his partner, who moved to the passenger side of the patrol car and got in. "Thanks for your help, Captain."

Dieter waited until the second officer climbed in and the patrol car drove away, and then hurried across the gangway onto the ship. He expected Okawna to come out to thank him, but it didn't happen, so he grabbed his suitcase and strolled off the ship into the fog.

***

PRINCE RUPERT AIRPORT:

While waiting for Henry and David to arrive, Alex and Mike were in the VIP reception area of a private aircraft hangar. It came with a self-serve bar, and they were watching the updated news bulletins about the extreme weather. Behind the news commentator was a satellite image of the expanding ice.

The sound of jet engines became louder than the television, so they got up off the chairs and looked through the window into the hangar. A white Gulfstream jet rolled across the gray concrete floor and stopped thirty-feet from the glass before the whine of the engines dropped to silence. When the side door opened, Henry came down the steps with

David, and then the co-pilot followed them down, pointing toward the VIP room.

Alex moved to the door and held it open, and was greeted with smiles from his friends as they came into the lounge. "Thanks for coming on such short notice."

David could not stop smiling. "Are you kidding? I would have been disappointed if you hadn't invited me."

Henry grabbed Alex's hand. "I just hope we can complete our mission before it is too late."

David wrapped his arm around Henry's shoulders. "Our mission, Doc? You sound like a spy. We're here to save the planet." He noticed the rips and stains on Alex's white coat. "What happened to you? It looks like you wrestled with a wild animal."

"I was attacked by blackberry vines."

Mike walked over and held out his hand. "I'm Mike Tanner. Whenever you're ready, we'll take both of you to the Mystic."

Mike led them outside to the rented SUV and helped load the luggage. Once everyone was ready, he started the engine and headed back to the ship.

* * *

***THE MYSTIC*:**

Bett, Rita, and Okawna had cleaned out the three cabins for their new guests and had dumped the contents into the dumpster on the pier. Joshua was still asleep after staying on the bridge all night until they had arrived in Prince Rupert, and Lisa had stayed in her cabin since they had left the island. Mike called to explain they were on their way, so the trio migrated to the bridge, watching for headlights in the fog.

Okawna explained what happened with Dieter, and then stared at Rita. "You looked like a seasoned combat veteran in the lounge yesterday."

A smirk formed on her lips. "I did a short stint in the military."

Okawna stared at her for a moment, his curiosity now peaked. "Come on, we know Bett was a helicopter pilot. What did you do?"

"You can handle yourself, so I could ask you the same thing."

"No problem. I was a Navy Seal. Your turn."

Lisa suddenly stepped onto the bridge. "I thought you and Alex were spies."

"That's right. It was part of our job. How are you holding up?"

"Much better, thanks."

"Mike wanted me to ask you something when you woke up. He wondered if you wanted to go home. We all understand what you went through, and we wouldn't blame you for leaving."

Lisa stared out the window, thinking it would be nice to hold her mom. It always helped, and Alex didn't take her advances seriously, anyway. She turned back to the group. "I guess I need to see my mom. I'll ask Mike about transportation when he gets back. I'd better get packed."

When Lisa went down the stairs, Bett opened a fresh piece of gum and traded it for the old one. "Poor thing. Scientists aren't supposed to experience those kinds of horrible things." She suddenly stood. "Here they come."

Bett went to the outside door and down to the deck, with Rita right behind. Okawna hurried down the inside stairs and looked down the lower stairs to the cabins. "Hey Lisa. They're here."

Lisa was suddenly running up the stairs while Okawna waited for her, and together they went out to the stern. Okawna left her on deck with Rita and Bett and hurried across the gangway to help with the luggage. He nodded hello to Mike, then to a short, gray-haired man as they moved past him onto the ship.

Alex opened the rear hatch of the SUV, grabbed Henry's suitcase, and waited while David grabbed his, then shut the hatch and led the way across the gangway to Lisa. "This is my good friend, David Conway."

Lisa stared at David, and a shy grin crept across her face as she reached out to shake his hand. "I'm Lisa. Lisa Harding."

David smiled and accepted. "Yes, you are."

Lisa turned to look up at Alex. "I'll show David where we're sleeping. I mean, to his cabin."

"Great. See you when we're underway."

Okawna noticed Lisa and David smiling at each other as they strolled across the deck, so he stopped next to Alex. "A little while ago, she was packing her bags to go home. Is she going to stay on board now?"

"I guess so. I see my dock arrived in one piece. I guess we're ready to leave. Who's got the first watch?"

"Bett said she'd take it so you and I could get some sleep on the way back. I'll get us untied and tell her we're ready, and then I'll meet you in the lounge when we're underway."

***

Alex carried Henry's suitcase into the lounge and set it next to the short wall by the stairs. Mike and Henry were talking while moving around the room and Rita was sitting at the table, so he strolled over and sat next to her. "Where is Josh?"

Rita pointed at the floor. "Still sleeping."

"That's where I'm headed next. Care to join me?"

Rita reached over under the table to squeeze his thigh. "Are you sure you're not too tired?"

He grinned at her. "I'm sure I can stay awake for a while."

The *Mystic* began moving just as Okawna came in to join them. "It looks like I won't be arrested. I'll see you all later."

When Okawna headed down the stairs, Alex stood up and stretched his arms out as he yawned, then looked over at Mike and Henry, still talking. "I need some sleep, too."

When they ignored him, he held his hand out to Rita. When she accepted and got up from the chair, he smiled as he led her to the stairs down to the cabins.

Mike suddenly realized he and Henry were alone. "Well, Henry. It will take many hours to reach the island, so I suggest we join the others and get some sleep."

"Yes, that would be good for me as well."

Mike moved to the stairs and grabbed Henry's suitcase. "Follow me and I'll show you to your room."

Chapter 51

SPARROW VALLEY:

Robert Cave drove his old blue pickup truck into town, but had to stop at the intersection near the school. Several kids were stringing a white banner across the road between two light poles, and he waited for them to finish. Derek had told him about the encounter with the sheriff, and he knew it was useless trying to get Arnie to cancel the track meet, but he had to try.

The banner became taut between the poles, and *SPARROW VALLEY GOUGARS RULE* commanded attention in bright red letters on a white background. He continued through the intersection and past the high school, where the parking lot was already crowded with supporters from Darrington. Several motorhomes and camping trailers were parked on the football field north of the track area, and even the parking lot at the restaurant was crowded with vehicles, including the sheriff's patrol car.

He parked down the street and then strolled back to the restaurant. As he approached the door, the aroma of hamburgers and fries drifted out through the open windows. The bell above the door tinkled when he stepped inside, and a few of the customers glanced up at him as he continued to the counter and sat on a stool.

Molly set a mug on the counter and filled it with coffee. "Hey, Robert. Can I get you something to eat?"

"No, thanks. Just coffee."

"Everyone's getting excited about the track meet this afternoon. Since Darrington won most of the events in last year's playoffs, we all want to kick their butts this year."

Robert grinned and then took a sip of coffee. The room was suddenly quiet, so he set the mug on the counter and heard a familiar voice.

"Hey, Cave?"

Robert swung his stool around as Arnie strolled across the room and stopped next to him. When the sheriff slapped money onto the counter, he looked down at the one-hundred-dollar bill next to his coffee mug.

"There's my bet, Cave. Put up your money and let's make this official."

Robert slowly looked up at him. "That's my tax dollars you're betting with, Arnie. I'd be betting against myself."

Arnie heard a few chuckles behind him as he stared at Cave. Everything about him always irritated him. "So what? I earned it."

Robert looked around the room, where all eyes were on him, then up at Arnie. "It's not too late to cancel the track meet."

"Don't tell me you believe that crap Patterson was spouting about the dam breaking. Has that old hermit suddenly become a psychic? Or are you just afraid of losing the bet?"

Robert looked around the room at the expectant expressions. The rivalry between the two schools was more powerful than common sense, so he knew to argue the point would be useless. He stood, pulled out his wallet, and laid five twenties on the counter.

Arnie grinned and looked around the room, satisfied he had gotten the best of Cave, and decided to take advantage of the situation. He leaned forward and took a long, animated sniff of Cave's clothing. "I guess Patterson's not the only one full of horseshit."

Robert's hands clenched into fists, and the smirk on Arnie's face made it difficult to resist his urge to knock it off his face. He tried to step past him, but when Arnie shoved his palm against his chest to stop him from leaving, he could not take it anymore.

Arnie did not see Robert's fist flying at him until it was too late, and he staggered backward from the punch. It was the first time anyone had hit him since high school, and he wasn't used to it. He grabbed his jaw and moved it from side to side as he watched Cave walk out of the restaurant, and for a moment, he was tempted to follow him and continue the fight. The expressions from the people in the room let him know he deserved it, so he let the matter go.

Molly watched the sheriff turn and look at the money on the counter. When he reached down to grab it, she snatched it up. "I'll hang onto this until after the games, Sheriff."

Arnie heard a few chuckles and walked out of the restaurant. When he saw Cave strolling along the street back to the old truck, he climbed into his patrol car, ready to follow him, but a school bus load of Darrington students stopped behind him and he couldn't back up to leave. By the time the students entered the restaurant and the bus moved away, Cave's truck was gone.

***

SPARROW VALLEY HIGH SCHOOL:

Derek fidgeted in his chair, finding it impossible to concentrate on the teacher's instructions. He had not been able to contact Wesley since yesterday, and felt like leaving the room, but wasn't sure what to do if he did.

The school bells finally rang, and the classes were over for the day. Derek grabbed his backpack and leapt out of his chair, then ran to the door before anyone else. He slipped and lost his footing as he turned the corner into the hallway, nearly driving Jessica into the lockers on the far wall. "Sorry about that."

He continued down the hallway at a slower pace, but was eager to get to his motorcycle. It was only a half-hour ride to Wesley's barn.

Jessica hurried to catch up with him. "I just got a message from Jamie."

Derek stopped. "What's going on?"

"She said they're opening the dam, and you need to get your grandfather away from the ranch."

"This is bad, Jessica. It's not just the ranch. If they need to open the dam, it means the lahar is about ready to come down the mountain. I need to pick up Kristy at the middle school first, so tell anyone who will listen to leave the valley!"

"You know they won't leave."

Derek looked up and down the hallway at the students rushing to put their books away and get outside to the track meet. "Then it's not our problem."

He sprinted down the hallway and out of the building to his motorcycle. A moment later, the rear tire threw gravel into the air as he raced out of the parking lot. First, he had to make sure Kristy was safe, and then he would go to the ranch and warn Robert.

***

Derek slammed on the brakes when he arrived at the grade school and saw the buses were already gone. He circled the buildings in case Kristy was waiting for a ride, but the school grounds and buildings were deserted. He stopped and put his feet down while looking around, trying to decide what to do. "Where are you, Kristy?"

He realized she might already be at the ranch, so drove back onto the highway, thinking he might still have time to get Kristy and Robert away in the old truck. He shifted gears to slow down as he passed the store, turned onto the bridge, and once across, shifted gears again and raced down the road toward the ranch.

Two miles further, he slowed to stop. The river had crested its banks, and the water was streaming down from the mountain on his left, forming a twenty-foot wide, shallow river across the gravel road. From there, it continued down to meet up with the main river below the pasture.

It did not appear too deep, so he slowly drove down into the water, holding his feet up, until on the other side. He opened the throttle, and the motorcycle roared out of the water, leaving a long wet trail in the gravel. He stood on the pegs to see over the white fence at the water flooding the lower pasture and realized he was running out of time.

With the water acting as a level, he could see Robert was correct. The house and barn were sitting on a mound, but he thought relying on the island as protection would be foolish. Wesley said the lahar would destroy everything in its path, and the ranch would be washed away.

When he drove up to the porch and shut off the engine, he felt the weight of the satellite phone in his backpack, and was frustrated Wesley had not called back. He leapt off and ran up the steps into the kitchen, grabbing the screen door before it slammed shut.

When he didn't see Kristy, he draped his backpack over a chair and hurried into the living room to Robert. "Is Kristy here?"

Robert stood up from the recliner. "I haven't seen her. Did she go to the track meet?"

"No. She's smarter than that and knows what could happen."

Robert walked into the kitchen. "We had better go to town and find her."

"The road is already flooding."

Robert continued outside, and Derek followed him across to the garage, where they climbed into his pickup and headed for the bridge. Just over two miles from the house, Robert slowed down for the water across the road and stopped.

"When I came across on the motorcycle, the water was a lot lower."

"That's what makes this an island. This is always the deepest part when the river floods. It's about five-foot deep right here, and tapers up to the bridge, so we're too late to get across in the truck. Let's go back, and I'll call Arnie."

***

Jessica was correct, and nobody believed her story about the dam breaking. She climbed into her mustang and started the engine, then drove out of the parking lot. As she turned the corner in front of the main school building, she eased the accelerator down, anxious to get to their home on the hillside.

When she recognized a small yellow backpack on the ground in front of a little girl, she stomped on the brake pedal. The tires squealed to a stop, and she shoved the shifter into park, then threw open her door and climbed out, looking over the top as she waved her arms. "Kristy! Over here!"

Kristy slung her yellow backpack over one shoulder and ran across the grass to the Mustang. "I can't find Derek."

"How did you get here?"

"I made the bus driver stop here at the school."

"Get in. We have to warn your grandfather the ranch is going to flood."

Kristy climbed in and Jessica drove to the stop sign. When Jessica turned left onto the highway, Kristie stared through the right window. "I heard grandpa say he doesn't need to leave the ranch because it's on an island."

Jessica's phone rang, and she grabbed it out of her purse and handed it to Kristy. "Answer that for me, so I don't have to stop."

Kristy smiled and took the phone. "Maybe it's Derek?"

"I doubt it. He doesn't have a phone."

"My uncle Alex gave him a fancy one. He can reach all the way to Alaska."

"Answer it and find out."

"Oh. Right."

Kristy saw a picture of a young man on the screen. "I think it's your brother."

"Put it on speaker." Kristy held it out toward her. "I'm here, Danny."

"Jessica called and said she tried to call you. What's going on up there in the valley?"

"Everything is going to be flooded, and nobody believes me."

"I didn't understand everything Jamie told me, except you should drive up to the park as soon as you talk to somebody named Derek Cave."

"Already done. I'll call her when I'm on my way. Thanks, Danny."

Kristy closed the phone and set it on the seat. "I guess I should have stayed on the bus."

Jessica glanced over, and Kristy had slumped down in the seat. "You're safe, and that's what matters. We'll meet Derek at the ranch."

Kristy sat up as they approached the grocery store. "We might be too late, Jessica. The water is already all over the pasture."

"It looks like the road on the other side of the bridge is still good, so we'll be okay."

Jessica turned onto the bridge and noticed the water was ready to overflow the banks. Once on the other side, she stepped on the pedal and the mustang shot forward, but it wasn't long before she was stopped by the water over the road. "We'll have to go back."

Jessica backed the car up until she found a place to turn around and then headed back toward the bridge. When she arrived, the river was overflowing the banks, tearing massive chunks of asphalt from the road on her side of the bridge.

She stopped to shove the shifter into reverse as more of the road washed away in front of the car, then backed up onto the shoulder to turn around. She shoved the shift lever into drive and stepped on the accelerator, but the mustang didn't move, so she let off the gas and stared at Kristy. "We're trapped!"

"We can walk back and cross the other water. It wasn't moving so fast."

"You're right. Let's go."

Jessica grabbed her purse while Kristy got her backpack, then they climbed out of the car and hurried along the road as fast as Kristy's short legs could move. One hundred feet further, Kristy suddenly stopped and ran back toward the bridge.

"Where are you going?"

"I left your phone on the seat. Be right back."

Jessica thought about following her, but Kristy was faster than she imagined, so she crossed her arms and tapped her foot while Kristy disappeared around the mustang. She heard the door slam shut, and then watched Kristy run up onto the road, her little yellow pack bouncing across her back. She uncrossed her arms and smiled at how cute she looked, then her eyes went wide and her mouth hung open when the mustang disappeared. "Kristy! Run!"

Kristy looked over her shoulder at the road washing away behind her. "Jessica!"

Jessica tossed her purse on the ground and ran down the road, desperate to reach Kristy, as more of the road disappeared behind the little girl. When they met, she slung the backpack from Kristy's shoulders and grabbed her hand, dragging her along the road.

After several hundred-feet, Jessica looked back and slowed to a walk, then stopped to catch her breath. "Whew. That was close." She noticed the frown on Kristy's lips and the fear in her eyes. "Are you okay?"

Kristy looked up at Jessica and indicated she was, then turned and started walking away. Jessica caught up with her in two long strides, and then placed her hand over Kristy's shoulder as they continued toward the ranch.

Chapter 52

MYSTIC:

Joshua was on the bridge after a nice long sleep and a hearty meal. He was checking the controls when a flash of blue light caught his attention, so he grabbed the binoculars and aimed them north. His jaw dropped open for a moment, and then he grabbed the microphone for the intercom. "You'd better get up here."

Alex came up the stairs first. "What's going on?"

Joshua gave him the binoculars. "The ice wall is only twenty miles north of the island."

Alex brought the binoculars up to look. "Damn. We're running out of time. How much longer to the island?"

"Fifteen minutes."

The entire crew was crowding onto the bridge to find out what was happening. They took turns with the binoculars, looking from the ice wall to the small brown dot on the horizon. When they were within one mile, they saw the whirlwind was visible, swirling up from the crater.

***

THE ISLAND:

Alex was in the motorboat with David and Okawna, towing the wooden platform across to use as a permanent dock for the motorboat. The rest of the crew was watching them from the stern, except Joshua, who was minding the bridge.

The water level was even lower, exposing three feet of vertical wall below the beach, as Alex eased the bow against the shore and Okawna held one end of a thick rope as he jumped across onto the beach. When David jumped off, Alex backed the boat away from the shoreline.

Okawna and David lifted one end of the platform and dragged it across the gravel until five-feet hung over the edge in the water. When they lowered their end onto the gravel, the other end rose up out of the water, hanging four-feet out from the edge of the island.

David ran across the platform as Alex eased the side of the boat against the new dock. He knelt down and held the boat in place while Alex traded places with Okawna, then pushed the boat away.

Okawna drove across the water, then eased the motorboat against the stern of the *Mystic* and held it in place while Mike helped Henry climbed in. A few moments later, he eased the side against the dock, and David secured the boat with the rope.

Alex helped Henry out onto the dock and put his arm around his shoulder. "You're going to love this, Doc. Follow me."

Alex climbed the steps to the V with Henry behind him and then led him up to the top. When the Doc's eyes lit up and his mouth hung open, Alex smiled.

Henry closed his mouth. "Can you believe this, Alex? That spaceship was once deep inside the planet!"

"I know. Lewis's relatives sure knew how to build them rugged."

"I would never have dreamed a manmade object could survive the temperature of molten rock."

Alex was waiting for Okawna and David to come up, but could tell Henry was eager to get started. "This way, Doc."

When they stepped down onto the rusted deck, Alex and Henry waited until Okawna and David joined them. "This deck is thin in some areas, so walk where I walk."

The cold breeze from the whirlwind twenty-feet above their heads lightly tugged at their hair as they walked across the remains of the steel deck. Once down the gangway, there was only a light breeze and a soft whirring noise from the device as they continued up the beach to the side of the spaceship.

Henry was excited to show them his secret, then smiled as he reached into his coat pocket and brought out a small handheld alien device. When he placed it against the side of the spacecraft, a six foot high by two foot wide area of the mirrored surface shimmered and became an opening into the ship.

Henry looked inside, then turned and smiled. "It is the control room, just like the one at Groom Lake."

Henry spun back around and stepped through the opening onto a slightly slanted floor, but most of the room was too dark to make out any details. He shifted to one side when David walked past him further into the room, studying the interior.

Outside, Alex saw Okawna was eager to join them. "Go look around. I'll take the boat back and get the rest of the crew. I have a lot of people to inform about our progress."

"I'll go with you back to the dock and show them the way across the ship. That way, you can leave the area and make your calls."

They returned to the dock and Alex drove across to the *Mystic*, where the crowd was waiting on the stern. Alex tied the boat to a cleat recessed into the deck, climbed out, and looked at the expectant faces. "We got inside, and it's in better shape than we expected. Now they need to find a way to turn off the devices."

As Alex started moving across the deck, Lisa stepped in his way. "You said we could go over and see the spacecraft, Alex."

"I'll take all of you over, but you'll need flashlights. Give me a minute to get my phone and I'll be right back."

Lisa watched Alex hurry away and smiled at Rita and Bett as Mike went to a locker to get flashlights. "Can you believe it? A real spaceship!"

Neon blue light flashed overhead, and they heard crackling and popping sounds echoing from the north. With the wall of the crater blocking their view, they could not see what was going on and looked up at the bridge.

Joshua stepped out of the bridge and looked down at them. "The ice wall just got closer!"

Alex was coming out onto the deck and stopped to look up at Joshua standing at the railing behind the bridge. "How close is it now?"

"Only ten miles, Alex, but it doesn't seem to be expanding as far south each time it activates."

Alex ran over to the motorboat and climbed in, then looked up at the four people on the deck. "We're running out of time. Get in and see if you can help the Doc and David, and I'll let my people know what's going on."

Alex helped Lisa into the boat, and then Mike, Rita, and Bett climbed in. Alex drove them across to the island, and when they were safely on the dock, he shoved the throttle forward to full speed and headed out to open water so he could make his phone calls.

Chapter 53

RANGER STATION:

Jamie could not stand still and paced in front of the counter. She didn't want to leave in case Wesley showed up, but staying here made her feel helpless and frustrated and she kept wondering if she could have saved him somehow.

Larry was in his office taking phone calls, and Frank was sitting at his desk on the other side of the counter answering his phone, but she had nothing to do, and it was driving her crazy. She could not even search for Wesley without knowing where to start.

She stopped pacing when Larry jumped up from his desk and hurried over to the counter. "What is it?"

"I've just received a report a wall of water is rushing down the river. It seems someone opened the dam."

Jamie felt a sense of hope. "It was Wesley's idea, so it has to be him! I need to get up there!"

"Go. I'll call the Sheriff and tell him what's going on."

When Jamie spun around and ran out of the building, Larry heard his phone ringing and went back into his office. Four lights were flashing on the phone console, so he sat down and pressed one. "US Park Service."

***

TRACK MEET:

Arnie sat on the bleachers while staring at the parking lot, realizing he had not seen this big a turnout in five years. That was the last time Sparrow Valley was in the championship playoffs with Darrington. The visiting team buses had arrived thirty minutes ago, with the athletes now warming up at their various events, and cheerleaders from both schools were practicing in front of the bleachers.

He heard his phone ring and pulled it from his shirt pocket, but did not recognize the number. "Sheriff Parker."

"This is Larry Cob, up at the park. We're opening the dam so the river's going to flood. You should start sending people down the mountain before the main bridge washes out."

"Who in hell is opening the dam?"

"Your niece, Jamie, and Patterson."

"Patterson? Get up there and stop him. We've got a competition going on."

"It's not just the flooding, Sheriff. If that dam is destroyed, it's all coming down the mountain into the school grounds."

"That Cave kid told me about Patterson's paranoia, and I don't believe him."

"I've seen it myself, Sheriff. If it breaks, it's coming down the mountain, so you had better do something."

Arnie turned off his phone and stood to look around, then hurried down the stairs and across to the parking lot. Two of his fishing buddies were getting out of a pickup, so he walked over. "I'm evacuating the valley, and I need your help."

"Is that a joke, Sheriff?"

"I'm serious. What did the river look like down the mountain?"

"It was close to overflowing past the bridge, and we were wondering why."

"Listen, we've got to get these people out of here. One of you stays here with me and starts telling people to leave. The other one goes down to the bridge and stops more from coming up, and I'll send the cars down in both lanes."

"They're going to want to know why, Sheriff."

"Just tell them the valley is going to flood."

When Arnie's phone rang, his friends walked away to help with the evacuation then he checked and recognized the number. "Hey, Cave. The bet's off."

"I don't give a damn about your bet, Arnie. I'm trying to locate my niece, Kristy. Have you seen her?"

"Uh, no, I haven't. Listen, Robert. You were right, and I'm trying to get people to leave. I'll tell everyone to keep an eye out for her."

"Thanks."

Arnie watched two motorhomes drive into the parking lot and knew it might be impossible to make the visitors leave. He hurried over and told them to go back, but they thought he was trying to give his school an edge in the competitions. They didn't believe him, so he threw his hands up in frustration and headed for the bleachers.

***

THE DAM:

Wesley heard a car engine gradually getting louder and watched a cloud of dust billowing up into the air through the trees down below. Suddenly, a green Park Ranger vehicle raced up the road and slid to a stop in front of the concrete building. He stood when a car door slammed shut and Jamie ran around the corner.

Jamie ran up to Wesley and threw her arms around his neck, pulling him close and hugging him tightly. "I was so worried that I lost you forever. What happened to you last night?" She heard a soft groan and let go. "I'm so sorry. I forgot about your injury."

"I'm okay. I spent the night in the lady's room at the campground."

"What? Why the lady's room?"

"Have you ever seen the floor of the men's room? That many germs could kill a person."

Jamie grinned and lightly shook her head in wonder. "I'm just glad you're all right. How did you get the dam open? Larry and I both tried to move the wheel, and it wouldn't budge."

"You need to step on the release lever at the bottom. Otherwise, it's locked in place."

"I knew it was you when we heard the dam was open. Is the water level dropping?"

"Not fast enough. It just about killed me turning that wheel, and I couldn't get it open all the way. Give me a hand letting more water out before it's too late."

They hurried into the building, where Wesley pointed at the base of the wheel. "That's the release lever. I'll hold it down and pull on this side while you push up on the other."

Wesley stepped on the lever and heard the thud, then pulled on the wheel, and with Jamie pushing, it was much less painful. The chains and gears loosened with the repetition, and soon the dam was all the way open. He released the latch and let go of the wheel.

Jamie was impressed. "How did you know about the release lever?"

"I read about it on the internet a few years ago. It's a pretty amazing design for 1906. They used the weight of the concrete block to seal the dam, and they could bring it up to whatever height they needed for the right amount of outflow."

"Speaking of which, we'd better go down the mountain and check on the flooding."

"What about the Caves? Did Derek get my warning?"

"I called Jessica and left a message to warn them about the flooding, but I don't know if she got it in time."

Wesley hurried out of the building. "Let's go. I made a promise to look after Derek and his family, and I intend to keep it."

Jamie pulled the door closed as she left the building, then climbed into the SUV. Once Wesley had eased himself onto the passenger seat, she started the engine and headed down the mountain.

Wesley looked around the inside of the vehicle. "Do you have any water in here? I didn't have any when I walked out of the campground, and it was a long hike up here to the dam."

"Sorry, I don't. I'm just surprised you even made it this far with your ribs and all."

"It's nice to see you again, Jamie. How's my Hummer? I already lost my hat and snow cat, so I don't want to lose the Hummer, too."

Jamie stared at him. "Really, Wesley? With all that's happening, you're worried about your Hummer?"

"That's right. I won't be happy until I get my snow cat back, either."

Jamie shook her head in wonder as she drove down the mountain. "I'd better find out if my sister found Derek." She reached into her pocket, felt two phones, and brought them out. "I almost forgot. I grabbed your phone this morning." She held it out to him.

Wesley took the phone and stared at her. "You stayed at my cabin?"

"I hope you don't mind. I didn't want to go all the way home, and I hoped by some miracle you would show up."

Wesley stared through the windshield for a moment, then dialed Derek's satellite phone. Jamie pressed the speed dial number for her sister, and they both waited for someone to answer as they continued down the mountain.

Chapter 54

THE ISLAND:

David strolled around the interior of the control room, studying the different consoles. "I recognize most of these controls, Doc."

"The one we want will be different on this ship."

Okawna stepped into the spaceship with Lisa, Rita, Bett, and Mike, and was surprised to see the four chairs were designed to fit humans, but another thing bothered him. "If this thing crashed, where are the bodies?"

Henry looked at David, then at Okawna. "That is an interesting question."

***

THE MOTORBOAT:

Alex held the satellite phone up to stare at the screen, searching for a signal, and then one bar appeared. A moment later, he had two, and when he had four bars, he pulled the throttle back and shut off the engine.

The cold wind was whipping across the water, so he took a moment to put up the canvas top, then sat on a bench seat, entered his code for messages, and waited. After a few moments, two appeared on the screen and he pressed play.

"Alex, this is Sonja. Things are getting bad. Please call me."

"Alex, Martin here. The President wants an update, so call when you can."

Alex entered Sonja's number first for more information, and she answered immediately. "I just got your message."

"It is starting, Alex. The earth's axis has shifted one-degree off center, and the wobble will increase magnitude if we do not stop the expanding ice sheet. Our latest satellite image shows the bottom edge is almost down to the Aleutian Islands."

"I know. I'm just south of the islands right now, but we found something that might help. It's only a matter of time, but it's up to my friends, and there's nothing more I can do."

"Thank you, Alex. Bye, love."

He entered Donner's number and his receptionist answered. "This is Alex Cave. Is Martin available?"

"He's in a meeting with the President, Mister Cave. Can I take a message?"

"Tell him Doctor Heinz has entered and to sit tight."

"I'll give him the message as soon as he returns. Should I have him return your call?"

"He won't be able to reach me. Just give him the message."

Alex turned off the phone and slipped it into his pocket. For the moment, there was nothing more he could do, so he started the outboard motor and headed back toward the island.

*****

THE MYSTIC:

Joshua hated not being in contact with Bett and the others. He checked his distance from the island and adjusted the thrusters, and then brilliant blue light filled the bridge for an instant. He looked north, where sunlight glistened off the surface of the water below the wall of ice.

At first, it was interesting, but something was wrong, and it looked like the glistening was quickly moving toward him and the island. He jabbed his finger on the horn button and kept pressing it repeatedly while staring out the side window, hoping they could hear him and walk over the top of the crater.

Okawna was suddenly waving at him, and he used the thrusters to move closer to the beach, then ran out from the bridge to the railing and jabbed his finger toward the ice. "It's coming our way!"

Okawna was waving both arms away from the ice, and he heard him yelling to get out of there, but he hesitated, knowing Bett and his friends could be trapped in the ice if he left the island.

He heard Okawna yelling at him to get the *Mystic* out of there, or they will *all* be stuck, so he ran inside the bridge and used the thrusters to spin *Mystic* around, away from the approaching ice. He held the joystick and stared through the rear window, hoping the freezing would stop before reaching the island.

*****

THE MOTORBOAT:

Alex saw the flash of blue light on the other side of the island, but he was already at full throttle and still four miles away. All he could do was hope the ice did not reach his friends before he got there.

In the distance, he saw the *Mystic* off to one side of the island and knew Joshua was being cautious of the approaching ice. From his low elevation, Alex could not tell what the ice was doing, and relied on the actions of the *Mystic* as a guide for what was going on.

His knuckles turned white on the steering wheel, frustrated at not closing the distance fast enough. He watched the *Mystic* racing away from the island and saw the sun sparkling on the surface of the ice, moving straight at his boat at an incredible speed. The boat abruptly stopped, hurling him against the steering wheel and nearly driving his head through the plastic windshield.

He pushed himself back onto the seat, heard the engine screaming, and then it quickly overheated from lack of liquid water and died. He stood and ran to the rear canvas, unzipped the plastic flap, then stepped out onto the rear deck and held his palm up against the glare. He saw the top of the island was still another four miles in front of the boat, then looked toward the Mystic, only two miles away.

He felt the ice rising into the air and was knocked off balance, then crashed onto the deck. He got back onto his feet and stared at the island, as it slowly sank out of sight under the sheet of ice. When the ice stopped moving, he shook his fists at the sky. "No!"

He felt emotionally drained as he brought his fists down and opened his hands, and then stared across the empty expanse of ice. There was nothing to see except the horizon, and he realized he was now alone on an ice sheet, helpless to save his friends and family.

***

THE ISLAND:

Okawna watched the *Mystic* race away across the water, but he could not see what was going on and remained on the flat area above the beach. He jumped back, nearly falling over the edge as the water near the beach turned to ice. "Oh, shit!"

He climbed down the steps onto the dry section of beach, covered his eyes against the glare, and looked across the frozen expanse in all directions. Several miles away, he saw the small outline of the *Mystic* on the horizon.

He heard Mike hollering his name, so he climbed back up to the V and stared down into the crater at Mike and Bett at the bottom of the gangway. "We're trapped in the ice. I think the *Mystic* managed to stay ahead of it, but she's a long way from here, so it looks like we're on our own."

The sound of crackling and popping echoed inside the crater and Okawna spun around, and then fell back onto the ground as a wall of ice rose up from the beach. He could feel the ground shake as the ice wall crawled higher, and he knew if it was like the other times, it still had a long way to go to reach one-hundred-feet.

A moment later, the ground stopped shaking, and the wall of ice had remained outside the crater, now only ten-feet above the top. He stood and looked down at Mike and Bett getting up off the gravel. "Is everyone all right?"

When Bett and Mike waved up at him, he looked over at the spaceship. The rest of his friends ran out onto the beach and stopped to stare up at him. "It seems we're going to be here for a while."

Chapter 55

CAVE RANCH:

Jessica was holding Kristy's hand as they stopped at the water rushing over the road, then looked down at her. "I know we have to go across, but I'm a little scared."

"I can see Derek's motorcycle tracks in the dirt on the other side, so it can't be too deep."

"Okay, let's go for it."

Kristy heard music in her pocket. "I almost forgot."

She held out Jessica's phone and nearly lost her fingers when it was snatched from her hand. She looked up when her new friend put it on speaker.

"Jamie, I'm in big trouble. Where are you?"

"Up on Baker. What's wrong?"

"I was trying to get to the Cave ranch with Kristy, but the river overflowed and we're trapped."

"Can you get to the ranch?"

"The road is flooded, but we were just about to try. What good would that do if the dam breaks?"

"Wesley and I got it open, but the water we released is roaring down the mountain, and it will flood your location real soon. You have to get to the ranch as soon as possible."

"It's flooding already. That's why we're trapped."

"Where is Derek?"

"We saw fresh motorcycle tracks in the dirt on the other side of the water, so I think he's already there."

"Wesley is calling Derek right now, but you need to get going before it gets too high and you both drown."

"Okay. I'll call you back when we get out of here."

She turned off her phone and slipped it into her front shirt pocket as she looked down at Kristy. "They're going to call Derek to come and get us."

Kristy looked back along the road. "The river water from the bridge is coming this way."

Jessica turned around, and the road behind them was underwater. "We need to do like my sister said and keep moving before the water gets too deep and we're trapped. Are you ready?"

"Yeah, but don't let go of my hand. I'm not as tall as you."

Jessica reached down and put her hand around Kristy's. "I won't let go. I promise."

Kristy smiled bravely, then they headed into the water, but the farther they walked, the deeper it became. Jessica felt Kristy's hand tighten on hers as they continued, but it was already knee deep for her and up to Kristy's waist. "Are you okay?"

"How come the other side is getting farther away?"

Jessica looked up and the motorcycle tracks were gone. She looked behind them, and the road was completely underwater. "You're right. We need to move faster."

"Jessica, it's up to my waist. I can't go any faster."

"I know. It's pushing harder against us, too. Hey, the trees! If we can make it to those fir trees, we can climb up out of the water. Let's go."

The water started moving faster, driving against Kristy's lower body. "Jessica, I can barely touch the ground, and I'm slipping."

Jessica pulled her close. "Grab my belt." She felt the pull on her waist. "That's it. We're almost there."

She gained a few more feet, and then she was nearly pulled down into the water when Kristy's full weight yanked on her belt.

"Jessica!" Kristy hollered as she clung tightly to the belt when she lost her footing.

"Just hang on. We're almost there."

Jessica held her arms forward for balance as she dragged Kristy through the water, as it continued to rise, and small branches and leaves piled up against her waist. "Just a few more feet, Kristy."

Each agonizingly slow step was a battle to move forward. The branches and leaves kept building up against her waist, creating drag to force her backward from the trees, so she had to keep shoving them aside. When she finally grabbed a large branch of the tree, she was exhausted, but elated. "We did it!"

Jessica pulled them closer to the trunk and twisted around so Kristy could start climbing. When the weight was gone, she grabbed a higher tree limb and pulled herself up until she could stand on it, then reached down and pulled Kristy up to the next limb. When she thought they were high enough from the rising water, she stopped and gave her a shaky smile. "Wow. Okay. That was intense. How are you doing?"

Kristy looked up at her. "I'm freezing."

"Yeah, me too, but we'll be okay now. We just have to wait for Derek to come and get us."

"Jessica? I heard about the dam breaking and what will happen to the school, so I'm glad you found me."

"We're not any safer here, Kristy."

"Maybe. But if my brother knows we're here, he'll come and get us. I know he won't stop until he saves us."

***

TRACK MEET:

Arnie was having difficulty getting people to leave the school grounds, and most of the visitors gave him a hard time saying he was afraid of losing to Darrington, so they would not get up from the bleachers. Even the locals thought he was being paranoid and refused to leave, so he was pissed off with himself for not acting sooner, and frustrated with the spectators.

He had an idea and called the volunteer Fire Chief, Tyler Masterson. "Where are you right now?"

"Hello, Sheriff. I'm in the bleachers, waiting for the games to start."

Arnie walked to the bottom of the bleachers and searched for Tyler among the dozens of faces sitting in the benches. When he saw Tyler stand up, he turned off the phone and waved him down onto the field. A few moments later, Tyler stopped in front of him. "You need to activate the fire alarms."

Tyler shook his head no. "The alarms will be like forfeiting the games. We can beat Darrington this year, Sheriff. We can't let them win by default."

"I know, but we have an emergency. There's a chance the dam could break, and it will come straight down into this field. I've been telling people to head back down the mountain, but they won't listen. If we set off the alarms, they'll have to leave."

"Who told you about the dam?"

"Larry Cobb, from up at the park."

"That dam has been there for over a hundred years, Sheriff. Are you sure about this?"

"Patterson's the one who told Larry about it, and I know what you're thinking. He's a crazy old hermit, but Robert Cave's son, Alex, was here a few days ago, and he thinks it could happen, too. I would rather play it safe and get everyone out of the valley."

"All right, but if it doesn't happen, it could ruin your chances for re-election."

"That's the least of my worries right now. Just turn the alarms on so we can get these people out of here." He saw the skepticism in Tyler's eyes, but the fire chief nodded assent, and then headed toward the school buildings.

Arnie turned and looked at all the kids enjoying the games. "I just hope this works."

Chapter 56

THE ICE SHEET:

Alex stared across the empty expanse of frozen water to where the island had disappeared as he considered his situation. His friends were dead, the mission was a failure, and he was alone on thousands of miles of ice. It felt as if something was deliberately blocking his every attempt to shut down the devices. For now, his only option would be to make it to the Mystic.

When he swung his foot over the side of the boat, he suddenly remembered Sonja telling him about people stepping onto the ice and immediately freezing. He gently lowered the sole of his shoe onto the surface and jerked it back, then did it again for several seconds with the same result. He sighed with relief and stepped out onto the ice.

Without the protection of the boat, the frigged air seeped through the thin protection of his jeans. He brought the sat phone from his coat pocket and turned on the power, but the signal was erratic and the GPS was not working. He realized he was too close to the device on the island, so he needed to go back at least a mile to get a signal.

He knew his boat was pointed at the island, and remembered seeing the *Mystic* through the left rear window before the ice rose up. He slowly turned in a circle, searching for some sort of landmark, but the ice disappeared over the horizon in all directions.

He headed toward the *Mystic*, using the boat as a point of reference, and hopefully, he would get a signal before he lost sight of it. If not, he might walk in a circle and never get a signal. He glanced over his shoulder at the boat and then quickened his pace across the ice.

***

THE ISLAND:

Okawna walked down the gangway to the beach, then over to his friends standing outside the spaceship. "Any luck with the shutdown program, Doc? We could sure use it right now."

"Yes, I think we have found the problem. The ship crashed when the control system failed because of some sort of interference, which caused every electronic system on this ship to fail at the same instant. Whatever interfered has stopped, and David and I were just about to begin the startup procedure."

"You mean it still works?"

"Possibly. We will not know until we start each system."

Rita got Okawna's attention. "Did you see Alex before the ice rose above the island?"

"No. The only boat was the Mystic on the horizon."

Henry turned and headed back into the ship. "We need to hurry, David. Come, come."

Rita had been following Henry and David's every move as they talked about how the ship functioned. She knew the information might come in handy in the future, and wasn't going to let the two scientists out of her sight, so followed them back inside the alien craft.

Mike shoved his hand into his pocket and brought out his flashlight. "No sense waiting out here." He turned and entered the ship, followed by Lisa, Bett, and Okawna.

***

In the center of the forty foot circular room, four high-backed padded chairs were facing a control console. Henry stepped in front of it, touched a button, and a seven-inch square tray with four slots slid out, then he held a three-inch diameter by one inch thick crystal out for them to see. "When we entered our first spaceship in 1948, there were small remnants of these crystals in each of the slots. We did not know what they were at first, but over years of testing, they kept getting smaller, and three of them went dark. We realized they were the power source, but we had no idea what kind of mineral it was, or how to get more."

With a sense of reverence, Henry slowly placed one new crystal into an empty slot. It immediately turned light blue and glowed, and then the ceiling shimmered for a few seconds before becoming transparent. The interior was suddenly illuminated by the sun, but there was no heat from the radiation. The exterior wall around the control room became transparent, and they could see the volcanic rock from inside the ship.

Henry smiled and clasped his hands together. "We are one step closer to shutting down the devices."

Okawna went outside to do some exploring. He stared at the narrow tornado swirling up from the tip of the device and then walked over to find out how powerful the wind would be up close. When he was within five-feet, the suction pulled at his coat, dragging him closer, which made the wind pull harder, dragging him even closer to the tornado. "Oh, shit!"

He felt his belt tighten as he was yanked backward onto the ground below the tornado. He rolled away and stood up, then gave Bett a thankful smile. "When we get back to civilization, I'm buying you a crate of gum."

Bett smirked at him. "That wasn't real smart, Okawna. For a minute there, I thought you were a goner."

"I was getting a little worried myself."

"What's in the cave?"

"I saw a skeleton just inside, wearing an old German Officer's uniform. It must be Dieter's relative."

***

David walked over to an odd-looking control console, which appeared to have been smashed against the floor. "I don't recognize it, Doc."

"I do not recognize it, either. Lewis said it would be different from the others. It must be the control for the devices."

Rita was looking over their shoulders. "Who is Lewis? It sounds like he's flown one of these before."

Henry knew the Dead Energy mission was still classified as top-secret, so he couldn't tell her that Lewis was an alien. "He is a very intelligent man."

David knelt down next to the two-foot long by two-foot wide oval cylinder. When he set it up straight, the back cover fell onto the floor and he looked inside. "The optical cables are still attached to the floor, and it has power."

He looked closer at the interior, noticing one of the tiny optical cables was dark, not neon blue, like the other cables. "I think I found the problem."

He pinched the tiny end between his fingers and shoved it into the only empty hole in the connection board. It turned blue like the others, but when he let go, it fell out and went dark. "The tip of this cable has broken off inside the connector. If I hold it in place, everything works, but I received a slight electrical tingle before it shut down. We need something to hold it in place. Something nonconductive."

He stood and looked around the interior of the spaceship. "I don't see anything in here that could work." He looked over at Rita. "I don't suppose you have any electrical tape in your pocket."

"No. Isn't that a little old fashion for a ship this advanced?"

"You're right, but I left what I need on the Mystic. I didn't know we'd get stranded."

He looked over at the entrance as Okawna and Bett walked in, then Bett turned around and faced the doorway, ready to get rid of her gum for a new piece. "Stop!" he yelled, and hurried across the room.

Bett turned and stared at David. "What's the matter?"

David held out his hand. "I need your gum."

When Bett reached into her pocket to get the package out for him, David stopped her hand. "No, I need the piece you're chewing."

Bett gave him a quizzical stare, then pulled the piece of gum from her mouth and dropped it into his hand. "I guess you're not the squeamish type."

David went back to the control console, knelt down behind it, and then wrapped the gum around the optical cable. He pushed it into the hole while pressing the gum tight to the connection board and the interior systems lit up, then he stood to study the illuminated touch pads on top. "Do you recognize any of these symbols?"

Henry stared down at the controls for a moment and rubbed his chin, then reached down and held his finger above one of the touchpads. "I believe this is the one for deactivation."

"Okay. Push it and let's see what happens."

"Hang on a second," Okawna asked, then stepped into the exit so he could see the device near the cave. "All right. Go ahead."

Chapter 57

SPARROW VALLEY HIGH SCHOOL:

The ringing of the bells got everyone's attention, but nobody stood from the bleachers, and Arnie could not believe no one seemed worried. "Are you people stupid or something? That's the fire alarm, damn it! Get out of here!"

A few of the men stood and looked back at the school buildings, and then one turned back to Arnie. "I don't see any smoke, Sheriff."

One fan from the Darrington bleachers stood up. "What's the matter, Sheriff? Afraid of losing this year?"

Arnie placed his hands on his hips as he stared at the ground. "Damn!"

***

CAVE RANCH:

Derek paced in front of the porch, frustrated he could not locate Kristy, and then looked up at Robert in the swing. "Aren't you going to do anything?"

"What would that be? We're safe here."

Derek climbed onto the motorcycle and put on his helmet. "Kristy isn't safe, and I can't stand sitting around, so I'm going back to the water to see if it's gone down."

Robert knew it was a waste of time, but it would give the boy something to do. The engine roared, and then he watched Derek drive away. He pushed himself in the porch swing, while waiting for a call from Arnie with information about Kristy.

He heard a strange sound and looked around, but could not locate its origin. Something kept beeping, so he stood from the swing and followed the sound through the screen door into the kitchen. The muffled noise was coming from inside Derek's backpack, so he opened the zipper and saw the strange-looking phone inside. He reached in and grabbed it, then studied the key pad and saw one green button and one red. He figured green was good, so pressed it. "Hello?"

Wesley did not recognize the voice. "I'm trying to reach Derek Cave."

"This is his grandfather, Robert."

"Robert, my name is Wesley Patterson. Your granddaughter and Jessica Parker are trapped between the highway and your ranch, and they're in big trouble. We opened the dam, and you're going to be flooded soon."

"Are you crazy?"

"I don't have time to explain, but you need to get on your horses and go get them. When this water hits, they'll be drowned, so you had better hurry."

"I'm on my way to the barn right now."

"Good luck."

Robert pressed the red button and set the satellite phone on the table, then headed out onto the porch and down the steps. It had been a while since he had saddled a horse without help, so he hoped Derek was a fast learner.

***

When Derek reached the water, it was higher than before. Frustrated, he gunned the engine, slipped the clutch to spin the rear tire around in the dirt, and then headed back toward the house. When he drove into the driveway, he noticed Robert headed across to the barn and drove over beside him. "What's going on?"

"Kristy and that Parker girl are trapped between here and the bridge, and we have to hurry. Some idiot named Patterson opened the dam, and the water is headed our way."

Derek shut off the engine and climbed off the motorcycle. "Tell me what to do."

"Just watch and do what I tell you, and you'll be fine."

***

MOUNT BAKER PARK:
Wesley led Jamie into the ranger station and stood at the counter while looking into Larry's office. "Any word from the Valley?"

Larry stood from his desk and went out to join them. "Glad to see you alive, Wesley. The Sheriff just called. Nobody believes him, and they wouldn't leave the track meet. When you opened the dam, it flooded the road on the other side of the main bridge, and now no one can get down the mountain."

Wesley felt helpless as he looked at the concern in Jamie's eyes. "I didn't have a choice. It was either flooding the river or destroying your town, so I made an informed decision."

Jamie crossed her arms over her chest, leaned back against the counter, and stared at the floor. "What we need is a helicopter." She heard Wesley grunt. When she looked up, he was grinning. "What?"

"Time to ask a favor. Remember that friend of mine, Alex Cave? He's Derek's uncle, and he has connections."

He turned his phone on and selected Alex's number, but was told to leave a message. He was about to put the phone away when he noticed a second number for Alex. He pressed it, and a moment later, a woman answered.

"Tanner Company. How can I help you?"

"My name is Wesley Patterson, and I'm trying to reach Alex Cave. I'm a friend of his, and I need some help."

"Hold, please."

A moment later, he heard a voice say hello. "Hello? Who am I talking to?"

"This is Carl Gregory. Who am I speaking to?"

"I'm Wesley Patterson, a volcanologist working with Alex Cave."

"I remember him mentioning you. What can I do for you?"

Wesley explained what was going on. "Alex's nephew and niece are in trouble, and we could use a helicopter ride."

"I'm a friend of Alex, too, and I've got a helicopter at my disposal. Where can I meet you?"

"That's great. The Mount Baker State Park Ranger Station has a big enough parking lot for you to land. Hang on and I'll get you the GPS location."

Larry looked at him, shrugged, then Frank handed a piece of paper over the counter and he read the numbers to Carl. "I really appreciate this."

"I'll be there in twenty minutes."

"I'll be waiting."

He turned off the phone and looked at Jamie. "Help is on the way."

***

CAVE RANCH:

Derek's feet felt like ice, and his jeans were soaked halfway up his legs, as the horses sloshed through the five-foot deep rushing water. He and Robert followed a line of fir trees along the submerged road, but their speed was limited to the footing of the horses, both acting spooked by the leaves and branches rushing past in front of them. He turned to look at Robert riding on his right side. "They could be anywhere."

Robert did not reply and stared straight ahead. He kept thinking he could have done something earlier, like keeping Kristy home this morning. He had plenty of warning, but he did not know they would open the dam.

Derek saw a flash of bright yellow in one tree and pointed. "There they are!"

***

Jessica and Kristy clung to the branches, watching snags of vegetation and small trees sweep past beneath their feet. Kristy looked over at Jessica standing on another thick tree limb next to hers. "I, can't stop, shivering," she said through chattering teeth.

Jessica realized her jeans were wet, but her jacket and shirt were still dry. She carefully shuffled along the tree limb and stepped around the trunk to stand behind Kristy, then knelt down and wrapped her arms around the small shoulders to pull her back tight against her body. "Derek should get here soon. We just have to be patient for a little while longer."

Kristy suddenly turned her head toward the ranch. "Do you hear that, Jessica? It sounded like a horse snorting."

Jessica leaned around the tree trunk. "It's Derek and your grandfather! They're almost here!"

Kristy saw the face of a horse appear beside her and smiled up at Jessica. "I told you he'd rescue us."

Derek slid back on the saddle as he held his hand out to his little sister. "You look cold. Get on in front of me, and I'll warm you up."

Kristy stepped off the tree limb onto the saddle, then felt Derek's warm arm wrap around her waist under her coat. "I knew you'd find us."

When Derek's horse moved out of the way, Robert moved his horse up next to Jessica. "We've never really met. I'm Robert. Slide down behind me."

"I've never been on a horse before. Won't he move away? I saw that in a movie."

"No, he won't move. Go ahead and slide down behind me."

Instead of sliding across, Jessica leapt from the limb onto the back of the horse, grabbing Robert's shoulders for balance and nearly throwing him off the saddle. "Wow. That was intense. Sorry about that."

Robert turned his horse back toward the ranch and rode up beside Derek, then smiled and reached over to put his hand on Derek's shoulder. "Good job, son."

Derek looked over and smiled, but it quickly slipped away. "We're not safe yet. Wesley said even with the dam open, it may not hold back the water if that logjam tears loose. I think we should head up to his place. It's up past the park and away from the water."

"That's too far for the horses, and we'd never make it out of the flooded areas. Our best option is to get back to the house and barn. Please, just trust me. We'll be safe there."

Derek knew it was the only option and indicated he understood. He switched arms around Kristy, giving her fresh warmth, then looked over at Jessica and nodded his appreciation. When she smiled, he stared ahead as they made their way back to the ranch.

Chapter 58

MYSTIC:

Joshua paced across the bridge, frustrated there was nothing he could do or see with the forty-foot wall of ice looming beside the ship. He suddenly remembered Alex leaving in the motorboat, which was probably frozen to the surface, and it suddenly dawned on him Alex had important connections, and was friends with the Director of National Security. All he needed was the name and phone number.

He entered the question into the computer terminal and the information appeared on the screen, so he grabbed the sat phone and entered the numbers. A moment later, a woman's voice answered.

"Director Donner's office. How can I help you?"

"I'm a friend of Alex Cave, and I'm trying to get a message to Mister Donner."

"He's busy at the moment. I can give him the message when he's done."

"Tell him we had a setback, and Alex is stranded on the ice north of my position. Here is my phone number and GPS coordinates. And be sure to tell him something up here interferes with all the electronics."

"I'll make sure he gets this as soon as he comes out."

"Thank you."

Joshua set the phone back in its bracket and stared at the wall of ice. It wasn't as high, and he wondered if the device was running out of juice. He thought even alien batteries must run out of power eventually. He sighed in frustration and sat on the chair. For now, there was nothing he could do but wait.

***

THE ICE SHEET:

Alex brought the sat phone out of his coat pocket again and stared at the screen, but still didn't have a signal. He made a mark on the ice with his pocket knife, and then held his hand up as a visor over his sunglasses as he slowly turned in a circle. He had lost sight of the boat a long time ago, and did not know if he was walking in a straight line or a circle. Without a point of reference, it was impossible to tell.

He turned back toward his mark and then continued on to where he thought the *Mystic* might be located and knew Joshua would be waiting somewhere close. It was difficult distinguishing the ice from the sky, and he could not see an end to the transparent block of frozen water. He just hoped he was walking in the correct direction.

One hundred yards further, he heard the sat phone beep and brought it up to look at the screen. The signal was weak, but he was getting close, so he began jogging while staring at the screen. When four bars appeared, he stopped and entered the number for the *Mystic*.

***

THE MYSTIC:

Joshua heard the sat phone ringing and grabbed it. When he saw it was Alex, he jumped off the chair. "Man, I'm glad you called. Where are you?"

"I'm still on the ice and trying to get to you. My GPS works now, and I'm at these coordinates." He read the numbers from the screen. "What's your location?"

Joshua studied the readout on the computer monitor. "You're only a quarter mile north of me. Here are my coordinates. I should be able to nudge the *Mystic* close enough to the ice wall for you to jump onto the roof."

"I don't understand. Did you say jump?"

"Yeah, the ice is only about forty-feet high this time."

"I'll be there in a few minutes."

Joshua set the phone down and took *Mystic* off automatic, then used the thrusters to spin her sideways and slowly moved closer to the ice wall. When he was within five-feet, he stopped and pressed automatic again, then waited a few moments to make sure it was working. When everything was normal, he grabbed the sat phone and binoculars as he walked out of the bridge.

When he climbed the ladder onto the roof, he could see over the top of the wall. He looked through the binoculars and scanned the surface, then focused on a shiny black ball bouncing a few feet above two dark blue poles, and knew it was Alex in his white coat running across the ice.

***

THE ISLAND:

Okawna looked back inside the spaceship at the expectant faces and shook his head no. "It's still working, Doc."

Henry and David turned and looked down at the control pad, trying to decipher the symbols. They both knew those early humans used a different vocabulary, and Henry was still learning the language from Lewis.

Henry looked up at the people standing around him. "I am sorry, that was my mistake. It is this one."

Henry pressed the symbol and quickly turned to look at Okawna, who was staring out at the device. While he waited for the news, the moment seemed to drag by.

Okawna watched the tornado vanish, and the soft whining inside the crater was suddenly silent. He grinned, then turned and looked inside. "It stopped, and the whirlwind is gone. We did it!"

Henry clasped his hands under his chin and was all smiles. "Hopefully, the radios will work, and once we upload the shutdown command through the satellite system, we will turn the other device off as well."

Okawna heard a strange sound from outside the ship and went out onto the beach to listen. Faint crackling sounds echoed in the crater, so he walked over to the gangway and up onto the old ship. The sound was louder, and he climbed up to the V and looked down at the space between the ice wall and the beach. Some water had thawed and was lapping at the gravel, but the cracking sound was not coming from below, it was coming from above the ice.

Something was happening up there, but he was helpless to see what was going on. He jumped back when fracture lines rippled through the ice like melting spider webs, then huge pieces crashed onto the beach. Within moments, the ice was dissolving around the island.

***

MYSTIC:

Joshua watched Alex getting closer, now only four hundred yards and closing fast. With his help, they might get their friends off the island. Now that he no longer needed them to see Alex, he let the binoculars hang from the strap.

He heard something cracking and then watched a massive slab of ice break free from the wall and crash into the water. More cracking sounds pierced the air, followed by huge chunks of ice slamming into the sea. A massive wave from the falling blocks slammed into *Mystic*'s side, driving her sideways away from the wall while tossing Joshua off the roof.

He hit the deck rolling, jarring the sat phone from his hand as he slammed against the steel surface. He quickly sat up, crawled over to the phone, and grabbed it. "Run, Alex! Go back! The ice is falling apart. *Run!*"

He scrambled onto his feet and ran into the bridge as the water around the *Mystic* clogged with large chunks of ice. He flipped the thrusters off auto and eased *Mystic* through the thick chunks until she was free to maneuver, and watched helplessly as the ice disintegrated, with Alex somewhere on the surface.

Chapter 59

CAVE RANCH:

The water began to shallow as they rode closer to the ranch, then the gravel road was dry all the way to the house and barn. Derek looked over at Robert, thinking so far so good, but he was still worried about the logjam.

They stopped the horses in front of the porch, where Derek slid off his saddle and looped the reins around the wood hand railing. He grabbed Kristy off the saddle and set her on the ground, then helped Jessica down from Robert's horse. Robert climbed down and looped the reins around the handrail, and then sighed with relief his family was safe.

Derek noticed Kristy waiting for him, so went over to hold her hand as they walked up the steps. "Are you okay?"

"I am now. I love you, Derek."

"Yeah, I love you, too. You should change clothes. I'll meet you out here when you're done."

"What about you? Your pants are wet."

"Only up to my knees, so they'll dry in a little while."

Jessica walked past Derek and sat on the porch swing then sniffed her fingers and made a sour expression as she looked up at him. "I smell like a horse."

"You can change into a pair of my jeans, if you want to."

"Thanks, but the rest of me is still dry, so I'll be fine."

Robert grabbed both sets of reins from the porch railing. "I'll take the horses to the barn."

Derek had paid little attention to the horses until now. "Should we take the saddles off so they can dry?"

"That's all right. I'll take care of it."

Derek spun around and leapt over the steps to the ground beside his grandfather. "I'll give you a hand."

Jessica stood from the swing. "Does it stink over there, too?"

"It smells like a barn."

Jessica hurried down the steps to walk beside him. "I already smell like a horse, so I might as well go, too. I've never seen the inside of a barn."

"You're kidding, right?"

"I never had the opportunity until now."

Derek grinned. "It's not too bad."

***

RANGER STATION:

Wesley, Jamie, Larry, and Frank stared through the window at the dust billowing up from the parking lot. The bottom of a white helicopter dropped from the sky, and then gently touched down on the asphalt.

Larry slapped Wesley on the back. "I'd like to meet Alex sometime. He must be well connected for someone to fly a helicopter up here for you."

"Sure." He headed for the door and the Rangers followed.

***

Carl set the engine on idle, then climbed out and walked toward the people coming out of the building. A big man with shaggy hair stepped forward and extended his hand, so he reached out to shake it. "I'm Carl."

"Wesley. I really appreciate this. Let's go inside and I'll show you where we need to go."

Everyone followed Wesley into the station and watched as he pointed out locations on the big wall map. "Up here is where the logjam is located, but we need to go southwest first to check the Cave ranch and find out if everyone's okay."

Carl studied the location of the Cave ranch on the map. "I saw that area when I flew in from the west. Not much showing above the water on the south side of the town, but I didn't pay attention to that area. Let's go check it out."

Larry and Frank followed them outside and wished them good luck, then waited while Wesley and Jamie climbed into the rear passenger section of the helicopter. When the rotors picked up speed, they stepped back inside the station and watched the helicopter leap off the ground, and then Larry grabbed a portable radio. "Keep an eye on things here, Frank. I'm going up to check the dam."

"Give me a holler and let me know what's going on."

"I will."

***

SPARROW VALLEY HIGH SCHOOL:

When the alarms stopped ringing, Arnie saw Tyler walking back to the bleachers and hurried over to him. "What are you doing?"

"They're not listening to them anyway, so what's the point?"

Arnie spun around when he heard the cheers from the bleachers. He tried to think of something else to motivate these people to leave the school, but knew until something happened, no one would leave.

***

It did not take long to reach Sparrow Valley by helicopter, and from the air, the town was dangerously close to the vast expanse of water covering everything south. Wesley stared down at the high school and saw the crowd watching the games. "Oh, crap!"

Carl looked over his shoulder at his passengers. "I see a house and a barn up ahead."

Wesley leaned forward between the front seats and stared down at the ranch, but did not see anyone outside the house or the barn. "Is that area big enough to land?"

"No, that barn's in the way. I'm sorry."

"Let's go check out the logjam."

Wesley leaned back and looked over at Jamie. "There isn't anything else we can do right now."

Jamie nodded, slumped down in her seat, and stared out the window. When Carl swung the helicopter back toward Mount Baker, Jamie reached over and grabbed Wesley's hand. "They might have been in the house, so we can't be sure what happened."

***

THE DAM:

Larry parked in front of the concrete building and climbed out of his SUV, then strolled to the fence on the outside edge of the concrete and stared down at the water. When he looked to the far end of the reservoir, the watermarks and green algae on the sides showed it was still over half full. He had no idea how much water would race down the mountain, or how much the dam could handle. In fact, he had no idea if or when it would happen. All he could do is hope the logjam holds until after the games.

***

Carl brought the helicopter up the canyon for two miles, then hovered sixty-feet above the massive tangle of logs and debris. Wesley stared out the window at the water pouring over the top, and more rushing out from the bottom, but the massive body of water was still being held back by a precarious tangle of downed trees.

Wesley's heart sank when he thought about all those kids and their families enjoying the games. If the full force of the water lets loose, it would overwhelm the strength of the dam, and hundreds of people would die.

Because of the noise from the rotors and jet engines, they did not hear the snapping and popping of shattering timber, but watched the pile split down the center, releasing a torrent of water, mud, and trees rushing down the canyon. Carl didn't wait to be asked and swung the helicopter up above the lahar, then followed it down the mountain.

***

Larry flinched when the sound of splintering timber echoed down the canyon. The air was filled with a multitude of crashing sounds as the lahar tore away everything in its path, getting louder by the second. He spun around and ran back to the SUV, jumped inside, and started the engine, and stomped on the accelerator, spinning the rear tires before racing down the road.

Four hundred yards further, he turned onto the road going back up the side of the canyon, and then stopped at the lookout point above the reservoir. He shut off the engine and climbed out, then ignored a few smashed aluminum cans as he rushed around a large fire pit. He stopped at the edge to look down on the dam and reservoir, then up the canyon at a massive dark river of mud, boulders, and trees.

***

SPARROW VALLEY HIGH SCHOOL:

The roar of the lahar got everyone's attention and most of them stood up on the bleachers, staring up at the canyon while trying to see what was going on, but Arnie knew and spun around to the crowd. "Everyone out!"

The valley people had heard about the possibility and ran down the bleachers, trampling some of the stunned visitors from Darrington. Panic erupted on the school grounds as people desperately tried to reach their vehicles, knocking each other to the ground to escape.

The visitors had no idea what was going on, but were caught up in the throng of people running around the bleachers and the parking lot. The crackling and snapping sounds filled the air as the lahar raced down the canyon, only adding to the panic. Car horns blared from frustrated drivers trying to get out of the parking lot, but Arnie knew it was too late, and did not try to enforce an organized exit from the school grounds. He resigned himself to the inevitable destruction that would soon destroy Sparrow valley, and just stared up the canyon.

Chapter 60

THE ICE SHEET:

Alex slid to a stop when he heard Joshua's warning and stared toward the *Mystic*, but could not see what he was talking about. He suddenly recognized the crackling and popping sound of fracturing ice, then watched the zigzagged edge of the ice sheet quickly moving in his direction. "Ah, shit!"

He spun around, slipping on the surface as it melted and crashing onto the ice, but quickly got back on his feet and shuffle-skated across the slippery surface. As the snapping and crackling grew louder, he glanced back over his shoulder, and the zigzagged edge was only twenty yards behind him. "Crap!"

He struggled to gain traction, but the ice water just got deeper. It was difficult keeping his balance, but he desperately fought for every inch.

***

Joshua was still on the bridge when he heard a strange sound. He reset the autopilot and ran outside the bridge, then climbed up onto the roof air as an orange and white Coast Guard helicopter raced past overhead. He saw Alex sliding on the surface, only seconds from being swallowed by the crumbling ice sheet and crushed by the slabs, and held his breath while the helicopter seemed to take forever to reach his friend.

***

A deep thumping drew Alex's attention, and he looked back over his shoulder. He saw the helicopter, but knew they could not land to pick him up, so he kept sloshing across the surface.

He heard Joshua's voice suddenly yell from the sat phone in his coat pocket. "Alex! Behind you! Behind you!"

When he turned to look, the edge of the ice was only three feet behind him. He lost his footing and started to fall, then a rope ladder swinging across the ice smacked against his shoulder. He grabbed the rungs as he looked up at a helmeted face staring down at him, and then felt the pressure through his hands as the helicopter gained altitude.

He stepped onto a rung, taking the strain off his arms, as his adrenaline level dropped closer to normal. He smiled and sighed with relief as the helicopter swung him around back toward the *Mystic*.

***

Joshua saw Alex suddenly swinging below the helicopter and raised his fist into the air. "Yes!"

When the helicopter began moving in his direction, he climbed down and waited outside the bridge. A few moments later, he grabbed Alex from the swinging ladder, set him on the deck, and wrapped his arms around him for a quick hug. "You are one lucky teacher."

"A few moments ago, I was wondering about my luck."

They both looked into the bridge when they heard someone calling on the radio. They hurried inside, and Joshua grabbed the microphone from the clip. "This is the Mystic, come in, over."

"This is Coast Guard Search and Rescue. Can we be of further assistance?"

Joshua stared at Alex. "What do you think?"

"We can't take the chance the electronics will go out if they head toward the island. We'll just have to make our way back as the ice continues to fall apart."

Joshua keyed the microphone. "That's a negative, Coast Guard. Thanks for the help, and you should keep south of our location"

"Understood, Mystic. Good luck."

***

THE ISLAND:

Okawna stared at the rapidly melting ice, hoping Alex was still in the motorboat. A few minutes later, it had dissolved around the island, and he saw the *Mystic* slowly moving in his direction. He turned and smiled, expecting everyone to be standing outside the spacecraft, but no one was there.

He climbed down the steps and over the gangway, then up the beach to the entrance into the spaceship. "All the ice has melted."

Rita hurried across the room. "Did you see the motorboat and Alex?"

Okawna stopped smiling. "No, but the *Mystic* is coming for us. Maybe he's with Josh. You never know with Alex."

***

THE MYSTIC:

Alex stared forward from inside the bridge as the ice melted much faster than it had frozen. He noticed a blue object floating to the right of the island, then recognized the motorboat bobbing on the water. "Over there. She'll need a new motor before we can use her again. That one seized up when the water froze."

"She's useless without a motor, so we always carry a spare. It's in the locker with the rest of the deck equipment."

When they were close to the motorboat, Alex walked out of the bridge and down the steps to the stern, while Joshua backed the *Mystic* up so he could grab the bow line. He tied it off to the stern with a long towrope and then went up to the bridge. "All set."

"The interference is gone, Alex. I bet they shut down the device."

"That would explain why the ice melted."

Alex stared out the window as they headed toward the island, but decided not to call Donner until he knew more about his friends. Just like before, they did not take a portable radio to the island, so he could not call them.

***

Joshua brought the *Mystic* fifty feet from the beach and pressed the horn button several times. A moment later, everyone on the island climbed over the V, smiling and waving before they climbed down the steps to the beach.

As Joshua set the *Mystic* to hover, Alex shoved his sat phone into his pocket and they both left the bridge and went down to the stern. Alex climbed into the boat and tied it close to the deck, then Joshua handed him the new outboard motor. Once the engines were swapped, he slowly drove across.

Because of the higher water level, Alex nosed the boat onto the gravel next to the partially submerged dock, then stepped out onto the dry section of wood to greet his friends, who were smiling at him. When Rita approached, he stepped down onto the beach.

Rita threw her arms around Alex's neck, pulling him close for a passionate kiss. "I thought I'd never see you again."

"Rita, my dear, you have no idea."

Alex shook hands with everyone and gave Okawna a quick hug and a slap on the back before stepping back and hugging Lisa, and then he looked at Henry. "I take it you shut down the device?"

"Yes, and when the ice suddenly started melting, we were worried about you."

Henry grabbed Alex by the upper arm and gently pulled him toward the V in the crater. "Come, Alex. It is in better shape than we imagined."

"In a moment, Doc."

Alex looked at Okawna, who had climbed into the motorboat. "Once you get Rita, Bett, Lisa, and Mike back on the *Mystic*, bring the ladder for the sub and a pry bar back with you. I want to check out the hatch covers on the old ship."

"I noticed something odd about them, too. I'll be back shortly."

Alex looked down at Henry. "Lead the way, Doc."

***

Joshua paced across the stern, watching Bett, Rita, Lisa, and Mike climb into the boat with Okawna. He stopped pacing when the boat finally drove away from the dock. A moment later, the boat bumped against the stern, and Bett jumped out and leapt into his arms.

The others climbed out onto the deck and waited while Okawna tied the boat to the stern. When Bett let go of Joshua, Rita walked up to him. "How did the Mystic hold up through all this? Is there anything I need to fix?"

Joshua grinned. "She's purring like a kitten."

Okawna climbed out and shook Joshua's hand. "You did the right thing by leaving, but thanks for coming back."

Chapter 61

THE DAM:

The roar of the lahar drew closer as Larry watched a twenty-foot high mass of mud and debris plunge into the reservoir. He watched the churning mass of brown sludge and branches forcing the clear water toward the dam, causing it to rise like a tsunami as it was compressed against the concrete.

He held his breath, waiting for the dam to give way to the massive torrent of debris, and then clear water sloshed over the rim of the concrete and the banks of the reservoir. The water continued flowing in at a slower pace, but still tossing trees around like toothpicks on the surface. It slowly calmed down and the water going over the dam finally stopped.

Larry did not realize he was holding his breath, and let out a long, slow sigh of relief. The road alongside of the reservoir was blocked by a tangled mess of branches and vegetation, but only a small section near the water was washed away. An accumulation of vegetation rose to the surface of the thick brown water, and near the outside of the dam, a small stream of water gushed out from the lower part of the opening beneath the sliding blocks of concrete, now temporarily blocked by the debris.

He looked up at the helicopter as it flew down the canyon and hovered above the dam, and smiled and waved at Jamie, staring out the window. When the helicopter continued down the mountain, he went back to his SUV and headed for the station.

***

SPARROW VALLEY HIGH SCHOOL:

The roar of the lahar was suddenly gone, but Arnie continued to stare up the canyon for several moments. The cars had stopped honking, and as he turned around, he saw the crowd of panicked people had settled down. He helped the injured get up from the ground, and then his shoulders slumped as he realized it was over and the valley was safe.

***

RANGER STATION:

Wesley and Jamie thanked Carl for his help, and stepped out of the helicopter onto the station parking lot. Once they were inside the building, they watched through the window as the helicopter took off.

Larry arrived just as the helicopter was flying away and parked in front of the building. As he climbed out, Wesley, Jamie, and Frank walked outside, so he closed the door and leaned back against the hood. "That'll be something I'll always remember."

Wesley indicated the side of the mountain. "How does the dam look up close?"

"It's a lot tougher than we thought. We'll need a little roadwork done, but everything looks okay. The outflow has slowed down a lot, too, but it's only temporarily blocked by debris. I'll take Frank back with me to close the dam before the blockage is washed through the opening, and the water in the valley should start draining in a little while." He looked at Jamie. "Did you find your sister and the Cave family?"

"We couldn't tell from the helicopter."

Wesley held his hand out to Jamie. "I need my keys so I can get my boat."

Jamie looked over at Larry. "I'll be back as soon as I can."

"Don't worry about it. Go take care of your family."

Jamie wrapped her arm around Wesley's, and then they headed toward his Hummer. When he stopped at the driver's side door, she handed him the keys and ran around to the other side to get in.

***

CAVE RANCH:

Kristy walked through the kitchen and noticed Derek's fancy phone on the table. She remembered Uncle Alex said it could reach all the way to Alaska, so she picked it up and stared at the buttons on the front. One button said power, so she pressed it, and the small screen came on. She wished she knew Uncle Alex's phone number and then remembered something he had said about speed dial.

She pressed number two and held it to her ear, heard it ringing, and then heard a click. "Uncle Alex?"

"No, this is Wesley. Who are you?"

"I'm Kristy Cave. Are you with my uncle Alex?"

"No, I'm up near Mount Baker. Is everyone all right?"

"Yeah. We got wet, but we got out of the water. I'm at my grandpa's house."

"Tell everyone that Wesley and Jamie are coming to get you?"

"Okay. Bye."

***

THE CABIN:

Wesley turned off his phone and looked across the seat at Jamie. "They're okay. They made it to the ranch and will wait for us."

Jamie had been sitting on the edge of the seat, and now she leaned back and sighed with relief. "Thank goodness."

When they were near his cabin, Wesley backed up to the barn doors, shut off the engine, then looked over at Jamie. "Once we get your sister and the Caves back on dry land, how about letting me cook dinner for you tonight?"

"That would be nice, Wesley, but from what I saw in your refrigerator, I didn't think you liked to cook."

"Actually, I do, but I only did it for my wife. Now I'd like to cook something for you."

Jamie smiled. "Thanks, Wesley. Does that mean you're thinking about getting a haircut?"

"Don't push your luck, Miss Park Representative."

Jamie grinned. "I didn't say you had to do it."

"Fair enough."

Chapter 62

THE ISLAND:
Alex followed Henry and David into the spaceship, then over to the odd-looking control pad. "So this controls the devices. What about the rest of the ship, Doc? You said it's in good shape. Can it fly again?"

"I am not sure yet, Alex. We have only started the basic systems."

"It would be nice if we could fly this thing to Nevada."

***

Once the rest of the crew was on the *Mystic*, Okawna grabbed what he needed, and then drove the motorboat back to the dock. He carried the ladder and the pry bar down into the crater and over to the side of the old ship, then leaned it against the side, next to the rusted hatch covers. He hung the pry bar on one rung, then went back to the spaceship and stepped inside. "Ready when you are, Alex."

Alex stepped out of the spacecraft and followed Okawna to the side of the rusted ship, then climbed up the ladder and wedged the pry bar into the crack separating the two sides of the hatch covers. When he hauled back on the bar, the screeching and popping of rusted hinges echoed in the crater.

The pry bar suddenly slammed down against one cover, as the other side broke away and slid down the side of the ship. He leaned over the remaining cover to look inside, but the angle was too sharp, and the interior too dark, so he climbed down onto the beach.

When Alex stepped down, Okawna grabbed the ladder and leaned it into the opening of the missing cover. He let Alex climb back up into the cargo hold, and then went up, stepped inside, and saw him kneeling on the deck, next to a large pile of bones.

Alex used a rib bone to separate the pile, then hooked it under something white and eased it out of the tangled remnants of bones, and then stood and held it out toward Okawna. "These are human, and this is the captain's hat Burk was wearing in the movie."

Okawna moved closer and knelt down to grab a large femur bone, then carried it back to the opening and into the sunlight for a closer look.

"There are teeth marks on this one, and there aren't any polar bears on this rock."

"Colonel Dieter was the only skeleton in the cave, and it was still in one piece. I guess he became a cannibal."

Okawna tossed the leg bone onto the pile. "I can't really blame him. I think anyone desperate enough would do the same thing."

Alex felt something strange on the side of the rib bone, so walked to the opening. In the sunlight, he saw a half-round notch in the side of the bone. "This person was shot."

Okawna moved around the pile. "I don't see any skulls."

"He probably felt guilty looking at the faces of the people he was about to eat and threw them into the ocean."

"I wonder who managed to escape in the skiff with that movie we watched."

"It's hard to say. Maybe one of the pirates found it."

Okawna moved back to the opening. "It stinks in here, and I've seen enough."

Alex tossed the rib and hat onto the deck and followed Okawna down the ladder to the beach. "I found something in the cave when I was marooned here yesterday, and I want to check it out."

He turned and walked up the beach with Okawna and entered the cave, and then his breath caught in his throat. The rock was gone from the entire wall, and the mirrored side of the spacecraft followed a narrow path at a down angle deeper into the cave.

He led the way down the curved outside of the spacecraft until he saw light radiating from an eight foot square opening in the side and smiled at Okawna. "This is the outside door for the airlock into the cargo hold of the ship."

Alex moved onto the slightly slanted deck in the four foot deep airlock, then continued through the inside door into a large room, with a three-foot diameter cylinder in the middle. He saw the last of the four devices lying against the far wall, next to a six-foot diameter silver sphere with a mirrored surface.

Okawna followed him inside. "What's that ball for?"

"I have no idea. This ship is different from the others."

Alex walked across the room and stopped next to the device on the floor. "These four devices operated together to clean the atmosphere. Once we retrieve the other two from the water, we can use this ship to let them do what they were intended to do, and clean up the mess we've made in our atmosphere."

"Hold on a minute, Alex. Haven't they done enough damage?"

"We'll have to learn more about how they work first."

"Those things are pretty old, Alex. What if they don't work as planned? It could make things worse."

"Henry and Lewis will figure it out."

Okawna walked across to the silver ball and looked at his distorted reflection on the surface, then placed one finger on the smooth surface and jumped back when the sphere moved. "This thing is really lightweight. I barely touched it, and it rolled along the wall."

Alex stepped closer to the silver sphere, and when he tapped the side with his knuckles, a hollow sound echoed from the inside. "I'll have to ask Lewis what this was used for."

When Alex placed both hands on the silver surface to roll it away from the wall, he received an electrical shock. For a moment, he thought he saw a shimmer in his peripheral vision just as he let go.

Okawna noticed some strange-looking clothing on the floor behind the sphere. "I think we've found the crew. One of them, anyway. Take a look."

Alex knelt down next to the mummified remains of a human body wearing a one-piece silver suit. "There should have been four people on this spaceship. I wonder what happened to the other three." He stood and looked at Okawna. "I'd better call Donner and let him know what happened."

Alex and Okawna stepped through the airlock back into the cave and then continued outside. Alex selected Donner's number on the sat phone and was transferred to his office, so he put it on speaker.

"I'm so glad you're alive, Alex. I didn't know if the helicopter I sent would get there in time, but they let me know they left you on the Mystic."

"I really appreciate it, too. We did it, Martin, but we need some support out here. We know those pirates had connections, and I'm sure we aren't the only ones who know about this island."

"I already have the Coast Guard on standby. Someone named Mason told them to stay away from the island, so I'll call them right away."

"What about military support?"

"That will take a little more time, but I'll make the call."

"One more thing. I need you to call the Canadian authorities and have Okawna Jamison removed from their wanted list. It was self-defense, and

I don't want him sitting in jail until the authorities figure out what happened."

"His last name is Jamison?"

"No, Okawna is his last name, but the pirate who filled the charges thought it was."

"Okay. I'll take care of it. Is he with you right now?"

"Yes, he's listening."

"Okawna, your father had a fatal heart attack two days ago, and you need to call home right away."

Okawna's jaw went slack for a moment. "Oh. All right. Thanks, Martin."

Okawna took the phone from Alex and stepped away, then entered the number for the family ranch in Stillwater, Wyoming. His cousin answered, explaining what had happened, and asked him to come home as soon as possible. When he finished talking, he ended the call and handed the phone back to Alex. "I need to get home, but I don't want to leave you with no backup."

"Rita can handle herself, and I've got Josh, David, and Mike to help. Let's get back to the ship and have Bett take you to the airport in Seward."

Okawna hesitated. "That's not much help, Alex."

"The sooner you leave, the sooner Bett can get back to increase my odds. Let's go."

Alex and Okawna climbed into the motorboat and drove it back to the *Mystic*. Once they bumped against the stern, Alex tied off while Okawna hurried into the lounge. He checked the gas gage, and it showed ¾ of a tank, but he opened the gas cap and looked inside to be sure.

***

The flowing curls of Rita's red hair jostled back and forth as she tiptoed up the stairs to the bridge. In order for her plan to work, Alex had to be here on the *Mystic* while she was on the island with Henry and David. From what she had just heard, Joshua wasn't feeling well, so Bett was going to give him a ride to Seward.

She peered carefully over the last step to make sure no one was inside, then hurried up the stairs, grabbed the satellite phone, and hurried back down. She checked her pistol, tucked it into the back of her pants, and tugged her coat down before stepping out onto the stern.

***

Okawna entered the lounge, where he found Mike, Bett, and Lisa sitting at the table, and Joshua lying flat in one of the chairs. "I hate to impose on you, Mike, but I have a family emergency, so I was wondering if I could get a ride to the mainland?"

"You saved this ship and our lives, Okawna. It's the least I can do."

Bett was listening and looked over at Josh. "Are you feeling any better, sweetie?"

"No, in fact, I'm feeling worse."

"It's settled then. You're going with us to the hospital in Seward. Okawna, let's get my baby ready to go."

When Bett and Okawna left the lounge, Lisa got up and stared out the window at the island. "Do you think the pirates will come back?"

Mike stood and moved up beside her, as he considered the possibility. "Someone filed murder charges against Okawna, so whoever that was must know the location of this island, or they wouldn't know about the murder."

"I wonder if there are any charges against me because I shot that poor man."

He turned his head to look at her. "Poor man, Lisa? He was a pirate. Hell, all of them were going to kill you and everyone else, so it was self-defense."

"I've never even fired a gun before." She was silent for a moment. "I just remember opening my eyes and seeing that man on the floor and all the blood."

"I'm sorry that happened to you, Lisa."

"Can I get a ride back to the mainland with Bett? I just need to go home for a while."

"I understand, and I'll let her know. Use the company credit card to get to your family. What about David? Does he know you're leaving?"

"Yes. He's a nice guy, and we'll try to get together when he's finished with the spaceship."

***

Alex was surprised when Rita jumped into the motorboat. For some odd reason, he suddenly didn't trust her. It was nothing he could explain, really. It was just a simmering hatred in the back of his mind.

"Can I get a ride back?"

Alex hesitated. "Can you wait until Okawna leaves?"

Rita held out the sat phone. "Henry needs to talk to someone named Lewis, so I told him I'd be right back."

"Okay."

He shoved off and started the engine, then sped across and eased the boat against the shore. When she leapt off the bow, he back up and headed back toward the *Mystic*.

Rita waited until Alex had climbed on board the ship, and then headed to the steps up to the V in the crater. She knew Henry would not be a problem, but David would try to stop her. She brought the pistol out from the small of her back and slipped it into her coat pocket, then grinned as she headed down to the spacecraft.

***

Alex climbed out of the motorboat and heard the helicopter's engine whine, so went over to Okawna. Lisa and Joshua came out from the rear doors and they helped him into the back seat.

Alex gave Lisa a hug. "You're very brave. Take care of yourself."

He smiled when she gave him a quick kiss on his cheek before climbing into the helicopter, then he turned to his best friend. "Let me know if there is anything I can do to help."

"Thanks, Alex."

After Okawna climbed into the helicopter next to Bett, Alex moved into the ship and the helicopter took off. When Bett flew them away from the island toward the airport in Seward, he looked at Mike and realized they were the only ones on the ship, so they headed up to the bridge while their friends played with the spaceship.

***

DISCOVERY:

Carl set the helicopter down on the landing pad and shut down the systems. When he climbed out of the helicopter, Janice and Victor came running up the stairs, both smiling.

Janice ran up to Carl and wrapped her arms around his neck, holding him close, then stepped back and smiled up at him. "We got a signal from *Celeas* a short time ago!"

Victor shook his hand. "I asked one of the other operators about it when I heard a beeping, and he said only the camera was damaged. It was amazing, Carl. We were watching the video from another rover and the ice just melted. They're bringing *Celeas* on board right now. Let's go watch."

Carl didn't know if he could smile any wider as he followed them down the stairs. When he saw his girl being hoisted onboard, tears blurred his vision.

Chapter 63

CAVE RANCH:
Kristy carried the satellite phone out onto the back porch and everyone was gone, including the horses, so she walked down the steps and over to the barn. When she went inside, she saw Jessica sitting on a bale of hay, and heard Derek and her grandpa arguing in the tack room, where they stored the saddles, then she sat next to Jessica. "What are they arguing about?"

"Your uncle Alex. Something about Robert blaming him for your parents' accident."

Kristy heard the strange phone ringing and pressed the green button. "Hello?"

"Hi, Kristy. It's Alex. Is everyone all right?"

"Yeah, I was pretty scared, Uncle Alex, but Derek saved us."

"That's good news."

She stared at the tack room when she heard Derek and her grandpa yelling at each other. "Can you wait a minute?"

"Sure."

Kristy stomped across to the open door and walked into the room. "Just stop it right now!" she yelled. "You're acting like the kindergarten kids." She held the phone out to Robert. "It's Uncle Alex."

Robert hesitated as he stared down at her wet hair and her determined expression. He thought about almost losing her a short time ago, and how it was his fault. He slowly took the phone and brought it up to his ear. "Alex? Listen, I uh. I want to apologize. I had a hard time dealing with things, but I'd just like for you to come home to the ranch when you have time."

"I understand, Dad. I might be a little busy for a while, but I'll come home once I'm finished. I'm just glad all of you are safe."

"Okay. Goodbye, son."

Robert pressed the red button and smiled down at Kristy. "He said he'll get here once he's done."

When Kristy smiled and walked to him with her arms open, he knelt down and hugged her tightly. "Thank you, Kristy."

Chapter 64

MYSTIC:

On the bridge, Mike wasn't paying much attention to Alex talking on the phone when he heard the deep thumping of an approaching helicopter. He grabbed the binoculars and looked toward the sound, and when he focused the lenses, he smiled and looked over at Alex, who ended his call. "The Coast Guard helicopter is coming our way."

Alex took the binoculars from Mike and focused on the orange and white helicopter half a mile from the island. At least he had some support, although they probably wouldn't have much firepower. Still, it was better than no support at all until the military arrived.

His smile turned into a frown as he recognized a trail of white smoke streaking through the sky and he stood up. The helicopter was suddenly a massive ball of fire, with flaming pieces dropping into the ocean.

Mike jumped out of his chair and stared at the smoke over the water. "What just happened?"

Alex aimed the binoculars toward origin of the trail of smoke and saw two large helicopters headed toward them. "We're being invaded." He grabbed the microphone for the portable radios. "Are you listening, Rita?"

"I heard an explosion. What just happened?"

"Two helicopters just shot down a Coast Guard rescue helicopter, and they're coming our way."

"What do you want me to do?"

"Tell Henry and David to stay inside the spaceship until we know what's going on. I'll be there in a minute, so meet me on the dock." He looked at Mike. "I'll grab the shotguns and take the motorboat to the island while you get the Mystic away from here."

"That's a bad plan, Alex. I can help."

"Thanks, but the Mystic's too vulnerable."

Alex grabbed the binoculars and stared out the window for one last look at the approaching helicopters. "You can come back when they leave."

"And do what? Collect the bodies?"

"I hope not."

***

Rita shoved the radio into the chest pocket of her coat and placed her hand on the butt of the pistol inside her coat pocket. She knew in a few minutes, all hell was going to break loose, so she stepped inside the spaceship.

David heard the explosion and was moving toward the exit when Rita stepped in his way. "What's going on?"

"We're going to have company in a few minutes. Just stay inside, and I'll go find out what happened."

Rita hurried back to the dock and could see Alex standing in the motorboat at the stern of the *Mystic*, collecting shotguns from Mike and placing them on one of the seats. She waited while Alex drove across to the island, keeping her pistol hidden in her pocket.

Alex eased the motorboat against the dock. "One helicopter is a troop carrier, and the other one is for cargo. I brought shotguns for you and David."

He reached down and grabbed one shotgun, then handed it to Rita. As he reached down for the other two, he heard the distinct sound of the pump handle inserting a round into the chamber of a shotgun. When he looked up, Rita was aiming it at his chest. "What are you doing?"

"Throw the shotguns into the water."

Alex stared at her. "We're in a lot of trouble, so don't do this." He eased his hand down to his jean pocket.

Rita brought her shotgun up to her shoulder and sighted down the barrel at Alex. "Don't even think about it! I know about your pistol. Take it out slowly and toss it into the water."

Alex knew he didn't stand a chance and held her gaze and did as she asked. "Why are you doing this?"

"Get rid of the shotguns."

Alex reached down, grabbed the barrel of a shotgun, and then looked at Rita. He thought about using it as a club, but she shook her head no, so he tossed both of them into the water. "What now?"

"Go back to the Mystic and take it away from the island." She saw the rage building in Alex's eyes. "I don't want to see the Mystic full of holes, so just do what I say and no one will get hurt."

Alex moved forward to the steering wheel, but hesitated to sit down. "What do you want?"

Rita brought the shotgun down even with her waist, but kept the barrel aimed at Alex. "We want the devices."

"Who are you working for?"

"Not working *for,* Alex. Working *with,* and you don't need to know. Just leave and I won't hurt anyone."

"Right, like your friends didn't hurt anyone in the Coast Guard helicopter a few minutes ago?"

"I had nothing to do with that. Now leave!"

Alex reluctantly drove the motorboat away from the dock, while the deep thumping of the approaching helicopters was getting louder. He knew if they didn't leave the area right away, the invaders might capture the *Mystic*. If that happened, he could not come back and get his friends. He didn't trust Rita to keep her word, and his friends might be dead when he returned, but he knew he had no choice.

When he reached the stern of the *Mystic*, he tied the motorboat off to a cleat and ran up the stairs onto the bridge. He didn't answer the question in Mike's eyes. He switched the engines from thrusters to jet pumps, then shoved the throttle to full speed and steered away from the island.

***

Rita waited on the dock until the *Mystic* was racing away, then headed back toward the spaceship. If everything went according to plan, in a few months she would be wealthy enough to buy a small island.

***

David stood in the entrance of the alien craft, watching Rita walking up the beach. "Where's Alex?"

Rita stopped just outside the spaceship. "He'll come back once the helicopters leave. Get back inside."

David hesitated to do as she asked. "I don't understand. What's going on?"

"We're taking the device in the cave. Just do what I say, and no one will get hurt." When David didn't move, she aimed the shotgun at him, but he just glared back. "I'm not kidding."

David slowly turned and went back inside, and saw the questioning expression from Henry. "Alex isn't coming. They want one of the devices, so just stay calm, and maybe we can find a way out of this."

David got an idea and slowly walked to the four chairs in the center of the control room. He saw Rita watching him through the opening as he sat down and waited for her reaction, but she didn't pay him any attention. He knew if he could shut down the power and seal them inside this ship, they would be safe from whoever was coming. He figured if the exterior of this alien craft could survive in molten rock for one-hundred and eighty-million years, a shotgun blast would not hurt it.

Rita turned and looked up as a helicopter suddenly appeared over the edge of the crater, then four thick nylon ropes dropped out of the open side door. An instant later, four armed men slid down them to the beach.

Rita saw David reaching down to the control pad and stepped inside, holding the shotgun waist high, and aimed it at David. "Come over here, Henry. We're going outside."

Henry's mouth opened slightly as he looked at David for help. David lowered his hand toward the control panel to cut the power before Henry made it to the exit, but flinched and jerked his hands away when the deafening roar from the shotgun's warning blast filled the room.

David stared at Rita as she swung the shotgun around from the exit and aimed it at him, then raised his hands. "All right! You've made your point." He saw the imploring look in Henry's eyes. "I'm sorry, Doc."

Henry's shoulders sagged as he slowly shuffled across the room and out through the entrance. "What do you want, Rita?"

"Just stand over there away from the ship until we're done."

***

Using a pair of binoculars, Alex stared back at the two helicopters hovering over the island, frustrated there was nothing he could do. He watched as four men dropped down ropes from the first helicopter and disappeared into the crater, and then the aircraft moved off to one side of the island to allow the second aircraft, a Sikorsky S-94 cargo helicopter, to move into position. Two thick cables with slings quickly descended, and a few moments later, the device from the entrance of the cave was hoisted into the air, swaying below the helicopter as it moved away.

The first aircraft returned and hovered over the crater, and Alex watched as two people in harnesses on the end of a rope were pulled into the helicopter. For an instant, he thought one of them had gray hair. Four more people were hoisted out of the crater, and he recognized a full head of red hair. "Damn you Rita!"

He watched as the last four people disappeared inside the aircraft and both helicopters swung away from the island. "Take us back, Mike."

Mike brought the *Mystic* close to the island and set the controls on autopilot, and then he and Alex ran out from the bridge and hurried down the stairs to the motorboat, still tied to the stern.

When Alex looked across at the island, he saw David walking down to the dock, and sighed with relief he wasn't dead. He jumped into the boat, and motored over to the island. As the boat bumped against the dock, he noticed David's angry expression. "Get in. We'll wait on the *Mystic* until help arrives."

"That bitch Rita took the Doc, Alex."

"I know. Now get in so we can figure out where she took him."

Alex took them back to the *Mystic*, where Mike was waiting on the stern. They all walked up the outside stairs to the bridge, and no one spoke for several long moments until David broke the silence. "At least we have the location of the other three devices."

Alex gave him a somber look. "I'm more worried about what Rita has planned for the device she did get. They may have been designed to clean the atmosphere, but we know how potentially destructive they can be as well. Once we get some support out here, I'm going back to the mainland. The only way to find the Doc is to find out whom Rita is working with, and if he comes to any harm, she'll wish she had never met me."

David had seen that look in Alex's eyes once before, when he had talked about the six men who had murdered his wife, Sevi. Alex had killed each one without mercy.

The end of part 1.

I hope you enjoyed Cold Energy, and I would be grateful if you would take a moment to write a short review.

Thank you.

James M. Corkill

Here is a preview of part 2.
Red Energy.

Chapter 1

WYOMING:

When he felt a thud from the tire, Henry opened his eyes and looked at one of two guards sitting in the back of the cargo truck with him. The other guard sitting beside him had his head tilted back against the wall, snoring softly. At least they had respected his age, or perhaps Rita had told them to be considerate, but they had not even tied his hands.

He hadn't seen Rita since the helicopters had landed at a private airport in Yakama, Washington, and had no idea where they were taking him. He looked down at the device strapped onto a wooden pallet, wondering what had made her do this. She appeared to enjoy working for Mike on the research ship, so was it for money?

He felt the truck slow down as it turned a corner and stopped, then he heard men talking outside, but the conversations were muffled. When the truck began moving again, the road felt rough, tossing him from side to side. When it stopped again, one of the guards stood and opened the rear door, allowing the dwindling sunlight to illuminate the interior.

Rita looked at Henry sitting on the bench seat against the far wall. "Sorry for the rough treatment, but there was only enough room in the cab for two."

Henry remained seated. "I will not help you, Rita."

"Fine. Come with me and I'll take you somewhere for dinner. I even have a place for you to sleep."

Henry felt his stomach rumble when he thought about food, then slowly stood and moved past the device to the rear of the truck. When Rita reached out to help him down, he shrugged her off and climbed out on his own. "I could use something to eat, but I will not change my mind."

Rita knew Henry was tired and didn't push the issue. "That's okay. I'll explain everything in the morning. Follow me."

When Henry walked around the truck, he froze and stared at Rita. "Are we going underground?"

"That's right. It's an old research facility."

Henry felt his heart rate increase. "I do not do well underground."

"I promise you, it's safe."

Henry turned and stared at the entrance into the facility. It was an arched shaped concrete opening, twenty feet high and fifteen feet across at the bottom, similar to a tunnel entrance on a highway. The letters C.O.B.R.A. were imbedded in the concrete above the opening. "What is COBRA?"

"It stands for Complex Organisms and Biological Research, Alien." She indicated the waiting golf cart with her hand. "Get in. It's a long walk to the facility."

Henry hesitated. He was not claustrophobic, but was afraid of being buried alive. As a young boy in Germany after World War II, he had been trapped for three days in a flimsy old bomb shelter, hastily constructed during a raid, and he was not eager to be below ground again.

A big man put his hand on Henry's shoulder. "I'll make sure you're safe, Doctor Heinz."

Henry turned and looked up at a different guard. "Forgive me, but I do not even know your name, sir."

"Chris Jenkins and I'll be your escort while you're here, Doctor. I'll do my best to make you as comfortable as possible."

Henry turned and reluctantly climbed into the rear seat. Once Rita sat in the front, Chris climbed in behind the wheel and drove into the entrance. As they continued down a long, level tunnel, Henry felt a knot form in his stomach as fluorescent lights flashed by overhead, illuminating the concrete floor and walls curving up to form the arched ceiling.

Three-hundred-yards further, the tunnel ended at a fifty-foot-square, steel-framed opening. On the left side, massive hinges supported a two-foot thick steel door for sealing the facility, which only added to Henry's anxiety.

They drove through the opening and entered an enormous circular chamber three hundred feet across at the bottom, with a ceiling shaped like a dome, fifty feet high. A grid-work of steel rails with several mechanical hoists was hung from the ceiling with thick steel rods.

Chris stopped the golf cart just inside the entrance, and the three of them climbed out then he led them into the lounge and indicated the table and chairs. "Why don't you two take a seat and I'll fix us something to eat."

After they sat down, Henry stared at Rita. "Will you at least tell me why you brought the device to this facility?"

"We need a safe place to conduct our experiments. This facility is leased from the government by the D.A.R Corporation. DAR is short for Demolition and Reconstruction. They contract with the government after any major disaster, such as hurricanes, tornadoes, bombings, and just about every major catastrophe here in the states. It's a billion dollar industry for those who get the contracts."

"I do not understand. Why do you need the device?"

Rita knew why, but also knew if she told Henry, it would only strengthen his resolve not to cooperate. "All in good time."

Henry thought about the heavy steel door. "Did you see the movie, The Andromeda Strain?"

Rita grinned. "Both versions, and you're right to make the association. During the beginning of the space program in the sixties, the government was worried about bringing samples back from the moon. They set up this abandoned gold mine as a place to study the material, and in 1970, the facility was sealed. One day, a congressional representative convinced the government this place was outdated and a wasted resource, and it should be leased under contract to the highest bidder. The owner of DAR, Steve Preston, underbid his competitors, and now has full use of this facility."

Henry found it odd this complex would be sealed and abandoned without a reason. He was about to bring it to Rita's attention when Chris walked out of the kitchen and set a platter of sliced club sandwiches on the table.

"It's the best I could do on short notice. I'm actually a pretty good cook."

The conversations ceased while they ate. When they finished, Chris took the platter back to the kitchen and returned to the table, but did not sit down. "I'm sure you're as tired as I am, Doctor. Let me show you to your room. You'll find an assortment of blue coveralls in the dresser, and I'll show you where the restrooms are located."

Henry slid his chair back and stood, as did Rita, and then they followed Chris to the back of the lounge through another door. After showing them the washrooms, he led them into the small dormitory style sleeping quarters.

***

When he awoke the next morning, Henry searched through the drawers and found the smallest coverall he could find, and then carried it down the hall to the showers. When he returned to the lounge, he saw Chris sitting at a table.

Chris looked up from his magazine and grinned when Henry entered the room. The coverall he was wearing hung loosely over his small frame, and the pant legs were rolled up above his shoes. "Good morning, Doctor Heinz. Would you like something to eat?"

Henry continued across the room and sat at the table. "Yes, thank you. Toast and coffee would be nice."

Chris stood. "I'll try to get you a smaller size coverall while you're eating."

Henry stared after Chris as he walked around the counter. For being so robust in build, around two-hundred and fifty pounds and perhaps six foot tall, Chris carried the weight well. When he returned with the toast and coffee, Henry noticed Chris's nose had been broken at one time and never properly reset, and a slight scar ran through his right eyebrow. When Chris set the plate of toast on the table, Henry saw the scars on his knuckles.

Chris notice Henry staring at his hand and moved it away. "I'll go look for some different coveralls that might fit you better, Doctor Heinz."

Despite being held captive, Henry appreciated Chris's courteous attitude. "Just Henry will do, Chris. Thank you."

When Chris left the lounge, Henry slid the magazine over and read the title. Better Homes and Gardens was not what he had expected.

A few moments later, Chris returned clutching a pair of light blue coveralls and set them on the table. "These are the smallest size I could find, but they should fit you better than the ones you have on. Mister Preston just arrived, and he's eager to meet you." Chris noticed the magazine was face up and grinned. "I enjoy gardening in my spare time."

Henry found Chris to be a curious individual. Perhaps he was just a man with a job to do, and did not bear him any ill will. When he realized Chris was waiting for him to change clothes, he got up and hurried back to the bunk room.

***

After parking the golf cart at the entrance, Rita ran over to the helicopter as Steve Preston climbed out. It had been two months since she had left him to work for Mike on the Mystic. She threw her arms around his neck, pulling him close. "I've missed you so much."

Preston stared at the entrance, hot Rita. "Missed you, too. Take me inside. I want to see what this alien device looks like."

***

When Henry walked in, Chris set the magazine down and stood from the table. "Much better."

Henry followed him into the massive main chamber and saw the device positioned vertically on a support base with the pointed end up. A framework of one-inch fiberglass rods held it in place.

He looked across the room and was relieved to see the heavy steel door was still open, and then saw Rita standing in front of an elevated control console. Apparently, Rita had brought a suitcase and was dressed in blue jeans and a light blue sweater, and beside her was a handsome man dressed in a white shirt and black jeans.

Rita looked up when Henry and Chris entered the room. "Come over here and join us."

Henry strolled beside Chris to the console, and the Steve Preston held his hand out to him, but Henry refused to accept it. "I do not appreciate being kidnapped, Sir." When the man's eyes showed his hostility, Henry raised his chin defiantly and returned his stare.

"I don't give a shit. Teach us how to control this device and you'll be treated decently. Refuse and I'll strip you naked and put you on display to the outside world. There are thousands of sick people on the internet who would enjoy seeing you humiliated."

Since he had always been very modest, Henry's jaw dropped slightly when he realized the man was serious. He closed his mouth and gave Preston a nod of acceptance.

Chris's right hand unconsciously made a fist when he heard Preston's threat and placed a reassuring left hand on Henry's shoulder. "Just do as he asks. Everything will be okay. I promise."

When Henry looked up, he saw the sincerity in Chris's eyes. "Thank you, but I will only do what is necessary."

Preston turned to Rita. "Do you really need this old man's help?"

"He knows more about this device than I do."

Preston glared at Henry. "Fine. Just let me know when he's no longer of any use and I'll get rid of him." When he saw the fear in Henry's eyes, he grinned sadistically. "Glad to see you'll give us your full cooperation."

Rita shifted her stance when Henry stared at her, his eyes begging for help, and then she looked at Preston. "I'm sure he won't be a problem."

Preston gave her a quick kiss. "I'd better get going. Chris? Drive me back to the helicopter."

Once Chris and Preston drove down the tunnel, Henry stared at Rita. "I do not know as much as you think I do. You have seen how unpredictable they can be, and the repercussions of your experiments could have devastating effects. Please stop this before it is too late."

"Sorry, Henry. I think you know more than you're telling me. Just help me get it right and nothing bad will happen."

Henry sighed in frustration and headed for the lounge. "You will be the death of us all, Miss Harrow."

Award-winning author James M. Corkill is a Veteran, and retired Federal Firefighter from Washington State, USA. He was an electronic technician and studied mechanical engineering in his spare time before eventually becoming a firefighter for 32-years and retiring. He has since settled into the Smokey Mountains of western North Carolina and has a fantastic view from his writing desk.

He began writing in 1997, and was fortunate to meet a famous horror writer named Hugh B. Cave, who became his mentor. In 2002, he rushed to self-published a dozen copies of Dead Energy so his wife could see his book published before she was taken by cancer. When his soul mate was gone, he stopped writing and began drinking heavily.

His favorite quote. "When you wake up in the morning, you never know where the day will take you."

In 2013, he met a stranger who recognized his name and had enjoyed an old copy of Dead Energy, except for the ending. When she encouraged him to start writing again, he realized this chance meeting was just what he needed to hear at the right moment. He quit drinking and began the rewrite of Dead Energy into The Alex Cave Series, and thankful for that fateful encounter.

Other books by James M. Corkill
Dead Energy. The Alex Cave Series Book 1.
Red Energy. The Alex Cave Series Book 3.
Gravity. The Alex Cave Series Book 4.
Pandora's Eyes. The Alex Cave Series Book 5.
DNA. The Alex Cave Series Book 6.
Parallel. The Alex Cave Series Book 7.
Impact Yellowstone.

Movie scripts available from the author.
You can contact him at: Jamesmcorkill@gmail.com